OPEN FOR BUSINESS

The Seaview Series

Barbara Angermeier Malcolm

Barbara Writes

Barbara Angermeier Malcolm

eBook: ISBN 978-1-970552-11-9
Paperback: ISBN 978-1-970552-12-6

Cover design by: GetCovers
Published by Barbara Writes
Printed in the United States of America

To my late husband, Don, who always encouraged me to follow my dreams. You had faith in me when I doubted. I'm doing it, Dear, just like you said I could.

CONTENTS

CHAPTER 1

My beachside bed-and-breakfast, Seaview, was supposed to be empty. I'd just come back from seeing my daughter Marie off at the ferry terminal in Blowing Point across the Caribbean island of Anguilla, and I was waiting for Janet Fielding, my first guest, to arrive. I kept hearing a noise upstairs. Granted, Seaview was an old building with only four guest rooms, and in the trade winds the place groaned and complained regularly. This sounded as if someone was up there. I grabbed the baseball bat that my son Will had propped behind the registration desk, "just in case you need it," and climbed the stairs. I was startled to see a pair of legs jutting out of one of the bathrooms. "Who's there?"

There was a grunt and the sound of metal hitting the floor. "Oh, Rosie, you are back. I am just checking over the plumbing." Calvin levered his bulky form off the floor. He had been banished ever since he'd tried to force me into having a relationship with him.

"Get out," I said. "Iggy told you to leave and not come back."

"I want to make sure that a job with my name on it is done right. Besides, I wanted to see you again since Iggy is not here." He reached out toward me. I backed up, brandishing the bat.

"Stay away. Just gather your tools and get out before I call the police."

He hitched up his sagging jeans and swaggered another step my way. "You will not call the police. What are you going to tell them? That I am a conscientious plumber, making sure that the work is done right? Best get used to seeing me because I plan to keep coming around until you agree to be friends."

I kept the bat raised, ready to smash his grabbing hands. Here I am, a sixty-seven-year-old retired widow with brown hair and eyes. Sure, I could pull off a swimsuit, but I'm no magazine model. Why he would want the little old white girlfriend of his best friend who consistently beat him off was beyond me. Maybe I was a challenge to be conquered. "We're never going to be friends. You're not my type, and you're a married man. I like your wife too much to ruin that relationship."

"She does not mind if I have something on the side. I want to have you. Nothing you say or do is going to change that."

When he got close to me, I could smell his bad breath. Didn't he brush his teeth? He reached out and took hold of my left wrist. I cracked the baseball bat down on his forearm with all the force I could muster. He yelped and let go, his face a grimace of pain.

"You broke my arm."

"I did not. But I will break it and the other one if you don't gather up your tools and get out of here." I raised the bat to show that I meant it.

"All right, all right, I will leave now. But I will be back. You can be sure of that." He used his left hand to pick up the wrench that he had dropped and weighed it in his hand for a minute. I braced, expecting him to take a swing at me with it. After a tense few seconds, he put the wrench into his tool bag, picked up the bag, and came out of the bathroom. He was cradling his right forearm against his stomach. "If my arm is broken, I will sue you."

"You go right ahead. I look forward to telling a judge that you're trying to force yourself on me. Everyone would know what kind of predator you are if they don't already. Now get out of here."

My boyfriend, Iggy, already knew Calvin's obsession

with me. I didn't think that bringing him into the conversation would help. I used the baseball bat to point the way downstairs. I backed up to give him room to walk past me.

He left muttering under his breath that he'd be back.

I couldn't let that happen. I needed to be more careful about keeping the doors locked when I wasn't at home. I heard Calvin's truck tires crunch the gravel alongside the hotel and was relieved that I'd gotten him to leave so easily. I hefted the baseball bat in my hand, glad that Will had thought I might need it, and went downstairs to await my guest.

The front doors were open, and the Caribbean breeze brought in the sound of small waves on the sand at the foot of the stairs into Seaview. I had dreamed of this day for years, and after months of rebuilding, today was opening day.

I stood at the registration desk fiddling with the pens that were in my late husband's favorite mug. Then I straightened the shadowbox frame with the Hemingway letter and fishing lure that hung next to the registration desk. Hoping that my first guest would arrive soon, I mentally checked my bank balance. It cost a lot more than I thought it would to refurbish Seaview. I'd spent a lot buying building supplies at home and ended up spending more at the hardware store on the island. Island prices were almost double home prices, which really put a dent in my finances. And that's not even counting the cost of buying the bed-and-breakfast itself. I'd stretched Jim's life insurance money as far as I could, and I needed more than one paying guest to refill my coffers.

I had my laptop open, and the check-in program that Marie had set up booted up. I also had a notebook alongside because I was nervous about using the program for the first time with someone standing there impatient to begin their vacation.

The sound of wheels on gravel alerted me to a vehicle in my little parking area beside the hotel. My hand strayed toward the baseball bat, afraid it was Calvin returning. Then I heard the scrunch of sandals and suitcase wheels on the patio block path alongside the building.

"Here I am," Janet poked her head in the open door and came in.

"I'm glad to see you again. Can I help you carry anything?"

She shook her head, her thick light brown hair swinging as she moved. "No, I've got my suitcase and my laptop case."

I pulled a ring with two keys from the pigeonhole behind the registration desk. "Then let's get you up to your room."

Janet followed me upstairs. I unlocked the door and ushered her inside. The sun was streaming in through the curtains, making the room look golden.

"We can move the desk away from the window if you think the view will be too much of a distraction when you're writing." I wondered if this was the room Hemingway had stayed in when he was here all those years ago.

"Oh no," Janet said, "that view is why I chose this room."

I put the keyring on the desk. "Come back to the lobby when you've got your things settled, and I'll get you checked in."

I went into the kitchen and pulled out the cheese and fruit plate I had made as a welcome for my guest. I thought it would be a way to make people feel refreshed after traveling. Even though Janet had only moved from her too big, too expensive vacation rental across the island in Shoal Bay, I wanted to treat her as if she had just arrived in Anguilla.

"Hello? Rose?" Janet called from the lobby.

I picked out a small bottle of wine from the fridge, laid a napkin on the plastic-wrapped plate, carried it into the lobby, and set it all on the nearest small table. Going behind the registration desk, I said, "I need to see your driver's license and a credit card, please."

Janet rummaged in her purse for her wallet and slid the cards across the desk to me. "Here you go."

I wrote the information down in my notebook. I'd enter

it into Marie's program later. Handing the cards back to Janet, I said, "I made a cheese and fruit plate for you, and there's a split of white wine to go with it. You're welcome to sit here in the lobby, or you can take it to your room."

"That's very nice." Janet smiled. "I think I'll take it to my room to eat and drink while I enjoy the view."

"Great." Gesturing to the other side of the room, I said, "Please set the plate and glass on the sideboard when you're done."

"I'll do that." She picked up the items and went up the stairs to her second-floor room.

In the kitchen, I mixed up a batch of mango-lime muffins for tomorrow's breakfast. I was grateful to my chef daughter-in-law, Elizabeth, for developing a simple recipe that I could put almost any fruit into and have it turn out. I'd use the silicone pans that made six big muffins each. Those pans wouldn't rust in the salty Caribbean air. I had to set the pans on a cookie sheet so that they stayed level when they baked. The first batch had come out slanted because the cups tipped on the oven rack. The practice muffins were wedges rather than domes. Iggy and I had to eat them all ourselves. What a pity. I needed to get back to my regular yogurt and granola breakfast because my waistbands were getting a little snug.

After tapping on the back door frame, Iggy stuck his head into the kitchen.

"Hi, Rose, did your guest arrive?"

Ignatius Solomon, Iggy, was the electrician I hired when the renovation of Seaview began. The place had been a mess. The roof leaked for years; the wiring was frayed and in danger of catching fire, and most of the pipes were split or leaking at the couplings. Over the months, our relationship had changed from employer and employee to friends and then to lovers. He was nearly seventy years old, with close-cropped salt and pepper hair and a trim, muscular physique. A native of Anguilla, Iggy was a big help in finding reliable workmen and what few building materials I hadn't brought to the island in containers.

"Yes, she did." I wiped my floury hands on my apron. "She's up in her room getting settled. How come you stopped by today?"

He walked over and put his arms around me. "I came to see my best girl."

I slid my arms around Iggy's neck. "I'm glad. Calvin was in here when I got back from putting Marie on the ferry, and I used Will's baseball bat to encourage him to leave. I only had to whack him once. He makes me furious."

Iggy's arms tightened around me. "Calvin was here? What was he doing?"

"Fiddling around with the pipe under one of the bathroom sinks. I turned on the water after he left, and I don't think he damaged anything. Will you check the pipes before you leave, please?"

"Sure. What are you doing right now?"

"I'm mixing up muffin batter for tomorrow's breakfast."

Iggy peered over my shoulder at the countertop. "What flavor? I am rather partial to the mango-lime ones."

I laughed. "Funny you should say that because that's the flavor I'm making today. If you behave yourself, I might send some home with you since I have one guest and the recipe makes twelve."

Iggy leaned down and kissed my cheek and worked his way down to my neck.

I sighed and leaned into him. "Oh, if you keep doing that, the muffins won't get baked."

Iggy hummed against my skin. "I think there are things I would rather do than bake muffins on a nice warm Saturday afternoon."

I pushed away from him. "Now, Iggy, I have a guest. We can't be dallying around in the afternoon in bed when there's someone else in the house."

He put his lips near my ear and said, "You have a lock on your apartment door. We can lock the door and be very quiet.

Your guest will never know."

Though tempted to drag Iggy into my bedroom, I had that bowl of muffin batter to consider. "Tell you what, let me bake these and then we can retire for a short time."

Iggy smiled. "I like how that sounds, muffins and lovemaking all in the same afternoon." He walked over to the sink and washed his hands. "Can I help?"

"Sure."

It only took a few minutes to finish mixing up the batter, adding the lime zest, and the mango chunks. I asked Iggy to put the papers into the muffin cups and set the prepared pans on the cookie sheets. Elizabeth had tested the recipe and said to bake the muffins for about twenty to twenty-five minutes, checking with a toothpick at twenty minutes and making sure that the tops of the muffins were golden brown. Since mango was a juicier ingredient than other fruits, I planned that the muffins would take twenty-five minutes and maybe even a little longer.

He bent over to watch through the glass pane in the oven door, trying to hurry them along.

"It's going to take the full twenty-five minutes for them to be done," I said. "You might as well stand up straight and not hurt your back hunched over like that."

"I want them to be done faster. I want to get to the second part of the afternoon's activities." He caught me around the waist and nibbled my earlobe.

I laughed. "I know you do," I said, turning my head to kiss him back. "I do too. We have to be patient and let the muffins bake so that they aren't raw in the middle. That mango is juicy, and it makes the muffins take longer to bake."

Iggy frowned. "Which are the fastest baking muffins?"

I considered. "Chocolate chocolate chip."

"Then those are my favorite," said Iggy with a laugh.

While the muffins were baking, we washed the dishes.

CHAPTER 2

I got the coffee started just before eight o'clock on Sunday morning. I heard Janet stirring in her room and thought that she'd be down soon. When she came down the stairs, I hurried out of the kitchen to greet her.

"Good morning," I said. "Sit wherever you'd like. Coffee?"

"Yes, please." She sat down at one of the three tables spread out in the lobby, with three brightly painted chairs at each.

"Cream or sugar?"

"Just cream, or milk works too."

I went to the sideboard and poured her a mug of coffee. Then, I excused myself to go into the kitchen for the cream and a basket of muffins. I set the cream and the muffins down, saying, "I hope you like muffins. These are mango-lime. I'll be right back with place settings." I went back into the kitchen thinking that I should have made a tray with everything I'd need instead of racing back and forth. Oh well, it was the first day and the first guest. Tomorrow I'd do better. I set the plate, butter knife, and pats of butter down in front of Janet. "Here you go. Enjoy."

"Will you join me for coffee?" Janet said.

"I'd be happy to." And went back into the kitchen for my mug. "What are your plans for the day?"

Janet set her mug down. "Oh, I think I'll just stay up in my room and write. I've been trying to write for a few hours each day. I found it hard to concentrate at the villa in Shoal Bay."

"How come?"

"Well, the beach in front of the villa is very popular, and there were volleyball games and loud music playing most of the day. Even with earbuds, I had trouble blocking out the sound. Your beach seems like it's much less noisy and more low-key. I have high hopes of being able to concentrate here." Janet picked a muffin out of the basket, peeled off the paper, cut it in half, and laid it on her plate. She opened a pat of butter and spread it carefully on the tender, cake-like pastry. "This looks luscious," she said.

I said, "My friend Iggy had one fresh from the oven, and he gave it a thumbs up." I got up and freshened Janet's coffee. "What kind of books do you write?"

"Mysteries. I write cozy mysteries. The one I am working on now is called *Three Cheers for Murder*."

"That's an interesting title. What's it about?"

Janet took another muffin. "These are so good I'm going to have another. I hope you don't mind."

"No, I don't mind. Eat as many as you'd like. Whatever is left, I'll take over to Johnno's Beach Bar for him and his son to eat. If they stay here, I'll nibble away at them, and my waistline doesn't need the help."

"I hear you," Janet said. "Anyway, *Three Cheers for Murder* is about the murder of three cheerleaders in a small town in Wisconsin. A local business owner and busybody tries to help the police solve the mystery."

"Wisconsin! I'm from Wisconsin, from Green Bay. Have you ever been there?"

Janet shook her head. "Not to Green Bay. I went to college at Lawrence University in Appleton."

"I'm familiar with it. I thought it was mainly a music school."

"Music is big, but it's also a liberal arts university. I was an English major with a minor in Creative Writing. I read and wrote my way through four years of school."

"Sounds like a good way to spend your formative years."

"I wrote a lot of emotional drivel during those years, and

then my grandmother challenged me to write something that she'd like to read. I did, and after a lot of work, I got published. The rest is history. I've been writing ever since."

"Can I get you some more coffee?"

"No thanks, any more and I'll be too buzzed to sit still and write. I think I'll take a shower and then get going."

"Sounds good. Let me know if you need anything."

Janet went back upstairs, and I went into the kitchen for a tray. Back in the lobby, I cleared the dishes and the muffin basket, and turned off the coffeepot.

I sat at the kitchen island talking to Silas and eating a sandwich when Janet's voice came from the doorway. "Sorry to disturb you, Rose," she said. "I wonder if I could use a corner of your fridge to store some lunch foods. Just cheese and fruit. I could keep crackers or bread in my room, but I'd like to keep the cheese cold."

I swallowed my bite, wiped my mouth with a napkin, and stood up. "Sure, I could clear out a corner of one shelf for you to put your food. I even have a plastic basket that you could put it in to keep it from getting mixed up with mine." I extended a hand toward the young man. "This is my friend Silas. He helped refurbish Seaview and works for his dad, Johnno, at the bar just a few doors down the beach."

Janet reached across the kitchen island to shake Silas' hand. "Pleased to meet you. You did a great job getting this place back in shape. I'll bet that it was a real challenge."

Silas's hand engulfed Janet's as they shook. "Yes, it was a big job, and Mrs. Rose here was a really good boss, kept us working hard all the time. No time for foolishness when Mrs. Rose is in charge."

"I wasn't that bad. We had plenty of foolishness, but we also got the work done in good time."

"That's true, and we did have fun at the jump-ups." He turned to Janet. "You need to come down to Johnno's today for the jump-up. There is music and dancing and rum punch all night long."

"Well, I wouldn't want to intrude on a party."

"It is not a private party; it is a party for the whole island, locals and tourists alike. Mrs. Rose and Uncle Iggy come and dance all night. If you are staying on the island, you are welcome. Come on down tonight."

"I just might do that. Maybe watching people dance will give me ideas that I can put in my novel."

"If you come to the jump-up, you won't just watch the people dancing; you will be one of the people dancing." Silas did a little dance step. "Everybody dances at Johnno's jump-up."

Janet looked at me to check that what he said was true.

"Yes, if you go to Johnno's jump-up, you dance. Didn't you go to the jump-up at Captain Mike's last week? You must have been there."

"I heard the music and the laughter, but I didn't go down the beach to check it out. I guess I should have."

Silas put his hands on his hips. "Captain Mike's jump-up is pretty fine. A lot of the little tourist girls are there shaking their booties, but Johnno's jump-up is more of a neighborhood party. Young and old, locals and tourists, everybody comes to Johnno's. You have to come."

"Okay, okay." Janet put up her hands as if to ward him off. "Tonight, I'll be at Johnno's, and I'll dance. Cross my heart."

"Now that we have that settled, I'll clear out a corner of the fridge for you right away. I'd recommend keeping your bread or crackers in there too so that you don't attract anything to your room. The kitchen is always open. I have pitchers of cold water and iced tea in there for you too."

"Great. I'll get my purse and head up to the market on the hill to get something for lunch. I'm starved even though I ate two muffins not that long ago."

After Janet left, I turned to Silas. "Well, what do you think?"

"She seems like a nice lady. A good person for your first

guest."

"Agreed."

After lunch, I drove up to Vista Market to pick up a few things. Walking in, I nearly bumped into a local woman coming out.

"Oh, excuse me."

"Humph." She stepped back to let me pass.

I realized she was Mrs. Whiting, Iggy's neighbor in West End Village, who saw herself as my chief rival for Iggy's affections. I shrugged, picked up a basket, and went down the aisle. I picked out some bananas and oranges and stopped at the end of the aisle to see if there was a loaf of Amy's coconut bread on the shelf, and there was. I put it into my basket. When I turned the corner to go down the next aisle, I glanced up and saw Mrs. Whiting glaring at me and whispering in the owner's ear. I supposed she was telling Evelyn that I had usurped her place in Iggy's life. In the wine aisle, I got a bottle of Pinot Grigio for my consumption and a six-pack of mixed white and red wine splits to welcome my guests.

"Hello, Evelyn," I said when I stopped at the counter to pay. "I hope you're having a good day."

She didn't smile as she had in the past. "You can call me Mrs. Richards."

I couldn't figure out what had changed, but people in Anguilla tended to be more formal than Americans. When I tried to hand her my credit card, she said, "Cash only."

"What? Oh, okay." I fumbled in my wallet for bills to pay for my purchases. Thankfully, I had enough cash, took the change, bagged my purchases, and went out to my car. Mrs. Whiting was sitting in her car, watching me and smiling when I came out of the market. It occurred to me she might have had something to do with my not being able to use my credit card to pay today.

CHAPTER 3

That evening, when I saw Janet standing at the edge of the packed beach bar, I stood up and waved. She made her way through the crowd, excusing herself as she came, and finally reached the big round table.

Edward stood and said, "You sit here, Miss Janet. I will not need it. I be dancing all night."

"Oh, I couldn't take your chair."

I laughed. "Edward isn't lying; he'll dance every dance all night. Please sit down."

Iggy stood up with his hand extended. "Hi, Miss Janet, I'm Ignatius Solomon. People call me Iggy. Can I get you a drink?"

She reached into her pocket for money to give him, but he waved her off.

"The first one is on me." He strode away through the crowd.

Janet looked like she wanted to object, but I told her, "Johnno is Iggy's brother. He won't charge him for the drink."

"Oh, okay. I'll buy the next one."

I introduced Janet to the men seated around the table. "You met Silas in my kitchen earlier. These two, Luke and Melvin, scraped and painted all of Seaview, inside and out. And Edward helped just about everywhere. Most of all, he helped keep the Customs man happy."

Iggy came back with the drinks on a tray. They were tall glasses with pink liquid in them and a spear of pineapple sticking out of the top.

Janet looked at hers. "What is it? It looks delicious."

"It is Johnno's rum punch," Iggy said. "He puts fruit in the blender and then adds soda. Oh, and a good shot of rum, that is the punch. I hope you like it."

Janet took a sip, and her eyebrows went up. "Oh, that's good. I can see that I'm going to have to be very careful not to have too many of these. I'll get tipsy fast if I do."

Just then, the band crashed into the first song. The calypso rhythm filled the room and made my toes tap. The dance floor filled up fast. Edward reached out and took Janet's hand. "May I have this dance?" he said with a courtly bow.

"I don't know how to dance to this."

Edward pulled her to her feet. "Then I will teach you. Come on." And he led her to the dance floor, put his hand on her waist, and started slow. Soon their feet were flying. They danced up next to Luke and me.

"Are you having fun?" I had to shout over the loud music and the sound of feet on the sandy wooden floor.

Janet laughed. "I'm having a blast."

Then Edward whirled her away.

As the evening wore on, the room heated up even though it was open to the air on two sides. There were too many people crammed together in a fairly small space. The air smelled of sunscreen, cologne, and sweat. It was a heady mixture. The sunset colors streamed in through the seaside wall and tinted the dancers' faces pink and orange. I thought it was like dancing in a kaleidoscope.

The crowd was a mixture of tourists and islanders in about equal measure, and everyone seemed to have a good time, except a group of middle-aged local women standing near our table who were whispering to each other and looking at me.

Iggy leaned over toward me. "Pay no attention to those women. They have been trying to catch my interest since my wife died, but I am not interested in them. I am interested in you." He took my hand and kissed my fingers.

The young men paid the most attention to the young

tourist girls who whirled and dipped with the best of them. Older couples stayed at the fringes of the dancing and looked like they were having just as much fun as the energetic youngsters.

I spied Calvin leaning on the doorpost, watching me dance. He didn't say anything or come any closer; he just watched. I could feel his laser focus on me, his dark eyes never blinking. Seeing him there sent a shiver up my spine.

When the band switched to a slow song, Julius, the local gigolo, came up to Janet with his hand out. "Would you like to dance with me?"

Iggy claimed my hand.

"Did you see Calvin is in the doorway?" I said. "Seeing him there gives me the creeps."

"I will keep him away from you; do not worry." Iggy's grip tightened.

I watched Julius lead Janet onto the dance floor, and as he held her, he started to talk. I leaned close to Iggy's ear. "I wonder what he's saying to Janet."

Iggy turned to look and smiled. "He is saying the same thing he always says. 'I can show you a good time on the island.' That line is his stock in trade."

"Do you think she'll fall for his line? I don't know if I'm ready to see Julius at my breakfast table."

"I wouldn't worry about her. She seems like she's here for a purpose. Didn't she move from Shoal Bay for the quiet of Sandy Ground to concentrate on her writing?"

I nodded but kept my eyes on the dancing couple just the same. When the song ended, Julius escorted Janet back to the table. We got to the table just as Janet turned and said, "Thanks for the offer, but I'm on the island to write."

As we sat down, Silas arrived with a tray full of baskets heaped with Caribbean delicacies. He unloaded a feast.

"Here are some conch fritters with Daddy's dipping sauce, some plantain chips, and some chicken nuggets with barbecue sauce. Help yourself."

Janet's eyes widened. "Really? It smells great. All that dancing made me hungry. Thank you." She grabbed a napkin and helped herself to something from each basket. "I've never been brave enough to try conch fritters, but here goes." She dunked one in the sauce and took a bite. A smile lit her face. "It tastes like the sea."

"Oh good. Food. I'm famished." I filled a napkin with something from every basket, too. "Have you tried the conch fritter sauce?" I said to Janet. "I'm determined to weasel the recipe out of Johnno one of these days."

"Good luck. I'll bet he guards the recipe for something this good pretty closely."

I nodded. "He does. He swears that it's a secret. I'm determined to catch him at a weak moment." I took another bite and wiped my mouth with a napkin. "Don't you think it would be good drizzled over an egg bake for breakfast? I do."

Iggy laughed at me. "Do you really think that Johnno will tell you how he makes his famous sauce? He started with Mama's recipe years ago and has refined it since. He will not share; I am sure of it. You can keep trying. It amuses him to have you pleading for it."

"I amuse him, do I?" I pretended to be offended. "Well, I'll have to give him a piece of my mind the next time I see him."

"I hope I am here when that happens. I think that you and Johnno will have a fine argument over that sauce recipe."

I raised my eyebrows and pointed at Iggy. "I know what I'll do. The next time Elizabeth and Will are here, I'll ask Elizabeth to figure it out. I bet she'll work it out easily."

Iggy grabbed my pointing finger and looked doubtful. "I do not think so; he has a secret ingredient that she will never figure out."

"We'll see; we will just see."

At that moment, the band came back from their break, and everyone got up to dance. Edward claimed Janet's hand. "You dance with me again, Miss Janet, you a good dancer."

And they were off.

The band quit playing at midnight, and the Seaview party reluctantly said goodnight to their dance partners.

Luke, Melvin, and Silas each kissed me on both cheeks, saying, "Good night, Mrs. Rose." They shook Janet's hand and thanked her for dancing with them.

Edward kissed me and Janet on both hands and then on both cheeks. "You a good dancer, Miss Janet. I like dancing with you. You have to come back next week to dance again, okay?"

Janet laughed and kissed Edward's cheek. "I loved dancing with you, Edward. I'll be sure to come back next Sunday night."

Janet, Iggy, and I walked down the beach to Seaview.

"How did you like your first jump-up, Miss Janet?"

Janet stretched out her arms and twirled around. "I loved it. I've never been to such a fun party with so many strangers. I don't know how I'll feel in the morning. Tonight, I feel great. Tired but great." She went up the steps, unlocked the door, and let herself into the lobby of Seaview.

Iggy and I lingered on the sand, our arms around each other, our bodies touching from hips to toes.

"Am I staying over?"

I turned to nuzzle his neck. "Oh, I think you have to. It's too late to drive all the way down to West End Village tonight."

He hummed his approval of the idea, and we walked up the steps arm in arm. I was careful to lock the front and back doors, and Iggy made sure to lock the door to my apartment. I was already undressed when he walked down the short hall to my bedroom.

"Oh, what a good idea," and hurried to join his clothing to mine on the bedside chair.

It was a while before we slept.

CHAPTER 4

I checked Seaview's website the next morning and found a couple of emails asking about availability of rooms. One was a last-minute inquiry from a woman who said she was an executive looking for a quiet retreat from the rat race and hoped that Seaview might be what she was looking for. I composed my reply saying that I thought Seaview would be an excellent place to get away from her busy life, that the bed-and-breakfast was situated on a sweep of white sand along the bay with quiet restaurants and small shops within walking distance. I asked for her credit card information to secure the reservation and got a quick reply. Iggy was sitting across from me at the kitchen island, leaning on his elbow and sipping a mug of coffee.

"That's great," I said, "another single woman coming to stay on Saturday."

"You better be careful, or you will get a reputation as a sanctuary for single women," Iggy said, laughing.

"I wouldn't mind that in the least. Seaview doesn't have the atmosphere for the party crowd or space for diving couples. A steady stream of women coming to stay would suit me fine. Now let's see what this one says."

The second email was also from a single woman. This one was arriving on the island in two weeks. I emailed back to say that she had a room and asked for a credit card to reserve the space. It didn't take long for the woman to call Seaview's number with her reservation information and a credit card number to guarantee the room. She said she was planning to stay for a week. I told her that would be fine. It was a good thing that Marie had worked hard the last ten days to set up my website and take pictures that showcased the area around my little hotel. It was also a good thing that I had more reservations and deposits to start refilling my nearly depleted bank account.

I was sure that my son Will would call or email soon to find out how things were going. I hoped that spending ten days on the island, meeting the building crew, and helping finish the remodeling would give Will confidence that I hadn't made a huge mistake investing most of the money from my late husband Jim's life insurance policy on "a ramshackle hotel on a Caribbean beach." That phrase was in frequent use in Will's emails. He had tried his best to talk me out of buying Seaview. His early emails were full of links to reports of people being victimized by con men on tropical islands. I had been smart and hired reliable workmen, insisting that the electrician and the plumber be licensed.

"The second one is from someone looking for peace and quiet. I think I can assure her of that here. And not one email from Will, full of doom and gloom. Maybe working him hard the last ten days finally set his mind at ease about Seaview."

"Maybe, or maybe he is just gathering strength for a new campaign."

"Oh, don't say that. I hope he's convinced that I can look after myself after seeing how professional you are and how nice the hotel looks. Having a first guest soon should go far to reassure him, don't you think?"

Iggy reached across the kitchen island and patted my hand. "I am sure that he was impressed and will become your biggest cheerleader. Elizabeth will see to it."

Just then the timer dinged, and I went to the oven and removed the egg casserole that I had made for breakfast that day. I was glad that I had worked with Elizabeth to adjust a couple of recipes so that I had some that made smaller quantities of food for when there were only one or two guests. Food was too expensive to waste, especially here on the island where nearly everything had to be imported.

I heard Janet stirring and made a fresh pot of coffee so that the aroma would let my guest know it was nearly time to come down for breakfast.

Iggy pushed back his stool and stood up. "I need to get to work, Rose. I will stop by to see you after I finish the job."

"Good," I said, "I'm hoping to hear about the grill that your friend is selling. Maybe we can take your pickup truck to get it later."

He came around the kitchen island and kissed me. "That is fine. Call me when you hear from him." He hitched up his jeans and went out. I enjoyed watching him leave.

"Good morning," Janet's voice came from the lobby.

I got up and went to greet her. "Good morning. I hope you rested well after your strenuous evening at Johnno's jump-up."

Janet poured a mug of coffee and added creamer. "That was some party. I had a great time. I don't know when I danced so much. My feet are still tired."

"Maybe you can rest today. I have an egg casserole just out of the oven. I'll bring you a piece along with some fruit and a muffin from yesterday if you'd like."

Janet sat down at one of the lobby tables. "I'll have some egg casserole and fruit. No muffin."

"I'll be right back with your breakfast." It didn't take me long to assemble a wedge of egg casserole on a colorful plate, scoop some cut-up fruit into a small dish, and place it all on a tray with silverware and a napkin. I carried the tray into the lobby and served Janet her breakfast.

"Sit with me. Keep me company while I eat."

"Are you sure? I can leave you to eat in peace."

"No, I'd like the company."

We spent a pleasant half-hour chatting while she ate her breakfast. Janet said that she would write most of the day but thought that she would start off with a walk down the beach and back, "just to flex my feet in the sand."

"I know what you mean. Walking on that soft sand is good exercise. I stick to the wet sand when I'm in a hurry."

"It feels good when the little waves lap over your feet, doesn't it? Maybe I'll take my notebook down to the beach with me and prop myself against that palm tree I can see from my window and try a little writing by hand. It makes me stop and think before I put something on paper. Sometimes I get better results when I slow down the process. My brain isn't in such a rush to get words down my arms and out my fingers when I'm holding a pen or pencil."

"Does it really make that much of a difference?"

"It does. I try to do a little of each every day to see what different ideas come to me." She put down her fork and wiped her lips with her napkin. "That was excellent, baked to perfection, and the fruit bowl was just enough. Thank you."

"There's a pitcher of sun tea and one of cold water in the fridge that you can help yourself to whenever you like."

"Sweet tea?"

I shook my head. "No, I like it unsweetened. There's sugar available in the container there on the sideboard."

"That's okay, I like my tea unsweetened too."

I picked up the tray. "Enjoy your walk and your writing." I went through the door into the kitchen.

I started washing the dishes when there was a knock on the back door. "Yes?" I walked over to the screen door, drying my hands on a towel. A man with a clipboard stood outside on the back porch. "Can I help you?"

He looked up at me and frowned. "I have had a complaint about the cleanliness and food safety practices here. I am Gerald LeMoinette from the Anguilla Health Department here to inspect your operation."

"I remember you from when you shut us down a few months ago." I reached out and pushed the screen door open. "Come in. I have nothing to hide."

LeMoinette spent the next hour going over every inch of my kitchen, from the way I stored serving pieces to the inside of my refrigerator to the range hood. He was especially interested in looking under the stove and cupboards to make sure that they were clean and there was no evidence of rodent or insect infestation. All the while he was checking over everything, he kept questioning me about how I maintained food safety.

"Do you keep your refrigerator at 45 degrees Fahrenheit or below?"

"Yes, I do. I have a separate fridge thermometer to double-check that."

He inspected the seal on the refrigerator door to make sure it was tight by closing a dollar bill in the door and trying to pull it out. It didn't budge. He ran his fingers across the edge of the range hood, checking for grease.

"Rancid grease is a big bacteria host. You need to clean this hood at least once a week."

"I do. I'm very careful about that."

He kept checking things off on his clipboard. "What do you do if your guests want to cook?"

"They can use the microwave in the lobby to reheat their doggie bag leftovers, and I'm buying a grill for the patio that they can use. I have separate baskets they can store their food in in the fridge so that it's contained and doesn't mix with my food. They are not allowed to cook in the kitchen. It's against the Health Department rules."

He looked at me from under his eyebrows and scowled. "You have an answer for everything. I wonder what you are hiding."

I stood straight on both feet, my arms folded across my chest. "Mr. LeMoinette, I am not hiding anything. I'm doing my best to abide by the Health Department rules to keep my certification and to keep my guests healthy and happy. You're welcome to stop by anytime to inspect my kitchen and quiz me about my food safety practices. My daughter-in-law is a chef and has to get certified every year in food safety. She shares what she learns with me, and I do my best to implement it. If you have any recommendations, I'd be happy to hear them."

He flipped the pages on his clipboard and said, "I see nothing that would pose a problem. I think I have been misled."

That caught my attention. "Has someone been telling you that my kitchen isn't clean and I'm not careful to keep food safe?"

"No. No, this was a standard inspection."

"Oh really? Then why did you say when you came in that you had a complaint?"

His lips curved in a wry smile. "I always say that to scare people into being careless."

"And does it work?"

He tucked his clipboard under his arm. "Most of the time." He extended his hand. "Thank you for your time, Mrs. Lambert. I will be by again, I am sure."

I shook his hand and walked him to the door. "Thank you for stopping, Mr. LeMoinette. I'll see you around."

CHAPTER 5

I was just finishing putting the dishes away when the registration desk bell rang. I went out to see who was there. He was a preppy-looking man of about fifty with sandy-blond hair. "Can I help you?"

"Is Janet Stanesford—I mean Janet Fielding—staying here?"

I looked down to make sure that the notebook that I'd used to check Janet in was closed. "I'm sorry. We make it a policy not to divulge our guests' names."

"You make it a policy." An ugly look contorted his face. "I'm surprised that a dump like this has a Health Department clearance, much less a privacy policy."

I felt as if someone had thrown cold water on me.

"Please leave."

"I know my wife is staying here. I saw her stupid notebook outside. Tell her that her husband is looking for her." He turned and strode out of the lobby.

I heard his steps thud on the stairs down to the beach and crept to the door to make sure that he was gone. Instead, I saw him pick up Janet's notebook and start paging through it.

"What are you doing here?" I heard Janet's voice. "Give me my notebook. How dare you look at it without my permission?"

I could overhear the exchange and see them through the front window as I was standing at the registration desk answering emails and checking hits on my website.

I heard the book hit the sand. "Just checking that you're really here to write and not to tumble around with some hot island man. Did you think you could escape me that easily?"

Janet picked up the notebook and shook off the sand. "I didn't come here to escape you, Nathan. I escaped you when I filed for divorce six months ago. I came here to write. Go away."

Nathan stepped forward and grasped her wrist. "I won't go away. We're married. You belong to me. Forever. Remember the vow you took? 'Til death do us part.' Remember that, Janet?"

She wrenched her arm away from him. "You mean the vow that you broke with your string of mistresses and one-night stands? You don't have any claim on me anymore, Nathan. Go crawl back under your rock and leave me alone."

He leaned down until his nose almost touched Janet. "You'll regret divorcing me. You won't get a dime from me. And you won't get any of my father's money either. I'll make sure of that."

"I don't need your money or your father's money. I have my own. That's enough for me."

He laughed and flung a hand at Seaview behind him. "Enough to put you up in this dump for a week or so? If this is the best your money can afford, I'm sorry for you."

"Go away, Nathan. Just go away."

She stepped around him and started up the steps into Seaview. Janet picked up her pareo and grabbed her pencil off the floor. She made it to her room before I heard her sob.

I hadn't known that Janet was married, not that it mattered, and hadn't told her husband that Janet was staying there when he came into the lobby and asked. How had he known? I wondered as I watched her flee up the stairs.

Janet came back downstairs almost at once and stood waiting for me to look up.

"Can I help you?" I said with a smile.

"Yes, I need to know if you told my husband that I'm staying here." Her tone of voice was flat. She was frowning.

"No, I didn't. I told him it was against company policy to reveal our guests' names, and he stormed out the door."

"I was afraid that you had told him. Then I would have left and lodged a complaint with the Chamber of Commerce."

"Nope, not revealing guests' names, how long they are staying, nothing. He must have seen your things on the porch." I looked at her. "Would you like a glass of wine? I have a bottle of Pinot Grigio in the fridge that might just smooth out the day."

"I'd love a glass."

I closed the laptop. "Come into the kitchen. We can have some wine."

It wasn't long before Janet poured out her heart to me. She told me about falling in love with Nathan when she was a typist at his father's law firm. Nathan was in law school, clerking for the summer, and he asked her out for drinks one Friday afternoon.

"I fell hard. He's so handsome, and he can be charming when he wants to be. In college, Nathan was a party boy, always off with friends for weekend trips to Vegas or Chicago, hitting the bottle pretty hard, and sloughing off his studies. I think his father thought that if he married quiet little typist me, he would suddenly become responsible. That he would hit the books, get better grades, and pass the bar." Janet took a drink of her wine. "He didn't finish law school. He flunked out, and I think he barely made it out of undergrad. That left him working as a perpetual clerk in the firm." She twirled the stem of her wineglass between her fingers. "I kept working until my books started to sell, and by then Nathan's father was embarrassed that his daughter-in-law was a typist, so Nathan asked me to quit. That was all right with me. I was ready to write full time by then. I didn't argue."

I offered to refill her glass, and Janet nodded.

"Thanks."

"Where did you live?"

"Oh, we lived with his father. He has a huge estate with an enormous mansion. We lived in one wing and met him for dinner in the evenings." Janet laughed. "It reminded me of a British manor house novel. Most of the time it was just the three of us, just his father and me when Nathan was off with friends. It took more than a few years for me to realize that most of the friends he was off with were young, beautiful women who thought they had a chance to marry a rich man. I think his father always knew and pitied me for being dim."

"Any children?"

"No, thank heavens, no children."

I refilled my glass halfway and looked at Janet. "Why do you think Nathan followed you to Anguilla?"

"I think his ego took a hit when I left and maybe his father told him I might be worth hanging on to. Mr. Stanesford and I always had a good relationship, which surprised me since I wasn't of their social class." Janet swallowed the last wine in her glass. "I'd better get back to my writing or I won't make my word quota for the day. Besides, I'm expecting a call from my lawyer."

I lifted my glass in a toast. "Well, here's to lots of words."

We both laughed, and Janet went up to her room.

An hour later, I heard shouting from the lobby and ran to see what was going on. Nathan stood at the foot of the stairs and yelled up at Janet. "Come down, I want to see you."

Janet pulled open her room door and glared down at him. "What are you doing? I'm not coming down. Go away."

"I won't go away. Come down here and talk to me."

"No." He started up the stairs, and she slammed the door and locked it. "Stay away," she said from behind the closed door.

He got to the top of the stairs and pounded on the door with his fist. "Dammit, Janet, open the door. I want to talk to you. We're still married, and you have to obey me."

I saw his fist raised for another barrage. I hurried up the stairs and pulled on his arm, spinning him around. "You can't be here making a scene. If Janet doesn't want to see you, you'll have to leave, or I'll call the police."

He flung my hand off his arm. "Go ahead. Call the police. See if I care. That's my wife in there, and I have a right to see her and talk to her."

"Not if she doesn't want to see you. She's filed for divorce; you signed the papers; that should be it. I can't help it if you've had a change of heart. You'll have to leave." I reached out again and pulled at his shoulder.

He shoved me away and turned back to the door. I stumbled backwards, nearly falling down the stairs, but I caught myself on the handrail. Raising his fist to pound on the door again, he caught sight of the door to the front gallery. He rushed down the short hall, pushed open the door, and went out onto the narrow porch that fronted the seaside rooms. Janet's windows were open. Nathan pushed at the screen until it broke, then he stuck his head through it and started to climb in.

"Help," Janet said, "get out of here." She shoved at him, but he was too strong for her to repel.

I followed him and saw what was going on, then pulled out my cellphone to call the police station. It was only a few doors down the street so that whoever was on duty could be there fast.

I could hear the commotion in Janet's room and debated whether to wait for the police or use my master key and try to stop him. Heavy footfalls came through the lobby, and Officer Matthew leaped up the stairs two at a time to my side.

As soon as I unlocked the door to Janet's room, the policeman and I saw Nathan backhand Janet, knocking her to the floor. Matthew pushed past me as I stood stunned in the doorway. The officer grabbed Nathan by the upper arm and pulled him away from Janet.

I helped Janet get back on her feet. A tiny trickle of blood seeped from the corner of her mouth. "Are you all right?"

Janet reached up to touch her face. "I think so. That's the first time I've ever been hit."

"I'm sorry, Janet, I never meant to hit you. When you

slapped me, I just reacted. I'm sorry, can you ever forgive me?" Nathan reached toward Janet but was held in place by Officer Matthew's firm grip.

"No, I can't. Just go, Nathan, and don't come back. We're done."

The police officer tugged on his captive's arm and led him out of the room. "Come along, sir, you heard the lady. She wants you to leave."

Nathan turned back toward Janet, who shied away as he passed. "Janet, tell him I didn't mean it."

Janet stood with her hands hanging at her sides, her cheek fiery red, tears rolling down.

I said the only thing I could think of. "I'll get you an ice pack," and I hurried to the kitchen and came back with the frosty blue rectangle wrapped in a clean towel.

"He hit me."

"Here. Put this on your cheek. It'll help with the pain and swelling."

She sat on the edge of the bed and laid the ice pack on her cheek. Her breath hissed through her teeth. "Cold. Nobody ever hit me before." She looked up at me. "If you'll excuse me, Rose, I'd like to be alone."

"Of course." And I left the room, closing the door behind me.

CHAPTER 6

An hour later, Janet came down to the kitchen with her water bottle and poured herself a bottle of tea. "I hope you don't mind, but I love your tea. What kind of tea is it?" She handed me the now-warm ice pack without a word. Her cheek was still red from the slap.

I smiled at her. "I make it with plain old tea bags that I get from the IGA. Kind of the British equivalent of Lipton, I guess. It makes good sun tea, I think." Evidently, we weren't going to mention the morning's excitement.

Janet looked at the bottle of rich brown liquid in her hand. "I wonder if I can get this tea in the States."

"I'm sure you can, probably on Amazon, and they'll ship it right to your door."

"That's good because I'm crazy about it. I'm going to drink it all if you aren't careful."

"No problem, I can brew up another jug of it in just a few hours. In fact, I'll get it started right now. The sun is streaming in the lobby windows and shining on the sideboard. I'll put the jug there, and it'll be ready in no time."

"You really brew it in the sunshine?"

I nodded yes. "My grandmother taught me how to make it when I was a girl. I remember sitting and watching the water turn from clear to brown in the strong afternoon sun on her kitchen table. It works the same if you don't put it in the sun; it just takes longer."

Just as I finished repairing the screen that Nathan broke, I got a call from Iggy's friend, Jamison Gard, that afternoon.

Jamison had a grill that he was selling, and I wanted a grill for my back patio. I told him I had to wait until Iggy finished working because there was no way I could get a grill into my car.

"That is fine, Mrs. Rose," Jamison said. "I can wait until Ignatius comes to cart it off. She is a good little grill and will serve you well."

I knew Iggy wouldn't let me buy a grill that wasn't in good shape. I didn't need a big, half oil drum grill like Johnno had lent me for the end of construction party last week. I just needed a small family-size grill for my own personal use and for my guests to use if they wanted to. It had always been nice to be able to grill lobsters when I stayed at Sydans. It had been convenient to be able to cook and not have to go out for every meal. I knew Seaview was a bed-and-breakfast, still I wanted to provide a few amenities like refrigerator space and a grill for my guests to use. The Health Department had been very clear that I could not allow the guests to cook in my kitchen, but they had no objection to guests grilling food on the patio.

I stood at the kitchen island folding towels when a man cleared his throat behind me. I jumped. "You startled me," I said. "Can I help you?" I turned to face Nathan Stanesford. "Oh. What can I do for you?"

"I want, no, I need to apologize to Janet for my behavior earlier. I tried calling her. She won't answer her phone. I was wondering if you would be so kind as to ask her to come down to meet me."

I leveled a hard stare at him. "I don't want more trouble. If you're here to start another fight, you can turn right around and go back where you came from."

Nathan lifted his hands as if to ward off the thought. "No, I don't want a fight. I just want to talk to my wife."

I finished folding the towel. "I'll go and ask her if she'll come down and see you. Wait in the lobby, please."

He followed me from the kitchen to the lobby and

watched me walk up the stairs.

I knocked on Janet's door. "Janet? Can I speak to you?"

"Just a minute." She opened the door and looked at me. "Is there a problem?"

I shook my head. "I'm not sure. Your husband is in the lobby, and he'd like to speak to you."

Janet looked shocked. "Nathan's here in the lobby?"

"Yes, he is."

"And he said he wants to speak to me?"

"That's what he said. I told him I don't want a fight, and he said he's not here to fight with you."

Janet was quiet for a minute, staring at the floor. "I guess I'll come down to see him."

"You don't have to. I can make him go away if you'd like."

Janet shook her head. "No, that's all right. Tell him I'll be down in a few minutes."

I nodded and went back down the stairs. "She said that she'll be down in a few minutes. Can I get you something to drink? Iced tea?"

"A glass of water would be great."

I took a glass off the sideboard, ran the water in the sink for a few seconds, and filled the glass. "Here you are."

"Thank you."

I went back into the kitchen, but I kept my eye on them and could hear what they said.

Janet came quietly down the stairs and stood at the bottom. "What do you want, Nathan?"

He set the glass down on the nearest table. "I just want to talk to you."

"We have nothing to talk about. We're getting a divorce, and that's that."

Nathan put his hands in his pockets and pulled them back out. He reached toward Janet. "What if I don't want a divorce? I never wanted a divorce. I love you."

"You have a funny way of showing it. You went out partying almost every night. You flirted with every woman you saw. You went to bed with most of them. Those behaviors are not the behaviors of a man in love with his wife."

He put his hands back in his pockets. "I've been seeing Dr. Harriman again, and this time I got tested for Attention Deficit Hyperactivity Disorder, and I have it. The doc gave me medicine that's helping. It's a natural supplement, not a stimulant, and I am taking an antidepressant too. I'm much better, much calmer."

"I'm happy for you, Nathan. That doesn't change my mind. We're getting a divorce."

He reached out as if to touch her arm, but Janet backed up. "Come on, can't you give me one more chance?"

Janet shook her head. "I don't know, Nathan. I've spent the last fifteen years being hurt by you. I don't think that I can just forget all of that and pretend to be happily married because you say that you've changed."

"I have changed. I'm changing. Ask Dr. Harriman; he'll tell you. The meds are helping me focus. I'm not depressed. I'm not restless and jittery. I'm getting better. Even Father has noticed that I'm doing better at the firm."

"I'm happy for you, really I am, but I spent too many years sitting alone at home while you were out partying to go back. I'm sorry, Nathan, no." She looked at his face and saw tears in his eyes.

I saw the tears too and wondered if they were crocodile tears. Nathan seemed like the kind of guy who'd use any lever he could to get his own way.

"Please, Janet, please come for a drink with me. Just one drink."

"No, not even for one drink." She shook her head and went back upstairs.

Nathan's shoulders slumped. He turned, glanced toward the kitchen with a small smirk on his lips, and left Seaview alone.

I wasn't sorry to see him go.

CHAPTER 7

I sat at the kitchen island and didn't know what to do. I had unpacked all the things in my apartment. I had arranged and rearranged the kitchen and would probably do it again before I had it the way it worked best. Throughout all the months of construction, I had longed for the day when it would all be finished, and I could relax as the owner and operator of a bed-and-breakfast on a Caribbean beach. Now the day had finally arrived. My first guest was in residence, and the second one was arriving on Saturday.

Nothing needed to be cleaned. The lemon fragrance of dish soap competed with the lingering scent of the baked egg casserole I'd served for breakfast. I washed the breakfast dishes, let them air dry, and put them away. I mixed a batch of muffin batter and put it in the fridge. Tomorrow morning, I'd stir in banana slices and bake them. I had put nutmeg in the batter and doubled up on the vanilla so that the muffins would taste like the Jamaican banana pancakes we had at a villa in Montego Bay. Those trips to Montego Bay were fun, but I was glad that we had learned to dive and gone to other islands. Maybe being my own boss meant I could take some time to have fun myself.

I checked the time. It was twelve thirty. It was a beautiful sunny day, and I wondered if Tamarind had an afternoon dive boat going out. I headed to the dive shop next door.

My friend Lomira was working, and I was happy that there was an afternoon dive boat going out with room for me. I asked her to put my name on the list and hurried back to Seaview to change. I wriggled into my two-piece swimsuit, slid a long-sleeved sun shirt over it, and got my dive bag out of the back room. I unloaded the bag and repacked it to make sure that I had all of my gear. Yes, mask, fins, snorkel, buoyancy control device (which divers call a BCD), regulator, weight pockets, and wetsuit. All were in the bag. All were ready to go. I wore my water shoes so I could just slip on my fins on the boat.

I scribbled a note that I was going diving and would be back in a few hours that I taped on the registration desk in the lobby. I locked the doors of the bed-and-breakfast after I stuck a note on the front door saying when I'd be back, shouldered my dive bag, and walked over to Tamarind. I had all my own gear except for the tank and weights, so I didn't have to rent equipment. Tamarind had a "locals" dive package that I'd bought when I first arrived on the island, and I still had dives left.

I leaned on Lomira's desk to fill out the Medical Release forms before the dive. As I was working through that, she talked. "You know that Eleanora Whiting is spreading rumors around that you are trying to cheat people? She is angry that Mr. Solomon has chosen you for a friend instead of her, so she has gotten her friends together to badmouth you to all the merchants on the island."

I gaped at her. "Are you kidding me? Do I seem like a cheat and con woman to you?"

"No, you don't, Mrs. Rose, but I have known you since you and Mr. Jim used to come down to dive with us, long before you moved here and bought Seaview. I also think that Ignatius Solomon is a grown man, and he can choose who he wants to spend time with, and he has chosen you. Eleanora Whiting is spiteful and has a mean mouth on her. You need to watch out that she does not ruin you in Anguilla."

"Thanks for telling me, Lomira. That explains a lot of what's been happening."

There were gulls squabbling over a dead fish on the beach right next to the boat hull, and I thought that someone should clear it away. Dougie had put a tank on board for me and was waiting with the boarding ladder lowered at the stern of the dive boat. "I know you do not like to climb up on the bow, so I am all ready for you to come around to the stern," he said when he saw me come out of the dive shop.

I slung my dive bag onto the boat deck and waded around to the boarding ladder and climbed up the metal rungs. There were already six divers on board, four men and two women, getting their gear set up. None of them were young, and none of them looked confident. From the trouble they were having assembling their equipment, I surmised they were fairly new to diving. I found a spot along the side in front of a tank and got busy setting my gear up too.

Dougie called for everyone's attention to start the pre-dive briefing. "Today we are visiting the MV Ida Maria." He had to shout over the engine noise. "She lies in forty to sixty feet of water on a sandy bottom. The bow is twisted ninety degrees to the west, and the holds are collapsed, so there is no penetration opportunity."

There were several groans at that. I'm not a wreck diver who enjoys swimming into the holds of ships. I didn't mind since I get claustrophobic in overhead environments.

"There are usually Atlantic Spadefish swimming over the ship, and lots of Damselfishes and Sergeant Majors tend their egg patches on the hull. Do not be intimidated by the school of Barracuda that patrols the perimeter of the ship. They will not bother you unless you have bait in your pockets, and I hope none of you do because I do not want to clean dead fish parts out of the rental BCD pockets." Everyone laughed at that.

The boat bounced from wave to wave, spray flying in the wind to douse us. I tried to introduce myself to the couple sitting next to me, but with the roar of the engine it was nearly impossible to hear each other. That gave me time to think about how I'd combat Eleanora Whiting's rumors about me. I tossed my hair in the wind, hoping that it would blow those thoughts away. I needed to focus on the dive.

Freddy slowed the catamaran and approached the mooring buoy. After shifting into neutral, he left the helm and went forward to the bow, where he expertly hooked the buoy and slid the mooring line over it. On his way back to the helm, he gave me a dirty look out of the corner of his eye. He must have heard the rumors too. He turned off the boat's motor. The stink of diesel exhaust washed over us when the boat swung with the wind.

"Let's get geared up and get ready to dive," Dougie said.

That set off a flurry of activity. I had put my wetsuit on halfway before we left shore. All I needed to do was pull up the top and slip my arms into the sleeves. Once it was zipped, the neoprene suit was tight enough to feel like a full-body hug.

Dougie came over to where I was sitting. "Mrs. Rose, do you have a dive buddy?"

"No, I'm here on my own. Does someone need a buddy?"

"Not really; they are all buddied up. Would you like to swim at the back of the group so that no one wanders off? It would help me keep them together."

I smiled at him. "I'd be happy to. I'll make sure there are no stragglers going off into the abyss."

The rest of the divers on the boat were fussing with their gear and having trouble getting organized.

I thought it was a good thing that I would swim at the back to keep them together.

"Let's get into the water," Dougie said. He escorted the divers to the opening in the boat's side and held them steady while they put on their fins, got their masks settled on their faces, and made their giant stride entries. "Swim over to the mooring buoy, and I will meet you there to begin the dive." He motioned to me. "Mrs. Rose will swim behind the group to make sure that everyone stays together."

He nodded at me, and I moved to the side of the boat while he went to gear up and enter the water on the other side. We splashed into the water at the same time, came up and gave Freddy the okay sign. I tasted the salty tang as the water washed over me. It took the other divers a couple of minutes to get their gear settled and to start their descent. I watched their faces to see who was nervous, who I'd have to keep an eye on underwater. I overheard one man say to the woman next to him, "Oh, all right. We can hold hands if you want." I memorized the color of her wetsuit and fins so that I could watch to make sure she was comfortable during the dive.

I waited until all the heads were underwater before beginning my own descent. This wasn't the first dive since moving to Anguilla that I'd been asked to swim at the back and keep watch. I thought that maybe I should have listened to Jim and gotten my Divemaster certification if I was going to be the safety diver trailing the group on every dive I did in Anguilla. Either that or I'd have to find myself a dive buddy.

Maybe one of my guests would be a diver. I knew Janet was not a diver because she had inquired about snorkeling or maybe doing a Discover Scuba while she was on the island. I wondered if the executive who was arriving in a couple of days was a diver. It would be great if she were. I could volunteer to accompany her on a couple of dives as another service of her Seaview stay.

While those thoughts were running through my mind, I was sinking into the warm Caribbean sea watching the silvery bubbles of the divers in front of me trail up like strings of mercury beads behind them. I felt the cool seawater seeping into my snug wetsuit and was glad that I wore it. I saw the resident school of silver Barracuda, shiny in the filtered sunlight, patrolling the perimeter of the wreck and a big school of twenty or thirty Yellowtail Jacks. One of the divers ahead of me spied a sleeping Hawksbill Turtle in the open hold of the ship and was excitedly pointing it out. She started to swim down to touch the turtle, but Dougie caught her in time and waved her off.

A powerboat roared overhead, and I felt the thrum of the motor in my chest. I kept my distance and watched as the six divers explored the exterior of the shipwreck. A lot of the stern was covered with cup coral, which looks like clusters of little pink toes when the polyps aren't extended. Every few minutes, I had to swim over and warn them with a shake of my finger not to touch the sponges or coral. On the canted bow, the anchor chain links were still attached, and they were big—four by six inches each—and encrusted with tiny sponges and fuzzy hydroids that gave the whole bow a fairy castle look.

Time passes quickly underwater. I looked on as Dougie gave the signal to ascend. He slowly swam back to the mooring line and started toward the surface, keeping a slow rate of ascent. I joined the group and began ascending alongside them, not needing to hold on to the line to maintain my position in the water.

Dougie stopped at fifteen feet for a three-minute safety stop, and all the others joined him. He watched his dive computer to time the stop while the divers watched the life on the wreck from above.

I ascended ahead of the group, caught the trailing drift line, removed my fins, and handed them up to Freddy. Then I climbed the boarding ladder, he handed my fins back, and I made my way across the boat to my seat. By the time I had shrugged off my scuba unit and stripped off the top of my wetsuit, the rest of the group was onboard.

Everyone exclaimed about the abundant life on the wreck.

"Did you see that school of Barracuda?" said one woman. "I thought they looked like a street gang patrolling their turf."

"I loved all the turquoise and pink Parrotfish munching on the coral heads surrounding the wreck," the other woman said.

A man bemoaned the fact that this was a single boat dive instead of a two-dive trip like the morning one was.

"Sorry," Dougie said, "we try not to get our dive staff bent from decompression sickness."

Everyone agreed that was a good reason to only do one

afternoon dive. As soon as the boat slid onto the sandy beach in front of Tamarind Dive Shop, I got up, put my dive bag at the bow, and hopped down onto the sand.

"Thanks for a great dive, Dougie. I'll be back in a day or two."

"Thank you, Mrs. Rose. I will see you again."

He waved to me, and I started off down the beach to Seaview, my mind a little clearer after the dive. I felt like the seawater had washed away some of my worries about the bed-and-breakfast's success in the face of Mrs. Whiting's mean mouth.

I stopped on the back porch to hang my wet dive gear, and as I reached to put my dripping wetsuit on a peg, strong arms slid around me and pulled me close. I smiled, thinking that it was Iggy. The voice that purred my name wasn't his, and all I smelled was sour sweat and bad breath. I tried to turn around but was held tight.

"Rosie," Calvin said, "I like you when you are half-naked."

"Let go of me." I shoved my elbow into his doughy stomach as hard as I could. "Let me go."

"Oof," he said when my pointy elbow sank into him. "I will have to hold you even tighter. You need a real man to control you."

I wriggled, trying to get free. He held me fast. I kicked at his shins, but my water shoes were too soft to do much damage. I dug my fingernails into his wrists where they crossed over my middle. He loosened his grip enough for me to turn around and knee him in the groin. Calvin let go immediately, grabbed himself, and bent over groaning and swearing.

"Dammit, woman, you cannot do that to me and get away with it."

He reached out toward me, but I stepped aside out of his grasp and grabbed the broom propped by the door.

"Leave. Leave now, or I'll hit you."

He laughed. "Hit me with a broom? That will not hurt much. I will take it away from you and then spank you with it."

I held the broom end, wound up and hit him across the shoulders with the wooden handle as hard as I could. I had gotten stronger from doing a lot of heavy work during the renovation. I could tell by the sharp sound it made and by his hissing intake of breath that I hurt him. I raised it to strike again, but he turned and, still holding his privates, limped across the yard and out onto the road. I followed him and watched him get into his truck and drive away.

"And stay away," I said to his retreating taillights. I didn't need more trouble after hearing the bad-mouthing from the Whiting woman. Still, I should report the incident to the police. At the very least, I'd let Iggy know Calvin was getting bolder.

With shaking hands, I put the broom back by the door and finished hanging my dive gear. It took me three tries to get the key into the door lock, and I was careful to lock it behind me. I entered, then leaned against the door and let out a long breath.

A sharp knock on the door made me jump. I turned around to see Iggy smiling at me through the window. Unlocking the door, I threw myself into his arms.

"I am happy that you are glad to see me. What is the cause of all this?" His arms went around me, and he held me close. "You are shaking. Did you have a bad experience on your dive?"

"No, the dive went fine. As I was hanging up my gear, Calvin snuck up behind me and grabbed me so tight around my middle that I couldn't move. I finally dug my nails into his arms and could turn around and knee him you know where. Then, I hit him hard across the shoulders with the broom handle, and he left. I know he'll be back." I felt tears rolling down my cheeks.

"I will talk with him again." His arms tightened around me. "He makes me so angry. Maybe I can make him see sense."

Wiping the tears from my face with my sleeve, I said, "I doubt it. I appreciate you trying. Are you done working for the day?"

"Yes. I got a call from Jamison about the grill. How about you get dressed and we can go look at it? He says it is in good shape and will make a fine grill for you and your guests to use. He even has a pail with a lid for storing charcoal and lighter fluid." Iggy kissed the top of my head, patted my back, and turned me around to face the kitchen. "Go get ready, and we can go. A little drive might do you good."

"Can we stop at the police station? I want to tell them about Calvin attacking me today."

"Alright."

CHAPTER 8

When the late afternoon American Eagle jet landed, I knew that my next guest would arrive soon. Being close to the airport was an advantage, but when the wind shifted directions, you could sometimes hear the planes. It never bothered me, and I hoped it wouldn't bother my guests. In less than an hour, there was the sound of tires on the gravel parking place alongside Seaview, then footsteps on the path to the door. I reached up and smoothed my hair and wiped my hands on my shorts. The old-fashioned bell on the registration desk dinged, and I called out, "I'll be right there."

A slender, dark-haired woman in her thirties stood at the registration desk looking a little travel-worn. "You must be Ellen Gage." I held out my hand. "I'm Rose Lambert, the owner of Seaview. Welcome."

Ellen shook my hand. "I'm glad to be here. It's been a long day, and I'm anxious to get out of these clothes and into shorts."

"Let's get you checked in, then I'll show you to your room, and you can get changed and start relaxing."

The phone on the desk rang, and I excused myself to answer it. "Hello? Seaview Bed & Breakfast. Rose speaking."

"Go home," the voice hissed. "No one wants your kind on Anguilla. We were doing fine before you came. Go home." They hung up.

I put the receiver down and stared at it for a minute.

Ellen leaned toward me over the counter. "Problem?"

"Uh, no, wrong number." I shook my head. "May I see your driver's license or passport and credit card, please?"

It took only a few minutes and a single minor hiccup caused by my shaky fingers to get Ellen registered in the computer system. "Now, you're booked into a seaside room. If you'd prefer a garden room, that would be all right too."

Ellen shook her head. "Oh no, I want to look out my window and see the ocean and the beach."

"I thought that might be the case." I turned, picked up a key fob, and walked to the bottom of the stairs. "This way."

Ellen followed me up the stairs. We turned left and stopped at her room. "This is your room." I opened the door and stood aside to let Ellen precede me into the room.

"It's pink."

"Salmon, but yes, it looks pink in the sunlight. I hope that's okay."

Ellen looked around, smiling. "When I was a little girl, I wanted my room painted pink in the worst way. Mama said that my room had to be white, so white it was. All the rooms in our house were white. It was cold and sterile-looking. This is perfect." She walked to the window. "And I can see the ocean and a little offshore island. Just what I was hoping for."

I handed her the keys. "I'll leave you to get settled. The bathrooms are in the hall, and there's a small sink in the corner for you to use to wash up. You'll have to carry your towels with you. Oh, I have a small fruit and cheese plate fixed for you. Would you like me to bring it up? Or you can come down to the lobby when you've unpacked and enjoy it there."

Ellen looked like she had been given an award. "Oh, bring it up, if you don't mind. I haven't eaten since Miami, and I'm starving."

"Can I tempt you with some wine too? There's a split of Pinot Grigio or Merlot with your name on it."

"That would be excellent. I'll have Merlot. Thank you so much."

"I'll be right back with your food and wine." When I returned, Ellen had the windows open, and the sea breeze made the curtains billow behind her. The tang of saltwater filled the room.

"Please bring it all down when you're finished. You can set it on the sideboard in the lobby and I'll take care of it."

"Thank you."

Janet poked her head out of her door. "Welcome to paradise. I'm planning to go to supper in about an hour and a half. Would you be interested in coming with me?"

An hour slid by as I worked on my account books. Paying the workmen had just about depleted my savings. I owed a fairly large amount to Henry's Hardware, and all of my credit cards were nearing their limits. There was only one reservation for a week's stay, but that wasn't for another week. That wasn't enough. I needed more guests pronto. What I didn't need was Mrs. Whiting and her friends spreading rumors about me all over the island. It hurt my feelings that so many people believed her lies.

Iggy and I were sitting in rocking chairs on the porch watching people stroll in the moonlight. I told him about the phone call I got that afternoon. It had to have been Mrs. Whiting or one of her group of friends.

He advised me to ignore it. "They will get used to you and stop harassing you."

I wasn't as confident as he was.

Janet and Ellen came up the beach.

"How was your evening?" I said.

"Fine," Ellen said. "We went to the Barrel Stave and had a delicious meal."

"Mrs. O'Neill is an excellent cook. She's especially skilled at preparing fish. I'm glad you enjoyed it."

Hearing that they ate at the Barrel Stave reminded me that Rebecca O'Neill had turned away from me the last time I called out a greeting. She must be another one of the people that Eleanora Whiting spread her spiteful rumors to. I needed to find the time to talk to Rebecca. I wasn't ready to talk to Mrs.

Whiting yet.

"We saw Nathan and a blonde embracing in the surf," Janet said. "It didn't take him long to find another woman after he professed his undying love for me. I'm glad that he didn't see me."

"Don't you worry. If he shows up again, I won't let him know you're in your room. He can leave a message."

"Good."

Ellen yawned. "I've had a long day and too much wine. I think it's time I turned in."

"Me too," Janet agreed.

They said good night and went inside.

Iggy turned to smile at me. "Well, both of your chicks are back in the nest. You can relax."

"I wasn't waiting for them to come back."

He touched my hand on the arm of the rocker. "All the same, you were wondering where they were and if they were having a good time."

"You're right, I was curious if they had found a nice place for supper and hoped that they were enjoying themselves. It's difficult to turn off the mom radar, you know."

He squeezed my hand. "I do know. Our mother tried to be very involved in all of her children's lives. She made Sunday supper for everyone who could make it every week, and you had better have a very good reason for not showing up."

"Every week? That's asking a lot of people who have busy lives and children to take care of."

"She did not think of it that way. She worked hard to make sure that we did not get into trouble growing up. I guess those Sunday suppers were her way of keeping on making sure."

I frowned. "Johnno's jump-up is on Sunday. He must never have made it to your mother's suppers."

"In those days, Johnno did not have a Sunday jump-up. It was a slow night at the beach bar, so he could get away for an hour to come over to Mama's house for a meal and to make an appearance."

"When did the jump-ups start?"

Iggy looked up at the moon as if he would find the answer there. "I do not know. Maybe ten years ago? Our cousin Maynard started up a steel pan band and needed a place to play, so he convinced Johnno to let them play at the beach bar on Sunday afternoons, thinking it would attract some business."

"Well, that sure worked, didn't it?"

"It certainly did. From the first, it was a big hit. Johnno was afraid that the neighbors would complain about the noise. Instead, they all came down to the bar to dance and party. The tourists at Sydans Garden Inn and Blue Harbour Resort started to come, and then tourists from all over the island came. It grew to be the big party with islanders and tourists that it is today."

I stood up. "I'm tired too. I think I'll lock up and hit the hay. Gotta get my rest before tomorrow's jump-up. I wouldn't want to miss a Sunday at Johnno's."

Iggy stood up and put his arm around my shoulder. "Are you in the mood for company?"

"I could be persuaded."

CHAPTER 9

I was pleased with the online response to my website. There were quite a few inquiries about dates and rates, but no more reservations yet. That needed to change so that Seaview would thrive and so my bank balance would thrive too. I had high hopes that Janet and Ellen would post glowing reviews and encourage their friends to stay at Seaview.

I started the coffee when heard the first stirrings from the rooms upstairs, and soon the aroma of brewing coffee had brought both Janet and Ellen downstairs.

"I hope you slept well." Hesitating before laying placemats and napkins on one of the lobby tables, I said, "Would you like to eat together?"

"Sure," they said in unison.

"I slept better than I have in months," Ellen said. "I left the window open and fell asleep to the sound of the little waves kissing the sand. Heaven."

"That's great." I wondered how I could turn that into something on my website. Could I persuade Ellen to put that in her review? "Janet, how did you sleep?"

"I slept okay." She yawned and stretched. "I stayed up too late writing, and the wine I drank with supper kept me up."

Ellen laughed. "Wine is supposed to put you to sleep, not keep you up all night."

"I know, but alcohol does weird things to me. I usually avoid it. Mm, that coffee smells wonderful." She crossed the lobby and poured herself a mug, adding creamer.

Ellen crossed the room to join her. "Is there any sweetener? I spoil my coffee with sweetener."

Janet pointed to the small box next to the coffeepot. "In there are all different kinds. And spoons are in the crock over here."

I heard the sounds of mugs filling with coffee and the clink of spoons as I set the table.

Pausing in the doorway to the kitchen, I said, "Are you ready to eat something? I have egg casserole with farm-fresh eggs and bacon, a tropical fruit bowl, and there's bread on the sideboard if you'd like toast and jam."

"Yes, please," said Janet.

Ellen sat at the table and put down her mug. "I rarely eat breakfast, but I'll try some egg casserole and fruit."

"Me too, and I'm making toast because I love that bread you get from Amy's bakery."

"Coming right up," and I went into the kitchen to fetch the food.

"What's so great about the bread?" I heard Ellen ask.

"It's coconut bread, made with coconut water from coconuts grown right on the island. It makes great toast. I can't get enough of it."

Carrying a tray, I let the aroma of the savory egg bake precede me. "Here you go. Fresh from the oven. I hope you enjoy it."

Iggy and I sat at the kitchen island having pieces of egg casserole and bowls of fruit.

"I guess your food is satisfactory," Iggy said. "No one has come back here to complain."

"Oh, you." I poked his arm. "Don't tease me. I'm too nervous about everyone enjoying their stay. I hope they like the food." I looked down at my empty plate. "I like it." I looked across at his empty plate. "You like it too. What's not to like about fresh eggs, cream, bacon, onions, bell peppers, and imported Dutch cheese?"

A figure appeared at the open back door, and a familiar voice said, "Do you have any left for a starving young man?" Silas looked particularly Caribbean in his tropical print shirt and cargo shorts.

I smiled at him. "Come in, Silas. Yes, there's some left for a starving young man. Didn't your mother feed you this morning?"

Silas nodded as he pulled out a stool and sat down. "Yes, she fed me. That was hours ago. I am a growing boy and need regular fuel. May I go make some toast?"

"Let me make you some. I think my guests are still finishing up. Be right back."

Silas frowned. "I will not scare them off."

"No, but I don't want them to think that there are random people who stop by for breakfast. Sit. I'll make your toast."

"And I am not a random person. I am a friend of the family and practically staff."

When I came back with his toast and jam, Silas looked at me from under his brows. "Mrs. Rose, I heard from a few people at Johnno's that you are here to cheat the Anguillan people. That cannot be true."

"Darn it." My hands clenched into fists. "Who did you hear that from?"

He shook his head and took a bite of toast.

"You don't need to answer." I loosened my fists. "That's Mrs. Whiting's doing. Lomira told me she's going around bad-mouthing me, and I'm not sure what to do about it. Evelyn at Vista Market won't talk to me anymore, and Rebecca at the Barrel Stave turns away when she sees me. Oh, it makes me so mad I could spit."

Iggy drained his coffee mug and set it down. "I am sure that it will all blow over soon. You should not make a big deal of it. I am not going anywhere."

"Blow over? It's got the potential to blow me and Seaview right off the island. If Mrs. Whiting had her way, I'd be run out of town on a rail, and you'd leave me in the dust. It is a big deal. There was that surprise visit from the Health Department inspector the other day, which I passed with flying colors, and now everyone looks at me out of the corner of their eye when I pass by. I have to figure out a way to counteract her rumors." I picked up my coffee mug, but my hand was shaking so much that the rim chattered against my teeth. All I needed was a chipped tooth.

Silas said, "You worry too much. Mrs. Whiting will get tired of making a fuss, and things will go back to normal."

I didn't think so.

Later that morning, I sat at one of the tables with my laptop open, hoping for more reservations when Ellen appeared.

"I was just accosted by a man named Julius who offered to show me a good time on the island. It kind of creeped me out."

"Oh, I'm sorry you were creeped out. Julius doesn't mean any harm. He has taken it upon himself to squire around women who come to Anguilla alone. He's done it for years and seems to make a sort of living at being a personal tour guide, if you get my drift."

Ellen's chin lifted. "You mean he's a gigolo?"

"Exactly, he's Sandy Ground's own gigolo. Like I said, he doesn't mean any harm, and he seems to take rejection well."

"So, I don't need to worry about him following me around?"

"No, although if you decide to come down to Johnno's jump-up with us later this afternoon, I'm certain that you'll see Julius and he'll probably ask you to dance, along with quite a few of the other local islanders. Iggy and I meet up with the crew who helped renovate Seaview, and we eat and drink and dance the night away. You're welcome to come along."

"I'll think about it. Right now, I'm going up to get my book, go back to the beach, and read in the sun."

"Be sure to put on lots of sunscreen; the Caribbean sun can be vicious if you aren't careful."

Ellen started up the stairs. "Oh, don't worry, I've been slathering it on and don't intend to stop."

Until now, there hadn't been any problems with the bed-and-breakfast facilities. Since we didn't have a dry run once all the work was done, I was a little apprehensive about whether things were done properly, especially the plumbing. After Iggy threw Calvin out, his crew had completed the work, and I didn't know if they were licensed plumbers or just assistants. I hadn't wanted to ask for fear that would bring Calvin back.

"Rose," Ellen called from upstairs, "the sink in the green and white bathroom is leaking."

I put my head in my hands. Just when I had been congratulating myself that everything was working, it turned out that it was not perfect after all. Or maybe Calvin had loosened it when I caught him here last time.

"I'll be right there," I said.

I went into the back room, grabbed a handful of towels and a bucket, and went upstairs.

Ellen was standing in the hall between the two bathroom doors.

"Which one?"

Ellen pushed open the door of the left bathroom. "This one, the green and white one."

There was a puddle on the floor under the sink. I threw down a couple of towels to keep the water from damaging the floor. I sopped up the water and wrung the towels out into the shower. Once I had the standing water mopped up, I positioned the bucket under the sink pipes and turned on the water. It immediately started coming out around the coupling. I chanted in my head, "lefty loosey, righty tighty" and turned the coupling ring to the right until it was snug. The dripping stopped. Using a fresh towel, I dried the pipes, turned the coupling ring a little tighter, ran the water again, and when it didn't drip, I leaned back on my heels.

"Well, it looks like they didn't tighten this enough. I'll leave the bucket here just in case. Let me know if it happens again."

"I can do that."

Before going back downstairs, I went into the white and green bathroom on the right side of the hall and double-checked that the coupling ring on that sink was snugged up tight. It was. All I needed was for the plumbing to start leaking all over the hotel.

By then, it was lunchtime. I toasted a slice of Amy's good coconut bread. I buttered it and then put a slice of Gouda cheese on it. There were cucumbers at the market, so I sliced one to eat like potato chips with my cheese toast. As I sat down to eat, Janet came into the kitchen.

"Hi, I'm just looking for a little something to eat." She opened the fridge and took out her basket of food. "May I use your knife and board to slice my cheese?"

"Go right ahead. Take one of those small plates too, if you'd like."

"Thanks. I'll leave you alone to enjoy your lunch."

"You're welcome to stay if you'd like."

"Okay, I'd like that. I hit a dead spot in the book, and I'm stumped. I thought maybe it was because I was hungry, so..." She motioned to the plate that she set on the kitchen island. "Are you and Iggy going to the jump-up this afternoon?"

"Of course. If we didn't show up, Edward would come down here to roust us out and chivvy us down to Johnno's."

Janet's face lit up. "I remember Edward. He's a real dancer. I think he danced every dance and danced with every lady in the place last week."

"Edward is a dancing fool. I think he goes to every jump-up on the island every week. He loves it. Johnno's is his favorite."

"There are more jump-ups?"

"Yes, there's that big one at Shoal Bay on Saturday. I know you heard it when you were staying there. The one at Blowing Point on Friday catches people off the last ferry from St. Martin, and there are smaller ones at beaches around the island every day except Monday. There are no jump-ups on Monday."

"That must be the day when everyone recovers so they can start again fresh on Tuesday."

I laughed. "I think it's the day that the steel band rests. The same band plays at all the jump-ups. They must be exhausted by the time Sunday night rolls around."

"Surely that can't be right. There have to be more bands on the island. Guys are always making up rock bands in their parents' garages."

Holding up a finger, I said, "Rock bands, yes; steel pan bands, I don't think so, and the steel drums are the reason the tourists come to the parties. The jump-up organizers learned early that rock bands bring young people, locals and tourists, and the neighbors complain. Steel drum bands bring together people of all ages. It makes for a better party, and the neighbors like it too. More fun and more profit."

"So how come you moved to Anguilla? What do you like about it?

"I've dreamed of owning and fixing up Seaview ever since I saw it in 1990 when we came here on a dive vacation. It was pretty rough then and only got worse over the years. A French businessman owned it and used it about three times a year, so maintenance was slipshod at best. Iggy, Silas, and the three guys you danced with at the jump-up spent the better part of the last year helping me refurbish the place inside and out. New wiring, new plumbing, new walls, and a new kitchen." I listened to what I was saying and hoped that I could overcome the rumors and bad feelings Mrs. Whiting was spreading. "What do you like about it?"

Janet was quick to reply. "The people. I've been here for

a couple of weeks, and the local people couldn't be nicer. I'm loving my stay at Seaview too. It's so homey and welcoming."

I grinned at her. "That's great. Thanks. Be sure you put that in your review."

"Oh, I will."

Janet finished up her cheese, crackers, and banana. "Time to go back to see if I can't string a few more words together before time to get ready for the jump-up. This week I'm wearing different sandals. I got a blister between my toes wearing leather flip-flops last week."

"Ouch," I said. "I have a pair of dancing sandals. I tried wearing sneakers. They stuck to the floor. See you in a while. Iggy and I go down around five o'clock. We'll save you a seat. Or rather, the guys will. They get there early to nail down that big table on the edge of the dance floor." Maybe I should put a dancing sandal recommendation on my website.

"Thanks. Later," said Janet as she left the room, her bottle of iced tea in her hand.

CHAPTER 10

It was raining when we woke up the next morning. Not too hard, but still no one wants a rainy day on vacation. Ellen and Janet were slow to come down to breakfast, and both of them seemed a little hungover from last night's jump-up at Johnno's. I had watched them dancing and drinking with the crew, just like I had the first time we went to the jump-up from working on Seaview. They both danced all evening and into the night with a wide variety of partners. Edward was in constant motion, as always. He didn't let either woman sit out a song if he noticed they weren't dancing, just like he'd done to me last year. Silas, Melvin, and Luke did their parts to keep the women on their feet until I said, "Stop. Let them catch their breath. Give them a chance to rest and have something to eat and drink." That brought the young men up short. They weren't used to needing to stop and recharge and thought that everyone was the same.

Julius had done his best to capture Ellen's hand for every slow song. I noticed that as the night wore on it didn't look as though she minded at all. By midnight her head was on his shoulder, and he was talking nonstop in her ear. In fact, I was surprised not to see Julius come down to breakfast with Ellen that morning. I thought about dancing like that with Jim when we were first visiting Anguilla, how it made me feel safe and loved. Dancing with Iggy was all about warmth, but a different warmth tinged with respect for my independence and drive to make my dream of a bed-and-breakfast come true.

I made sure that Janet and Ellen had mugs of fresh coffee before saying, "Can I bring you each a couple of slices of banana bread along with a bowl of berries?"

Janet perked right up. "Yes, that sounds lovely."

Ellen lifted her head from her hand. "I guess I'll have some too. Mostly I just want coffee and then I think I'll go back to bed since it's raining and all."

I went into the kitchen to make a tray with two breakfasts on it, thinking I was glad that I'd made something gentle for hungover tummies. Maybe I should make up a "hangover cure" breakfast option for Monday mornings. I had set the table with placemats and napkins when I made the coffee. As I put the plates in front of my guests, I said, "It rarely rains for long. I'm certain that the sun will be out in an hour or so."

Ellen groaned. "That's great. I'll sleep until the sun comes out."

"And I think I'll write," Janet added. "I didn't drink as much rum as Ellen did since I asked Johnno to put a half shot in mine. I don't feel as bad as you seem to."

"All the dancing didn't help. I haven't danced that much since I was in college, and that was over ten years ago. Pilates class has nothing on a jump-up at Johnno's."

Just then the rain increased in intensity and the wind picked up. I said, "You should probably make sure that the seaside windows in your rooms are shut. The rain comes from the sea, and it'll rain in." Would guests blame me if their possessions got damaged if it rained on them?

Janet and Ellen hurried up to their rooms. "Oh no, my laptop is on the desk by the open window," Janet said, running up the stairs.

They met in the hallway on their way back downstairs to finish their breakfast.

"Did anything get wet?"

Janet shook her head. "Nothing important. I had the curtains closed, so they got a little wet, but no rain got on my laptop, thank goodness." She turned to Ellen. "How about you?"

"The only thing that got rained on was a map that I got from the car rental place. I wiped it off and I'm sure that it'll finish drying just fine." She drained her coffee mug. "I think I'll go back up and lie down."

Around noon I was sitting in the lobby watching the weather on my laptop. I worried how the tropical storm would affect my fledgling business. Would I be able to flourish with such a handicap at the start? Thank heavens I had Iggy to help me prepare for it.

"What's going on?" said Ellen, coming down the stairs from her room. "Why is it so dark?"

I motioned to the screen. "There's a hurricane spinning toward Puerto Rico and we're catching the rain bands."

Ellen came to stand behind me so that she could look at the screen too. "A hurricane! They predicted it to swing north of Puerto Rico last I heard. I would never have made the trip if I thought a hurricane would come here too. What are you going to do?"

Trying to project an attitude of calm, I looked up at her. "I'm going to make sure that all the flashlights have good batteries in them and hope that the power stays on, so we don't have to use them."

"Flashlights. Is that all you are going to do? What about the wind? What about the storm surge? I've seen footage from hurricanes in Florida and no flashlight in the world could help with all of that."

"No, you're right, but flashlights are the first step. There are shutters for all the windows and latches to keep them closed. I'm waiting for Iggy to come over. He's lived on Anguilla his whole life and he'll be able to tell me more of what to expect."

I didn't need a hurricane in addition to no new reservations and Mrs. Whiting's rumors. Although maybe the storm would keep that creepy Calvin away for a few days.

With the edge of the hurricane hitting Anguilla, I would be feeding my guests two or three meals a day for the duration. I needed supplies. I asked Janet and Ellen if there was anything they'd like if I could find it at the grocery store. Janet said that she was sure whatever I found would be fine. Ellen wanted sunshine and no wind. I told her I couldn't promise anything. Everyone had the same idea. I wasn't surprised to see that the IGA parking lot was full. I had to park on the street. When I got into the store, I got the last shopping cart, one with a broken and squeaky wheel. The place was packed. People were throwing food into their carts, shoving each other out of the way to get to things. Most of the time, the people of Anguilla were polite and friendly. Not today.

I bagged tomatoes, cucumbers, bell peppers, and lettuce from the sorry-looking remains in the bins. The onions looked a little rotten. I picked out a few that weren't too bad. The woman behind me in the produce department kept running up on my heels. I turned and frowned at her the second time she did it. She didn't apologize; she just made a face. I figured she was another one of Mrs. Whiting's friends, believing her rumors.

The meat department was even worse. The coolers were stripped bare, and the service counter was nearly empty. I managed to get a kilo of beef shawarma, seasoned beef strips with onions, peppers, and celery that made a savory sauce when sauteed. I could cook that up with a big pot of rice and even have some to freeze if the electricity stayed on.

The canned goods aisle was nearly cleared out. I nabbed two last few cans of canned meat. That was precooked so it could be eaten without heating. I hoped that there would be loaves of bread. I got the last package of toilet paper, snatching it from under the hand of another woman.

Two women in the beverage aisle were bemoaning the fact that they were out of bottles and jugs of water. I never thought about the water treatment plant being damaged in a storm and no water coming out of the taps. I would have to fill all of my biggest pots and pails when I got back to Seaview.

When I turned the corner of the bakery aisle, I was pleased that there was bread on the shelves, but by the time I got there, almost all of it was gone. I took two loaves, leaving some for other customers.

The checkout lines were long and slow. Everyone was in a bad mood. There was none of the usual friendly chat and banter; people were serious-faced and tight-lipped. I looked at the woman in the next line. She had tears running down her cheeks.

"Don't cry," I said. "Maybe the storm will miss Anguilla."

The woman reached up and wiped her cheeks with her hand. "No, hurricanes always come where I am."

I didn't know what to say in the face of such fatalism. I turned back to my cart only to see someone trying to take a loaf of bread.

"I beg your pardon. Put that back."

"You have two, I have none. I need bread for my family," the woman said.

"And I need bread for my guests." Then I thought about the rumors going around about me. "Oh, take it." We could have open-face sandwiches.

The woman's angry expression changed to a look of triumph as she put the loaf of bread into her cart. But she didn't thank me.

The line moved slowly as full cart after full cart was unloaded, scanned, and bagged. My food budget took a hit. I paid and was happy to be out of the store. I loaded the groceries into the back of my car and left the cart in the corral at the edge of the parking lot. This was my first hurricane experience. I wished now that I had listened harder to the stories that Aunt B told of North Carolina and Florida hurricanes, about how to prepare and how to ride them out. It started raining again as I drove home from The Valley. Maybe this is the beginning, I thought.

I turned on the car radio and heard only music. I twisted the dial until I heard a voice say, "Hurricane Alphonso has stalled out twenty miles east of Puerto Rico. The storm has sustained winds of one hundred three miles per hour, making it a Category 2 hurricane. Residents of St. Martin, Sint Maarten, and Anguilla should be prepared for strong winds and heavy rain as the bands move across the area." My heart sank. The voice didn't say for how long we could expect the storm to affect Anguilla. Could they even predict things like that?

A gust of wind rocked the car as I slowed down for the roundabout. My windshield wipers were barely keeping up with the rain and I was getting nervous about the strength of the storm. What must it be like during the storm if this was just the bands of wind and rain that fanned out from the bulk of it? I was glad that I was almost home. I thought I saw Calvin's faded green pickup truck right behind me as I turned down the hill toward home, but it didn't follow me. Was it my imagination, or was I really seeing him everywhere? I chastised myself. The man had a business to run; he didn't have time to trail around after me.

I got soaked carrying in the groceries even though I had a rain jacket. The cold rain ran down my neck and nearly blinded me as I carried the groceries into Seaview.

Silas ran down the street from his dad, Johnno's beach bar, to help carry in the last few bags. "Everything all right, Mrs. Rose?" he said.

I used a towel to dry off my face. "So far, so good, but I don't know what I'll do if it gets any worse."

"I am sure that Uncle Iggy will come down soon and help you get ready."

"That's good. I'm not sure what to do."

I got busy putting away the groceries, and Silas left to keep helping his dad tie down the tables and chairs at the beach bar. I surveyed the food that I had bought and decided that now was as good a time as any to cook ahead in case the power went out.

I heard a vehicle pull up and park behind Seaview, then footsteps on the back porch, and Iggy came in wearing a slicker and a ball cap.

"You need a rain hat."

"No, this works fine," said Iggy, "it does not get in the way of me seeing where I am going."

"It doesn't keep the rain from trickling down your neck."

"I turn up the collar and I stay dry." He smiled. "Or drier anyway." He hung his slicker on the hook by the back door. He took my hands and pulled me to him for a kiss.

"Oh, I'm glad you're here."

"Me too. It smells good in here. What are you cooking?"

I waved my hand at the stove. "I bought some beef shawarma at the IGA and cooked that up. I have rice simmering and I made fettuccine. In the oven are two big meatloaves, so we can have meatloaf sandwiches. They're the best."

"Why are you doing all this cooking now?"

"Well, I figured if the power goes out, at least I'd have something to feed my guests. I made up an egg casserole to put in when the meatloaves come out, and then I'll make a couple batches of muffins. I want to be ready."

Iggy put his hands on his hips. "You have a gas generator. That will run things if the power goes out."

"Yes, I do, but what if I run out of gas?"

"It sounds as if you are preparing for Armageddon. I have another can of gas for you in the back of my truck."

"Hey, this is my first hurricane. I'm running scared and want to be prepared." I put my hand to my mouth. "Oh, I forgot. The IGA was out of bottled water and jugs of water. I need to fill up some kettles and pitchers, maybe some buckets too, in case the water treatment plant goes offline."

Iggy stepped forward. "I can do that. You keep cooking."

We worked side by side for the next hour. Iggy carried pails of water into each bathroom in case the water went off so they could flush the toilets.

"It's too bad that we don't have a bathtub to fill up with water," I said. "That would be a lot of water to have on hand."

"I will put a pitcher of water in each guestroom too for tooth brushing and face cleaning."

Just as the last pan of muffins came out of the oven, the power went out.

I had read in the instruction manual that I could light the stove burners with a match. The oven wouldn't work because the igniter needed electricity to function. That was okay. I had cooked and baked everything I wanted to before the outage. Unfortunately, that meant no coffeepot, no microwave, and no toaster. I needed a percolator so I could brew coffee on a stove burner. Also, no electricity meant no lights or air conditioning. Good thing I had laid in a stock of flashlights, small lamps, and batteries. I had a small gas generator, but I didn't want to start it up just yet. I hoped that the power would come back on soon.

Then I thought of all the food in the refrigerator. That appliance needed electricity to keep things cold. I had a lot of food in there that I couldn't afford to spoil. Better start the generator.

I put on my rain jacket and a hat because the generator was on the back porch. The rain and wind seemed to come from every direction. Even though I was under the porch roof and in a rain jacket, I still got wet. Staring down at the generator, I hoped it would start. I didn't want to have to have Iggy get it going because I needed to be independent. He wouldn't be there all the time. He had shown me what to do; I had written it down step by step. Fortunately, Iggy had filled it with gas, so I didn't have to do that. I was confident that it would start. I turned on the switch, turned on the gas feed, set the choke, and pulled the rope. Nothing. "Come on." I pulled the rope again. Still nothing but a strangled cough. "Come on. You can do it." Maybe I wasn't pulling hard enough. I tried again and this time I braced my hand on the generator and really yanked on it. It started. I didn't want to close the choke too soon. "Not yet. Not yet. Now." I waited until the engine had settled into a steady rhythm before turning off the choke and letting it run.

"Good job," Iggy said from behind me. "I knew you would get it going."

I put a hand on my chest. "Oh, you startled me."

"Sorry." He patted my shoulder. "When the power went out, I did not have a light. I had to feel my way downstairs. Then I heard you talking to yourself out here, so I came to see how you were doing."

"I'm doing fine. I was going to wait to start the generator. Then I remembered all the food in the fridge. I thought I'd better start it just to keep the food safe."

"Good thinking." He came closer and leaned down to give me a kiss. "Take care. I am going down to the beach bar. I will be back later when I am done helping Johnno and Silas."

"What else should I be doing?" I kissed him back and held on to him for a moment. "Tell me we'll be all right, that the storm will not intensify."

Iggy held my shoulders. "You know I cannot tell you that. The storm will do what storms do, which is whatever it wants, and we will have to cope with it. You can do this. You are a strong woman." He kissed me again and went up the road to his brother's beach bar.

When I got back into the kitchen, I hung my jacket on the hook by the back door and hung my hat over it.

"The power went out," Ellen said, shining a flashlight in my eyes. "It got too dark in my room to read."

I nodded and shielded my eyes with my hand. "Yes, the power went out. I started the generator so that the fridge stays cold. I'd prefer that you use a flashlight or one of these battery lamps." Taking a small lamp off the highest shelf in the kitchen, I handed it to Ellen.

"This isn't what I am paying for," Ellen said. "I want air conditioning and internet and light."

"I'm sorry, but with the edge of the hurricane here, none of us have those things."

Ellen folded her arms over her chest and thrust out her chin. "I wouldn't have come if I'd known this hurricane would hit the island. The weather people said it was going far north of here. Are you planning to give us a discount because of the inconvenience?"

I turned to face my guest. "Actually, I'm considering charging you more because I'll be feeding you three meals a day since you can't go elsewhere to eat, unless you prefer to take care of yourself. All the restaurants are closed, and the grocery stores are empty."

Ellen took the battery lamp off the kitchen island. "Humph, we'll just see about that." She left the kitchen, and I heard her stomp up the stairs. In a couple of minutes she was back downstairs wearing a jacket.

Ellen came to the kitchen door. "The front doors won't open."

"Yes, I know. They're locked, so the wind doesn't pull them open. If you want to go out, you'll have to leave through the back door."

Ellen stalked across the room and left without another word.

I watched my guest walk off and shook my head. I was certain that Ellen would leave a critical review on the website and any other place she could think of. I sat down on one of the stools at the kitchen island, put my face in my hands, and let the tears fall. This was not the way I had dreamed the second week of operating my bed-and-breakfast would be. I had imagined warm sunny days, laughing happy guests who ate my delectable breakfasts and then went off to enjoy themselves on the island, not torrential rains, high winds, and guests stuck in their stuffy rooms in the dark because the power was out. Tears made tracks down my cheeks as I let myself sink into disappointment and fear that this was a harbinger of bad things to come. In my imagination,

Hurricane Alphonso would shift course and bear down on poor little Anguilla, and Seaview in particular. The wind would tear off the new roof, peel off the siding, suck the shutters right off the windows, and finally flood the whole first floor, ruining all of our hard work. I wouldn't have the money or the heart to start over.

I heard the scuff of a shoe in the doorway behind me. I hurried to wipe my tears on a handy dish towel and turned to find Janet standing at the door.

"I'm sorry to interrupt. I came down for more iced tea."

I gave a watery smile and waved toward the refrigerator. "Help yourself, but be sure to close the door quickly. I have the generator running to keep it cool, and I don't want to waste the cold. We may need it for a long time." Just then, the power came back on. "Oh, good," I said. "I'll go shut off the generator to save gas."

"Ellen is really frustrated."

"Yes, I know, but I can't make the power stay on or make the rain go away."

"Yep, that's true. I think she's used to making things happen, to getting things in order and having them go her way. It's going to take her some time to get used to rolling with the punches."

I smiled at her. "How are you doing? Are you getting any writing done?"

"I am. I got my laptop charged up before the power went out and there is just enough light from the window for me to see what I am doing." Janet put the iced tea pitcher back into the refrigerator. "The sleuth is following clues, and the murderer is laying down false trails. It's moving right along."

"Good, I'm glad someone is having fun on their vacation." A powerful gust of wind rattled the windows and flung the raindrops at the glass with a sound like BBs hitting it.

She touched my shoulder. "Don't worry, I predict that once Ellen sees that there is nothing to be done but sit back and roll with the situation, she'll cheer up and be a good sport about the whole thing."

"I don't know. She seemed pretty angry when I said that I'm considering charging a bit extra because I'll be feeding you three meals a day instead of just breakfast until the storm passes." I braced myself for another negative response.

"That makes sense. I hope we get to eat some of the meatloaf that you baked earlier. It smelled divine."

"Oh, don't worry, the meatloaf and a salad are on tonight's menu."

"Great." Janet walked across to the doorway. "Back to writing."

I heard her climb the stairs, humming a tune. At least someone was happy. I realized I hadn't eaten since breakfast, and I was hungry. I sliced off a bit of Gouda cheese and toasted a slice of wheat bread. I reconsidered and toasted two slices of bread so that I could have one with cheese and one with jam. After that challenging grocery store trip, I deserved it. I was just finishing up my late lunch when Ellen came through the back door. She was soaked. Her hair hung in strings around her face, and her clothes were wet.

"Oh, you poor thing, let me get you a towel to dry off." I hurried into the back room and grabbed a bath towel, then handed it to Ellen, who rubbed it across her head and face.

"I'm sorry," Ellen said. "I walked all the way down to Blue Harbour Resort and you're right. Nothing is open. Even they say that they are only feeding their guests." She peeled off her jacket and dabbed at her damp arms and wet legs. "I was sure that you were saying you had to feed us to beef up our bills. I was wrong. Why did this have to happen now? I needed a break, needed to de-stress, and now I'm more stressed than ever."

I put on the kettle to make a cup of tea. "Why are you stressed?"

"Because nothing is going the way I expected it to. All of my plans are ruined. I can't go for walks on the beach because the surf is too high. I can't go snorkeling because the waves are too strong, and the visibility is nil. I can't even lie on my bed reading a book with the window open and a cool breeze coming in. I'm trapped."

I turned to face her, compassion pushing back my bout of self-pity. "You're right. Your vacation will not be what you expected, but you're still away from home and work and have nothing pressing to do. Have you ever thought of writing a book or short stories? I bet Janet would be glad to get you started. You could let me teach you how to play solitaire; that can suck up hours of time."

"No," Ellen said, "I don't like playing cards. There's too much uncertainty playing cards. You can't predict which one will come next or whether you'll get the one you need when you need it. Too risky, too chancy for me."

I held up my hand. "Okay, I get it, you aren't into playing cards. Do you draw?"

"No, I don't do anything but work. I boss people around and make corporate decisions. I don't do crafts, I don't play computer games or any kind of games for that matter; I just work."

I poured boiling water over a mint tea bag in a mug and pushed it across to Ellen. "What did you think you would do here?"

She picked up the paper tab and dunked the tea bag up and down in the hot water, watching the color of the water change from clear to brown and inhaling the rich aroma of the tea. "I don't know. I guess I hadn't thought about what to do in bad weather. I envisioned sunny days and balmy breezes." She looked at me. "I enjoyed meeting all those people at Johnno's jump-up on Sunday. I thought maybe I would spend some time with one of those guys. Edward seemed like fun, and Julius was eager to spend more time with me."

I poured myself a mug of tea water, too. "Edward isn't your type."

"How do you know?"

I took down a canister of herbal tea bags and picked

a cinnamon orange one out for myself. "Because Edward is a little simple. He doesn't have much conversation, and he's unable to drive. He's excellent when you tell him what to do every step of the way, and he's the best dancer on the island. Now Julius, on the other hand, is an excellent conversationalist, and he'd be happy to show any lady the sights of Anguilla."

Ellen took the tea bag out of her mug and set it on a plate on the table. "What do you mean 'any lady'?"

I swirled the bag in my steeping tea and put my tea bag on the plate next to Ellen's. "Well, remember I told you the other day Julius is a gigolo. He'll squire any single woman around the island, out to meals, into her bed; it's his job. One he has done for years."

Ellen's jaw dropped. "I didn't think you were serious."

I nodded. "Dead serious. He's been at it since I've been coming to Anguilla and that has been since the early nineteen nineties."

"He doesn't look that old."

"Oh, he's not very old, just in his mid-fifties, prime gigolo age, I think. He started when he was barely out of his teens. And I hear that he's very good at what he does. If you want someone to entertain you while you're here, you could do much worse than take Julius up on his offer."

Ellen looked shocked. "I didn't think that anyone did that except in the movies."

"I suspect that's where Julius got the idea, from an old movie, but being a gigolo is an old and honored profession, almost as old as the oldest profession, if you know what I mean."

"And to think that I considered taking him up on his offer to show me around. I guess I have Hurricane Alphonso to thank for that narrow escape."

"I'm certain by now that Julius is hooked up with another woman for the week. I think he does his best hunting at Johnno's jump-up. When I got here, Julius offered to squire me around, but I put him off, not wanting to get involved. Then I met Iggy and he changed everything."

"Don't you ever feel lonely?"

"I do. Sometimes I miss Jim so much I can't bear it, but I decided to make Anguilla my home. It's imperative that I make a success of my new business. That has to be my focus now."

While we talked, the storm intensified, and Seaview was creaking and moaning. Ellen looked startled at the sounds the hotel was making, and I glanced at the ceiling, hoping nothing fell through.

I put down my mug of tea. "I think I'd better go check that none of the doors and windows are leaking. I don't know how much battering they can take." I smiled as I crossed the room to the lobby door. "I don't know how much battering I can take either. Will you check the windows in your room for me, please?"

"Sure." Ellen drained her tea mug and set it by the sink. "I need to change into dry clothes, anyway. Thanks for the tea and the chat."

"Anytime."

CHAPTER 11

All the next day the rain came and went, but the wind stayed strong. It blew the doors back against the frames when they were opened and blew the rain in if the door stayed open for long. Having all the windows and doors on the front of Seaview closed made it hot and stuffy in there. I kept the side windows and the back doors open to mitigate the heat. It wasn't much help and not much rain came in. I knew my guests weren't happy with the weather, but there was nothing I could do about it.

Iggy arrived in the late afternoon wearing his old yellow slicker that flapped around his knees. The bottoms of his jeans got soaked in the dash from his truck to the back door of Seaview. Naturally, he arrived in the middle of a rainstorm not during one of the slack periods. "Do you have everything buttoned up?" he said as he shook the rain off his slicker like a dog.

"I have all the doors and windows on the front closed and latched. I have the side windows open for ventilation. Is that wrong?"

"Yes, you should have the place shut up tight. That wind will bring the rain from all directions." He took off his slicker and hung it on a hook by the back door. Then he charged into the lobby. I heard him closing the windows one after the other.

"Well, excuse me, I didn't know," I said to his retreating back.

Ellen and Janet came into the kitchen in Iggy's wake.

"What are you going to do if the power goes out again?" Ellen asked.

"I've been to the market and laid in lots of food. I have a gas generator that will provide a little power. We should be all right as long as the gas holds out, and there are always flashlights." I smiled at Ellen.

Janet said, "The internet is down. I tried to get online to check on the hurricane's track and got nothing."

Iggy's voice came from the bottom of the stairs. "Hurricane Alphonso is on track to strike Puerto Rico head on. That is one hundred twenty-five miles from here. Anguilla is getting the edge of the storm. The rain and wind are from the bands that swirl around the storm."

"How many hours can we expect it to be like this?" Ellen turned to look at him.

Iggy shook his head. "Not hours, days. It depends on the storm's forward momentum. They rotate at a fast speed but do not always move across the ocean fast. Sometimes they meander and stall and then you have this for what seems like forever."

Ellen's fists hit her hips. "This is my vacation. I'm supposed to be walking on the beach and going snorkeling, not hunkered down in a stuffy hotel room with no internet and nothing to do but sweat."

I shook my head. "I'm sorry. No one controls the weather. Check the bookshelf. Maybe there's something there you'd like to read."

"I should never have come to this backward island." She whirled on her heel and stomped up the stairs.

Iggy, Janet, and I watched her go in silence.

Iggy broke the silence. "It sounds like the rain is slacking off a bit. Maybe we can open the windows and let some air in soon."

Ellen's voice came from upstairs. "There's a puddle in front of the gallery door and it's spreading."

"Oh shit," I said, and I hurried to grab some towels and a bucket.

Iggy and I went upstairs and sopped up the water that

the driving rain had pushed under the door. "I knew we should have put a new sweep on this door," I said as I wrung out the towel and went back to mopping up the rainwater.

"Do you have a sweep?" said Iggy. "I could put it on for you."

"No, I don't have a sweep. Do you think that the hardware store would have one? I could go get one."

Iggy patted my hand. "I will go. I know where to look in the store. If one is there, I will find it."

"Get four if they have them, one for each outside door."

"I will get two for sure, one each for the front and back gallery doors. I do not think that the back doors on the ground floor will need them. The porch overhang will protect them from the worst of the driving rain coming from that direction."

"Okay, you're the hurricane expert." I finished mopping up the water and left a rolled-up towel across the bottom of the door, thinking it might slow down the rain coming in.

Iggy stood up and went back downstairs.

I followed him and went into my apartment. "Let me give you my credit card. I don't want you spending your own money on this."

He held out a hand to stop me. "That is unnecessary. You have an account at the hardware store, don't you?"

"Well, I did when we were working on the building. Now that we're finished, I thought it'd be closed."

Iggy laughed. "You are never finished with a building like this. I will tell Henry to put it on your account."

"Okay, if you say so. Tell him I'll come next week to make a payment." I thought that if I had to keep paying for repairs before I had enough guests, I'd be even farther in the hole than I already was.

"That is fine." He put on his slicker and snapped it. He pulled the wet ball cap out of a pocket and settled it on his head. Iggy leaned down and kissed me. "Be good while I am gone. If it stops raining, open the windows to let the air in, but keep an eye on the western sky." He opened the back door and stepped out onto the porch. "Hey, the sun is out. Go get things open. I will be back soon."

I hurried to the lobby and opened the doors and windows to let the breeze in. It immediately felt more comfortable in the room, and it was good to get the hot, stagnant air replaced by fresh air that smelled like the sea. The horizon was filled with gray storm clouds, but for now, the sky was blue over Sandy Ground. I went upstairs, rapped on each occupied room's door telling my guests that they could open their windows while the sun shone, and I went down the hall to open the bathroom windows. I checked in the back two guest rooms to make sure that there was no water from the windows or the roof that had leaked in. Everything was dry, and I sent up a prayer of thanks for Zeke's good, conscientious work on the roof.

I stood on the front porch of Seaview to see what the bay was looking like. Big waves rolled in and broke a lot farther up the sand than usual. Where before the waves had come to within ten feet of the bottom of the steps, now they were almost touching it. If there was a storm surge, the water would come right over the steps, across the porch, and into the lobby. I had never given thought to how flat Anguilla was. Now I wondered if a big storm surge could wash across the entire island. I hoped I had not put in all the work over the last months to have it washed away or ruined in a storm the second week I was open. I wasn't a religious woman, but I said a little prayer that Hurricane Alphonso would change course and track farther north. I knew that even if the storm did not hit Anguilla directly like Hurricane Gonzalo had, the surge could send seawater far inland. Even this hurricane didn't make me wish I'd chosen another island.

Iggy was back in an hour, and so was the rain. I made sure that all the windows and doors were closed again, and he and I hurriedly screwed the sweep to the outside of the front gallery door, getting thoroughly drenched. As we gathered up the tools and prepared to go install the sweep on the back gallery door, Ellen opened her door and said, "I'm leaving."

I was stunned. "Where are you going? To another hotel?"

"No, I'm going home. I didn't spend all this time and money to sit around sweltering and listening to the rain."

Iggy cleared his throat. "I am sorry to tell you that no planes will fly today."

"Are you sure about that?"

He shook his head. "I went past the airport to get to the hardware store and all the airplanes were gone or tied down. You can call Lloyd International Airport to ask about flights, but I am afraid that you will be out of luck."

She looked from him to me. "I know it's not your fault, but I can't stay here like this. I'm calling the airport." She took two steps back and closed the door. She immediately opened it again. "There's no cell service. Can I use your landline?"

"Go right ahead. Use the phone on the registration desk."

Ellen left her room and went down the stairs.

Iggy and I went to the back gallery door and installed the sweep on that door.

"I was lucky to get the last two sweeps in the store," said Iggy. "I hope you will not need them on the back doors onto the porch. That has a wide overhang that most likely will protect it from the storm forcing rain under it."

I looked at him. "Were there really no planes at the airport?"

Iggy turned the last screw in the sweep and closed the door to the storm. "There are usually no planes on Monday, but I am certain that the operation is shut down because of the wind." He ran a hand over his face to wipe off the rain. "Let's go downstairs and get dry. Maybe you can make some coffee. I am a little chilled."

I made a pot of coffee and then went into my bedroom and found an old tee shirt that was too big for me that Iggy could wear. "Here," I said, "take off your wet shirt and put this one on. I'm sorry that I don't have any dry jeans for you to wear."

"Thank you, I appreciate the dry shirt."

I went back into my bedroom and changed into dry clothes. By the time I was redressed, the coffee had finished dripping. I poured us each a mug and carried it into the kitchen.

"Do you have any muffins to go with this coffee?" Iggy said.

I got up and went to the refrigerator. "I have a couple left from the other day that Silas hasn't eaten. I'll take the chill off in the microwave." I put the two muffins on a plate and slid it into the microwave. Soon the microwave buzzed, and the room was filled with the aroma of banana bread. We sat drinking coffee and eating warmed muffins in companionable silence.

Iggy cleared his throat when he drained his coffee mug. "I need to tell you that Henry at the hardware store made me pay for the sweeps. He would not let me put them on your account."

"Why not? Did he say?"

"Yes. He said that you were not reliable and are looking to take advantage of Anguillans and their good nature, so your account was closed."

"That's not true, Iggy. I'm not taking advantage of people or trying to cheat them. Has Mrs. Whiting talked to everyone on the island? Lomira was right to warn me to be careful."

As I sat there brooding on the latest blow, I felt antsy. I felt like I should be up and doing something. All the doors and windows were sealed as best as we could manage, and I had laid in food enough for four people, food that could be eaten cold in case the power went out again and stayed out. My instinct was to make a pot of soup like I would have in Wisconsin when a blizzard was on the way, but without a way to heat it, soup was disgusting, and it was too darned hot to eat soup, anyway. Hm, what about gazpacho? I could make that or another kind of cold soup. Would it be as comforting as a bowl of hot chicken soup on a cold winter day? I didn't think so, but now that I thought of it, I wanted to make it. I probably had all the ingredients on hand. Standing up, I pulled down my recipe binder.

"What are you doing?" Iggy said.

"I want to make gazpacho, and I think I have a recipe in here." I pulled on the "Soup" tab and paged through. "Yes," I said. "Here it is." I scanned the ingredients list. "And I have everything I need. Now I just need the power to stay on for half an hour so I can make it."

Iggy drained his coffee mug and wiped his mouth on his napkin. "What can I do to help?"

I had my head in the refrigerator, gathering up vegetables. When I stood up, I handed Iggy a knife and cutting board and put a big bowl between us on the kitchen island. "You can chop up some of these vegetables for me."

"How small should I make them?"

I consulted the recipe. "It just says chopped so about half an inch should be good."

We got to work chopping an onion, a bell pepper, a cucumber, a few tomatoes, and two green onions that were in the bottom of the crisper drawer. I squeezed the juice from two lemons, minced a clove of garlic, and measured out red wine vinegar, dried tarragon, dried basil, and chopped fresh parsley. Working together, it didn't take us long to have the bowl full of all the chopped veggies and herbs.

I poured in a quart of tomato juice, sprinkled on a teaspoon of sugar and a little salt and pepper. I stirred it to combine all the ingredients, then scooped the whole bowlful of ingredients into the food processor in a couple of batches and blended it until it was combined but still chunky. I took a spoonful to taste. "Just right."

"Don't I get a taste too? I helped chop."

I grabbed another spoon. "Of course, you do. Tell me what you think."

He dipped the spoon into the soup and tasted it. "I think it needs a squirt of hot sauce."

I thought about it. "I'll leave that out until it's served. Others may not like things as spicy as you do. I'll put in a pinch of red pepper flakes just to brighten up the flavors." I did and gave it another whirl in the food processor.

"What are you making?" Janet stood in the doorway. "It's too hot and stuffy to write, so I came down to see what you're doing."

I motioned her to come in. "We're making gazpacho."

"Oh, yum, is it ready to eat?"

"Not yet, it has to chill for a couple of hours to let the flavors blend."

"Rats. What else is there to eat? I'm kind of hungry."

I checked the refrigerator when I slid in the big, covered bowl of gazpacho. "I have some leftover egg casserole and a couple of muffins. There's some roast beef."

Ellen spoke from the doorway. "Can we have roast beef sandwiches? I love them on white bread with mayonnaise."

I laughed. "Yes, we can have roast beef sandwiches with mayo. All I have is whole wheat bread. Will that do?"

Ellen smiled and nodded. Outside, the wind was roaring, and we could hear waves crashing on the beach in front of Seaview.

"I will go make sure that no water is coming in," said Iggy. "You make some sandwiches."

In the kitchen I was slicing roast beef to make sandwiches. Ellen stood across the island from me. I said, "I thought you were leaving."

Ellen folded her arms across her midriff. "That guy…"

"Iggy."

"Yeah, Iggy was right. There are no flights in a hurricane or even at the edge of a hurricane. I guess I'm stuck here for the duration. How long will it be?"

I kept slicing. "I don't know. This is my first hurricane too. Probably a few days. It depends on how fast the storm moves along."

"Days. I was hoping by now it'd be hours."

Iggy came back into the room. "We are getting the rain bands on the edge of the storm. They can sweep through for a few days if the storm is a slow mover. I heard on the radio that it stalled out east of Puerto Rico this morning, and we are east of Puerto Rico. I think we are in for at least a couple of days of this wind and rain. Nothing to be done about it." He turned to me. "Do you have a radio?"

"No, I don't have a radio. I suppose I should get one as soon as I can. I use my laptop for weather information. That's useless now that the internet is down." I looked up to see tears rolling down Ellen's cheeks. "Oh, honey, don't cry. This old place has gone through rougher weather than Hurricane Alphonso and stayed standing. We'll be all right." I handed her a paper towel.

Ellen wiped her tears. "It's not that. I came on this vacation because I needed to get away from everything. My career is stalled. I think I've hit a glass ceiling, and the stress is making me sick. I wanted a no stress, no problems vacation and look what I get, a hurricane."

Janet said, "I came down here to get away from home and my soon to be ex-husband. He followed me here. Talk about stress on vacation. I was all ready to hole up in my room here until I could be sure that Nathan had left. Now I'm afraid that he's stuck on the island too. I want to call Blue Harbour Resort to find out if he's still here, but I'm too chicken."

Ellen wiped her cheeks again. "I can make that call. I'll say that I'm from Nathan's firm and need to speak with him. Rose, can we use the phone? Let's do it right now. Put your mind at ease."

Ellen and Janet put their heads together and dialed the resort's number. Ellen put on her executive voice and got through to the manager immediately. They spoke for barely a minute.

"Ha," said Ellen after she hung up, "he's gone. You can relax, Janet. The guy said that Nathan left on Saturday."

A powerful gust of wind shook the hotel, and the lights

flickered. Janet looked up. "I'd better make sure that my laptop is turned off and unplugged. I can't afford for it to fry. It's the only place where I have my novel right now." She hurried out of the room and pounded up the stairs.

"I hope she backs it up on a USB drive," Ellen said. "It would be suicide not to."

"I'm sure that she does. Mention it when she comes back down. I hope the power stays on."

"Do not forget your generator," Iggy said, "it is full of gas and ready to go."

"I know. I don't want to start it again. It scares me."

"Sitting in the dark and having all of that food you made go bad should scare you more."

A particularly strong gust rattled the windows, and I heard a voice call out for help.

We raced up the stairs.

I unlocked Janet's door and had to push hard on it to get it open. A blast of wind and rain hit me in the face. Janet stood in a pool of rainwater and broken glass. "What happened?" I had to lean on the door to keep it from slamming shut.

"The shutters flew open, something hit the glass, and broke the window."

"Are you all right?"

Janet clutched her laptop to her chest. "I think I'm okay, but I can't move because I'm barefoot."

Iggy stepped past me, scooped Janet up in his arms, and carried her into the hall where he put her down. He looked at Janet. "Did you get cut when the window broke?"

Janet shook her head. "I don't think so. Maybe. My laptop got rained on and I'm afraid it's ruined."

I felt cold, not from the storm wind blowing in through the broken window, but from dread that I'd be liable for Janet's laptop and all her writing that was on there. I couldn't afford to replace her laptop, much less be responsible for her losing her livelihood if the computer was ruined. "Give me your laptop and I'll put it in rice like they do with wet cell phones. Don't try to turn it on. Let's just see if we can get it dry." I hurried downstairs with the dripping computer. I got out the big kitty litter pan that I used when I made a salad for a crowd, laid the laptop in it face down, and covered it with dry rice. I crossed my fingers that the rice would soak up the rainwater.

Iggy followed me into the kitchen. "I have a piece of plywood in the back room that should fit over the window. Can you come help me nail it over the opening?"

"Of course, it's my hotel and I have to do everything to keep it safe. Where's Janet?"

Iggy nodded over his shoulder. "I left her in the hall."

I grabbed the key to the lilac bedroom from its pigeonhole and hurried back upstairs. "Janet, let's get you into this other room where it's dry."

"My things…"

"Iggy is going to nail a board over the window and then I'll clean up the water and glass. We can get your things and move them into this room when it's safe."

"What about my laptop? I can't lose all that writing."

"Don't you back it up?"

Janet patted her pocket. "I do. I put it on a USB drive, but that's no good to me if the computer is toast. Is there a place in Anguilla where I could buy a new one?"

I shook my head. "Not really. The closest store is on Sint Maarten and I'm not sure that the ferry is running in this storm. I'll ask Iggy. Maybe we'll be lucky, and it'll be all right." I heard Iggy call me from the kitchen. "Gotta go. I'll get you some dry clothes once we have the window covered, then you can take a shower to wash off any tiny bits of glass that are stuck to you." I hurried down the stairs and found Iggy just finishing up pre-drilling holes in the corners of the plywood.

"I need you to come with me to hold the board in place while I nail it. That wind is going to make the wood want to fly away. You carry the hammer." He handed me the tool and slipped some long nails into his raincoat pocket.

I put on my raincoat and followed him upstairs to the

front gallery door. When I unlocked it, the door flew open toward us, letting in the wind and rain. We slipped out, pulled the door shut against the wind behind us, and wrestled the plywood over to the gaping window. Once we had it in place, the wind held it there. I leaned on it anyway to make sure it didn't move. Iggy pounded a nail in each corner and then examined the shutters.

"The latch broke," he shouted over the howl of the wind. "I will nail them shut so they don't pound themselves to pieces in the storm."

I nodded and helped him fold them over the plywood. The wind was strong in my face as I made my way over to the door back inside.

It took both of us pushing on the door to get it closed against the wind and rain. We stood in the short hallway that ran between the front bedrooms, breathing hard. I leaned on Iggy's chest and inhaled the spicy scent of his aftershave. "Did you shave before you came over today?"

"Of course I did. I always shave before I come to see you."

I wrapped my arms around him and laid my cheek on his chest. "I think you smell great. Right now, I feel like I look like a drowned cat."

He leaned back and looked me over. "Yes, you are a little wet."

"A little wet? I feel like I'll never be dry again."

"You need a better raincoat for storms like this."

I made a cross over my left breast. "I promise to get one just as soon as Hurricane Alphonso is done with us. Watch, I'll get a new, better raincoat and for as long as I live on Anguilla there will never be another storm like this, and it'll hang in my closet dry and pristine."

Iggy shook his head. "That will not happen. Every few years a hurricane, or the edge of a hurricane, or a tropical storm visits Anguilla. Your new, better raincoat will get a lot of use over the years that you live here."

I slapped my palm on his chest and splashed rainwater

back in my face. "Don't curse me like that. I can dream of a storm-less life of ease in the tropics if I want to."

"You can dream, but it will never happen."

I pushed away from him. "Let's go downstairs and get dried off. I could do with a cup of coffee and something to eat. Fighting that wind made me hungry."

"I could drink coffee, or we could..." He waggled his eyebrows at me. "Since we have to take off our wet clothes, anyway." He grinned.

"In the middle of the storm?" I looked over his shoulder at the guest room doors and lowered my voice. "Well, we'd have to be quick since they're liable to come downstairs at any minute. This is worse than having kids. I can't confine them to their rooms so mom and dad can have a nap."

We walked downstairs.

"Did you bring dry clothes along?"

"No, but you can put my clothes in the dryer while we are busy."

"Good idea."

An hour later we were in the kitchen, dry and refreshed, and making coffee.

"Are you still hungry?" Iggy said.

"Yeah, I could eat a little something. What time is it anyway?"

He looked at his watch. "It is three forty-five, past lunchtime but too early for supper."

"I don't remember eating lunch. No wonder I'm hungry. How about some cheese and crackers?" I rummaged in the refrigerator and brought out some cheeses and put them on the kitchen island. I grabbed the crackers from a wire mesh cabinet.

"Cheese and crackers sound good," Iggy said.

"Oh, here are some toasted baguette slices. They're better than crackers," I said and pulled out a plastic container with the slices.

I got out a small platter, arranged the baguette slices on it, and slid a cutting board and cheese knife over to Iggy.

"Please slice up some cheese while I make the coffee. Once our snack is done, I need to get that broken glass cleaned up so Janet can retrieve her belongings and move them to the lilac room."

"Is there enough for two more?" said a voice from the doorway.

I saw my guests peering in at us and smiled. "Sure."

CHAPTER 12

It took me over an hour to sweep up all the broken glass in the yellow guest room. I couldn't believe how far tiny pieces had flown. They were glittering all the way over to the door, and I was sure that the bedding had glass in it too. I thought I would hang the bedding to dry and then try to shake out the pieces of glass instead of attempting to launder them out. I didn't want glass shards and splinters in my washing machine.

It took even longer to get all the water mopped up. I did my best to dry the floorboards and the wall under the window. It would take time for the mattress and box springs to dry out, too. Soon I felt comfortable telling Janet that she could pack up her belongings to transfer them to the lilac guest room at the back of the hotel.

Every time the wind picked up, the hotel would shudder, and the old boards would creak and groan. At first, I thought that meant that the roof was peeling off, then I figured out that it was just the building moving in the strong wind. I could see the edge of the sheets of metal roofing, and it looked as if Zeke had nailed them down securely. It took Janet a few trips to get her things moved, and I noticed she flinched every time there was a creak of wood. It was no use trying to reassure her we were safe since she had a personal experience that there was every possibility that the storm would figure out a way to get in.

When I carried down the last armload of wet bedding, I stepped into a puddle when I reached the lobby. Where had that come from? I looked to see water seeping in around the front doors. We had installed new sweeps on the front doors, but they were evidently not enough to keep the seawater out when the waves came up high enough. The water was halfway across the lobby and spreading.

"Iggy," I called, "there's water coming in the front doors. What can we do?"

There was no answer. I went into the kitchen to find Iggy with his head down on his arms on the kitchen island. He was asleep. I went past him to put the wet bedding down in the back room and then went back into the kitchen. I laid my hand on his back and stroked it.

"Iggy, are you okay?"

His head popped up, and he looked around. "What... where..." his eyes met mine, "Oh, Rose, sorry. I just put my head down for a minute and must have fallen asleep."

"I'm not surprised. You've been running around, in and out of the storm, helping me, helping Johnno. It's no wonder that you're tired. Do you want to lie down?"

He shook his head. "No, I'm good. A little catnap was all I needed. What's happening now?"

I sighed. "Well, the waves must be washing up high enough to clear the front steps because there's water seeping in around the front doors. Is there anything we can do to stop it?"

"Not really. We can put down towels to keep the water from going far. That is about all."

I turned back into the back room. "I'll get some old towels rolled up and in place and put the washtub alongside for wringing out the towels."

My steps were slow and discouraged as I went back to the lobby with my burden.

"What's going on?" Ellen came partway down the stairs. "Now where is the water coming in?"

I gestured with my armload of towels. "The waves are breaking over the steps and seawater is coming in under the front doors. It's seeping past the weather stripping. The only way to keep it from spreading across the floor again is to roll up towels and keep wringing them out."

"I'm getting real tired of this storm," Ellen said.

I leveled a look at her. "You and me both, honey."

CHAPTER 13

The next afternoon, I was in the kitchen when the back door opened, and Janet and Ellen staggered in.

"You look like a pair of drowned rats," I said. "What happened?"

Ellen pushed her wet hair back. "We were walking on the beach during the last lull, and I got knocked down by a wave but couldn't stand up, so Janet had to help me. We both got soaked. It's started raining harder again too."

I nodded. "I hear the wind has picked up."

"Yes, it blew spray at us mixed with sand. I feel like I've been sandblasted. Is it okay if I go take a shower?"

Janet said, "Me too."

"There are two bathrooms, so you don't have to wait," said Ellen.

"It's okay. I want to get my things organized better in my new room before I shower."

"Suit yourself."

They went upstairs together and soon I heard the shower start. I heard Janet moving around in the lilac bedroom overhead.

This was not the way I wanted the second week that the Seaview Bed & Breakfast was open to be. I didn't want to have my guests trapped in the hotel needing to be fed three meals a day instead of one. Not that I begrudged them the food; I was happy to feed them. I also knew that I needed to figure out how much it was costing me and add it to their bills. That would not be popular, I was certain, but it was a fact of life that I hadn't planned to feed two extra meals a day to two extra people for I don't know how long.

Iggy came in from making a circuit of the outside of the hotel. "Everything except those shutters for Janet's room is holding tight. I nailed them closed, so they should stay that way until the storm passes and you can get Silas to fix the latch. He will probably have to install a new latch because that one looks pretty weak and rusted. That is why it failed."

"I thought you said that the nails had pulled out of the wood."

"I took a better look at it and the nails held fine; it was the latch itself that broke around the nails and pulled away."

I sighed. "I guess I'd rather replace the latch than have to replace the whole shutter. I imagine that after this storm shutters will be hard to find on the island."

"I imagine you are right."

I looked at the sandwich makings on the kitchen island that Janet and Ellen hadn't put away. "Are you hungry? I'm starving. I'm making a sandwich. Would you like one?"

Iggy hung his slicker on the nail by the back door. "I could eat a sandwich. Do you have any mustard?"

"I have mustard."

I laid out two plates, put two slices of bread on each plate, and dug a jar of honey mustard out of the refrigerator. "Is this mustard okay? I don't have any hot mustard."

Iggy shook his head. "It will have to be. I will bring over a jar of the mustard that I like so it will be here when I need it again. Maybe I will bring over some clothes too."

We each made a sandwich with meatloaf, tomato slices, and the spread of our choice.

"Oh, I have pickles too." I pulled a jar of pickle slices out. It was a very satisfying lunch.

I went to every window and every door, feeling around them for moisture. So far, they were mostly dry. There was that water seeping around the front doors, but with the strength of the wind I was not surprised that the rain and waves were sneaking around the sides of the doors. I'd keep an eye on it and remember to wring out the towels before the water spread. What surprised me the most was that no rain was coming in around the plywood over the front window that had broken when the shutters blew open. The wood must be just big enough to cover the opening completely. Thank God for Iggy.

When I went downstairs, I peered out the side window closest to the beach to see what the waves were doing. They were building and crashing all the way up past the edge of the sand. I figured they were breaking over my steps. Would the doors hold them out if the waves came up even higher? I thought that the only reason they might is because the doors opened out instead of in. Iggy and Silas told me it said in the fire code that all exterior doors had to open out so that in case of a fire the exit would be easier. No fires, please God, no fires. I was grateful that Seaview had all new wiring. The old wiring wouldn't have withstood the irregular stops and starts of power that the storm had brought. I went back through the kitchen to stand in the doorway and watch the storm from there.

Rain fell in sheets, and the wind whipped it every which way. The lights that Iggy had strung from the porch corners to the pole at the street had fallen. I slipped on my rain jacket and went out onto the porch to pull them back. I couldn't reach up high enough to unhook them from the posts, but I could get them out of the rain and unplug them. The back patio was littered with bougainvillea flowers like a red and pink carpet, and my mango tree was swaying like mad. As I watched, it swayed with the wind, and a powerful gust pushed it right over. It was not a big tree, but I imagined I felt the ground shake when it fell.

"Oh, no."

Iggy had brought the tree and soil as a gift to me, and there it lay with its roots exposed to the salt spray and the wind. Even if the storm stopped immediately and we could replant the mango tree, I was sure that it was doomed. It had only been there a few weeks, so it would not have settled into its new home. Another victim of the storm. I felt tears well up in my eyes. I blinked them away. It was just a tree. Things could get so much worse if the storm crept closer to Anguilla, if the wind got stronger, if the waves rose higher. A mango tree was easy to sacrifice in the face of all the possibilities of loss.

I went back into the kitchen to tackle washing the dishes. I was through the first sink full when a small voice from the doorway said, "Can I help?" I looked over my shoulder to see Ellen standing there.

"Sure, but you don't have to. I can get all this done myself."

Ellen walked over to the sink. "It'd go faster if you had someone to dry them."

"That's true. I feel guilty asking a guest to help do the dishes."

"You didn't ask; I volunteered. I tried reading in my room, but it's too dim and stuffy. And before you say anything, yes, I had the little battery lamp on, which helped. It's hot and close in there and I needed to get out."

I opened a drawer beside the sink and took out a cotton dish towel. "Okay, here you go."

We worked in companionable silence for a while.

Ellen piled the things she had dried on the kitchen island because she didn't know where everything went and because she knew they weren't completely dry. "Does anything really dry in this climate?"

I chuckled. "Not really. Oh, things seem dry, but the air has enough salt in it that it attracts moisture. That's why I have wire shelves and mostly open cupboards. I don't want anything enclosed to build up mildew."

"I wondered why you don't have cupboard doors on most of the cabinets."

I nodded to a closed cabinet next to her. "This one has a lining of screening so that I can put baked things in there to cool off without having bugs or lizards all over them."

"Bugs and lizards? What kind of bugs and lizards?" Ellen looked around as if expecting armies of critters to surround her.

"It's the tropics, so there are bugs and lizards all over. Down here you don't have to be a poor housekeeper to have bugs. Ants and roaches are facts of life, and those little anole lizards are usually in every room of the house."

Ellen shuddered. "Ick. I would have the exterminator here all the time to get rid of them."

"Then you would have a big bill for no outcome. It's impossible to keep them away. You just learn never to leave food out or dirty dishes sitting for very long. It keeps your kitchen clean, that's for sure." I rinsed the mixing bowl in my hand and turned it over on the draining board. "That's the last. Thank you for your help."

"You're welcome, but I came to ask you a favor."

"What's that?"

"Can you teach me to play solitaire?"

CHAPTER 14

I heard the static as Iggy tuned in the station and walked over to where he had plugged a radio in on the sideboard in the lobby. "What's this?"

He raised his hand, palm up, to showcase the small appliance. "This is a radio. You tune it to the local station, and it tells you the position of the storm and the weather report. I thought you might like to have that information." He grinned at me.

"I know that's a radio. Why did you bring it? I can get all that information on my cellphone."

"Which is not working because the internet is down in Sandy Ground. You need one. It should be battery-powered. This is the extra one I had at home."

"I know I need a radio. I'll get one as soon as I can. Thank you, I appreciate your thoughtfulness. It'll be good to have up-to-date hurricane news."

As Iggy fiddled with the dial, a voice came through the speaker. "Weather bulletin for the island of Anguilla."

I leaned forward to hear what the announcer said, my head right next to Iggy's. "Hurricane Alphonso has tracked to the northwest, moving past the north shore of Puerto Rico. That will begin pulling the rain bands away from Anguilla. Residents should expect the rain and winds to slack off over the next twelve hours."

I looked at Iggy, who was grinning back at me. "Well, that's great news. Maybe now the waves will start to ease, and water will stop coming in around the front doors."

"It will take longer than a few hours for the waves to

settle down, but it is a step in the right direction."

I went across the lobby to the doors and spent a few minutes wringing out the towels into the washtub. "I'm glad that Will bought a new washtub. It's nice and big, so I don't drip water all over when I squeeze out the towels."

"It will be heavy to empty though."

It bugged me that I both wanted and didn't want his help. "I don't let it get too full; that way I'm able to carry it and dump it out off the back porch."

"I can do that for you." He walked over to pick up the washtub.

I waved him away. "Hey, I wasn't done yet. Let me finish before you take over.

"I did not mean to take over; I just want to help." He straightened up and watched me finish wringing out the dripping towels.

"Now I'm done. Thanks for dumping the water for me."

"Are you certain you are finished?" When I nodded, he picked up the tub and carried it through the kitchen to empty it in the backyard.

As I watched him go, I thought about how I really needed his help, but my instinct was to do things myself. I'd have to get over that in this new, unfamiliar situation.

When he came into the lobby to put the washtub back in place, I said, "I forgot to ask. How's your house faring in the storm? Is there much damage in West End Village?"

"My house is fine. A flying palm frond dislodged one screen on the porch, but other than that, no damage. It looks like most of the houses in the village survived as well."

I sighed. "That's good. I'd hate for there to have been a lot of damage. Everyone was nice to me at the beach party, even the women warmed up a little bit by the end of the evening."

"Except for Mrs. Whiting. I do not think that she will ever forgive me for choosing an American friend over an Anguillan one."

I wondered if their relationship had been more than

neighborly. Was she a jilted lover? "Has she stopped baking coconut bread for you?"

"Oh yes, the loaf that she gave me the weekend you stayed with me was the last one I have seen."

"Amy's Bakery's coconut bread is almost as good as Mrs. Whiting's. I buy a loaf whenever I'm in the neighborhood if there's any on the shelf. I often find a loaf at Vista Market."

I glanced over at the front doors to see that the water was seeping out of the towels and across the floor again. Iggy and I went to wring out the towels, working together so that we could twist them harder and get more water out. The water was coming in so fast I felt like I should stay in the lobby and wring out the towels all day.

"The drier we make them, the longer they will absorb water."

"I'll be glad when we don't have to do this anymore. It's only been a day and I'm already tired of it."

"You are too close to the high-water line. You are always going to have trouble with seawater getting in during storms."

I made a face at him. "Well, that's not good news. I guess I should find some better weatherstripping before the next storm comes, even if I have to get it from the States."

"And you probably will have to."

Ellen came down the stairs in her swimming suit and water shoes. "I'm going stir-crazy up there in that room; even playing solitaire isn't doing it for me right now. I'm going for a walk up the road to see what's going on in Sandy Ground."

I opened my mouth to speak, but Ellen forestalled me. "I promise to stay out of the surf and stay on the road. If the wind and rain pick up, I promise to scurry right back here."

"That sounds good. When you get back, we can have supper."

"What's for supper today?"

"There's some of the gazpacho left, and I thought grilled cheese sandwiches would go well with it."

Ellen clapped her hands together. "Good. I love grilled

cheese sandwiches. Do you put more than one kind of cheese on yours?"

"I do. I put a little slice of every kind I have on hand in my grilled cheese. I come from Wisconsin; we do cheese right."

Ellen crossed the room and paused at the back door. "I promise not to go far. Oh boy, grilled cheese sandwiches and gazpacho. That might be my new favorite meal."

That night there was a tremendous crash that shook the building and woke everyone up. "What?" Iggy said as he sat up.

There was a second booming crash as I struggled out of the sheets.

"It sounds as if part of the building fell down." I swung my feet to the floor, grabbed a pair of shorts, and flipped on a flashlight.

CHAPTER 15

"Rose?" That was Ellen's voice.

"Coming." I opened the door from my apartment into the kitchen. I stumbled over the step up to the lobby to find two scared women, flashlights in hand, staring back at me.

"What was that?"

"I don't know. Did you hear where it came from?"

Ellen's flashlight beam shook. "It sounded like it came from below my room. I wonder if the palm tree fell over."

I could hear that the wind had picked up and the roar of the waves made it almost impossible to hear ourselves speak.

Iggy came up behind me. "I will go out and see what happened."

"No, it's too dangerous. Let's make sure that nothing is broken, that it isn't raining in anywhere, and wait until morning." I turned to Ellen and Janet. "Are the windows in your rooms intact?" I was glad that I could keep Iggy safe for once. He listened to me and didn't insist on going out in the storm like a stubborn macho man.

Ellen nodded. "That's the first thing I checked."

"I'm on the quiet side, away from the wind and waves. Mine is fine," said Janet.

I shone my flashlight around the room. "Something's banging into the front of the building. And water is seeping from a crack in one of the door panels. Just great."

"Let me go out with a flashlight and look."

I shook my head. "No way are you going out in that maelstrom. It sounds like the end of the world out there. Let's just stick together and we'll make it through the night. Come on into my sitting room. I've got some armchairs you can sit in that are more comfortable than these hard dining chairs."

We all trooped into my apartment where we dragged the chairs and the loveseat closer together and settled down to ride out the storm until morning.

It took quite a while for us to relax and stop talking about what might be happening outside. I handed out lightweight cotton blankets, and we all snuggled down in our little nests. Ellen and Janet were each curled up in an armchair, and Iggy went back to bed. I stayed awake long after everyone else was asleep.

When I woke up, I could hear the generator, not the wind. I uncurled from my squashed position on the loveseat and tiptoed out of the room. I opened the back door to a changed world. Leaves were scattered all across the backyard, and the little mango tree that Iggy had planted still lay uprooted and forlorn along the edge of the lot, but the sun was shining and the sky was clear. I was a little sorry to see the hurricane go since it had kept Calvin the plumber from trying to get into Seaview.

"It's like the Wizard of Oz," said a voice behind me.

I looked over my shoulder to find Ellen standing there. "What?"

"You know, when Dorothy opens the house door after the storm, and everything is in color?"

"Oh, yeah, I suppose it kind of is. Let's go see what crashed into the building in the middle of the night."

We walked across the kitchen and the lobby where I unlocked the front doors, but I couldn't push them open. "Something must have fallen across them. We'll have to go around."

Ellen and I went back to our rooms to put on shoes and then went out the back door and around the building on the path from the parking spaces. I moved palm fronds and tree branches out of the way. As I turned the corner of the building,

I stopped dead.

There was a boat on the steps and front porch of the Seaview.

I was stunned. "Well, that accounts for the loud crash, the crack in the front door, and the bumping in the night," I said.

"It sure does. I wonder whose boat it is."

"From this angle I can't see the name. I'm sure it belongs to someone who lives along the beach here. Somebody is bound to claim it."

Ellen and I stood staring at the small fishing boat lodged on Seaview's front porch. I thought it was a miracle that the boat hadn't broken through the front doors when it landed up there but just cracked a panel of one.

Ellen touched my shoulder. "What are you going to do about it?"

I shrugged. "I don't know. Hope that there's nobody in it and that the owner shows up to take it away, I guess."

Just then I saw movement in the boat and a hand reached up to grasp the gunwale.

"Oh my God," Ellen gasped. "There's somebody in there."

"Iggy," I hollered, "Iggy, get out here." I turned to Ellen. "Go get Iggy, hurry."

I ran over to the boat, but I was too short to see inside. Waves washed the stern, and I saw the sand washing away. The boat shifted, and the hand clutched even tighter.

"Hold on, help is coming. What's your name?"

A groan came from the boat, and another hand joined the first one. "I am Billy from Sandy Ground. Oh, this was a bad idea," Billy said from inside the boat.

Iggy and Ellen came hurrying around the side of the building.

"Who is it?"

"It's Billy the fisherman."

Sounding hollow from inside the boat, he said, "Iggy, can you help me get out of here?"

Iggy reached up and touched the hands. "Hold on, Billy, let me go get a ladder." He ran around to fetch the ladder from the back room and was back in a minute. Iggy set the ladder up at the stern of the boat next to the outboard motor and climbed up and over the transom. "Hold on, Billy, I am here."

With Iggy's added weight, the boat shifted again, and it knocked over the ladder.

"Be careful, that thing isn't very stable," I said.

I could see Iggy holding on to the side of the boat and trying to figure out how to get Billy out of there. "Can you move toward me?"

"I will try."

I heard Billy groan and shift his weight to the center of the hull. There was a sliding sound, and Iggy grunted as Billy crashed into him.

"Rose, can you stand the ladder up again?"

I righted the ladder and watched as the legs sunk into the sand a little before holding steady. "All set. I'll hold it while you climb down."

I heard grunting and shifting, and soon a leg came over the transom, the foot questing for the top of the ladder. I reached up to guide it to the step, and in a very short time Billy the fisherman was able to get out of the boat and climb down the ladder to the sand.

Ellen helped Billy move away from the ladder and sit down.

"I'll help you climb down too, Iggy," I said, as I saw him swing his leg over the back of the boat.

"I am good."

Why was it so hard for him to accept my help? I watched to make sure that he was stable on the ladder before I relaxed my grip on his ankle.

As soon as both feet were on the beach, Iggy walked over to where Billy sat and said, "What were you thinking to be out in your boat in that storm? You could have been killed, and then what would your wife do with those five children?"

Billy sat hunched over with his elbows on his knees and his face in his hands. "I know, man, I know, but I was sure I could fight the waves and keep my boat safe. It made it through most of it; only the last couple of hours were bad."

"And then you ended up on Mrs. Rose's front porch. What happened?"

Billy rubbed his hand over the side of his head. "A big wave washed under the boat; I lost my balance and hit my head on the side. Knocked me right out. I don't know how I ended up on Mrs. Rose's porch. Did I hurt the porch? And what about my boat? There's no hole in her, is there?"

Iggy started to laugh and couldn't stop. "Did you hurt the porch? I'm sure you did. The porch can be fixed, and you can patch your boat; it's your head you should worry about."

The fisherman's wife came running down the beach from the little neighborhood of houses.

"Billy! That's my Billy's boat," she called as she ran.

Billy's head came up, and he groaned again. "Oh, no, Caroline."

Caroline fell to her knees in the sand and wrapped her arms around her husband. She pulled him to her and rocked him, crooning his name and crying. "I thought you were lost."

He pushed her gently away and said, "I was almost lost. I am here now. I will be home as soon as I can move the boat."

"Oh no, you will not," said Iggy. "You are in no condition to move that boat right now. We will get a few of the neighborhood men together later and move it. Right now, you go home with Caroline and see to your head. Take a shower. Get the sea, sand, and storm muck washed off."

Caroline sat back on her heels. "What happened to your head?"

"I hit it on the boat and got knocked out."

"Come home right now and let me see to it. You can have something to eat, too. When was the last time you ate?"

"I don't know. Last night I ate a sandwich, I think."

Iggy grabbed one arm and Caroline took the other, and

between them they got Billy to his feet. He swayed a bit but stayed upright. Caroline put her arm around him, and he draped his arm over her shoulders. They turned, and the couple walked slowly up the beach toward their home at the end.

"That is one lucky man," said Ellen.

Iggy and Rose looked at her.

"He sure is," Iggy said, "to have such a loving wife."

"No, I meant to not lose his life riding out the storm in that little boat."

"That boat is the only way he has to feed his family. That boat is his life."

Ellen and I exchanged glances. I thought Billy was a lucky man in his way of life and could tell that Ellen thought he was going about life all wrong.

The waves were definitely smaller than they had been for days. They were still washing up the sand but stopped far short of the steps to my front door. It looked as though some of the sand had washed out around the base of the steps. I couldn't tell how much the steps and porch were damaged because of the boat resting on them. I was sure that the porch railing was splintered from the battering it took overnight.

"I'm going to go wash up," Ellen said, and we turned to retrace our steps.

I went into the kitchen and mixed up a batch of banana nutmeg muffins and got them into the oven to bake. I found a package of sausage links in the freezer that I thawed in the microwave and sizzled up in a frying pan. By then it was after eight o'clock. I went into the lobby and got the coffee brewing. Janet and Ellen would be down, just as soon as the aroma of brewing coffee wafted through the place.

While I waited for the coffee too, I thought about that fallen mango tree in my backyard. Iggy said that he would try to get it back into the ground. I had my doubts about whether that would work. Oh, I thought he could get it planted again. I was pretty confident that spending a couple of days on its side with its roots exposed to the wind and salt spray would spell the end of that tree. Would the hurricane and the storm of Mrs. Whiting's rumors about me spell the end of my attempt to sink my roots into Anguillan soil?

The last few spits and sputters of the drip coffee maker in the lobby interrupted my thoughts. I needed to get back into business mode, so I went out into the lobby, took placemats and napkins from the sideboard drawers, and laid two places for my guests. Then I went back into the kitchen to get the muffins out of the silicone pans.

"Good morning, Rose," said Janet from the kitchen doorway. "Are we back to breakfasting in the lobby today?"

I smiled at her. "Good morning. I thought it would make a nice change since the wind and rain seem to have moved away. I've got the front door open, and the waves stopped washing up over the steps, so I took the towels and washtub away too. I can't do anything about the boat though."

"What boat?"

I gestured toward the lobby. "There's a boat on the porch holding one of the front doors closed. I've got one door open so that the fresh air could blow through, but Billy needs to come claim his fishing boat."

Janet's face fell. "Oh, I thought we had turned from hotel keeper and guests to something more like friends over the last few days."

Ellen came up behind Janet. "Why are there places set in the lobby? Aren't we eating at the kitchen island again today?"

I wanted to get back into business mode, but I turned around to face my guests. "We can, you can. I just thought you might enjoy eating in the lobby with the doors open and the breeze blowing the stuffiness away."

Both women shook their heads. "No," said Ellen, "we want to eat back here with you." One big business lesson I needed to learn was to set limits and stick to them. But not today. I went into the lobby to get the placemats and napkins off the table, picked out one of each for myself and Iggy from the drawers, and carried them back into the kitchen. I set four places on the kitchen island, put out the butter, knives, and forks, and got the sausages out of the warm oven. I lined a basket with another napkin for the muffins.

"Pour yourselves coffee in the lobby and bring it back here; we're all set."

We settled around the kitchen island. I passed the basket of muffins and the plate of sausages to my guests before taking any for myself.

Iggy came in from outside. "Good morning, ladies."

"Good morning, Iggy," everyone said.

"Would you like some coffee and breakfast?"

"I would, thank you," he said, looking over his shoulder from the sink where he washed his hands. "Did you notice that the wind and rain seem to have left?"

I poured Iggy a mug of coffee and set it at the last place at the kitchen island.

Ellen said, "I'm going to go to Tamarind after breakfast to see if I can't get a boat ride out to Sandy Island for the morning. I've been itching to get out there since I arrived, and I don't want to wait another minute."

Iggy looked at her. "You know the waves washed over Sandy Island for the last few days. There will not be much left to see out there."

Ellen cocked her head. "What do you mean 'washed over'?"

"Well, the waves were powerful enough and high enough that they washed clear across Sandy Island and off the other side. They probably washed away most of the structures on the island. I do not know if Thomas will even consent to take a boat out today. You can ask."

Ellen finished the last bite of her muffin and picked up another sausage link with her fingers. "I intend to." She took a bite. "Are you interested in going out to what looks like Robinson Crusoe's island, Janet? You could take a notebook and write while I lay on the beach."

Janet nodded. "I wouldn't take a notebook because paper and water don't mix, but I'd love a few hours out in the sun and sand. I'll walk over to Tamarind with you as soon as I'm finished."

"Okay, great."

The two women finished their breakfasts and carried their plates, mugs, and silverware over to the sink.

I protested. "That's unnecessary; I can bus the table myself."

Janet said, "Well, it's done now so you don't have to. See you later." She sketched a small wave and followed Ellen out of the kitchen.

I had a lot to learn about island life, particularly island after a storm—this was more than just a vacation spot for me. To fit in and run a business, I needed to know how things work. "Do they need help over there, Iggy?"

He shook his head. "Thomas has weathered quite a few storms on the island. I am certain that he has his people working to get things set right."

I heard the guests climbing the stairs to their rooms and turned to Iggy. "Do you think Thomas will take them out there today?"

Iggy drained his coffee mug. "I think Thomas will be too busy cleaning up the sand that has washed into the shop and making sure that the storm did not damage his compressor and other equipment to take two ladies out to Sandy Island, but you never know. They might as well ask. Besides, you are not their mother. They can do what they like with their time."

I felt my cheeks flush and my stomach clench. "I know I'm not their mother. Still, I worry that they'll get into trouble now that the storm has passed and they can get out and about."

Iggy put his hand over mine and rubbed his thumb over my fingers. "You need to learn not to get attached to your guests. They are paying you to let them stay here; they are not your friends."

"That's a hard lesson to learn." I looked Iggy in the eyes. "What do you think can be done with that mango tree? Its branches are hanging over into the road. Pretty soon someone will complain, and I suspect it won't survive having its roots exposed to the wind and salt spray for days. Maybe Silas can cut it up and haul it away for me."

Iggy moved and put his own dishes in the sink. "I need to go down to Johnno's. I am supposed to help him get back up and running, and I have been sitting here eating muffins. Silas is there too. I will send him over when we are done at the beach bar, and he can look at the mango tree."

I picked up a paper sack. "Here are a couple of muffins for Johnno and Silas. Take them over as an apology for distracting you."

Iggy took the sack and looked inside. "Only two muffins? I don't get another one? They are my favorite."

I laughed and took the sack back. "You can have another. I thought the mango-lime ones were your favorite." I put a third muffin in the bag and gave it back to Iggy. "Now go to work." I tiptoed up and gave him a kiss on the cheek, then he turned his head and kissed me on the lips.

"All of your muffins are my favorite. I will see you later."

"Go. I have laundry to do, and I want to hang that damp and glassy bedding out on the line to see if most of the glass will shake off in the breeze. Then I can sweep up the glass off the patio blocks."

I took a laundry basket upstairs and gathered up all the towels from each guest room. I started the wash and then carried the bundle of rain-damp bedding out into the backyard. I wiped the wash lines with a rag to get off any dirt that had accumulated on them and hung up the wet sheets, taking extra care to hang the bedspread in the breeze. As I turned to walk back into Seaview, Ellen and Janet came up the road from the dive shop.

"Any luck?" I asked, but I could tell by their big smiles

that they were getting what they wanted.

"Yes," Ellen said. "Thomas said that the boat driver would take us out to Sandy Island right away and pick us up around noon. We're going to get our swimsuits on and get beach towels and sunscreen and hurry back to the shop. He said that the water is too churned up for snorkeling today. It may settle down by tomorrow. Fingers crossed."

I heard their excited chatter as they went upstairs to get ready. Thomas, the lanky American expat owner of Tamarind, came out the door of the dive shop and waved. I walked over to meet my neighbor in the parking lot.

"How did you survive your first hurricane?" he said.

"We had one set of shutters blow open and the window they covered got broken by a flying branch or frond. Then the waves were high enough that seawater seeped in around the front doors and across the lobby, and there's a fishing boat on the front porch. We didn't do too badly. How about you?"

Thomas shrugged. "Everything survived intact, but our building is built of concrete block. It's basically a bunker."

"I can't believe that you're going to take my guests out to Sandy Island today. Is anything left on there after the waves washed over?"

"Oh yeah, they're up and running already," he said. "They had everything tied down or off the island, so all they had to do was shovel the sand out of the building, put the chairs out, and fill the coolers. I don't imagine that they're going to be serving food just yet, but there will be drinks and shade for the ladies." As he finished his sentence, the ladies in question rushed out of the back door of Seaview with their beach bags over their shoulders and hurried across the parking lot.

"We're ready," Janet said.

Thomas smiled at them. "Go right out to the boat. Freddy is waiting for you."

I guess they didn't need my help after all. Iggy kept reminding me I wasn't my guests' mother, and he was right. I needed to develop a businesslike distance between myself and them. Be welcoming and helpful, but do not feel you've taken them to raise.

I spent the day airing out the Seaview, putting fresh sheets on the beds, and doing laundry. I thought about hiring someone to help with the housekeeping duties and I knew just the person. When Iggy and I were coming back from his place a few months back, we gave a ride to a young woman named Geneva whose car was in the shop. Geneva worked in housekeeping at a big resort and said that she'd like to work for me if I ever needed someone. There were more guests arriving the following weekend, which meant that I needed to get the window in the yellow guest room repaired and Janet moved back into there. Then that meant the lilac room needed to be readied for a new guest. Ellen would leave in a couple of days, which meant that the salmon room would need thorough cleaning. Of course, every day the bathrooms needed to be cleaned. With cooking and kitchen clean-up, I could use the help.

While I waited for the laundry to run, I calculated how much I could afford to pay someone and hoped that it would be enough to lure Geneva away from the big resort job. I'd have to discuss it with Iggy to see if the amount I could afford would be an insult. I hoped not.

CHAPTER 16

Silas stopped in to cadge a muffin.

"Do you know how to replace window glass?" I asked him, hoping he could do it, so I didn't have to ask Iggy to do another job for me.

"I do. Why, do you have a broken window already?"

"Yes, one pair of shutters blew open in the storm and something flew up and broke the window, scattering glass all over the room. What a mess that was to clean up."

Silas finished his muffin and dusted the crumbs off his hands. "I will go up and measure the opening, then go to the hardware store for a replacement pane of glass. Which room is the one with the broken window?"

I stood up. "I'll go with you. It's the yellow one, the right room on the seaside."

I grabbed the key when we passed through the lobby and went up to the yellow room where Silas used a tape measure that he had on his belt to measure the opening.

"The latch on the shutters broke free of the screws. You will need to get a new latch to fit on there too."

Silas nodded. "I will go out on the gallery and measure that too. How are you holding the shutters together now?"

"Iggy nailed them shut in the middle of the storm and he put a sheet of plywood over the window to keep the rain out. Please take it off carefully so we can use it again if we ever need it."

Silas wrote the measurements on a small slip of paper he pulled out of his pocket. "I will do that and put it into the back room. It will probably take a while to get the glass. I imagine there are many people needing to replace windows today. I will wait. They will put it on your account."

Thinking of Iggy having to pay for the door sweeps, I said, "Let me give you my credit card just in case." I put my hand on his shoulder. "Thank you very much. I really appreciate it. Do you have Johnno's all set up again?"

Silas nodded. "All set up and running smooth. It's an easy job because all the glassware and bottles are already in cabinets that have doors. They just got locked like they do at the end of the day, then we tied the tables and chairs down in a scrum to the bar and we were done. It was an easy task to undo it." I thought about having to do that with patio furniture if I ever could afford more than my current picnic table.

Once Silas left on his errand, I got back to the laundry. I went to the clothesline and shook out the bedspread from the yellow guest room that had glass sprayed on it, and ran my hands over it to see if I could feel any tiny pieces of glass left. When I was up in the yellow guest room with Silas, I checked to see how the mattress and box springs were drying. They still felt a little damp, so I would wait another day to make the bed. I made sure that the other two windows in the room were open so that fresh air was flowing through to help things dry. It was hard to get used to everything feeling a little damp all the time from the salt in the air and the constant humidity.

I took the bedding out of the dryer and folded the sheets. There were table linens that needed ironing. I set up the ironing board in the back room and got the placemats and napkins ironed and returned to the sideboard drawers. I was glad that I had insisted on having a clothes dryer in addition to the washer on the back porch. As much as I liked the way line dried things smelled afterwards, towels were much softer after a tumble dry rather than a line dry and sheets didn't look as if they needed ironing when they came out of the dryer although I usually gave the pillowcases a quick glide with the iron just to make them look more appealing and fresh. I was ironing when I heard Ellen and Janet come in through the kitchen door.

"We're back," one of them called.

I put down the iron and went into the kitchen to greet them. "How was Sandy Island?"

Ellen threw out her arms. "It was wonderful. They had cold drinks and sandwiches, so we stayed for lunch. We want to go back tomorrow. We've already set it up with Freddy."

I was puzzled. "What is there to do out on Sandy Island?"

Janet spoke up. "Absolutely nothing. We lay in the sand and walked around the entire island a few times. It was relaxing not being able to chain myself to my laptop like I've been doing for the last ten days. I'm certain that I'll be more productive the next time I sit down to write because I took a break for a couple of days."

Ellen was fidgeting with her swimsuit. "I need to go up, take a shower, and change. Can I hang my towel and suit on the clothesline, so they dry for tomorrow?"

I nodded. "Sure, go right ahead. I was just about to take down the sheets and bedspread. I think all the glass has fallen or blown off so I can safely put them in the washer."

The women walked through the kitchen and the lobby and upstairs to their rooms. Pretty soon I heard both showers go on and thought again that it was a good idea that I had installed tankless water heaters for each bathroom; that way I didn't have to worry about the hot water running out when the guests showered. I was just finishing the laundry and ironing when Silas came back from the hardware store.

"That was quicker than I thought."

"Me too. There was no line when I got there so he cut the glass right away. I got a tube of glass putty and some points to hold the glass in place."

I thought how lucky I was that his Auntie Anne recommended him to me when I first looked for workmen.

He handed me back my credit card. "Good thing I had this. Henry asked for payment up front."

"Thanks." I slid the Visa card and receipt into my pocket

and then put the rest of the laundry away on the back-room shelves. "Do you need a hand?"

"I don't think so, but I will call you if I do."

"Sounds like a plan."

"First, I will open the shutters and get that plywood off the frame. Then I can work all the old putty and any glass left in there out of the frame and get the new glass in."

"I have a putty knife. How about I work on cleaning the frame while you're getting the nails out of the shutters and the plywood? That way the job will go that much faster."

"Get your putty knife and get busy then." He grinned. "I will go up and put the glass pane on the bed and come back down for the hammer and a pry bar."

We got to work. It didn't take him long to get the shutters open, the plywood removed, and the shutter latch replaced.

I worked the putty knife under the putty that we had just put on the windows to make the glass hold more firmly in place. I was glad that only one window had broken in the storm. I put a piece of old canvas on the floor for the putty pieces to fall onto, and I was careful to avoid cutting myself on the glass splinters left in the putty. I only got a few little nicks.

Iggy stopped over just as we finished getting the glass installed. He approved of his nephew's use of glazier's points and puttying technique. I picked up the corners of the canvas and carried it carefully downstairs to empty it into the trash. When Silas came down to put the tools away, I handed him some money for his work.

"You do not have to pay me, Mrs. Rose. We are friends, and friends do favors for each other."

"Yes, I know we're friends. I don't want to take advantage of our friendship. Let me at least pay for your gas over to the hardware store and back, and maybe a little extra."

Silas looked at the bills in his hand, nodded, and slipped them into his pocket. "That is fair. You can pay for my gas."

Iggy spoke up. "Do you think you will have time in

the next day or two to come and cut up and haul away the fallen mango tree? Its branches are blocking the road and soon someone will complain."

"I can do it right now. There is a tree down at home that I have to take care of, and I have loppers and a saw in my truck. I will be right back."

I looked after him. "Well, that was easy."

While Silas went to get his saw and loppers, I hopped in my car to go collect my mail. I hadn't gone to the post office all week because I was too busy trying to keep Hurricane Alphonso out of Seaview. I put it all in a plastic bag and drove home to sort through it. Most of it was advertising flyers and junk mail, but there was one envelope from Henry's Hardware. I opened the letter and stared in disbelief at the bill. It listed all the purchases I had made for the last three months and demanded payment in full immediately. I was making regular payments on the balance, and Henry had seemed willing to be patient for me to pay it over time. Iggy said that I should just leave the account open because there's always something that needs fixing on a building as old as Seaview. I didn't have enough savings to pay the total bill. I supposed I could use a cash advance on a credit card to get the money I needed, but cash advances have much higher interest rates, and I couldn't afford that either. Besides, my credit card balances were already pretty high. Maybe if I talked to Henry, we could work something out. Had Mrs. Whiting's rumors spread to Henry at the hardware store already?

I was pacing around the kitchen when Iggy knocked once on the back door and came in. "What is the matter?"

Frowning and pacing, I brandished the bill. "Henry at the hardware store wants payment in full immediately, and I don't have the money."

"What?" He took the piece of paper from me and stood reading it. "Have you been making regular payments like you told him you would?"

"Yes, I have. Word must be going around that I'm not good for my bills. Come to think of it, I have to pay cash now at Vista Market and Rebecca O'Neill at the Barrel Stave turns away when I call out a greeting."

He was quiet while he read the letter and the bill. He paced around the room like I had been doing when he arrived. "Someone is spreading rumors about you. I have heard whispers." He stopped and looked sheepish.

"What whispers have you heard?"

He wrapped me in his arms. "I have heard that you are here to take advantage of us. That you are not what you seem to be."

I stiffened and pulled back from him. "I'm not what I seem to be? Lomira at Tamarind said something like that before the storm hit. After all the money I've invested in Seaview and all the time and sweat equity I've put in, Mrs. Whiting has spread rumors. It has to be her. Are you sure that you weren't involved with her before you met me? She's acting like a jilted lover." I started pacing again. "I've hired local labor, shop in local stores, and eat in local restaurants. I'm doing my best to become part of the community, and this is the thanks I get?"

Iggy watched me pace around the kitchen island. "You are going to make yourself sick with all of this frustration. You need to get to the bottom of these rumors."

"That means I have to confront Mrs. Whiting, and I'm not sure I'm ready to do that yet. Tomorrow I'll go see Henry and see if I can't convince him to reinstate my previous payment plan. I can't pay him what I don't have."

Iggy put his hand on my shoulder to stop me. "I could lend you my savings. That would cover your hardware store bill and leave you a bit of money in the bank. You could pay me back month by month, just like you planned to pay Henry."

I laid my hand on top of his and had to talk around a lump in my throat. "Thanks, Iggy. I can't take your savings. You need to hold on to that for emergencies. Eleanora Whiting has spread nasty rumors about me all over Anguilla, and I have to do what I can to counteract that. I had the Health Department inspector stop by the other day. He hinted that he'd had a complaint but backed off when I asked about it." I looked Iggy in the eye. "Do you think Mrs. Whiting would be capable of doing something like that?"

Iggy looked away. "I know that she and her friends are angry that I prefer your company over theirs."

I wrapped my arms around him. "Say no more. I won't press you to badmouth a neighbor, but I will get this straightened out. You'd better believe it."

The next morning after breakfast I put on lipstick and combed my hair, then drove over to Henry's Hardware to talk about my bill. Henry frowned when he saw me but consented to meet with me in his little office behind the counter. I told him the same things that I said to Iggy the day before. That I was invested in the island's prosperity. That I hire locals, shop in local stores, and that I have an account and safe deposit box in the local bank.

"I can't afford to pay you in full right now. I can increase my monthly payments a bit, I suppose."

Henry rifled through the papers on his desk and came up with my account. "I see that you have made regular payments on your account every month. I suppose if Ignatius says you can be trusted, I will believe him and continue to let you pay over time."

"Thank you." Then I thought about what he said. "You mean if Iggy says I'm good for the money you'll believe him?" That was a blow. I wasn't used to needing to have a man vouch for me.

"I have known Ignatius his whole life. You, I do not know. I trust him."

"Thank you, Mr., um, I don't know your last name."

He patted my hand, which lay on the corner of his desk. "Just Henry will do."

"Thank you, Henry." I stood up and put out my hand to shake. "I'll have Iggy stop by later today. I won't let you down."

CHAPTER 17

There were ten men standing around Billy's boat lodged on Seaview's front porch. I heard them discussing the best way of moving the boat without destroying my porch. I appreciated the consideration.

Finally, two of the men climbed onto the boat and then squeezed onto the porch to lift from there as the other eight arrayed themselves around the boat's sides and stern. They had taken the outboard motor off and laid it on a sheet of cardboard to keep gas and oil from leaking into the sand and removed any loose items from the boat. They didn't need things rolling around or falling on them as they maneuvered it. The men on the porch pushed the boat over away from the doors of the hotel, and the men on the ground shimmied it across the sand.

I watched in amazement as they slowly slid the boat away from the front of Seaview and got it settled on its keel on the sand. The wooden steps leading up to the porch were crushed and would have to be replaced, and the porch railing was splintered. All of that could be repaired.   Once the boat was on the sand, they rocked and slid it down to the water, holding it steady to make sure that it hadn't sprung any leaks from its hurricane adventure. Billy was careful climbing into the boat and examining every inch of it for water. "There is a little seepage where a few of the boards have separated, but I can fix them. Let's get her back on the sand where I can work on her."

Janet and Ellen stood by my shoulders at the lobby window watching the boat being moved.

"I can't believe that they can move that heavy boat," said Janet. "How do they do it?"

I shook my head. "I don't know. They have a long history of moving boats off the beach. Iggy calls it the 'Armstrong' method."

"Armstrong?" said Ellen. "Who's he?"

"Not who, what. Lots of strong arms to get the job done. Few of the boat owners have a trailer or a truck to tow it with, so they beach their boats and use brute strength to get them floating again."

Ellen folded her arms across her chest. "That's just crazy. They should save up for trailers or use a mooring, something to keep from giving themselves a hernia every time they move a boat."

"Moorings are scarce, and most people can't afford the rental fees. Take Billy, for example. He has a boat but no car. He can afford one or the other, and the boat lets him fish and feed his family. His customers meet him on the beach when he comes ashore in the morning to buy his catch; he doesn't deliver."

"How can they manage without a car? Don't they have a bunch of kids?"

I shrugged. "They walk places. People give them rides. I sometimes take Caroline to the grocery with me when I see her walking along the road and I'm going shopping. The kids ride the school bus, and they have a bicycle or two for the older ones to get around on. They work it out. It's what poor people do." I thought about Billy and Caroline's family. If no one told them they were poor, they wouldn't think it. They had enough.

"Not me. I'd never be without a car," said Ellen. "I need my wheels."

I turned to go into the kitchen. "I'm going to make something for those guys. They have to be thirsty and hungry after moving that boat."

Janet followed me. "I'll help."

Ellen stayed by the window and watched.

I was glad that there was an extra pitcher of cold water in the fridge, a big bag of shredded cheddar cheese, and plenty of bread since I'd shopped that morning. "Let's make pimento cheese sandwiches," I said. I had learned the recipe for pimento cheese from my Grandma Stephan. It was an old family recipe, simple, delicious, and quick to make. "It's supposed to sit in the fridge overnight. Let's just put in a little less mayo and I think it'll be all right."

I mixed the cheddar, mayo, undrained pimentos, garlic, and celery seed in a big bowl. Janet laid out slices of plain old white bread on a tray, and I went along behind her, scooping a heap of the mixture onto each slice. When they were topped with another slice and cut in half, we had a nice big tray of sandwiches to share with the boat movers. We carried our offerings around to the front of Seaview and arrived just as they'd gotten the boat back up on the sand.

"Food," I said, and ten sweaty faces looked at me and smiled.

Janet carried the pitchers of water and a stack of paper cups; she handed around. It wasn't long before there wasn't a crumb left.

"Thanks for the sandwich, Mrs. Rose," said Silas. "I will get my tools and get started fixing your steps right away."

"Oh, thanks, Silas."

Iggy came up chewing the last bite of his third half-sandwich. "These were good. Make them again sometime."

"I will."

"Silas," Iggy said, "I can help you with these steps. Why don't you go get the lumber and I'll start tearing down the broken pieces."

"Wouldn't it be smarter to tear things down first so that I know what to buy?"

Iggy looked shamefaced. "You're right, boy, that is a better idea. I must be getting tired."

"Not tired, Uncle Iggy, just old."

Iggy's face froze and then broke into a big grin. "I will

show you who is getting old. I can still work a boy like you into the ground."

"We will see about that."

And they both hurried around the building to get their tools from their trucks.

Ellen went down to Johnno's Beach Bar for a drink that afternoon. She had enjoyed being on Sandy Island and wanted to stay out of Seaview for the rest of the day. With all the days of forced sheltering from the hurricane, she said she was determined to explore and make the most of the remaining days of her vacation. She came in from Johnno's with rosy cheeks and went up to her room with a smile on her face.

She walked back downstairs, jingling her keys and walked past me. "I'm off on an island tour. I'll get supper somewhere."

I smelled rum on her breath. "Are you okay to drive?"

"I'm not driving. Julius is driving."

I swallowed my smile. "Okay. Have a good time."

"Oh, I will," Ellen said as she left through the front door, descending the new steps that Iggy and Silas had just finished.

I watched her go. "I'm sure that you will."

It was almost sundown when Ellen came in the kitchen door of the hotel and found me finishing assembling an egg casserole so that it could sit in the refrigerator overnight to be baked in the morning.

"How was your afternoon?"

"Very relaxing. We toured around a bit and then went to a secluded beach where we could swim and sunbathe. Now I'm going to take a quick shower, then Julius and I are going to Scilly Cay for lobster for supper."

I started running a sink of hot water to do the dishes that I had dirtied. "I love going there for supper. Cecelia makes the best sorbet that she serves for dessert, and the lobsters on the grill are delicious. You'll like it. I'm glad that the hurricane moved off so that you're getting the chance to go."

I heard the shower go on in the white and green bathroom as I stood with my hands sunk in the sudsy water. Hopefully Ellen understood Julius was a vacation fling kind of guy, not a forever kind of guy. I thought she did.

Janet popped into the kitchen from the lobby. "Hi Rose, how was your day?"

I dried my hands on a dishtowel and hung the dishrag over the faucet to dry. "My day was fine, busy with laundry and cleaning the rooms, but a fine day. How was writing this afternoon?"

Janet went to the refrigerator, took out the pitcher of iced tea, and filled her water bottle. "Writing was good. I'm so glad that getting rained on didn't ruin my laptop, and I'm glad that you had the rice and pan to dry it out in. I think I've figured out how the sleuth comes to realize the identity of the murderer and have set them up to come together, and not in a good way."

"That's excellent," I said. "I look forward to reading it when you've finished."

Janet laughed. "Oh, that will be a while. What I'm writing now is just the first draft; next comes rewriting, rereading, and rewriting, which can take more than a year. Then it goes to the publisher, and their editor takes a crack at it. I make the changes they want, and finally it goes to the printer. It's a long process. I will let you know when it's published. If it's ever published."

"What do you mean 'if it's ever published'?"

"Well, sometimes a writer gets done with all the work and the book never becomes what she hoped. It goes on the shelf and never again sees the light of day."

My hand flew to cover my mouth. "Oh, I hope that never happens to you. I'd be disappointed if I put in all that work and nothing became of it. What are you doing for supper tonight?"

Janet smiled. "I have a hankering for a cheeseburger. I'm going down to Johnno's for one. I overheard Silas and his friends say that Johnno's makes good burgers and fries, so that's where I'm headed. Or maybe I'll order some of those conch fritters like we had at the jump-up. They're so good, and I can't get them at home. I can get French fries any time at home but not conch fritters."

"Good idea," I said. "Might as well eat them while you can. I made a shepherd's pie and Iggy is coming over for supper. He's making a salad and there's a little key lime pie left that we can split."

Janet licked her lips. "Mm, that sounds good too. Enjoy your supper and say hi to Iggy for me." She walked to the doorway into the lobby and waved over her shoulder. "See you later."

"Bye."

I heard her say, "Hi, Ellen, how was your afternoon?"

"Dreamy. I hooked up with Julius for an island tour, a little swim in the sea, and now we're off for grilled lobster at Scilly Cay. What about you?"

"I wrote all afternoon and now I'm headed to Johnno's for a burger and conch fritters. Enjoy your evening," Janet said.

"You too."

Ellen came through the kitchen and walked over to me, holding out her key fob. "One of these keys opens the front door, right?"

I nodded. "Yes, the one with the blue key cap on it."

"What time do you lock the doors for the night?"

"About eleven when I turn in, and please remember to use the front door. The porch steps and railing are fixed and ready for use. I put this back kitchen door on a deadbolt when I go to bed."

"Okay, good to know. I've gotten used to using this door because of the high surf. I suppose now you would prefer us to use the front door into the lobby."

I nodded. "Yes, I'd prefer that. The kitchen feels a bit like my turf. I don't mean that you're not welcome to use the fridge or get some iced tea, but the lobby is where I planned for my guests to eat. This last week with the hurricane and needing to feed you and Janet all meals was an exception."

Ellen sniffed the air. "What are you making? It smells good in here."

"I'm making a shepherd's pie for me and Iggy. It does smell good, doesn't it? I can't wait to eat it. It's one of my favorites."

Ellen turned around and went back through the lobby, calling out, "It's time for me to meet Julius. See you tomorrow." And she was gone.

I let out a breath and sighed. This was how I had envisioned my bed-and-breakfast to be: independent guests going about their days, leaving me to make their breakfast and then having the rest of the day to tend to housekeeping chores. I would remember to ask Iggy at supper if he would tell Geneva that I would like to talk to her about working here. More guests were scheduled to arrive on the weekend, and I didn't want to be cleaning the bathrooms and laundering towels and sheets all day every day. I was still stewing about Henry's Hardware and him needing Iggy to vouch for me. If there were another hardware store on the island, I'd go there, but Henry was the only game in town.

The timer buzzed, and I took the shepherd's pie out of the oven and set it on a trivet to rest. While I waited for Iggy to arrive with the salad, I checked to make sure that the bacon had thawed out so that I could fry it up while the egg casserole baked.

"Knock, knock," Iggy's voice called from the back door.

"Oh good, you're just in time. The shepherd's pie is out of the oven."

He handed me a covered bowl. "Here's the salad. I didn't bring dressing; I figured that you have some."

"I do."

I cut the shepherd's pie into wedges and served us each one. Using tongs, I heaped salad alongside and set one plate in front of Iggy at the kitchen island, taking the other for myself.

Iggy took a bite and raised his eyebrows. "Mm, this is good. I don't think that I have ever had this before."

"It's something I made often at home. It's been too hot to make it here. I got hungry for it when I saw ground beef at the market, so I got some potatoes and carrots and made it, anyway."

"I like it. You can make it for me anytime." He liked it well enough that he had another wedge.

"Save room for pie. There's a quarter of a key lime pie that I'm willing to split with you."

Now his eyebrows really went up. "You will split pie with me?" He reached across the kitchen island to touch my forehead. "Do you have a fever?"

I swatted his hand away laughing, "Get away. No, I don't have a fever. It's a pretty good size piece of pie, so yes, I'm willing to split it with you."

I shouldn't have been surprised to see three people sitting in the lobby sipping coffee and waiting for breakfast. Janet was at one table alone, and Ellen and Julius were at another table. I was glad that I had peeked into the lobby before carrying in the tray of plates. Not that I disapproved of Julius spending the night with Ellen, I knew Julius had the habit of escorting single women around the island and taking them to bed. Since Ellen had spent the day and evening with him, I kind of expected it. I hurried to prepare a third plate of egg casserole with bacon on the side. I put a smile on my face, picked up the tray, and walked into the lobby to serve breakfast.

Once I had served the plates, I offered to refill coffee mugs and to pour anyone some juice.

"Good morning, Mrs. Rose," Julius said. "I hope you do not mind my being here."

I shook my head. "No, I don't mind. Good morning, Julius."

Ellen looked sorry that she had brought him to the table. It was too late to change that now. She kept her eyes on her plate and ate quickly. "Be quiet."

"Why? Mrs. Rose is my friend, and I can greet her if I want."

"Just eat and we'll get out of here."

Julius put down his fork and knife and looked at her. "I embarrass you being here? You were not embarrassed last night at supper or last night in your room."

Ellen's eyes darted to Janet. "Will you just be quiet and eat?"

He wiped his mouth with his napkin, took a sip of coffee, and stood up. "I believe I will be going. I am sorry that my presence embarrasses you." He stood still for a moment as if waiting for her to protest. When she stayed silent and focused on her plate, he strode across the room and went out the front doors, which stood open to let in the morning breeze.

Ellen laid down her fork and looked up at me with tears in her eyes. "I am so sorry that I brought him back here. I didn't mean to embarrass you."

I shrugged. "You didn't embarrass me. You're a grown adult woman, and you can invite whoever you'd like to spend the night with you." I reached for the tray and loaded Julius' abandoned breakfast plate and coffee mug onto it. "I'll take these into the kitchen and leave you to finish your meal." I turned around and left the room.

I heard them talking as I washed the breakfast pots and pans.

"What are you doing today?" said Janet.

"Packing," Ellen said, "I'm going home tomorrow."

"Aw man, that's too bad," Janet said. "Hurricane Alphonso took up most of your vacation. We should do something fun today. You can throw all your stuff in your suitcase tonight after supper. Why don't we see if we can go snorkeling? I've only been once and would love to try it again."

Ellen carried her plate and mug over to the sideboard and put them there. "What a great idea. Are you finished eating?"

"Yes."

Ellen said, "Let's go to Tamarind to see if we can schedule a snorkeling trip today."

I met Ellen at the desk in the lobby the next morning. She had her suitcase and carry-on and wore slacks and a nice shirt to travel in. "Still wearing sandals, I see."

"Yes, I have shoes in my carry-on. I'm not quite ready to give up on vacation," she said, looking down at her feet.

I had printed out Ellen's bill earlier and had it ready to hand over. "Since you were stuck in here for days and couldn't go anywhere else to eat, I decided not to charge you for the hurricane meals. Eating with me was cheaper than going out."

"Oh, thank you, that's nice of you. Did you add Julius' breakfast?"

I shook my head. "No, I didn't. He didn't really eat it, so I didn't charge for it either. I don't begrudge him a mug of coffee and a few bites of egg and bacon."

Ellen blushed. "I really want to apologize for bringing him here. It never occurred to me on Thursday night that he would still be here on Friday morning."

"Let it go. We're all adults. No apologies necessary."

Ellen took out her credit card, and I finalized the transaction.

"Thank you for coming to Seaview. I hope you enjoyed your stay despite Hurricane Alphonso."

Ellen put her credit card back in her wallet. "It certainly made for an interesting week. At least I had the first and last days to walk the beach and go snorkeling. The middle weekdays were kind of a bore, but at least I learned how to play solitaire."

I laughed. "Now you know one card game."

Ellen leaned on the registration desk. "I've already downloaded a free solitaire app on my phone so I can play on the plane."

"Uh-oh, I've created a monster."

Ellen checked her watch. "I'd better get moving. I have to return my rental car first. Or maybe I'll check in first and then return the car. Thanks for everything, Rose. You're a good host, and you make great muffins."

"Thanks, I'm glad that you liked them. I hope we see each other again." I handed her a small stack of brochures. "Please share these with your friends. And don't forget to leave a review on my site and other travel sites. I'd appreciate it." I followed Ellen to the front door and waved as she walked around the building on the patio block path to her car.

"Did I miss her?" Janet came down the stairs at a run, skittering on the last step as she hit the floor.

"Almost. She just walked around to her car. I'm sure that you can catch her."

Janet hurried out the door.

CHAPTER 18

I was glad that my guests had gotten along. Now I had to clean the salmon room and get it ready for the next guest. That reminded me I wanted to get in touch with Geneva to see if she was still interested in a job. I had to call Iggy. I had gotten a few new reservations and deposits, so I still thought I could afford to hire help.

I spent the rest of the morning going through the salmon guest room, dusting all the surfaces, changing the sheets, putting fresh towels with salmon trim in the room. Then I cleaned both bathrooms after starting to wash the sheets that I removed from Ellen's bed. I told Janet that she could move back into the yellow guest room if she wanted to, and she started immediately. That meant that once Janet had moved, the lilac room would need to be cleaned and made ready for the next guest. That meant more sheets and towels to wash. I really needed Geneva's help. The next guests were arriving later today, probably on the flight that Ellen was going home on. I needed to hurry to get the rooms ready.

Iggy arrived while I was moving the laundry around. I was happy to have help to fold sheets, especially the fitted ones.

"How do you know how to fold these?" Iggy said, carefully following my directions.

"I don't know. I figured it out a long time ago; now it's second nature." I reached over to help. "Here. It's easier if you lay the sheet down on a flat surface once you get the corners all nested together. I wiped off the top of the washer so it's clean and won't get the sheets dirty again."

We got all the sheets folded and put them together in sets before stacking them on the shelves in the back room. By then the towels were ready to come out of the dryer. We folded those too. I sorted them by color so that they went with the room colors to make it easier for guests to remember which were theirs.

We were in the kitchen enjoying a glass of iced tea when I heard a car drive up slowly, stop, and then turn into the parking place alongside the building. "Playtime's over," I said, "I'll bet that's one of my new guests."

"You call all the cleaning and laundry you do playtime? You work too hard."

I snapped my fingers. "That reminds me, can you have Geneva get in touch with me, please? I could really use some help with all the laundry, cleaning, and cooking. I'm already overwhelmed."

"I will do that today." Iggy walked over and put his glass in the sink. "I saw her a few days ago, and she asked me about Seaview and whether you would need help."

"Great."

"Hello?" came a voice from the lobby. Then the little bell on the registration desk dinged.

"Coming." I went to greet my new guests. "Hi, I'm Rose Lambert. Welcome. You must be the Andersons."

"We are," the man said, he reached a hand across the registration desk to shake. "I'm Dave and this is my wife, Marty. We're glad to be here and glad that you didn't get storm damage. We read about Hurricane Alphonso being in the area and worried that Seaview wouldn't be here when we got here."

I reached up and shook his hand. "We just had a broken window and a little seawater seepage around the front door because we're right on the sand. Oh, and a fishing boat was on the front porch. The owner moved it and fixed the steps for me." I checked the reservation. "I've put you in the salmon room. It's on the seaside overlooking the bay."

"Does it have a king size bed?" Dave asked.

"No, it has a queen size. None of our guest rooms are big enough for a king bed. They are all queens."

Dave smiled and nudged his wife. "Guess that means we'll have to be less energetic."

Marty blushed and poked him with her finger. "Oh, for god's sake, Dave, don't say stuff like that."

I would die of embarrassment if Iggy talked like that. I hoped they were at least quiet about it.

Dave looked around the room. "Do you have any information about deep-sea fishing? I want to go fishing while I am here. Marty doesn't enjoy fishing, but I do, so I'm going."

I took a brochure from one of the pigeonholes behind me. "Down at the other end of Sandy Ground, just before you get to Blue Harbour Resort, is The Hook. They have fishing charters. You can walk down there and see what they offer once you get checked in."

Dave leaned down and picked up their suitcases. "That sounds good. Let's get settled and get to vacating."

"Vacationing," said Marty.

"Whatever."

I took the key fob out of its pigeonhole and led the new arrivals up the stairs. I opened the door and ushered them into the room.

"Oh, this is nice. Look at that view, Dave. You can see right out to a little island in the bay. It looks like it ought to be Gilligan's Island."

"That's Sandy Island. You can catch a launch out to the island at the pier in the middle of the bay. They have food and drinks, and it's a fun place to snorkel."

Dave set the cases down and opened all the windows to let in the breeze. "That's better. Let the fresh air blow in."

I pointed up. "There's a ceiling fan if it gets too warm at night and there's air conditioning if the fan doesn't do it for you."

Dave flung his arms out. "I love real air when I sleep."

Marty looked at him and smiled. "And I am getting to the

age where I need cooling off at night. We'll be discussing the use of the air conditioner," she said with a meaningful look at her husband.

I turned and walked to the doorway, glad there wasn't a hurricane predicted and wondering what kind of guests they'd be. "I'll leave you to get settled. There's a pitcher of iced tea in the refrigerator in the hotel kitchen that you're welcome to help yourself to. There are small plastic baskets next to the fridge for you to put any food into that you buy and want to keep cool. Please don't keep food in your room; it draws bugs and mice. There's plenty of room in the fridge for your doggie bags or leftovers. There's a microwave in the lobby on the sideboard that you are welcome to use."

Marty stopped me. "Is there internet?"

"Yes, there is. The password is on the little cardboard tent on the desk." I stepped through the door and went back downstairs to get ready to greet the next guest who was arriving on the mid-afternoon ferry from St. Martin. It wasn't until I got to the lobby that I realized that I had forgotten all about the welcome plate of cheese and fruit that was waiting for them in the fridge. I put a couple of napkins on top of the plastic-wrapped plate, picked up a split of white wine and two glasses, and went right back upstairs. I tapped on the door and when Dave answered, I handed over the snack and the wine.

"Hey, thanks, this is great. I was just telling Marty that I was getting a little hungry and this will do the trick nicely."

"Oh good, I hope you enjoy it. Please bring the plate and glasses down and put them on the sideboard when you're done. See you later." I turned and went back downstairs.

I waited and waited, but the next guest never arrived. I checked my email and texts; there was nothing. No communication to indicate that there was a problem. Finally, the phone rang. "Hello, this is Seaview. Rose speaking, can I help you?"

"I'm lost," said a woman's voice.

"Is this Faith Macklin? I've been expecting you."

A disgusted sigh came through the phone. "I've been trying to find you for over an hour. I think I've driven all over this blighted island, and I can't find Seaview."

"I'm very sorry. Where are you now?"

"I'm in the parking lot of a place called Vista Market. The woman in the store couldn't tell me how to get to Seaview. Vista Market is up on a cliff."

It frustrated me that Mrs. Richards, believing what Mrs. Whiting told her about me, wouldn't help my guest, but I was grateful that I wouldn't have to drive off to find her and lead her back. "And it's right near us. Do you see the roundabout in front of the market?"

"Yes."

"All you need to do is go around the roundabout to the third exit that takes you down a steep hill. Be aware that the second exit is not a paved road; it's a gravel track, but it counts. At the bottom of the hill bear to the right and we're about half a mile down Sandy Ground Road. You'll see the sign. We're just past Johnno's Beach Bar on the left."

Faith let out a relieved breath. "Thank you. I'll be there shortly." And she hung up.

I had to smile. Signage was not a big priority in Anguilla. It was so small that everyone knew where everyone else lived, worked, and played. They still gave directions like "turn onto the gravel track just past Emil Fischer's old place." It made it hard for newcomers to make their way around the island without having to stop every other mile to ask directions. I wondered how I could go about making amends with Mrs. Richards. I needed to catch her when there were no other customers in the store.

A car came slowly down the road and turned into the gravel lot next to Seaview. That had to be Faith, my next guest.

Soon a blond head popped around the doorway and said, "I made it!" The person who followed the head looked like I imagined Peter Pan looked. Small and slender, and with that cap of blond pixie-cut hair, she looked like an imp.

"I'm glad to see you. I was getting a little worried when I didn't hear from you."

Faith walked over to the registration desk and set down her one suitcase. "I was getting a little worried that I couldn't find you too. The island looks so small on a map. It's a lot bigger in person when you're in a car trying to find someplace."

"Well, now you're here. Let's get you checked in." I took down the rest of Faith's information and put it into the computer. It hadn't taken me long to get used to entering guest information directly into it. "Both of the garden-side rooms are available. You can pick your color if you would like to."

"What are my choices?"

"Lilac or turquoise, neither one too bright, muted colors."

Faith put a finger to her lips and tapped them. "I think I'll take the turquoise one. Turquoise always reminds me of the ocean, which is where I want to spend most of my time this next week."

I entered her choice and closed the check-in program. I grabbed the keys to that room and ushered Faith up the stairs.

"I love the old-fashioned look of your check-in setup, especially that wall of pigeonholes behind the desk. Reminds me of an old black and white movie."

"I love it too. I was glad that we could save it and replace the rotted and broken parts. The sideboard across the lobby is also original. We just evicted the lizards and mice, and Iggy put in plugs. The little sink and tap are new too. It makes making morning coffee a breeze."

I stopped in front of the last door on the right side of the hall. "Here you are." I fitted the key into the lock and pushed open the door.

"Oh, it's just the way I imagined it."

"There's a gallery across the front of the hotel where you're welcome to sit to watch the bay and sunset if you'd like. There are two shared bathrooms, one on each side of the hall.

BARBARA ANGERMEIER MALCOLM

Your towels are color-coded to your room, so you don't forget which ones are yours in case you leave them behind. And there is a sink in the corner here so you can wash up in privacy and only need the bathroom for showering and using the facility."

"That's great. I bought a new bathrobe, so I won't have to take all my clothes into the bathroom when I shower."

I held out the key fob. "You have your room key on here; the front door key has the blue key cap on it. When you go out, be sure to have your keys with you, as I keep the door locked and turn in around eleven."

Faith reached for the keys. "I won't forget."

"I'll bring up a cheese and fruit plate and a little bottle of wine to welcome you."

Faith's face lit up. "Oh good, I'm starving. I didn't eat lunch, and it's way past lunchtime."

I stepped back out of the doorway. "I'll be right back." I brought up the plate along with a split of wine and a glass. I gave her my canned speech about iced tea, baskets for food in the fridge, and being able to use the microwave in the lobby.

Faith was taking big bites of cheese and fruit. "Mm, this is good. Thanks. What time do you serve breakfast?"

"I start the coffee around seven-thirty and serve breakfast when I hear people come down for their coffee, usually around eight. I can be flexible if you're a late sleeper."

Faith shook her head. "I'm an early riser. I get up early and run, then I'll be in for breakfast. Eight o'clock will work."

"Good, I'll leave you to unpack and get settled."

For the next few days, everything went smoothly. The guests seemed to have a pleasant stay and a good time on the island. I was making egg casseroles and muffins, both of which were very popular with my guests. They even liked the canned pork omelets that I made one morning when I couldn't get bacon or sausage anywhere on the island. It's kind of like ham, I told myself, as I stirred the cubed pork meat in the skillet.

I lay awake, staring at the ceiling of my bedroom. I checked the time, after two o'clock. I was going to be a wreck tomorrow if I didn't get to sleep soon. I hadn't been able to fall asleep and was lying there regretting that last glass of iced tea I had in the afternoon. It must have been too much caffeine, and it was keeping me awake.

I heard Faith's bed moving in the room above me and thought that I might see Julius at the breakfast table again in the morning. Maybe Faith would hurry him out the front door when they were finished. That rhythmic squeaking made me wish Iggy was there. It had been a while since he stayed over. I would have to invite him for the weekend. There, it was quiet overhead. I listened for footsteps in the hall and soon heard them; only one set, and they didn't come down the stairs and leave by the front door. Oh no, was Dave creeping around? Was it Janet? Or Marty? One of my guests had been having sex with another of my guests, and it was not the married couple. Was that going to interrupt the friendly atmosphere that I had worked so hard to encourage? It was going to be hard to look at them in the morning. I would wonder who Faith was having sex with and hoped it was Janet. I liked Marty and Dave too much for their marriage to be in trouble. I hated conflict and avoided it at all costs. That was it; I would ignore what I heard and just go on as if nothing had happened. I rolled over and eventually fell asleep.

CHAPTER 19

I grumbled when my alarm went off at seven. I had not fallen asleep until nearly two-thirty in the morning, and four and a half hours of sleep just was not enough. I took a shower hoping that would help me wake up, dressed, and got the coffee brewing. I was not sure when my guests would be down for breakfast because at least two of them were up in the middle of the night. I got the breakfast casserole into the oven and stirred up a batch of muffins to go with it. There were three past their prime bananas in the basket, so I made banana muffins. I loved the aroma of vanilla and nutmeg as they baked. Almost as soon as the coffee finished dripping, I heard someone come down the stairs. I peeked through the door into the lobby and saw Dave making his way across the room.

"Good morning," I said, and he jumped. "Oh, sorry, I didn't mean to startle you."

"That's okay, I startle easily. I'm just getting coffee for my bride and me to have in our room, if that's okay."

"That's perfectly fine."

"What time will breakfast be ready?"

"It will be about a half hour, so right around eight o'clock."

"Great, we'll be down at eight." He picked up a mug in each hand and went back upstairs.

I watched him go and thought, well, I guess it wasn't Dave creeping down the hall in the middle of the night if he's taking coffee to his wife this morning.

The timer for the muffins dinged, and I went back into the kitchen to take them out of the oven and let them cool in the screened cupboard. The breakfast casserole needed to bake for another fifteen minutes, so I went out into the lobby to get my own first mug of coffee for the day. Janet came down as I was pouring out my coffee. "Can I pour you some?"

"Yes, please," Janet said, "I had a late night writing. Didn't get to sleep until after two o'clock."

"I had trouble falling asleep myself. I think I had too much caffeine yesterday. And here I'm starting off my day with more of the stuff. I should probably drink decaf, but I just can't get going without it in the morning. It's probably all in my head."

Janet smiled at me. "I don't know. I can feel my brain kick in with my first cup of the day." She turned her face toward the kitchen and sniffed. "Something smells good. What are we having today?"

"Today we have a breakfast casserole with onion and bell peppers and ham in it, and fresh banana muffins. Maybe it'll give us all energy after our nearly sleepless night."

Everyone was down in the lobby, coffee mugs refreshed, and sitting at the tables just after eight o'clock. I heard them all talking and laughing. I was relieved that no one seemed angry or disturbed by what had happened last night. Maybe the squeaking that I heard was the wind moving the old building around. During the hurricane, the building had creaked and groaned almost continually. No, that was hopeful thinking, and I knew it. What I had heard was good, old-fashioned sex. Well, everyone here was an adult, and I was the innkeeper, and it wasn't my business to monitor what the guests did.

I carried out a tray with baskets of muffins and dishes of butter, then I went back into the kitchen for the plates of egg casserole. The egg custard had set beautifully, and the pieces of onion, bell pepper, and ham peeked out enticingly. It smelled delicious; I hoped it tasted as good as it smelled. I knew it would; it was one of my daughter-in-law Elizabeth's recipes, and what Elizabeth made always tasted great. I wondered how she and Will were doing and when I'd see my family next. Hopefully, there wouldn't be another surprise visit like when we weren't finished working on Seaview.

As I served each of my guests a plate of egg casserole, they were talking about their plans for the day. Marty and Dave were taking the launch out to Sandy Island to snorkel and have lunch.

"We love to snorkel," said Marty. "And I hear that lunch out there is worth the trip."

Faith was planning to drive around the island, stopping at a local restaurant or food stand for lunch.

"I'm going to sit under the palm tree to start today's writing and probably end up hunched over my laptop by lunchtime," Janet said.

Faith looked at her. "You should come with me. You've been here for weeks and can keep me from getting lost."

Janet laughed. "I've been here writing most of the time and the rest of the time Hurricane Alphonso kept me trapped indoors. Maybe I will come along; we can get lost together. And there is a good barbecue ribs stand at Shoal Bay where we can have lunch."

Faith clapped her hands. "Great, we all have a fun day planned." She picked up her fork and finished her egg casserole.

I asked how everyone's food was and received rave reviews.

Dave said, "I wasn't sure that I would like this girly egg casserole stuff, but it tastes great, and the muffins are good too." He turned to his wife. "Marty, you should get Rose's recipes, then you can make these for me when we get home."

"Maybe. Rose, these muffins are excellent. What do you do differently?"

I smiled. "I got a banana bread recipe from the cook at a villa in Montego Bay, Jamaica, years ago. He used half white and half brown sugar and put nutmeg and extra vanilla in his bread, so I just transferred that to my standard muffin recipe.

Easy."

"Well, it sure makes them taste good," said Marty. She patted Dave's hand, which rested on the table. "Drink up, Dave, the launch goes in about fifteen minutes, and I want to brush my teeth again."

Dave emptied his coffee mug and stood up. "Let's go. I'll get the towels, snorkel gear bag, and sunscreen ready while you do your teeth." They got up, wished Faith and Janet a fun day, and hurried upstairs.

Janet turned to Faith. "Would you mind if I wrote for an hour before we go? It's a small island so sightseeing won't take long, and I have an idea I'd like to get down on paper first."

Faith shook her head. "No, I don't mind. You go ahead and write under the palm tree. I can take a walk down the beach. How about we plan to go around ten o'clock? That will give us plenty of exploring time before lunch. I really want to try the ribs place."

"Yes, it's a great place for lunch. They have the best johnny cakes I've ever eaten, and they make it all right in their little shack on the beach."

I overheard their plans and said, "There's a local market that sets up in the middle of town, right on the main road. They have straw things and wood carvings, most locally made. That's a fun place to shop for gifts and souvenirs."

Faith smiled. "That's great to know. We'll definitely stop there. I can always use a few little things to give as gifts."

Janet carried her plate and coffee mug to the third table and put them onto the tray that I had left there. "I'm going to get my notebook and pencil and get out to that palm tree. I'll see you back here at ten."

Faith carried her dishes to the tray after Janet did. "Great. I could use a walk after that breakfast. I wasn't going to have a muffin, but they smelled so good that I gave in. Eating here is not going to do anything for my waistline."

Janet looked at her. "You're slim enough that you can afford to eat a little on vacation, plus you run every morning."

"I didn't this morning. I didn't fall asleep until after two, and it was hard to get up for breakfast at eight." Faith twisted her fingers together.

"I guess everyone had a hard time sleeping last night," said Janet. "Rose said she was awake in the middle of the night too."

Faith turned pale and excused herself to go walk down the beach.

Dave and Marty came down and left for their snorkeling day while I was clearing the tables. I wished them a fun day and was pleased to see them holding hands as they walked down the beach to the pier where they would catch the launch. I carried the tray of dirty dishes back into the kitchen. I bagged up the remaining muffins and ran a sink of dishwater. It must have been Janet leaving Faith's room in the middle of the night. I shook my head. No, I thought, don't even think about it. I'm not their mother, and it's none of my business. "Put it right out of your mind, Rose," I said aloud.

"Put what out of your mind?" asked Iggy from the doorway.

"Oh, I heard one of my guests sneaking out of a different room last night and I can't stop thinking about it."

He came up behind me and put his arms around my waist. "I have been missing you," he said as he nuzzled my neck.

"I've been missing you too. Would you like to spend the weekend here?"

Iggy chuckled. "I was just trying to figure out how to invite myself and here you do it for me." He squeezed me. "Yes, I would be happy to spend the weekend here. And Geneva will stop over this afternoon when she gets off work. She is very interested in working for you."

"That's good news. I'm feeling overwhelmed by all the cleaning and laundry, cooking and washing up. I hope we can come to an agreement. I'll be full again next week and could use the help, especially with the laundry. People use a lot of towels on vacation."

"I imagine they do. Any handyman jobs that need doing? I could bring my tools."

"I don't think so. So far everything is holding up just fine."

Iggy kissed my neck and then turned me around for a kiss on the lips. "I have to go do a job in The Valley. I will come back this afternoon with my grip. I have a couple of lobsters that we can grill if you want to fix up a salad."

"That's a great idea. I would love a lobster supper. Now go off and get your work done."

He patted my backside. "We sound like an old married couple."

"We sure do." I wasn't sure that was what I wanted at this stage of my life, but it felt like that was the direction we were headed in.

I was paging through my recipe binder when I heard someone come in the front door and go right upstairs. The footsteps were fast, and the ones that followed them were slower, more plodding, but they went upstairs too. Marty and Dave must be back, I thought. I checked the time, and it was just past noon. The launch from Sandy Island had just come into the pier and must have dropped them off. Then I heard raised voices coming from the upstairs room that Marty and Dave shared. I couldn't help but hear.

"You could at least control yourself when you're with me," Marty said.

"I'm sorry, hon, my libido got away from me."

"It always does. I can't believe that you lost control and fondled that woman right in front of me."

"Oh, you know me, Marty. I get caught up when I see a ripe young woman and just lose it. I flirt with all the women, you know that."

"Flirting is one thing, but fondling is another whole ball game. You could have been arrested."

"Come on, we were just playing."

"You started out playing, but it turned into something else real fast. Kissing and fondling. I was so embarrassed."

Dave laughed. "Why were you embarrassed? You weren't the one making a spectacle of yourself in front of a beach full of people. I was." Then he said, "Don't cry, Marty, don't cry. You know I can't stand it when you cry."

There was a long pause.

"Don't touch me," said Marty. "You do not get to touch me when you've spent the last two hours fondling some other woman. Just keep your hands to yourself for once."

I heard noise in the lobby and went out to find Faith and Janet standing stock still in the middle of the room. It was obvious that they too had heard Marty and Dave's conversation. Faith was pale as milk, red spots standing out on her cheeks.

"I have to go," she said, and she hurried up the stairs.

I hoped she made it to the bathroom before we heard her retching.

Janet and I looked at each other.

"What's going on?"

"Um, I saw Dave leaving Faith's room last night, well, early this morning," Janet said. "I guess they had a little interlude and Marty must have found out."

I looked up the stairs. "What a mess. I never counted on things like this happening with only four rooms at Seaview."

"I think things like this happen no matter how few rooms you have."

We could hear Marty crying and Faith retching. I was glad that Saturday was tomorrow, and everyone was leaving, even Janet, who had been there since the day I opened the doors. I wished I could specify that only women could stay at Seaview, but that wasn't a good idea. Even women had flings. I didn't have the customer base to allow me to be that selective. Most of my guests were single women, but every once in a while, a couple made a reservation, and I couldn't afford to refuse.

By the end of the day tomorrow, there would be four new women checked in. Tomorrow would be a very busy day. I had to strip and remake all the beds, even though the lilac room was currently empty, go through each room to dust and sweep, and wash yet another double armload of towels. The next time Will and Elizabeth or Marie came down from the States, I would have them bring more white terrycloth towels so that I could sew fabric strips or shapes on them to match them up to the rooms. When I made the first sets of towels and sheets, I had assumed that only one person would stay in each room, that one set of towels could be in use while the other one was being laundered. That hadn't worked out this past week because I needed two sets of salmon-marked towels for Marty and Dave every other day. Fortunately, I had brought a couple of extra sets of towels that I had hurriedly decorated with salmon motifs, but now I was out of plain white towels. I wondered if I could find plain white towels at the local home goods store.

Janet and I had been standing silently in the lobby while I was thinking about all of that.

Janet stirred. "I had better get started packing. I've really spread out in my room since I've been here so long. I never meant to stay for four weeks. I was getting so much writing done I hated to leave for fear that the words would stop."

I smiled at her. "I'm glad that you've gotten a lot done while you were here. I'm sorry that this mess has marred your last day on the island."

"Oh, it's all right. When I saw Dave leaving Faith's room last night, I knew that nothing good would come of it. Maybe I'll put a philandering husband in my next book. I'll make him the murder victim."

I touched her arm. "You won't set the next novel in a bed-and-breakfast in the Caribbean, right? I don't need that kind of publicity."

"No, I won't put it in the Caribbean." Janet laughed. "I'll

put it in some small Wisconsin town or village like my other books. There are philandering husbands everywhere."

"I meant to ask you, do you have any of your books along? Could you leave a copy of one here?"

"Sure, I have a couple with me I can leave here. I leave copies behind me like Hansel and Gretel's breadcrumbs. It's cheap advertising." Janet put her beach bag on her shoulder. "Now I had better pack. I don't want to leave anything behind." She went upstairs and turned left toward the yellow guest room, which had been her home for the last four weeks.

Almost as soon as Janet's door closed, the door to the salmon guest room opened, and Marty came out and plodded down the stairs.

I stood behind the registration desk and pretended that I had been checking emails and not listening to the argument.

Marty came over to the desk. "Can I ask a favor?" she said in a small voice.

"Sure, what can I help you with?"

Marty took a pen from the cup on the registration desk and fiddled with it. "Um, Dave and I have had an argument and I'm wondering if I could stay in the other guest room tonight. I'm happy to pay extra for it."

I wasn't sure what to say. There was that empty room, and I planned to remake the bed tomorrow anyway. The sheets were fresh, so Marty might as well sleep there. "You can certainly sleep in the lilac room tonight. I'm sorry that you and Dave had an argument." I handed over the keys to the lilac guest room.

"Thank you. I'll get my things." Marty trudged up the stairs as if she were going to the gallows. She opened the door to their room, and I heard her say, "I'm not sleeping here tonight, Dave. I've had enough and will spend the night in the empty guest room. I'll be calling my lawyer when we get home. I'm done."

She had left the door ajar. Their voices carried down to the lobby.

"What do you mean you're done? Why do you need a lawyer?"

Marty sighed so loud that I could hear. "I'm done looking the other way at you running around. I'm filing for divorce. I should have done it years ago, but I thought, silly me, that you'd outgrow your need to bed every woman that you take a shine to."

I heard the bedsprings creak.

"Aw, come on, Marty, you don't mean that. You and me, we're a team. We belong together."

Marty's voice was suddenly louder as she stood in the doorway. "We aren't a team. We haven't been a team in a long time. I'm sorry, Dave, we don't belong together anymore." Marty walked down the hall, rolling her small suitcase behind her. She unlocked the door to the lilac guest room, went inside, then shut and locked the door behind her.

Nothing like that had ever happened to Jim and me, and I was going to make sure that would never happen to me. Better to enjoy someone's company, like Iggy's, as long as it never got serious.

CHAPTER 20

I stood at the registration desk listening to Janet come down the stairs. I would be sorry to see her go. She'd been at Seaview as long as it had been open and had started to feel like a distant relative. I had to shake off that feeling. Iggy was right, I couldn't afford to get emotionally involved with my guests no matter how much I liked them or how long they stayed. I wanted them to come back and either tell or bring their friends. "All packed?"

Janet bumped her suitcase down the stairs and rolled it over to the registration desk. "I think so. I went over my room twice, maybe I should do it again," she said looking up the stairs at the door of the yellow room. She handed two paperbacks across the registration desk to me. "Here are a couple of my books for your bed-and-breakfast library. Thanks for asking." Janet shifted her laptop case strap on her shoulder. "I'm relieved that you could dry this thing out. I'd have been in a world of hurt if my laptop had been ruined."

"I don't think it got soaked but I'm glad the old rice trick worked too." I reached across the registration desk to shake her hand. "I really enjoyed having you stay. I hope you come back, and I hope you give me good reviews online."

She cocked her head. "Did Ellen leave good reviews?"

I grimaced. "Her reviews were okay. Not negative, but the whole hurricane experience colored her opinion, I think."

Janet laughed. "Not even a day and a night with Julius improved her review. I'm shocked."

I laughed too. "Yes, Julius is an Anguilla experience not to be missed. You got to dance with him at the jump-ups, so you had a little taste of his charms."

I had totaled up Janet's bill and printed it out. I slid the sheet across the registration desk. "Make sure all is in order."

"Oh, I trust you." She took the time to peruse the sheet and nodded. "You forgot to add the hurricane food."

"I didn't forget. I decided not to charge you. My treat."

"Thanks. Maybe someday I'll write a book set in the Caribbean and have a hurricane descend on the place. Having everyone trapped in a hotel by a storm would make a good, locked room mystery."

"That reminds me of the old Humphry Bogart and Lauren Bacall movie, *Key Largo*. Don't they get trapped in a small hotel in the Keys with a bunch of mobsters?"

"I don't know. I'll look it up when I get home. I love old movies like that, especially with Lauren Bacall." She handed over her credit card.

I scanned it, then handed it back and gave her a receipt. "Here are a few brochures. I'd appreciate it if you shared them with your friends or left them lying around in places where writers congregate. Thank you so much for staying at Seaview. Come back anytime and let me know how the book is going."

She checked her watch. "I'd better get moving so I'm not late for my plane." She picked up her suitcase handle and rolled it toward the door.

I came out from behind the registration desk to walk with her.

When she got to the door, she leaned over and gave me a one-armed hug. "Thanks for everything, Rose. I hope you have continued success. Tell Iggy goodbye for me."

I hugged her back and smiled. "I'll tell him. Thanks for choosing Seaview. Have a safe trip home. Stay in touch."

She lifted her suitcase and carried it down the porch steps, raised the handle, and rolled it toward her car.

I needed to attract more guests like Janet to keep me in business. I should have Marie put something about Seaview being a good place to host writing retreats and other special small groups on my website.

Almost as soon as Janet left, Faith came down with her bag. She still looked pale, as if she hadn't slept well.

"Thanks for choosing Seaview." I handed the receipt across the desk. "Please make sure that this is correct."

She barely looked at it. "It's fine. I just want to go." She looked up as if afraid that Dave and Marty would come down while she was still there.

I scanned her credit card and handed it back. "Have a safe trip home and come back sometime. Tell your friends about Seaview. Take a couple of brochures." I handed them across to her.

Faith nodded, picked up her bag, and left.

Dave was next to come to check out. He kept looking over his shoulder at the door to the lilac room and mumbling. "She had better get down here or I'll go without her." He turned and shouted up the stairs. "I'll go without you, Marty. Get a move on."

The door to the lilac room opened, and Marty came out pulling her small suitcase behind her. "Coming, Dave."

Dave looked at the bill and stabbed a finger at the last entry. "I'm not paying for her to have her own room. She can pay for that herself."

"I said I'd pay for it, Dave, and I will." Marty had reached the bottom of the stairs. She got out her wallet and handed me a credit card.

"Is that our joint account?"

"No, Dave, it isn't. I've had my own credit card for quite a while. I have a bank account too."

"Your own account, huh?" Dave shoved the receipt into a pocket on the outside of his bag. "I guess you've been planning this for a while. Too bad you had to ruin our vacation."

Marty just shook her head, put her credit card back into her wallet, and started for the door.

I didn't know what to say. 'Thanks for staying at Seaview' seemed like the wrong thing to say. 'I hope you enjoyed your stay' seemed wrong too. "Safe travels."

As I watched them go, I wondered if there was a way to vet future guests. That was probably wishful thinking.

Geneva arrived at the back door dressed as if she were going to church. She wore a nice floral-print dress and a hat.

"Come in, I'm so glad you came." I escorted her to a stool at the kitchen island. "Would you like a glass of iced tea or maybe water?"

She kept her eyes on her hands. "No, ma'am, thank you. I do not need a drink."

I sat down opposite her, folded my hands, and plunged right in. "I'm looking for daily help cleaning, doing the laundry, and help in the kitchen doing dishes and making breakfasts. I hope we can agree on working hours and salary. I'm hoping that you're available four or five days a week. What were you thinking?"

"Well, Mrs. Lambert, I am wondering how long you will be here in Anguilla." She fiddled with the clasp on her purse. "I have heard that you might not be here long, that you are a speculator who will leave if things do not go your way."

I felt the blood pound in my ears. Mrs. Whiting had obviously been spreading her rumors all across the island. I took a deep breath. "Geneva, as far as me staying in Anguilla, I intend to be here running Seaview until I'm a feeble old woman. I have sunk all of my savings into the refurbishing and running of this bed-and-breakfast, and I need guests to come to build my bank account back up. I have reservations and deposits for the next few months and realized that I need a right-hand woman to help me run the place, someone to work alongside me. I hope you are that person."

"Mrs. Whiting said..."

I interrupted her. "I'm sure that Mrs. Whiting is saying many negative things about me. She and her friends have had their eyes on Mr. Solomon since his wife died six years ago.

They aren't happy that Mr. Solomon has spent time with me instead of them. I'm not sure what I can do to combat their rumors except hold my head up, pay my bills, and do my best to be a part of the community. Are you willing to help me with that?" I thought but didn't say that my best revenge would be to make a success of Seaview and keep my relationship with Iggy despite the bad-mouthing of Mrs. Whiting and her friends.

Geneva lifted her chin and looked me in the eye. "Mr. Solomon should be able to spend time with whoever he chooses."

"I agree."

"Mrs. Whiting is a churchwoman. Spreading false rumors and lies about you is not the Christian way to behave."

"No, it isn't."

She took a deep breath. "I think I would like to work with you, Mrs. Lambert."

"Please call me Rose."

We spent the next hour going over the salary I could afford to pay her, her hours, and what her duties would be. I finally convinced her to have a glass of iced tea and a muffin with me, but she persisted in calling me Mrs. Rose. I'd work on that.

After we agreed on hours and pay, I walked her to the door and shook her hand. "I'll see you next week. I know that we'll get along just fine."

"Thank you, Mrs. Rose. I will see you next week."

CHAPTER 21

I woke up feeling blue and couldn't figure out why. I did all the things that usually perked me up—drank a mug of coffee while standing on the beach in front of Seaview, dressed in my favorite khaki shorts and red tee shirt, wore my red Keen sandals—nothing did the trick. I was quiet as I served the guests their breakfast of mushroom omelets and coconut bread toast. I didn't ask when they planned to leave; I bid them good morning and then left the lobby. No one noticed I was quiet; they were too busy talking about what they had done during the week, where they had been, what they planned to do when they got home.

I stood at the kitchen island watching Geneva start on the breakfast pots and pans. I was glad that I had hired the young woman. Paying her strained my budget a bit, but I'd recently gotten a raft of reservations and deposits for the next six months so I could afford her salary. Just.

Geneva was a quiet presence in the bed-and-breakfast. She was always moving. She stayed on top of the cleaning, getting through the bathrooms as soon as the guests left for their day. We worked together to keep the laundry moving. Now that Geneva was there, we could hang the sheets on the line so they smelled fresh, and we took turns ironing the pillowcases so they looked neat.

I heard the guests get up and go upstairs to pack. I went into the lobby to collect the dirty dishes and take them into the kitchen to be washed. Then all the guests came down to check out at the same time. They were still talking about the things they had done and how they planned to keep in touch. I presented them with their bills and scanned their credit cards one at a time. "Thank you for choosing to stay at Seaview. I hope you enjoyed yourselves and will come back again. And tell your friends." I handed out the colorful brochures that I'd had printed, asking them to pass them to friends and family.

They all agreed that they'd had a good time and would be sure to leave glowing reviews on the travel sites.

Once the last happy tourist had left for the parking area, I went back into the kitchen. "I'll take over the dishwashing," I said to Geneva, "if you want to get a start on the bathrooms. Everyone has left."

"Yes, Mrs. Rose," Geneva said, "I will get upstairs as soon as I dry these dishes." She gestured to the pile of baking pans and skillets in the dish drainer.

There was a light tapping on the back door frame, and Silas said, "Do you have any spare muffins for a poor, starving man?"

I turned away from the sink and smiled. "Yes, there are a couple of muffins in the fridge if you want them. I'll warm them in the microwave for you."

Geneva touched my arm. "I will get them for Silas, Mrs. Rose."

Silas came into the kitchen and leaned against the kitchen island. He smiled at Geneva. "How are you liking your new job?"

Geneva put two muffins on a plate and slid the plate into the microwave. She pressed the buttons for the time and turned it on. "I like it fine, Silas."

"Mrs. Rose not working you too hard, is she?"

Geneva peeked up at him from under her eyelashes. "No, Mrs. Rose is easy to work for." I stood at the sink drying the dishes with my back to the pair.

Silas went on. "Because if she is, I will have words with her."

The microwave dinged, and Geneva took the plate of muffins out and slid it in front of Silas.

"Do not be saying things like that. I am happy working here for Mrs. Rose. We work together and get things done. You used to work for Mrs. Rose, and you know she is a good person to work for."

"I know, I know, I am just teasing you." He polished off the first muffin in a few bites. "Maybe you can stop at Johnno's later when you get off work. I will be there. I could make you a special drink."

I heard the smile in her voice. "Maybe I will do that. I will see how the day goes." She turned and left the room.

I heard her in the back room getting the cleaning supplies, then she walked back through the kitchen to head upstairs to clean the bathrooms. "Mrs. Rose, I will throw down the dirty towels so you can get the washing started."

I stood the last plate up in the dish drainer. "That'll be fine."

I left the dishes to air dry a bit and filled two big two-liter glass jars with fresh cold water and hung six tea bags in each one before putting on the covers and standing the jars in the shaft of sunlight that streamed in the window.

"Why do you bother making tea like that?" said Silas. "It is much easier to make it with the powdered tea."

"Yes, it is easier and quicker, but this way tastes better. It's easy to do, and I like it. My guests like it too. I can't tell you how many of them think that I have a special way to make iced tea that is better than the way they make it. Maybe it's the British tea that I make it with. Whatever the reason, I won't quit."

"Okay then," he said laughing, "I won't try to talk you into making it any other way."

"While you are here, will you help me tighten the clotheslines? We're using them to hang the sheets and the lines are stretching. I'm afraid that the sheets will be dragging on the ground soon."

Silas and I went out into the backyard, and while I leaned my weight on the lines to tighten them, Silas retied the knots that kept them taut. "I have to get back to Johnno's. Dad will wonder where I have gotten to." He walked away down the road, waving goodbye.

I watched him walk away, admiring his confident strut. I thought that Jim would have liked the young man and his easy manner.

Jim. I still missed Jim every day. The grief was not as painful as it had been a year ago. I had resolved to find a good memory when I thought of him, but today his memory only brought sadness. Then I checked the date on my watch. Oh, that's why I was so blue. Today would have been our forty-third wedding anniversary. It was a surprise to realize that nearly five years had passed since Jim died and it was six weeks since I had opened Seaview.

That second week was a doozy, what with Hurricane Alphonso trapping me and my guests in the hotel for four days. I thought that my time as a hotel keeper would be over before it really began but the storm moved on and the damage was limited to seawater flooding across the lobby, a broken window in the yellow guest room, a cracked panel in one front door, and the latch on one set of shutters. There was the small matter of a boat that got washed up onto the front porch too, but Iggy and Silas repaired or replaced the crushed and broken steps and railing. Billy the fisherman helped with the repairs and paid for part of the materials. I almost forgot the mango tree Iggy planted for me that had toppled in the relentless storm winds and left a giant hole in the corner of the backyard. I needed to get some soil to fill that in. One of these days someone would stumble into it and get hurt. I had seen an ad on the community bulletin board at Vista Market for a local landscaper. Maybe I would drive up there and call him. Right now, I decided, right now while all the guests were out, and Geneva was busy cleaning.

I hurried into the lobby with a laundry basket and gathered up all the towels that Geneva had thrown down for me. I went out onto the back porch and got them into the washer. While the first load washed, I grabbed a dish towel and dried the dishes, and put them away in the cupboards. I was glad that I had bought stainless steel shelving and cupboards for the kitchen. The sides of the cabinets and drawers were mesh, so that air flowed through them. I waited out the half-hour wash cycle and put the first load in the dryer and the second load in the washer. Then I called up the stairs to let Geneva know I was going to Vista Market and would be back shortly.

"Okay, Mrs. Rose, I will be finished up here by the time you return."

Mrs. Richards frowned at me when she saw me standing at the community bulletin board, but there was a handful of customers in the store, so I didn't want to talk to her about the rumors and my intentions on the island. I had to sort through a few overlapping notices to find the landscaper's sign, but eventually found it. I put the number into my phone and called it when I got outside.

"Jed's Landscaping," said the voice on the other end of the phone, "Jed speaking. How can I help you?"

Already I was impressed with the professionalism of the operation. "Hi, this is Rose Lambert. I own Seaview Bed & Breakfast in Sandy Ground. I had a tree fall in the hurricane. It left a big hole where the roots were, and I need someone to bring a load of soil to fill the hole. I'm afraid someone will stumble into the hole and get hurt."

"Hello, Mrs. Rose, I heard all about your new hotel in Sandy Ground. My dad did your plumbing. I can probably help you with that. I am just wrapping up most of the hurricane work so I can get right on it. It sounds like a quick job. How big is the hole?"

Something sounded wrong, but I dismissed it. I was eager to get that hazard fixed. "I don't really know, maybe as big as a washtub and twice as deep."

"Here is an idea. Measure the hole width and depth and

call me back. Then I will know about how much fill you need."

"I can do that. I'll call you back within the hour."

"That will be great. If you get the dimensions to me today, I can be there early on Monday and get it filled in."

I thanked him and then hung up. As I pulled out of the parking lot, something Jed had said sunk in. Jed said that his dad did the plumbing for Seaview. That meant that Jed's dad was Calvin Brooks. Oh no. Just thinking about Calvin gave me a flashback to him pressing himself into me and trying his best to kiss me until Iggy came into the room and pulled him off. All the other times Calvin had grabbed me played like a movie in my mind. I wondered if Jed was the same kind of person as his father. I dearly hoped not. Maybe I should have Silas or Iggy around when Jed came, just in case. I thought about my safety without a man and didn't like the thought that I might need one.

I drove back down the hill to Seaview, dug around in my toolbox for a tape measure, and went out to measure the hole. It was nearly two feet deep and three feet across, bigger than I thought it was. I was glad I had found someone to fill it in for me without asking Iggy or Silas to do it. I felt I relied on their good graces too much and needed to stand on my own more. Finding Jed to do the landscaping was the first step, but only if he wasn't like Calvin. I called Jed and gave him the dimensions of the hole, and he promised to be there on Monday with the fill. That done, I went to see what Geneva was up to.

Geneva had the second load of towels in the dryer and was just getting ready to put the first load of bedding on the line. I hurried to help hang the sheets.

"Thank you, Mrs. Rose," Geneva said.

"No problem, this job is easier with two people. One can clip the sheets on the line and the other one can keep them out of the dirt. Silas helped me tighten the clotheslines this morning so we shouldn't have to worry about them dragging in the yard as they dry."

"Silas is a good boy."

I smiled at that. "I think Silas has graduated from boy to man. Silas is a good man."

Geneva was behind the sheet she was hanging up, but I could tell she was smiling. "Yes, Silas is a man."

I heard gnawing in the night. I lay in bed looking up at the ceiling, but the sound was coming from under the bed. What could it be? It was a rhythmic sound, like something was chewing on the wood. Termites wouldn't be that loud. Could it be a rat? I knew that there were rats on the island. I had seen one climbing up the palm tree next to the hotel, so I knew they were in the neighborhood. I touched Iggy, who lay peacefully sleeping beside me.

"Iggy," I whispered, "wake up. There's something eating Seaview."

His voice came soft and clear, no groggy sleepiness in it. "What do you mean?"

"Shh, listen."

We were both quiet; the only sound was our soft breathing. Then it came again. Crunch, crunch, crunch.

"Did you hear that?"

"Yes, it sounds like a rat is gnawing on the supports under the floor. I will set some traps tomorrow and maybe put out rat poison. We cannot get rid of them all together. We can make it unpleasant for them to stay around here." He put his arm around me and pulled me close. "Now go back to sleep. I cannot do anything about the little beastie right now." His breath ruffled my hair as he tucked me under his chin.

I felt his strong arm around me and relaxed back into sleep. We woke up still entangled and spent the first few minutes of the day enjoying the closeness.

CHAPTER 22

On Sunday I served an egg casserole to my new guests for breakfast with a side of bacon and coconut bread toast and jelly. As I knew would happen, as soon as the aroma of brewing coffee made its way upstairs, my guests stirred. I made sure that the cream pitcher was full, and the packets of the various sweeteners were easily accessible in the coffee service area. It was not long before all four of the guests were in the lobby. I invited them to help themselves to coffee while I set four places on the lobby tables.

"I'm Millie," said the woman staying in the lilac room, "Millie from Indiana."

"Hi Millie," said the woman from the turquoise room, "I'm Sue from Michigan."

The woman from the yellow room turned around with her coffee mug in both hands. "Oh, I'm so glad to have coffee. Can't start my day without it," she said. "I'm Connie, and I'm from Illinois." She turned to the fourth woman, who was just pouring her coffee. "This is my friend Dianne," said Connie.

Dianne raised her mug in a salute and said, "Hi, I'm from Illinois too. Looks like we're a quartet of Midwesterners."

I left the lobby and came back carrying a tray with four plates and sets of silverware. "We're all Midwesterners," I said. "I'm from Wisconsin. Welcome to Seaview."

I had finished eating my breakfast when Dianne poked her head into the kitchen doorway. She held an empty coffee carafe.

"Sorry to disturb you. The regular coffee is all gone. Can

you make some more?"

I set down my fork. "I sure can." I took the pot to rinse it before making a second pot. When I carried it back into the lobby, I said, "Am I the only one drinking decaf?"

"Yes, I like high test," said Millie.

"Me too," the others chimed in.

"Well, then, I'll make two pots of regular and make my decaf in the kitchen from now on." I turned to survey all the empty plates. "How was your breakfast?"

"It was good."

"Just the right amount."

"Delicious."

I started gathering the plates and stacked them on the tray which I had left on the sideboard.

I had given them my little welcome speech when they checked in, letting them know that there was room in the refrigerator for them to stash a small amount of food or doggie bags if they wanted to bring them back.

I didn't mention the rat that I thought was trying to gnaw its way through my bedroom floor. "Enjoy your day," I said as I carried the full tray through the door and into the kitchen.

Connie and Dianne asked for directions to the nearest church and went to enjoy the service at Pastor Davis's Anglican church. Millie and Sue took off in a rental car to tour the island. They all planned to be back in Sandy Ground to attend the weekly jump-up at Johnno's.

Edward stopped by to make sure that Iggy and I would be there. "I wants to dance with you, Mrs. Rose," he said, snapping his fingers and shuffling his feet.

"I'll be there. I want to dance with you too, but you have to promise to dance with my guests as well. I told them what a wonderful dancer you are, and they can't wait."

Edward nodded. "I will give them all a twirl," he said, spinning in place with one hand out like he was holding a partner's hand.

"Thanks, Edward, we'll see you later at Johnno's."

I did a load of towels and swept the lobby. I took the broom upstairs to sweep the bathrooms and the hall. Then I did a quick clean of the bathrooms since it was Sunday and one of Geneva's days off.

Soon enough it was four thirty, and my guests were back getting ready to go down to Johnno's for his weekly party. I had told them they should go down early to nab a table, or they would spend the evening on their feet. They all changed into clean shorts and tees, put some money into their pockets, and walked down the beach to see if they couldn't get a table. They told me later that they were lucky and got the last free table in the place.

Edward, Silas, Luke, and Melvin had already claimed the big table at the edge of the floor and guarded the two empty chairs for me and Iggy. When we got there, the steel band was just tuning up, and as soon as Iggy got back with our drinks, the music started.

Edward grabbed my hand and pulled me to my feet. "Come on, Mrs. Rose, let's go."

I barely got a quick sip of my rum punch before Edward swept me into his arms and whirled me away across the dance floor. As we spun by, I saw Silas, Luke, Melvin, and Iggy ask the four guest ladies to dance.

When the music ended, I felt a hand on my shoulder and turned, smiling, thinking that Iggy would be my next partner. It was Calvin. He gripped me in a vise grip and would not let go when I squirmed to get away. "Leave me alone, Calvin," I said, almost yelling to be heard over the music. I kept my feet still and made Calvin drag me. He pulled me off balance, and I stumbled and would have fallen except for the hold he had on me. Calvin pulled me to him and squashed me to his chest. He wrapped his arms around me and let his hands roam over my back and backside. I could feel his erect penis through our clothes, and it nearly made me sick.

"Let me go," I said, pushing against his chest.

"No," he said, "you will get used to me in time. You are mine now."

"I." "Will." "Never." "Be." "Yours." I pushed as hard as I could with every word, but he didn't loosen his grip. As the song ended, I saw Iggy coming up behind Calvin and relaxed. Calvin thought I had given up my resistance and loosened his hold enough for me to slip away. I stepped back from Calvin as Iggy pulled his shoulder and spun him around.

"You need to leave Rose alone, Calvin," Iggy said, "or else."

Calvin's face changed from a smile to a scowl. "Or else what, Mr. Big Man," he said.

"Or else this," said Iggy as his fist came up and hit Calvin a fierce uppercut that knocked his head back and sent him reeling into the crowd. People backed up fast to get out of the way of the stumbling man. Calvin landed on his back on the dance floor and lay there stunned for a moment. Then he got up roaring and lunged for Iggy, but Officer Matthew, who had been standing in the doorway watching the crowd and enjoying the music, grabbed him and pulled his arm up behind his back.

"That is enough, Mr. Brooks," said Matthew. "Mrs. Rose is not interested in your attention. You need to come with me." He escorted Calvin out of the beach bar, keeping his arm in a tight grip.

The place was silent as the policeman and the plumber left the floor. As soon as they stepped down onto the sand, the band launched into the next song, and the people began to dance.

I was embarrassed when the song ended, and I realized all eyes were on me. No one said anything, but I could feel the gaze of the crowd scorch my back. I knew that most of them had heard Mrs. Whiting's rumors about me, and having Calvin assault me in front of them just added to the shame. What were my guests thinking? Maybe now they knew why I was so adamant that they lock the doors when they left Seaview.

Iggy sat beside me, holding my hand with one hand and rubbing my shoulder with the other. "Now that Calvin will be in jail, you will feel safe, I think," he said.

I shook my head. "I don't know if I'll ever feel safe again. Calvin is obsessed with me, and I don't know how to deal with it."

"Soon he will turn his attentions elsewhere," said Iggy.

"That's easy for you to say. You aren't the target of his obsession." I gave a small laugh. "How can I ever face Dru again?"

"You do not have to worry about Dru; she has had years of her husband chasing skirts. You are just one more skirt he is chasing."

"No, I'll wager that he has never been this... this insane about it. This is a whole other level of crazy."

Iggy cocked his head and looked me in the eye. "Maybe you are right. I do not remember him ever being this persistent. I will stay with you until you feel safe. How is that?"

I squeezed his hand. "I really appreciate it. Thank you." Then I straightened my shoulders and shrugged off Iggy's hand. "Now it's time to get back to the party."

The band started to play a ballad. "Let's dance," I said and stood up, pulling Iggy up with me. Edward, Silas, Luke, and Melvin had each claimed one of my hotel guests' hands, and the five couples moved onto the dance floor.

The jump-up went on for another few hours, but Iggy and I left before ten o'clock. We walked down the beach to Seaview and let ourselves in the front door. I had locked it when everyone left for the party because I didn't want to come back to find Calvin lurking in my apartment. Even though I knew that Officer Matthew had taken Calvin away, I didn't know if he was in jail or had been set free. I insisted Iggy accompany me around the place, making sure that no one was lurking anywhere.

"He will not be here," Iggy said, "Matthew took him off to

jail and he could not be out so quickly."

"I know, but I want to check anyway."

And I set off up the stairs to check the bathrooms, the guest rooms, and the front and rear galleries. Once I was certain that no one was hiding upstairs, I checked all the rooms downstairs, even the kitchen where there was really no place to hide. In my apartment, I checked the wardrobe in the bedroom and under the bed just to be thorough.

"You see, I told you that no one was here, that Calvin could not have gotten out of the jail already."

"Yes, what if they didn't charge him, just took him away from the jump-up? What if they gave him a stern warning and turned him loose? Where would he go then?" I pointed to the floor. "I think that he'd come right here, so I'm not letting down my guard until I know for sure that he's in custody."

A rustling sound came in through the window over my bed. "Aha!" I whispered, "What's that? It's probably Calvin lurking around."

"It is probably a cat."

I turned and hurried out of the room toward the back door. I unlocked it and quietly edged out onto the porch, creeping to the corner of the building, and peeking around. I saw the looming shadow of a man under my window and backed away.

Iggy met me at the back door, and I whispered, "I was right. There is a man under that window. I'm going inside to call the police."

"Let me," Iggy started to say, but I interrupted him.

"No, he could hurt you. I'll call Officer Matthew and he can come down to get him." I used my cellphone to dial the police station and reported Calvin's presence under the window.

Officer Matthew sighed and said he would be right there. Iggy and I stood in my bedroom talking about nothing until we heard a shout and a scuffle outside.

"Now you are going into a cell," Officer Matthew said,

and they heard the click of handcuffs being applied. "Mr. Brooks, you are under arrest."

"What for?" Calvin bellowed.

"For trespassing, first off, and then for stalking Mrs. Lambert. You cannot be hanging around her windows and listening to her in the night."

"I will sue you," Calvin said.

"You can do that," Officer Matthew said. "You will do it from a jail cell."

We heard a grunt and then footsteps rustled around the corner of the building, across the yard, and up the gravel road to the police station a few doors away.

I sagged against Iggy's chest. "I don't think I'll ever feel safe here alone again. Is it eleven o'clock?" I checked my watch and then grabbed my keys to make sure that the doors were locked. As I made my way into the lobby, I heard a key in the lock, the front door opened and my guests, all four of them, came in giggling and dancing. I reined in my fear and smiled at them. "I see that you all had a good time."

Connie threw her arm over my shoulders. "Are you okay? That big guy who grabbed you was scary."

"I'm fine. The policeman took care of him, but I need you to make sure you lock the door when you come in or leave." I didn't mention that Calvin had been lurking outside my window when we got back from the jump-up. No need to worry the guests too much.

"I don't remember when I've danced so much. That Edward is a whirling dervish. Thank goodness there are four of us because he spread himself around, so we got a rest every once in a while."

"Didn't the others dance with you too?"

"Oh yes," said Millie. "Edward is the most energetic. He tired me out."

All four heads nodded in agreement.

"Edward is a dancing dynamo, I'll grant you that."

Dianne nudged Connie and said, "I'm bushed. I'm

heading up to bed. See you in the morning."

"I'm right behind you," said Connie.

"Me too," said Sue and Millie together.

"My feet are throbbing," Sue said. She slipped off her sandals and reached down to pick them up. "I have a new rule. No more dancing in thong sandals." She turned and followed the others upstairs.

I called after them, "See you in the morning." I locked the front door, turned out most of the lights except for the small lamp on the registration desk, and went through the kitchen to check that the back door was locked. When I had locked all the outside doors, I went back into my apartment to find Iggy in bed waiting for me. "All of your chicks back in the nest?"

I smiled at him. "All present and accounted for." I got undressed, put on a nightshirt, brushed my teeth, and slid in beside him. "Goodnight, Iggy, thanks for rescuing me on the dance floor."

He reached to pull me close. "My pleasure."

The four women staying at Seaview that week were tidy people. They didn't leave messes in the bathrooms, and when I replaced their towels, their rooms were neat as well. I dreaded the day when I'd have slobs as guests. It didn't fit into my dream of how the bed-and-breakfast would run, but then having one guest's husband fooling around with another guest hadn't been in my plans either. Now I just had to worry about what would happen on Monday when Jed's Landscaping came.

CHAPTER 23

I waited for Jed's Landscaping to arrive. He said that he would be there around nine in the morning, and it was nearly nine thirty. I was about to go inside to call his number when a truck came slowly down Sandy Ground Road and pulled to a stop outside Seaview. There were two men in the truck, and one of them was Calvin. Damn. I thought he'd be in jail longer, not just overnight.

"Are you Mrs. Lambert?" asked the driver.

When I said that I was he opened the door and stepped over to shake my hand.

"I am Jed Brooks. Thank you for calling on me to fix the hole in your backyard. I have some clean fill in the back of the truck and my dad volunteered to help me today."

"How nice for you to have your dad helping you. I'm glad that you could come right away."

As I talked, we walked across the patio and over to the corner of the yard where the hole left by the falling mango tree gaped.

"Oh, that is a nice size hole. We will get it filled in quickly." He turned and motioned to Calvin to get out of the truck. They met at the back tailgate where they lifted down a wheelbarrow and a couple of shovels. Jed immediately filled the wheelbarrow with shovels full of sandy soil. Calvin leaned on his shovel and gave orders. When the wheelbarrow was full, Jed speared his shovel into the mound in the truck bed and grabbed the handles to push the wheelbarrow across the yard to dump it into the hole. Calvin followed him, then stood by the hole and watched. He had his shovel on his shoulder like a rifle and did not appear ready to use it.

"Good morning, Mrs. Rose," he said. "I hope your hotel survived the storm undamaged."

I stepped back from him. "Good morning. I had a little damage and this new mango tree Iggy planted for me blew over. It wasn't salvageable. Silas cut it up and hauled it away. Now I just need the hole filled and things will be as good as new."

Calvin leaned closer to me and said, "I could fill your hole for you anytime you would like."

I felt heat rise up my cheeks. "No, thank you. I told you before that I'm not interested." I watched Jed shoveling more dirt and trundling the wheelbarrow across the yard. "Aren't you going to help your son, or did you come along just to proposition me again?"

"Oh, I am going to help. I wanted to let you know that I have been thinking about you." He took the shovel off his shoulder and used the back of it to tamp down the dirt that Jed had dumped into the hole.

"Well, I haven't been thinking of you. I appreciate the good work you and your crew did in replacing the plumbing in Seaview. That's all. I'm not interested in a relationship with a married man."

Jed stopped with the wheelbarrow half tipped toward the quickly filling hole. "Dad, you told me you were done with all that, then you got arrested for stalking her, and now I hear you trying to make time with Mrs. Rose. Stop it." He tipped the wheelbarrow all the way over, and the soil slid out and into the hole, nearly filling it. Jed stepped into the hole and used his booted feet to stamp the dirt down firmly. It compressed, and he stepped out of the hole and went back for another wheelbarrow load.

Calvin leaned on his shovel. "I am just being friendly," he called after his son. Calvin shook his head. "These young people do not understand friendliness."

I folded my arms across my chest. "You aren't being

friendly, Calvin. You're trying to get something going with me and I've already said no more than once. Give up."

He grinned a wicked grin. "No, I like the way you look, Rosie. I am not giving up."

"You're wasting your time and effort. I'll never agree to do anything with you."

Jed stormed up, pushing the filled wheelbarrow ahead of him. "Dammit, Dad, are you trying to ruin my business before it even gets started? If I had known why you wanted to come along today, I would never have let you. Leave Mrs. Rose alone and get to work."

I looked at Jed. "I have work to do in the kitchen. Please knock on the back door when the job is done."

"I will do that. I am nearly finished now. It will not be long."

I finished washing the breakfast dishes and had started on the pots and pans when the knock on the back door sounded. "That didn't take long at all," I said as I dried my hands and went over to the screen door.

"It was a small job. I sprinkled some grass seed and fertilizer over the place and watered it in. You should water it a couple times a day, just get it wet do not soak it, and soon the seed will sprout."

"Thank you. How much do I owe you?"

Jed repeated the price he had quoted me. "The grass seed is on me," I paid him in cash, thanked him again, and he left. Once I had the dishes all done, dried, and put away, I went out and pushed small sticks into the ground around the fresh dirt, hoping to keep people from walking on it until the grass seed had sprouted.

Back inside, I heard sounds from upstairs. I thought it was Geneva cleaning the bathrooms. All four of the guests left after breakfast. Millie and Sue went out on the launch to Sandy Island, and Connie and Dianne took books out to read on the beach.

"Stop that," Geneva said.

I hurried to the bottom of the stairs. "What's the problem, Geneva?"

The young woman stepped out of the bathroom on the right of the hall and looked down at me. "Mr. Brooks is in here fussing with the pipes. I think he is loosening the connection. He will not stop."

I charged up the stairs, forgetting the baseball bat, and burst into the white and green bathroom. "What do you think you're doing, Calvin?"

He held up his hands away from his body. "I am just checking that the connectors are tight. I do not want you to have any trouble with your pipes." He leered at me, which made me feel cold.

"Leave, Calvin, just leave. Do I need to call Officer Matthew again? Tell you what, let me call Dru right now to come and pick you up."

Calvin reached up and grasped my wrist and pulled me down close to him. "I will not leave, not until I have your word that you will spend some time with me. I mean to have you and I will."

I shook my head. "No. No number of threats will get me to cooperate with that." I turned to the young woman hovering in the doorway. "Geneva, go call the police. Mr. Brooks is threatening me, and I want him out of here."

Geneva nodded and turned away. I heard her quick footsteps down the stairs and across the lobby.

"It will take her some time to convince a policeman to come with her. We have that time to get reacquainted." He shoved his hand up my tee shirt to my breast and squeezed. "I can have you out of that sports bra in a minute."

I used my free hand to push him away, but he still held my wrist in a vise grip, and he was blocking my path to the door. "Stop it, Calvin, stop or I'll scream."

Calvin grinned at me. "Scream. No one will hear you."

A muscular arm reached in through the door and snaked

around Calvin's throat.

I looked to see Jed pulling his father off me. "For God's sake, Dad, leave Mrs. Rose alone. Do you want to get arrested again for assault?"

Calvin staggered to his feet and stumbled backwards into Jed. "I want to have her. She threw herself at me."

Jed pulled his father out of the room. "No, she did not. She told you no. She said that she did not want your attention, that you should stay away from her. I heard her."

"But she hired me to fix her pipes. I want to finish the job." Calvin kept talking as Jed led him down the stairs and out through the kitchen.

I stood shaken in the bathroom listening to their receding footsteps, then I bent down to make sure that the pipe connector that Calvin had been touching was tight. It wasn't. He had been loosening it, just as Geneva said. I turned it to the right until I couldn't turn it anymore.

"Hello?" a man's voice called from the lobby. "Mrs. Rose, are you all right?"

I walked out of the bathroom and looked down to see Officer Matthew at the bottom of the stairs. "Yes, Officer, I'm all right." I walked down the stairs and said, "Calvin Brooks wouldn't leave me alone, wouldn't leave Seaview. I sent Geneva to get you to move him along. His son, Jed, came up and hurried him out. He scares me."

Officer Matthew put his hand on my shoulder. "Maybe you should not be here alone."

"I will not let that old lecher make me afraid to stay in my own home. Is there such a thing as a restraining order in Anguilla?"

Matthew told me what I would have to do to swear out a restraining order on Calvin, saying that I needed a witness to attest to my claims.

I was sure that Geneva and Iggy would be more than happy to back up my claim that Calvin would not leave me alone.

Iggy came back from doing a quick electrical job for a friend to find me sitting on the end of my bed, rocking back and forth. "What is the matter?"

I looked up at him with tears in my eyes. "Calvin was here, and he said he won't leave me alone until he has me." I showed Iggy my reddened wrist from Calvin's vice grip. "Officer Matthew and Jed helped get rid of him. I'm afraid of him. He's strong and persistent, and he scares me."

Iggy crossed the room, sat beside me, and put his arm around me. "I know Calvin thinks that every woman wants him. I will talk to him again. What was he doing here?"

I leaned into Iggy's shoulder. "He came with Jed, the landscaper. I knew Jed was Calvin and Dru's son. It never occurred to me that Calvin would come along with him today. Then he was up in one of the guest bathrooms loosening the pipe connector under the sink. I think I need to call another plumber to have all the pipes checked to make sure that Calvin has not sabotaged them."

Iggy tightened his hold on me and smoothed his hand down my back. "You do not need to hire another plumber. I can check the connections that are visible to make sure they are tight. I will do it right now." He got up and went first into my bathroom, then into the kitchen, and then upstairs to check those bathrooms. He came back downstairs and said, "All tightened. You were right, he had loosened the coupler under each sink and turned off the water feed to all the toilets." Iggy shook his head. "I cannot believe that he would do such a thing."

"Like I said, he scares me. Don't forget the sink in the lobby. I don't think Calvin had time to mess with the sinks in the guest rooms. I'll get the master key and you can check them all the same."

Iggy nodded. "That is a good idea. Remember the sink in one bathroom leaked the first time Ellen Gage used it. I will check them all and make sure they are seated correctly."

I kissed Iggy's cheek. "Thank you. You do not know how

much safer that makes me feel. I asked Officer Matthew about swearing out a restraining order, and he said I would need a witness to his threats. Will you be my witness?"

"I do not think that I can be. I have only heard from you what he said. That is hearsay. Did Geneva hear him threaten you?"

"Yes, she did. I'll ask her when she's done with the cleaning. Maybe we can get a restraining order done today."

Soon Geneva had finished sweeping up tracked-in sand and putting fresh towels in each guest room. She was willing to be my witness, so we walked down to the police station to talk to Officer Matthew and get the process started.

Officer Matthew had the forms all ready for me and said that they would need to be notarized before the restraining order could be filed.

"Where do I go to have it notarized?"

"To the bank or the courthouse. You will have to wait until tomorrow." He looked at the clock over the counter. "It is late in the day, and they are both closed."

"I'll get it done first thing tomorrow." I looked at the thin sheaf of papers in my hand. "I hope that this works. I don't want to be constantly looking over my shoulder to see if Calvin is lurking behind me."

By the time we got back to Seaview, Iggy had checked all the plumbing. He came down the stairs and met us in the lobby. "The guest room sinks were all fine, tight and secure, but the sinks and toilets in the rest of the hotel had been tampered with. I have all of them back to the way they are supposed to be. There will be no leaking pipes as far as I can tell."

I stepped up to him, put my arms around his neck, and kissed him on the lips. "You have no idea how much better that makes me feel."

Geneva excused herself and went into the kitchen. Iggy put his arms around my waist and drew me to him. "I can make you feel even better. Why don't I stay here for a few days to make sure that Calvin does not come back? All of my tools are in my truck, and I can bring over a few clothes for convenience to keep from having to drive down the island every day."

I laid my head on his chest. "That's the best idea I have heard in a long time."

Iggy made a quick trip to the hardware store for rat traps and poison. I stood on the porch looking around to see if I could see any little paw prints in the soft dirt of the backyard. I didn't see any, but that didn't mean that there wasn't a rat living under my hotel. Then I heard scratching and turned to see something furry climbing up the fence that surrounded the yard. It was too small to be a cat and too big to be a mouse; it must be a rat. Living this close to the sea and on a bay where freighters docked, it made sense that rats would leave the ships and live there. As long as none of them came into Seaview, I guessed I could put up with them.

Iggy came back. By then, the last load of laundry was in the dryer. He had a bag with three big snap traps and a canister with a skull and crossbones on it. "Do you have any rubber gloves? I don't want to get this poison on my hands."

"Sure, I have a box of medical gloves left over from when Jim was sick. I'll get you some." I went into my apartment and came back with a pair of blue nitrile gloves. "These should do the trick. What will you use for bait? Do you need some cheese or peanut butter or something?"

Iggy shook his head. "No, the poison doubles as bait. You spread it onto the trap and set the spring, the rat eats the bait, and SNAP."

I flinched. "Yuk. I hope you'll be around to empty the traps if we catch anything. I don't think that I could deal with a dead rat."

"Better than dealing with a still alive rat." Iggy got a long piece of wood out of the back room and used it to shove the baited and set traps under the building. "There. I will check them in a day or so."

"Okay. Thank you. I don't know what I'd have done if you

hadn't been here. Lain awake all night listening and wondering what was trying to get in, I guess."

Iggy pulled off the gloves inside out and stuffed them into the trash bin by the back door. "You would have called an exterminator like everyone else has to. You have me, I will be your exterminator, Mrs. Rose." He gathered me in his arms and kissed me soundly.

I wrapped my arms around his neck and kissed him right back.

"Oh, excuse me," said a voice from the road.

I looked over the bougainvillea to see Connie and Dianne standing there. I cleared my throat. "This is my friend, Ignatius Solomon, ladies. You met him at the jump-up last night. What can I help you with?" I walked across the yard and around the end of the bougainvillea hedge.

"We want to find the craft market," Connie said, holding out a brightly printed map.

"It's easy to find." I pointed out the roundabouts and the roads they needed to follow to get to the market.

"Thanks," said Dianne. "Is there a place to eat there?"

I nodded. "There's a good stall at one end of the market that sells patties, meat pies that are delicious."

"Are they spicy?"

"A little spicy but not too bad. No spicier than a regular American taco. I think you'd enjoy them."

Connie and Dianne looked at each other. Dianne spoke up. "Is it safe? I mean, is the food safe to eat?"

"It is. I usually stop there for patties when I go by after running errands and I've never had a bad one."

Connie folded the map, and they turned to get into their rental car. "Thanks."

"My pleasure. Enjoy your meal. Bye." I waved as they drove up the road out of Sandy Ground.

I made sure that the doors of Seaview were locked and drove to the IGA. Monday was a good day to grocery shop, not as good as Tuesday but way better than Friday or Saturday. I parked in the lot, grabbed a cart from the corral, and walked toward the entrance scanning my shopping list. I bumped into the cart of a woman coming out of the store.

"Oh, excuse me. I'm so sorry. I wasn't looking where I was going," I said.

"No problem," the woman said, smiling as she turned to look at me. As her eyes met mine, the smile slid off her face and her mouth turned down. "No, I take that back," she said. "It is a problem."

My hands gripped the handle of the cart, and my stomach did a flip. It was Mrs. Whiting, and she had her cart butted up against mine and was pushing me backwards.

"You Americans come to Anguilla and think you can just take over. How dare you start a business on my island? And you have the gall to entice Ignatius Solomon so that he turns his eyes away from me. You are a bad, dirty woman who should leave us alone."

I felt my cheeks get hot, and I looked around to see if anyone was listening. "I didn't mean to take Iggy away from you. He came of his own accord. We started as friends, and our relationship grew from there. Neither one of us planned it; it just happened."

"You say it just happened? Ha. I am certain that you laid your eyes on that fine man and lured him into your bed."

As she spoke, she kept pushing her cart into mine, forcing me to back up into the center of the parking lot. People going into the store and people coming out of the store stopped to listen to her raving. I looked at her face with its ugly expression and thought if she could see herself and what her anger did to her, she would stop it.

"I'm sorry that you're so unhappy about my business. I've saved and scrimped for years to buy Seaview and refurbish it. I plan to be here in Anguilla, to be a part of the community until I'm too old to manage. I'm not giving up because you don't like me being here."

She flapped her hand as if to shoo me away. "Be a part of the community? A woman like you, a white American, will never be part of the community. Anguillans will see through your phony friendliness and your false bonhomie to the crafty, conniving woman inside."

The surrounding crowd was getting bigger, and I was afraid that others would join in her tirade. Mrs. Whiting had been spreading false rumors about me almost since I arrived in Anguilla, so most of the witnesses had to know that I was the subject of her rumors. People pressed in on me from all sides, nodding and agreeing with everything she said.

A hand reached through the crowd and touched my shoulder. I shied away from the touch until I heard a familiar voice. "What are you on about, Eleanora Whiting?" It was Iggy's sister, Anne. She put her arm around my waist and stood by my side.

Mrs. Whiting drew herself up to her full height. "How can you side with her when you know what she has done? She has stolen Ignatius from me."

"How can someone steal something that you never had? Ignatius was never yours. He is your neighbor, that is all." Anne shook her head. "When I heard your nasty rumors, I spoke with him about them, and he denied ever having a relationship with you."

"But he would have come around if she hadn't shown up." Mrs. Whiting's arm was extended, and her finger pointed at me like an avenging angel.

Anne looked at the gathered crowd. "Go about your business. Do not stand here in the hot sun drinking in this woman's poison." The people stood still. "Go on," Anne said. "You all have better things to do than to harass an innocent woman. Go." The crowd dispersed, and she drew me into the store with her. "Come along, Rose, let us get to shopping."

I unstuck my feet from the parking lot and followed her into the IGA.

When I got back to Seaview, I was gratified to see that

I'd gotten everything on my list because I didn't remember shopping. All I remembered was Anne's quiet voice talking me up and down the aisles, telling me to ignore the hostile stares. The wad of wet tissues in my shorts pocket told me I'd cried most of the drive home.

I told Iggy about Mrs. Whiting's tirade in the IGA parking lot and how she had accused me of stealing him away from her.

"I was never hers," he said.

"That's what Anne said. She came to do her shopping after school let out and saved me from Mrs. Whiting and her mob. A whole crowd of people had gathered around to listen to Mrs. Whiting rant and rave. I was afraid they'd beat me up, but Anne intervened before it came to that, thank God."

"What did you say to her?"

"I said that we'd started as friends and our relationship grew from there, and that I intended to stay in Anguilla running Seaview until I was a feeble old lady. She wasn't happy and did not try to hide the fact."

"I do not imagine that she was. I suppose I should speak to her to set her straight, although I doubt it will do much good. She is a stubborn, headstrong woman." He encircled me in his arms. "Do not let her scare you away."

I nestled into that warm, safe space. "I won't. I can be stubborn and headstrong too."

Later that night, as we lay in bed, Iggy rolled over to face me. "I feel like taking a swim. There is a full moon, and all of your guests are in their rooms. What do you say?"

I thought for a moment. "I say yes. Did you bring a swimsuit?"

Iggy shook his head. "No, I forgot it and it is too late to go down and borrow Johnno's swimming suit. I will just have to swim in my birthday suit. You will too."

We rolled out of bed, stripped off our nightclothes, and each grabbed a beach towel to wrap around ourselves in case there were people on the beach. It was late, after midnight, and we thought we would be alone.

In the lobby, I quietly turned the lock in the front door and opened it carefully so it didn't squeak or scrape the floor. I peeked out the door and didn't see anyone. I motioned for Iggy to follow me.

We dropped our towels at the bottom of the steps and, holding hands, waded into the small surf, shivering as the cool water lapped on our warm skin. We both leaned forward and fell into the sea. The full moon made a glittering silver path on the waves that we swam along for a while. We swam out beyond the anchored fishing boats until the water was too deep to stand in.

I treaded water and looked at Iggy. "This was a good idea. I wasn't asleep. I can't stop thinking about the look on Calvin's face today when he had hold of my wrist and his other hand up my tee shirt."

Iggy frowned. "You did not tell me he put his hands on you. I will definitely talk to him about keeping his distance. I will go to church next Sunday and make sure to talk to him there where he cannot make a fuss."

"Won't Dru hear you if you talk to him there?"

"I do not care. She has to know that he was arrested. Everyone knows that, and Dru needs to know what kind of man her husband is. I cannot believe that she has stayed married to him all these years. He has always been a lecher, after other women, and Dru looked the other way. I think she needs to face the truth and admit the kind of man that he is. She needs a divorce." Iggy stopped treading water and sank below the surface. He came up gasping and sputtering. "I did not mean to sink. I nearly drowned myself."

"Are you okay?"

Iggy nodded.

I shivered. "Let's go in. I'm getting chilled."

I turned and began swimming back to shore. Iggy swam alongside me, keeping pace, until we reached the shallows and stood up to walk to where we had left our towels. We dried off and went back into Seaview, locking the door behind us.

When we reached the bedroom, Iggy leaned down to whisper in my ear. "I think Calvin is outside. I saw someone by the palm tree when we came out of the sea. You be quiet and I'll sneak around the back to check."

I nodded agreement.

Soon I heard Iggy's voice through the open window. "I thought Rose told you to go away and not come back, Calvin."

Calvin chuckled. "Oh, I was just checking to see that the soil Jed put in this hole in Rose's backyard was level."

"At one o'clock in the morning? It is a little late and too dark to be checking on a landscaping job. I saw you lurking behind the palm tree when we came out of the sea. Go home, Calvin, and do not come back. I will see you in church next Sunday."

"I will not be there. I do not go to church anymore."

"That is too bad," Iggy said, "church might do you good. Go next Sunday. I would like to talk to you in the daylight and in a crowd so that I am not tempted to bloody your nose like I did when we were children. If you are not in church, I will come to your house, and we will have our discussion in front of your wife. You would not want that, would you?"

I heard Calvin push past Iggy and round the bougainvillea hedge that outlined the backyard. "I do not care what Dru hears or thinks. I am done with her. Now I only want to be with Rose."

I heard Calvin's steps crunch on the gravel of the road as he walked down to his truck. Iggy came back inside and locked the back door to my apartment before coming into the bedroom.

He was slipping off his shorts when I said, "I heard what Calvin said. I'll go first thing tomorrow morning to get the restraining order notarized and filed. I'm glad that I live just down the road from the police station. He is going to be a continuing problem."

Iggy lifted the sheet and slid in next to me. "I am afraid

that you are right." He slipped an arm under my neck and pulled me close. "I guess I will stay here until we can figure out what to do about Calvin."

I sighed. "Thank you. I don't know how to thank you enough."

He whispered in my ear. "Maybe I will stay here forever."

CHAPTER 24

The next few days were quiet ones at Seaview. Iggy hung around when he wasn't on a job and essentially moved in. I filed the restraining order and also a complaint against Calvin alleging that he was stalking and threatening me. Both Iggy and Geneva were witnesses to his actions, so the judge made Calvin promise he would stay far away from me and Seaview until his court date. The legal distance he had to maintain was one hundred feet, and I was certain that Calvin knew exactly how far that was and would keep to it. I hoped so anyway.

Connie, Dianne, Sue, and Millie all left on the Saturday flight from St. Martin. Geneva and I worked quickly to remake the beds, replace the towels, and clean the rooms before the next group of guests arrived. That week it was a trio, which suited me just fine. I had settled into a routine of alternating egg casserole days with muffin days. One day I made my late mother-in-law's famous (in the family anyway) Never-Fail Coffee Cake and that was a big hit with the guests. It's a kind of strudel filled with butter, meringue, brown sugar, and cinnamon. What's not to love?

The three guests were a writing group from the States. Their visit grew out of my idea of mentioning writing retreats on my website. The success of that idea made it easier to be strong and stay on the island. In the mornings they would all find a place to write, sometimes out on the beach, sometimes on the galleries, and sometimes in their rooms. Then before lunch they would gather in the lobby at one of the tables to share what they had written and give each other critiques. Once they had finished with their writing practice, they went on driving tours of the island, for long walks on the beach, or out to Sandy Island on the launch. I was glad they made time for sun and fun, but I was also glad that there were more writers under my roof.

I heard from Janet Fielding that the book manuscript she had worked on during her stay was cleaning up nicely, in her words, and Janet thought it would go to the publisher within a few months. I was thrilled at the thought that words written in my bed-and-breakfast would be an actual book. I wrote back to tell her about this week's writing group guests and suggested she might spread the word about Seaview among writers that she knows. And I needed to figure out a way to confront Mrs. Whiting without crying. Now that I had more guests and more reservations and deposits, I wouldn't let her rumors chase me off the island.

I was cleaning up the kitchen after breakfast service, and Geneva was in the back room getting ready to tackle the bathrooms when there was a thump at the back door. I crossed the room, wiping my hands on the dish towel over my shoulder, to find my son Will and daughter-in-law Elizabeth standing on the back porch. I couldn't believe my eyes.

"What are you doing here?"

"Surprise," Will said, "aren't you going to invite us in?"

I reached to open the screen door. "Sure, but what are you doing here? Where are you staying?" I backed up to let Will come in, dragging a suitcase behind him. Elizabeth followed him with a carry-on bag on her hip.

"We're staying here. I was sure that you would have a room for us now that you're up and running."

I stood shocked at my son and his wife arriving with no warning. I gulped. "You're in luck. I have one open room this week. I guess you're welcome to it."

Geneva came into the room with her bucket of cleaning supplies. "I will go up to clean the bathrooms, Mrs. Rose. I will throw the dirty towels down for you, okay?" She stopped seeing two extra people with luggage in the kitchen. "Oh, sorry, I did not know that you had guests."

I turned to her. "Geneva, this is my son Will and his wife Elizabeth. They will stay in the turquoise room."

Will extended a hand to her. "Pleased to meet you, Geneva. I guess we'll be seeing you while we're here."

"Geneva is a godsend. She helps with the cleaning, the laundry, and the cooking. I'd be lost without her."

Will gave a chuckle. "Well, I guess you won't need me and Elizabeth to chip in while we're here."

I put my hands on my hips. "And did you think I wouldn't be managing without you?" I turned to Geneva. "Go on and get the bathrooms started. The guests have split up to write, so the bathrooms should be empty." I picked up a laundry basket. "I'll position the basket where you can aim the towels at it. Come on." I motioned to Will. "I'll show you to your room." By the time I led my unexpected guests up to the second floor, Geneva had gathered up the towels from the first bedroom and dropped them over the railing into the basket.

I turned right at the top of the stairs toward the back of the building.

"Oh no," said Will, "I thought we would have a seaside room, not one in the back with a view of..."

"A view of the garden and the salt pond. You get whatever's left and are lucky to have anything at all. You're going to have to make reservations in the future. Both of the ocean view rooms are rented to paying guests this week. My three guests are writer friends who spend their mornings writing. You'll have to hold it down not to disturb them."

Elizabeth clicked her tongue. "I told you showing up unannounced again was a bad idea. What would you have done if the Seaview was full?"

"I knew it wouldn't be full," he said with a confident tone.

I looked at him. "This is only the second week since I opened. I haven't been full. You're lucky not to be staying at

Sydan's like you did last time. I'll charge you the friends and family rate."

Will looked startled. "Charge... but I thought we could just stay here if you had an open room."

I gaped at him. "You think I can afford to feed and house you just because you're my son? This is a business, Will. It would be irresponsible and poor business practice."

"We came all this way, and the airfare wasn't cheap."

"Beachside hotel rooms in the Caribbean aren't cheap either, son. You should have thought of that before you came without telling me."

Will looked astonished that his secret plan was falling apart. "Okay, I guess we'll pay for our room. Geez, Mom, after all the work we did when you were fixing up the place, I thought we'd get a little break."

"And you will. Like I said, I'll charge you a discounted rate. I can't afford to give it away. Did you arrange for a rental car?"

Elizabeth crossed her arms over her chest. "Yes, Will, what are we doing for transportation?"

Will hung his head and talked to his shoes. "I thought we could use Mom's car."

I was beyond amazed that my son would be that presumptuous. It left me at a loss for words. "I'll leave you to unpack." I went downstairs to get the laundry started.

"Oh, Mom," said Will, "which one is our bathroom?"

I stopped on the stairs. "You don't have a bathroom, Will, you share bathrooms with the other guests. As you know, there is one on either side of the hall, so whichever one is available is your bathroom. Your towels are trimmed to match the paint color of your room. Remember that. There are towel racks in your room for you to hang them to dry between uses, and there is a sink in the corner of your room for quick washing up, shaving, and toothbrushing. Most guests use the bathrooms for toileting and showering only. It works out."

I finished walking down the stairs, picked up the

overflowing laundry basket, and went out onto the back porch to get the wash started.

I got the first load of towels into the washer and stepped through the screen door back into the kitchen. I heard raised voices. The voices got louder as I went into the lobby.

"What did you expect?" Elizabeth said. "We showed up here unannounced. I'm surprised your mom didn't kick us to the curb."

"How was I supposed to know that the place would be nearly full?"

Elizabeth snorted. "Well, maybe if you had contacted Rose to tell her you wanted to come down, that would have given you a clue."

Will and Elizabeth were having an argument. A loud argument. That would never do. I hurried up the stairs and down the hall to the door of the turquoise room. I knocked on the door and the voices quieted. Will's voice came from close to the other side of the door.

"Yes?"

"Open the door, Will."

"I'm not dressed," he said.

"Open the door, Will, or I'll let myself in with my key."

The door opened and Will peeked around the edge. "Geez, Mom, what do you want?"

I kept my voice quiet and my temper in check. "You need to keep your voices down. My guests spend the morning writing in their rooms, and they don't need to be witness to your argument."

Will rolled his eyes. "We're paying guests too, remember? You're charging us your 'friends and family' rate, you said, so we get the same consideration as the other paying guests."

I nodded. "Yes, that's right, but the others didn't pay to listen to you two argue. Keep it down or... just keep it down."

Will's eyebrows drew together. "Or what? You'll kick us out?"

"Don't tempt me, Will. Don't tempt me. Clean up your act, and maybe tomorrow I'll be glad to have you here." I turned and walked back down the stairs, through the kitchen, and onto the back porch to swap the first load of towels into the dryer and start the second load. "Damn you, Will," I said to myself, "I don't need a problem with you besides worrying about Calvin lurking around."

"Who's Calvin?" Elizabeth asked from the doorway.

She startled me, and I turned to face her. "Oh, Calvin is the plumber who worked on fixing up Seaview and now he's decided that he loves me. Actually, he's assaulted me twice and is stalking me."

Elizabeth looked shocked. "Rose! Oh my God. Iggy's still around, right?"

I sighed. "Yes, Iggy's still around. I'm still in love with him and he is with me. Calvin is married and obsessed with me. I've had to swear out a restraining order to keep him away." I looked down the road and spied Calvin's faded pickup truck parked just past Sydan's Garden Inn. "See that green truck down the road?"

"Yes."

"Well, that's Calvin in his pickup. He spends most of his days parked there watching Seaview, hoping to see me. It's creepy, and it's driving me mad. He's a hundred feet away, so I can't do anything about it."

Elizabeth walked out to the edge of the backyard and stared up the road. She wrapped her arms around herself. "You mean he's there every day just staring?"

"Yes, almost every day. I think he still does a few jobs. He mostly sits there, sweating and watching."

"And the police can't do anything about it?"

"No, he's over a hundred feet away. They can't make him move."

"What if you walk down the road to the beach bar?"

"Then he starts his truck and moves away. He's very careful to abide by the restraining order so far, but I can't live like this."

Elizabeth turned to look at me. "And us coming down unexpectedly just added to your stress."

I smiled at her. "I'm always happy to see you, but a bit of warning would have been nice. I'd have felt awful if I were full and had to turn you away. Don't say anything to Will about this Calvin thing, okay? He'll be even more certain that I can't take care of myself." I took the towels out of the dryer and folded them into the waiting basket.

"All right, I'll keep quiet for now." She reached for a towel. "Let me do that. It's the least I can do for showing up out of the blue."

I let her take over the folding while I moved the wet load into the dryer. "What made Will think I don't have guests? I've been emailing about how many I've had and how well things are going."

Elizabeth shook her head. "I think he's decided that you're not telling the truth. That you're inflating your numbers, so we don't worry."

I leaned an elbow on the washer. "I don't know what I can do to convince him I'm telling the truth."

"I'm sorry, Mom." Will's voice came from the kitchen doorway. "I got it into my head that you were down here all alone bleeding money and I needed to come down to save you."

I turned to him. "I've been sending you emails saying how many guests I've had and how well things were going. We even dodged a bullet with Hurricane Alphonso with only that one broken window, the flooded lobby, and the porch damage from the boat. I don't know how else to tell you that things are fine." I walked over and lightly gripped his upper arms. "I'm not sending you my balance sheets to reassure you. You're going to have to take my word that I'm not bleeding money, as you said, and doing all right. I've been full almost every week until this one, and I have reservations on the books, deposits paid, into the new year. I've become popular with writers and single women looking for a relaxing place to stay that isn't a hopping resort. Anguilla is a safe island that attracts a quiet crowd looking to have a quiet vacation on a sandy beach with wonderful restaurants nearby."

Will shrugged off my hands and examined his fingernails. "I'm sorry I assumed we could use your car. I'll call for a rental car this afternoon."

I shook my head. "That's okay, you can use my car. The same rules apply as when you were a teen: bring it back with a full gas tank. I'll need it for a grocery run this afternoon, then it's yours for a few days. How long are you planning to stay, anyway?"

"Until Saturday."

"Good, because on Saturday the current guests leave and by nightfall more guests will have arrived, and I'll be full again."

"More writers?"

"No, next week a yoga group is having a retreat."

"A yoga group?"

"Yes, there are six of them. They're planning to do yoga on the beach at sunrise and in the lobby if it's rainy. Should be interesting."

"You only have four beds."

"I told them that but they're coming anyway, said that they don't mind doubling up. I didn't argue."

Will reached out and hugged me. "I'm sorry, Mom, I'm glad that you're making a success of Seaview." He let me go and looked over my shoulder. "Can we go down to Johnno's for lunch? I'm starving."

"Sure. Come on, Elizabeth, the laundry can wait while we eat."

We went indoors to get shoes and wallets, then walked down the beach to Johnno's Beach Bar where we shared a basket of conch fritters and had crab salad sandwiches for lunch. Will and Elizabeth had rum punch because they were on vacation. I had a cola because I needed to keep my wits about me.

After lunch, Elizabeth and I went grocery shopping. We shopped at the IGA in The Valley, the outdoor market under a tree on the road out of town, and Vista Market on top of the hill above Sandy Ground. Mrs. Richards was just as unfriendly as she had been every time I stopped in lately and she still demanded that I pay in cash. I did my best to be polite and complimentary, but she frowned and didn't speak.

"Boy, that clerk wasn't friendly," Elizabeth said.

"That's Mrs. Richards. She's the owner."

"Is she always that crabby, or does she have something against Americans?"

"Actually, it's just me." I sighed. "Iggy's neighbor, Mrs. Whiting, is a widow too, and she thinks that I've stolen Iggy from her so she's spending her days bad-mouthing me all over the island. She's telling people I'm taking advantage of Anguillans, that I look down on them, and that I will not stick around once I've made money. Oh, and I only want Iggy for sex."

"Oh my god, that's ridiculous. You are the last person I would accuse of taking advantage of people or any of that stuff, and I'm sure Iggy doesn't mind the sex." She blushed. "What are you doing about it?"

"Not much so far. Lomira in the dive shop knows me and isn't paying attention to the gossip, but I'm not sure how to go about changing people's minds. I talked to Henry at the hardware store, and he was willing to let me continue to make payments on my account if Iggy vouched for me which made me angry, but I went along with it because I don't have enough money to pay him off. I've been thinking I'll go over to the Barrel Stave before lunch or between lunch and dinner one of these days when it's quiet to talk to Mrs. O'Neill. Lately she's turned away when I call out a greeting. It'd be a start."

"That doesn't seem fair. Maybe you could bake a batch of muffins for the lady in Vista Market and take them up as an excuse to have a chat. You could tell her you're in Anguilla for the long haul despite what Mrs. Whiting's saying." Elizabeth stashed the bags she was carrying in the car's trunk. "This is a lot of stops just for groceries."

"Yes, I'd go to more stores if I thought they'd have what I want. I learned the hard way that if it isn't in those three places, it isn't on the island. I'm pleased that Amy's coconut bread is often on the shelf at Vista Market, so I don't have to drive all the way to Blowing Point when I run out."

"How are the recipes I helped you with going over?"

I smiled at her across the roof of the car. "Oh, they're popular. I make muffins one day and then an egg casserole the next day, mix it up so no one tires of the same old stuff."

"I have an idea I'd like to try out one morning if you don't mind," said Elizabeth. "I found a way to make French toast on a sheet pan so that you can make enough for a crowd without having to stand at the skillet making two or three slices at a time."

I pulled out of the parking lot, drove around the roundabout, and down the hill to Sandy Ground. "That sounds great. Do it tomorrow morning. I plan to serve breakfast around eight o'clock. You'll have to figure out when you need to start." I looked in the rearview mirror. "Dammit, Calvin has been following us the whole time we've been out."

Elizabeth turned in her seat to look out the back window. "You're kidding."

"I wish I were. That faded green pickup was behind us all the way. There has to be a way to discourage him."

Elizabeth turned back to face front. "I hate to say it, but maybe he'll find a new fixation one day and be some other woman's problem."

"Wouldn't that be wonderful?" I smiled when I saw Iggy's truck parked next to the bougainvillea hedge. I pulled into my parking spot, and he walked over to help carry all the shopping bags into the building.

"What did you do, buy out the stores?"

I shook my head. "No. Will and Elizabeth are here for

the week and will use my car. I thought I'd lay in a few extra supplies so that I'm not caught short without wheels."

Elizabeth put the bags she was carrying on the kitchen island and said, "We can still call for a rental car if you'd rather have your car available."

"No, that's all right. I have enough food bought for the week's breakfasts and extra for lunches and suppers if the two of you are around for meals."

Elizabeth laughed. "We probably will be, you know how cheap Will can be."

Will stepped through the lobby door. "Hey, who are you calling cheap?"

"You." Elizabeth pointed at him.

Will frowned. "I'm not cheap, I'm frugal. There's a difference." He sorted through the bags. "Have you got anything to eat in here? I'm starving."

I swatted his hands away. "Again? We just finished a big lunch."

"That was hours ago. I walked all the way down to the Blue Harbour Resort and back while you were gone. I'm hungry. Thirsty too."

I said, "There's a pitcher of iced tea in the fridge and some fruit in the basket on the kitchen island. I'll make up a nibble plate with some cheese and crackers once all this food is put away."

Will poured himself a big glass of tea and grabbed a banana out of the basket. "What's in those little baskets in the fridge?"

"Those are where my guests store their snacks and lunch foods. The baskets keep everyone eating their own things and not cadging someone else's food, like mine."

"What a good idea," Elizabeth said.

"Yep, it's a tidy way to keep their things separate from mine and it keeps the refrigerator neat." I finished putting the food away and folded the shopping bags into the basket that I used for produce from the outdoor market. "This basket lives in the trunk of my car. Will, can you put it away for me?"

He nodded, stood up, and put his empty glass in the sink. "Sure, I'd be happy to." He took the keys off the hook by the door and went outside. We heard him yell. "Hey, get away from there."

The three of us rushed out onto the porch to see Calvin loping up the road.

"What was he doing?"

"He was letting the air out of Iggy's tires. I don't know if I caught him in time before he did any damage."

Iggy shouldered past me and went out to examine the tires of his truck. "This one tire looks low, and this one is flat." He stood up and shook his head. "It is a good thing I keep my spare tire and jack ready. I will change the flat tire and go get the low one filled up. Stupid man, if he wants to keep me away from you, he should flatten my tires when I am anyplace else but here."

Will said, "Do you need a hand?"

"No, you and Elizabeth go off and have fun. I will get this taken care of quickly. Rose, call the police station and tell them that Calvin was here much closer than one hundred feet."

CHAPTER 25

I was busy in the kitchen assembling a pan of chicken parts and vegetables to roast in the oven for supper when Iggy returned from getting his tires filled.

"I called the police station," I said, "and told them that Calvin had let the air out of your tires when your truck was parked out back. They were quick to go right over to confront him and roust him for violating the restraining order. Officer Matthew asked if I wanted to press charges, and I said yes. I hope that was the right thing to do."

Iggy walked over and laid his arm across my shoulders. "It was the right thing to do. Calvin needs to learn that his actions have consequences. Maybe a night or two in the pokey will wake him up."

I leaned my head over to touch his. "Wouldn't that be amazing? He followed us on our shopping trip this morning. I saw him in my rearview mirror the whole way. I told Officer Matthew that too."

I finished arranging the chicken and vegetables on the baking tray, sprinkled them with olive oil, salt, and pepper, then covered the tray with plastic wrap. "There, that's all ready to be popped into the oven later this afternoon. Until then I'll just slide it into the refrigerator." I stood up, went to the sink, and washed and dried my hands. "Now I have to finish the laundry."

Iggy shook his head. "No, you don't. Geneva and I finished it while you were shopping."

"Then I'll just run the iron over the edges of the sheets and towels, so they look nice."

"That's done too. Geneva showed me what to do, and I did it while she folded things the way you like them and put them away."

I flung my arms around his neck and pulled him close. "You are amazing. What can I ever do to thank you?"

Iggy ran his hands down my sides. "I have a few suggestions." He nudged me toward my apartment door.

I grinned. "Oh that. Well, we'll have to be quick. I expect the guests and Will and Elizabeth will be back shortly. I think we can manage something."

We managed admirably and were back in the kitchen having glasses of wine when Will and Elizabeth came in the back door.

"What's for supper?" Will said as he crossed the threshold. "I'm famished."

"Again? We're having sheet pan chicken and vegetables. Can't you smell it? It'll be ready in about half an hour. There's a nibble plate of cheese and olives in the refrigerator."

Elizabeth went to the bread cupboard. "I thought I saw some sliced baguette in here." She reached in and pulled out a plastic container. "Yes, here it is, and they're already toasted. Get out the cheese plate, Will, and I'll pour us some wine."

"I don't want wine. I want iced tea."

"Fine, I'll pour me some wine and you some tea." Shaking her head and muttering, Elizabeth arranged toast slices around the edge of the cheese plate, then pulled out a tall glass for Will and a wineglass for herself.

"What did you do this afternoon?"

"We drove around the island looking for Amy's Bakery. It was closed. We were going to pick up a lobster pie for supper as a surprise," Will said.

"She closes early on Saturdays. We can call on Monday and order a pie for later in the week. That way we'll be sure to get one."

Elizabeth said, "Then we went over to Shoal Bay for a

swim. That's a nice beach, but I don't think that it's nicer than Sandy Ground's beach, just noisier."

"My first guest, Janet Fielding, said that was why she moved from a villa in Shoal Bay to Seaview because Shoal Bay was too much of a party place. She had trouble concentrating on her writing with all the loud music and laughter."

Will looked across the kitchen island at me. "What did you do this afternoon?"

Iggy and I answered together, "Laundry."

Will gave us the side-eye but said nothing.

Iggy reached down and squeezed my thigh, which told me he knew what I was thinking.

Geneva came into the kitchen with her broom and dustpan. "We need some kind of rug at the front door for people to wipe their feet on. I am thinking that soon all of Road Bay beach will be in our lobby."

Everyone laughed, and I said, "I'll check in the hardware store for a doormat, maybe one of those palm fiber ones that scrapes the bottom of your shoes. I'll get one for the back door too."

"Check at the Eastern Store," Iggy said. "They have a lot of that kind of household thing."

Geneva went into the back room to put away her cleaning tools and came back out to say goodbye. "I am going down to Johnno's. Silas asked me to stop on my way home today." She blushed.

I kept my expression neutral. "That's nice. Enjoy yourself."

I could tell that Geneva had combed her hair and washed her face before she left. I knew Silas stopped down for a muffin every few days and that he always talked to Geneva, but hadn't realized that it might be more than friendship.

Iggy looked at me. "Well, that's an interesting development. I thought Silas would like a flashier woman. Geneva is quiet, a good girl, not the woman for Silas."

"No, I think you're wrong. I think Geneva is exactly the

woman for Silas. They both have their serious side, and I think Silas is looking to settle down. How old is he, anyway?"

Iggy scratched his chin. "I think Silas is about twenty, maybe twenty-one. I suppose he would look around for a wife about now."

Will let out a breath. "Sheesh, that's young to be looking to settle down."

"You met me when you were twenty and look where that ended up." Elizabeth frowned at him.

Will set down his empty iced tea glass, the ice cubes rattling as he did. "Yeah, look where that ended up." He stood up from the kitchen island and left the room.

I watched him leave and turned to Elizabeth. "What's going on? Is there something you need to tell me?"

My daughter-in-law crossed her arms on the kitchen island and rested her forehead on them. She spoke to the tabletop. "We had a big argument about money at home, so Will decided we should come down here to hash it out and come to an agreement."

"How's it going?"

Elizabeth looked up. "Not very well."

"I'm sorry you're having trouble." I touched her arm. "Is there anything I can do?"

Elizabeth put her head back down. "Not really. I want to expand my business from a home-based one to a brick-and-mortar storefront, and Will thinks it's the wrong time with how the economy is these days and way too risky. I ran the numbers and if things continue the way they are now, I can make it go. There's a building I've picked out on South Broadway where the rents are lower and the buildings older. This one has a kitchen that just needs a little remodeling to get it up to code. I know I can succeed, Rose. I know I can. Will is afraid that I'll sink all of my savings into it and then lose everything. You know how he is, always looking on the negative side."

While we talked, I assembled a salad of Romaine lettuce,

spinach, cucumbers, and tomatoes. "I know. Change is hard for Will, and risk is even harder. Do you still have that retired executive mentor you can call on?"

"I do. I've talked to him about it, and he went over the building with me. He thinks I can risk it."

"Did Will go along when you went over the building?"

"No, he had to work."

I thought for a moment. "Maybe Will's jealous of you relying on the mentor instead of him."

Elizabeth was quiet for a few minutes, sitting slumped over her folded arms, then she sat up straight. "I never thought of that. You're probably right."

Just then, the oven timer dinged. I slipped off my stool. "That means supper is ready. Iggy, why don't you go call Will while I put out placemats and napkins."

"Okay." Iggy got off his stool and left the room.

Elizabeth made a vinaigrette dressing and was shaking it in a pint Mason jar when the men reentered the room.

Will cleared his throat. "It smells good in here. I'm sorry I stormed out, Mom."

I ran a hand across his shoulders. "That's okay. Everyone has their moments. Can you please get out some silverware and spread it around while I deal with this pan of food?"

"Yeah, will do."

I looked at the sheet pan sitting on the stainless-steel counter, hands on my hips, and said, "I'm just going to leave this all on the tray. We can serve ourselves from here. Is that all right with everyone?"

"Sure."

"That'll work."

"Fine with me."

For a few minutes everyone was in motion, grabbing a plate, filling it with roasted chicken and vegetables, and using tongs to put some salad on the side of the plate. Once we were settled around the kitchen island, Will spoke.

"I guess Elizabeth told you why we're here." He fiddled

with his fork and knife but didn't take a bite.

I said, "She did. It really isn't any of our business what goes on between the two of you."

Will turned to look at his wife. "I'm afraid that you won't need me anymore once you're even more successful than you are now. You found the building without me. You made a business plan without me. What do you need me for?"

Tears brimmed in Elizabeth's eyes. "Oh Will, I'll always need you for moral support. Your confidence in me is what makes me brave enough to step off the cliff and try growing my business. Never think that I don't need you. I'll always need you. You're my rock." She laid down her fork, stood up, and reached out to embrace her husband.

He stood up and hugged her so tight she squeaked. They both laughed and stepped back from the embrace.

"Not too tight, you'll squeeze the stuffing out of me."

Will put his hands on her shoulders. "No, I won't. You're tougher than you think. After supper, let's go over your plan. You brought it along, didn't you?"

Elizabeth nodded. "It's on my tablet." They hugged again, more lightly this time, and sat down to finish their suppers.

I looked at Iggy and smiled. Crisis averted.

CHAPTER 26

I was in the kitchen the next morning cutting up fruit for breakfast when Elizabeth came into the room. She had a dreamy smile on her face, so I knew that she and Will had come to an agreement the night before. "Good morning, Rose."

"Good morning, Elizabeth. Did you sleep well?"

"Oh yes," she said, a slight blush tingeing her cheeks.

"Those new mattresses are comfortable, aren't they?"

She looked at me out of the corner of her eye and nodded. "Where are your sheet pans?" she asked, rummaging in the lower cupboards.

"They're too big for the cupboards, so they're on a high shelf in the back room."

When she came back with a pan, she wiped it out with a damp cloth and set it on the kitchen island. "This recipe is the same as frying French toast; you just bake it in a hot oven. Set the temp at 425 degrees, please, and I'll get started making the toast."

"How long will it take to bake?"

"Just about twenty-five minutes. It'll be done in time."

We worked side by side cracking eggs and dipping slices of Italian bread into the egg and milk mixture.

Elizabeth added a small splash of vanilla to the eggs. "For flavor." She spread a generous amount of canola oil in the pan and then started laying the soaked bread slices on it in rows. "There," she said, laying in the last slice, "that should be enough for the guests, you and Iggy, me and Will, and a couple to spare." She carefully slid the pan into the oven and set the timer. "What do you have for breakfast meat today?"

I showed her the pan of bacon slices that I was ready to put into the oven on another shelf. "Bacon, but we'll have to keep an eye on it so it doesn't burn."

She nodded. "I can do that while you get the coffee made."

I made two pots of regular coffee in the lobby and one of decaf in the kitchen. It didn't take long for the enticing aroma of freshly brewed coffee to fill the whole building. I heard stirring coming from all the rooms upstairs. Will was the first to come down. He drifted past the sideboard, poured himself a mug of coffee, and came into the kitchen to greet his wife.

"Good morning, beautiful," he said as he engulfed her in his arms.

"Good morning," she said, kissing his whiskery face. "You need a shave, and I need to get the bacon out before it burns to a crisp, and it's time to flip the bread slices."

He released her, and she saved the bacon.

"Good morning, Mom."

"Good morning, Will. I trust you slept well."

"Oh yeah. I left the window open, and we could hear the surf, which is quickly becoming my favorite lullaby."

Elizabeth was crouched in front of the oven door. She turned on the oven light to check the progress of her French toast experiment. "Almost done. What do you have to put on it?"

"I've got syrup, cinnamon sugar, butter, and powdered sugar. I hope that's enough because that's all I have."

"Put out the jams too in case someone wants a tropical taste on their French toast."

"Jam, huh, that might be good. I'll try it."

I heard footsteps down the stairs and voices in the lobby. I looked out and all three of the writers were clustered around the coffeepots, taking turns getting coffee. I stepped through the kitchen door.

"Good morning, all. Breakfast will be ready in a few minutes."

"What are we having? It smells great," said Laurel. Carol and Pam murmured their agreement.

"We're having French toast, bacon, and fruit."

Pam set down her coffee mug and clapped her hands. "Oh, I love French toast."

I smiled at her. "Well, have a seat, and I'll be serving in a minute."

When I went back into the kitchen, Elizabeth had taken the sheet pan out of the oven. The French toast looked perfect, so we served two slices onto three plates, put three slices of crispy bacon alongside, and set the plates on a tray. I had already laid out placemats, napkins, and silverware. I carried the tray into the lobby and served.

"I'll be right back with fruit. Please help yourself to syrup, cinnamon sugar, powdered sugar, or tropical fruit jam, however you like to top your French toast."

When I came back with the fruit bowls, everyone had a bite of breakfast in their mouths. All three, too polite to talk with their mouths full, smiled and nodded their approval of the food.

"Enjoy," I said and went back into the kitchen to try the new breakfast for myself. It was good.

Sunday had dawned bright, clear, and hot. Iggy went off to church to talk to Calvin.   "Let's go diving," I said when we were finished with breakfast. "If we hurry, we can make the two-tank morning dive. Did you bring your gear?"

"Just masks, fins, and snorkels," said Will. "We'd have needed another suitcase to bring it all, and I didn't want to pay for the overweight."

"Fair enough. Let me call Tamarind and see if they've got a boat going out."

Tamarind had a boat going out, and there was room on it for the three of us. I made sure that the front doors were locked in case Calvin violated the restraining order. I let the writers know that we'd be gone for the morning, and we headed out. We got rental gear for Will and Elizabeth, including thin wetsuits so they would be comfortable in the eighty-degree water. We were the last ones onboard. The other divers were all friends, and they were clearly excited about going diving.

Dougie the Divemaster would lead the dive, and he began his briefing right away since our destination was the nearby wreck, *Oosterdiep*. The purpose-sunk shipwreck had become one of my favorite dives in Anguilla. It had been on the bottom long enough to become home to innumerable small critters like the shrimp that defended their square inch of territory by snapping one of their claws, making a sound like popping popcorn whenever you got too close. There were also garden eels in the sand alongside. I loved watching them sink into their burrows when a diver swam by and then come back out, mouths open into the current to catch any passing morsel of plankton. It was great sitting on the open boat as Freddy, still giving me dirty looks, steered it away from shore. Seeing his frown reminded me I needed to go down the beach to the Barrel Stave to talk to his mother. The wind blew away all my cares for the time being.

There were six male divers onboard plus Will, Elizabeth, and me. The ride to the mooring was short. Freddy hooked the floating line and made the boat fast while Dougie finished his briefing.

"We will descend on the stern of the ship where you will see a lot of sponges and sea fans growing on the rails," he said. "As you slip down the stern, the rudder and propeller surfaces are host to male Sergeant Majors guarding patches of purple eggs, and there is a school of about forty Yellowtail Jacks that patrols the area. If we are lucky, there will be a sleeping Hawksbill turtle tucked under the propeller. If it is there, please do not disturb it. Sometimes there are lobsters sheltering where the hull meets the sand. Hands off, it is not lobster season." Everyone laughed.

Elizabeth leaned toward me. "I can't wait to have one of Amy's Bakery's lobster pies."

I nodded. "We'll call tomorrow and order one for later

in the week. Don't worry, you won't go home without having lobster at least once."

She grinned. "Good."

Will leaned across Elizabeth. "Isn't this the wreck where we had that ripping current the last time?"

"Yes, it is. Why don't you remind Dougie, so we don't get caught again?"

Will walked over to the Divemaster to have him double-check the current before we went in. The two men stood side by side at the stern, looking down into the water. Will came back to say, "All clear. The sea fans are waving like parade queens. All we've got is surge, not a big current, we can handle that."

That was a relief. We finished putting on our wetsuits and slipped into our BCDs to prepare for shuffling to the opening in the boat's side to enter the water. Since Hurricane Alphonso had passed by the island, the movement of the storm water had heaped a lot more sand on the leeward side of the ship's hull. There was sand caught in the nooks and crannies on deck and behind the wheelhouse. There were a few sponges and sea fans that had been dislodged and lay on the sandy bottom. I wondered if they could be reattached to the hull, and then I saw Dougie pick them up and wire them to the ship. The other divers were exploring the shipwreck too and finding little critters tucked into the sponges and the drifts of cup corals that lined the stern of the wreck.

As we were ascending the mooring line and hanging at fifteen feet for our safety stop at the end of the dive, a pod of three dolphins swam by, barely sparing us a glance. We were thrilled.

Will was excited to see them and watched until they disappeared into the distance. When we got onboard the boat, he ripped off his mask and said, "Did you see those dolphins? That's the first time I've ever seen them in real life. Oh, I wish they would have stayed around for a couple of minutes. I wish I had a camera."

"I have a camera," said one of the other divers, "and I think I got a shot of them. If you give me your email address, I'll send you a copy."

Will turned so fast I thought he'd give himself whiplash. "Thanks, that'd be great." And he hurried over to sit by the diver to look at his camera and ask questions.

The second dive was at Little Bay, a protected stretch of water that's bordered by a steep cliff that makes access only available by boat. The best part of the dive was combing the little niches and holes in the cliff underwater to see what lived in them. Tiny shrimp and little crabs waved their claws at me and tried to shoo me away.

Elizabeth tugged on my fin to get my attention. She pointed at the seagrass bed in deeper water in time for me to see a Flying Gurnard swim/fly by. It's a fish that wriggles along the bottom and then unfurls long, colorful pectoral fins to glide through the water like it's flying. So much fun to see.

It was a short ride back to the beach where they ran the boat up on the sand. It was easy to jump off the bow and make our way back to the dive shop where we rinsed and hung our gear. I packed up mine and took it back to Seaview, and Will made sure that he had all of their snorkel gear before we left to go back to the bed-and-breakfast for lunch.

"Make yourselves a good lunch because today is Johnno's jump-up, which means we won't have anything except bar snacks for supper."

"Oh boy, a jump-up," said Elizabeth. "I've been hoping that we'd go."

"We can't miss it, or Edward will come down and shanghai us all."

The kids and I were back from the dive shop in time to rustle up a lunch of sandwiches, sliced cucumbers, bell pepper strips, and drinks. We were all hungry after our two dives.

"That was a great way to spend the morning," Will said. "I hoped that we'd be able to do a dive or two while we were here."

"Yes," said Elizabeth, "the promise of a few dives is how you got me to agree to come."

Will shrugged and peeked at me under his lashes.

I shook my finger at him. "But you're never going to come down without warning again, right?"

"Right. I'm sorry, Mom. I was sure that you'd have room for us, and you did."

"Just by sheer luck." I put the lunch fixings away and started to wash the dishes.

Elizabeth elbowed me away from the sink. "Why don't you let me and Will do the dishes? You sit at the kitchen island and keep us company. You can tell us about your guests."

I dried my soapy hands on a towel and poured myself another glass of tea. "There isn't too much to tell that I haven't already emailed you. My first guest stayed for four weeks, and the others have only stayed for a week. One week a married couple broke up; that wasn't fun to watch. Otherwise, it's been pretty tame."

Elizabeth made short work of washing the dishes, and Will dried them. She said, "I'm really looking forward to having conch fritters tonight at the jump-up. That sauce is divine."

"That reminds me, I'm hoping that you can figure out the ingredients of the sauce so I can make some. I think it'd be good drizzled over an egg casserole."

"Can't you just ask Johnno for the recipe?"

I shook my head. "He won't give it to me. He won't even tell me if my guesses are right. Iggy says that Johnno started with their mother's sauce recipe and improved it, adding a special ingredient aside from the mango puree I detected."

Elizabeth smiled. "I'll get an order of conch fritters to go and work on the sauce tomorrow." She rubbed her hands together. "Oh goodie, I love a challenge."

When we sat down after dancing at Johnno's, I could tell that Elizabeth was working on figuring out the sauce.

Instead of just gulping down the fritters dredged in the sauce, she ordered her own basket of conch fritters and started by dipping her finger into the sauce and tasting it.

She looked across the table at me. "I was expecting to find something like sweet and sour sauce with mayonnaise in it, and that's what this is. I taste the mango puree in here, but there's something else in it I can't pinpoint, not yet. I'll get it."

There was a light in her eyes that I hadn't seen in a long time. It was the same light that was there when she had first opened up her prepared food subscription service, *What's For Dinner?* Unlike the services that send you ingredients and a recipe, Elizabeth made the food, packaged it, and froze it for reheating so that people who didn't have even the time to cook a meal from scratch could have quick and delicious food to put on the table for themselves and their family.

It was good to have Will and Elizabeth around for the week. At times I almost forgot about Calvin lurking just up the road in his disreputable pickup truck. Except Elizabeth couldn't keep my problem with Calvin a secret. About midweek, she must have told Will, and he threw a fit.

"Mom! I can't believe you didn't tell me that the plumber is stalking you. What are you doing about it? Have you called the police? Maybe you should sell out and come home. It doesn't seem safe for you here."

"Calm down, Will. Yes, I've called the police many times, and I've filed a restraining order, so he has to stay a hundred feet away from me. So far, it's working. I called Officer Matthew when Calvin let the air out of Iggy's tires because he was closer than one hundred feet and he spent a night in jail."

"But, Mom, it's not like you have a force field around you to keep him that far away. What if he ignores the rules and comes after you? What are you going to do then?"

I wrapped my arm around his shoulders. "First, Calvin will not chase me out of Seaview and off Anguilla. Neither are the nasty rumors that one of the local women is spreading about me."

He straightened up to his full height and turned to face me, his mouth open to speak.

"No, don't interrupt. The woman spreading the rumors has designs on Iggy, so she wants me to leave the island, and I'm not giving her the satisfaction. Iggy is staying with me to keep me safe, and I'm locking the doors when I'm here and when I leave. My next step is to figure out how to combat the rumors and get the local people to trust me again. I've got some ideas. Every day I get another reservation and a deposit or two. I'm doing okay. Don't worry, I've got things under control."

Will grasped my upper arms and leaned down to look me in the eye. "You don't have things under control if you've got a restraining order against one guy and a woman is bad-mouthing you all over the island. Maybe this whole bed-and-breakfast thing was a bad idea. Maybe you need to come home."

I shook my head. "No. I am not going home. This is my home now. This place is my dream, has been my dream for over thirty years and no one is going to take it away from me." I felt tears well in my eyes and I blinked them away. I didn't want to cry in front of Will. He'd see that as weakness and redouble his efforts to get me to sell out and leave.

He let me go and paced around the lobby, shaking his head, his hands in fists. "I can't stay here and keep you safe. I'd better go talk to Iggy." And he left the room in search of Iggy.

Elizabeth and I took the ferry over to Sint Maarten to the department store and found some white terry cloth towels that I could sew strips of fabric onto so that I had more than two sets of towels for each guest room. When we got back to Seaview, I had Elizabeth cut out leaf and flower shapes, and I set up my sewing machine on one of the lobby tables and sewed them onto the towels. It didn't take us long, and I was relieved to check that off my to-do list. Will stayed at Seaview to make sure that Calvin didn't take advantage of me being away and try to sneak in and do some damage or just hide. Iggy was still staying with me too. I appreciated his sacrificing his independence to keep me safe.

Will and Elizabeth left on Saturday, as did the trio of writers. Geneva and I worked all day stripping beds, washing sheets and towels, and cleaning rooms and bathrooms. It was a big job, and I was glad to have Geneva to work alongside me. The yoga group arrived on the afternoon American Eagle flight from San Juan, and there was a flurry of activity getting them settled in their rooms.

When I started doing my personal laundry on Sunday, I realized that about half of the clothes belonged to Iggy. When Iggy got back from church, I teased him that since he had so many clothes at my place, he should sell his house and move in.

"I do not think that would be a very good idea. I like my house and the neighborhood. I have more room to move around in my house."

I laughed. "Are you kidding? This place is much bigger than your little house."

"Yes, it is. All of it is bigger than my house, but your private apartment is much smaller, and there are always strangers roaming around day and night, in and out of the kitchen, needing more towels or looking for directions. You have very little privacy, and we have to be quick and quiet when we have relations."

That did it. "You mean you won't move in because having the guests cramps our sex life?" I snorted. "That's a laugh. It feels to me like we have relations, as you say, often and quite satisfactorily."

"We have to have all the doors locked and even in the night you've got one ear cocked to hear if someone is moving around."

I flung my hand toward the bedroom. "I'm listening for Calvin to be lurking under the bedroom window. I thought you were staying here to protect me from Calvin, not so that you can have sex on demand."

Iggy nodded. "Yes, I am staying to keep Calvin away; that

is the main reason. I also enjoy holding you in bed at night and being able to have relations whenever we want."

"And you can't have sex whenever you want? It seems like I agree every time you suggest it."

"Yes, but we have to be quick and quiet. Sometimes I'd like to spend the afternoon slowly enjoying each other like we did in the beginning. Or not have you leap out of bed early in the morning to make coffee and get breakfast ready for the guests. I'd like to linger."

My fists hit my hips. "It's a bed-and-breakfast hotel. I kind of have to get up in the morning and make breakfast. I wouldn't stay open long if I set out a couple boxes of cereal and a jug of milk so that we could dally in bed for the morning."

"I know, I know, I would like to come before the guests some days."

This was an argument that had only one logical conclusion in my mind. "Well, if you feel like that, I think it would be best if you packed up your things and went home."

I went over to the clean laundry that was on my bed and started separating and folding Iggy's clothes. "My guests will always come first. They pay the bills." Tears ran down my cheeks, but I kept my shoulders stiff and finished sorting the clean laundry into piles of his clothes and mine. "I thought you understood that my first responsibility is to my guests. I guess not, especially if you're here mostly for the sex."

Iggy reached out toward me as I left the room. "Rose, I'm not here mostly for the sex. I'm here because I want to be with you. I just want some time with you when you are not tending to guests."

I kept walking and lifted my hand in farewell. I heard him mutter and then pull his suitcase out from under the bed.

In a very short time, he walked past me through the kitchen and to the back door. "You know where I am if you need me, Mrs. Lambert."

I didn't turn to watch him walk out.

CHAPTER 27

What had I done? The last thing I really wanted was to break up with Iggy. I loved Iggy, but he needed to understand that my guests came first. I'd have no business if it wasn't for my guests. It's my job to keep them content and happy while they're in Anguilla. Tears blurred my vision as I pulled out the pitcher of sun tea and poured myself a glass.

I heard Peg say, "Let me go ask Rose." The leader of the yoga group came into the kitchen. "Hi, Rose, sorry to disturb you but could we use the back patio for a meditation hour this afternoon? It's too hot in the sun to meditate on the beach after lunch. The patio is nice and shady."

I blinked the tears back. "Of course, you can, Peg. It isn't very level so it wouldn't be good for yoga. If you're just sitting, it should work just fine. Or you could pull chairs from the lobby if you don't want to sit on the ground." I put the tea back in the refrigerator. "The laundry will be done by then. There should be no noise from the machines to interrupt your concentration."

She grinned at me. "Oh, thanks, we'll be sitting on the ground. We'll fold up beach towels or our yoga mats to pad our behinds and sit in the lotus position. No chairs required."

"That's fine then," I said. "I won't disturb you if I'm moving around in my apartment or the kitchen, will I?"

"No, we need to learn to ignore ambient sounds so you can go about your chores, and we'll be just great." She turned to go into the lobby, then turned back. "Are you going down to the jump-up at the beach bar tonight? I hear it's the best party on the island and we don't want to miss it."

The thought of going to Johnno's jump-up made me feel cold in the pit of my stomach. "No, I won't be going this week. You all go. Be sure to get there early if you want a place to sit. It fills up fast."

"Thanks for the tip." She smiled and left to rejoin her group. I heard her say, "We're all set, ladies."

I thought about making lunch but wasn't hungry. Darn that Iggy. He could be the most understanding man most of the time but for "having relations" he was just like every other man. He wanted it when he wanted it and to hell with the rest of the world. Well, I wouldn't cave in to his demands. I was a woman with a new business, that had to come first. First before Iggy, first before my children, first before my own needs, if it comes to that. A bed-and-breakfast is part of the service industry, and that service doesn't stop when the breakfast dishes get dried and put away. I needed to be available to my guests throughout the day. At least that's the way I thought about it.

I was standing at my bedside folding my laundry when the yoga group got themselves settled on the patio in the backyard. I could see them through the window. They folded something to sit upon and sat down on the paving stones. Peg led them through some breathing exercises that sounded relaxing. I had tried meditation a long time ago but could never get my brain off its hamster wheel. Thoughts bombarded me as I tried to center myself and turn it off. Lists of things to do, old grievances, retorts I should have made all crowded into my head and kept me from clearing my mind. After a couple of weeks of trying, I gave up. Maybe I'd ask Peg if she had any tips. It might help me think of a way to overcome all the rumors Mrs. Whiting was spreading about me. I could use some mental relaxation.

As I folded clothes, I saw Calvin appear at the gap in the bougainvillea hedge. He hesitated when he saw the group seated on the patio and then retreated. I'm sure he saw Iggy storm off with his suitcase and figured the coast was clear.

Damn the man. I'd have to call the police station and let them know he had been on the property. I refused to be a prisoner in my own home.

A couple of hours later the yoga group clattered downstairs laughing and chattering on their way to Johnno's jump-up. Peg stopped in the kitchen doorway. "Are you sure you don't want to come to the party with us?"

I shook my head. "No, thanks. I'm not in the mood for a party tonight. You all have fun. Oh, and lock the front door behind you, please."

"Sure thing." She jangled her keys at me.

Not half an hour later there was a pounding on the front door. Dreading who I would find, I went to answer the knock. "Who is it?"

"It Edward, Mrs. Rose. Open the door."

I unlocked the door and pulled it open. "What can I do for you, Edward?"

He grinned. "You can put on your dancing shoes and come to the jump-up."

"Not tonight." I put my hand on his shoulder. "Iggy and I had a fight today and I'm not in the mood for a party. Maybe next week."

"Coming to dance will put you in a good mood. I will see to it."

I shook my head. "Not tonight. Thanks for inviting me. I'll skip the party this time."

The next morning, I walked over to the Barrel Stave when I saw the windows were open, figuring that Mrs. O'Neill was there getting ready for the day. I called out, "Hello?" when I went in the door.

"We are not open," called a voice from the kitchen.

"Mrs. O'Neill, it's Rose Lambert from Seaview."

She came to the kitchen doorway. "What do you want?"

"I want to talk to you for a minute if you have the time."

"I am busy getting started cooking. I suppose you can

come into the kitchen and say your piece."

"Thank you." I followed her to the kitchen and stopped at the door.

"So, talk." She picked up a rolling pin and started rolling out the pie crust.

"Rebecca..." She squinted at me. "Mrs. O'Neill, I gather that you've been talking to Mrs. Whiting. I hear that she's spreading rumors about me. I have heard that she says that I'm here only to make money. That I don't care about Anguilla or her people. And that I'll leave when I've made enough money."

"Yes, I have spoken to Mrs. Whiting."

"Well, what she's saying just isn't true." I twisted my fingers together to stop them from shaking. "I've always loved this island and her people ever since Jim and I started coming here thirty years ago. When I saw Seaview on our first trip, I fell in love with it and our plan was to retire here and rebuild the place, then Jim got sick and died so I came alone, bought Seaview with the insurance money, and now I'm trying to make it a success. I've spent just about everything I have to buy it, refurbish it, and now run it. I can't afford to leave and I plan to stay here until I'm too old to run it."

"I remember you and Mr. Jim coming here for supper and talking about Seaview. I had forgotten." She slid the crust into a pie pan and started crimping the edge. "What about Mr. Solomon?"

"Getting involved with Mr. Solomon was unplanned. I hired him to redo the wiring, and we became friends. One thing led to another, and we started dating. I can't help it if he and I fell in love. Mrs. Whiting and her friends have done their best to attract Iggy's attention over the years since his wife passed. I can't change the fact that Iggy chose me." I could feel the heat of a blush rising in my cheeks. "And I'm not with him just for the sex like she's been saying either." I looked over at the other woman and could see that she was smiling as she worked on her pie.

"I have wondered if Eleanora Whiting ever enjoyed sex.

She has always been too prim and proper to be believed, even when she was a girl."

"I thought that you and I were building a friendship, and it hurt me when you turned away from me. Do you think we can begin again and get to know one another better? I'd like that."

She dusted the flour off her hands on her apron and came around her work counter. "I am sorry that I believed her nasty rumors, Mrs. Lambert. Yes, let us begin again." She put a hand on my shoulder. "Join me in a cup of tea?"

I let out a breath that I had been holding. "I'd love some tea and, please, call me Rose."

The yoga group had a good time at Seaview and on the island. They greeted the sunrise on the beach every morning and meditated in the garden in the afternoon. All six of them were cheerful and said they appreciated my food. They all hugged me when they checked out Saturday morning, saying that they'd had a fun time and that they'd be back. More groups like that would keep me in the black and help rebuild my savings. Marie and I need to brainstorm about how we can put something on the website that will attract more small groups like that.

Geneva and I hurried through the laundry and preparing the rooms for the next week's three guests. Geneva was a treasure.

I couldn't get Iggy off my mind. I told Mrs. O'Neill that we were lovers, but I'm sure that word has gone around the island that we broke up. Every time I reached for the phone to call him, I lost my nerve and didn't punch in the number. Maybe it was for the best that I had to stand on my own two feet without a man to protect me, but I sure missed Iggy. I wondered if he was missing me too.

CHAPTER 28

One of the new guests was a single man named Douglas, "everybody calls me Butta. Cause I'm smooth like butta." I could tell from the get-go that Butta was a party guy. When he checked in, he wore cargo shorts, flip-flops, and a Hawaiian shirt. He had that good-time personality, and I rarely saw him without a beer in his hand. He even asked for a beer with breakfast. I had to apologize that I didn't have a liquor license, so I didn't provide beer.

"But you give out a tiny bottle of wine when people get here. You could have a beer for guys who don't like wine."

I had to admit that he had me there, so I went up to Vista Market, where Mrs. Richards was still not speaking to me, for a six-pack of AXA Ale to serve him for breakfast. The thought made my stomach turn, but he was happy, and I guess that's what counts. Although the first time he let out a big, satisfied belch after breakfast, I regretted buying the beer.

The other guests, single women, glared at him. He just laughed and said, "Get used to it, girls, that's how real men finish a meal."

Life with Butta in the house was hectic. He played music in his room when he got back late at night and spent an hour in the bathroom after breakfast. As soon as he was dressed, he was out and down the beach to Johnno's, one of the other beach bars along Road Bay, or on the launch to Sandy Island. He quickly found other party guys to hang out with and spend the afternoon drinking beer with. Some days I thought that breakfast was the only non-liquid meal that he had in a day.

His room was a disaster. When I gathered up his used

towels, I found the bedclothes were a rumpled mess and half off the bed, but I didn't expect everyone to make their bed. Wet towels lay on the floor under the empty towel bar, accompanied by soiled briefs. I was slightly relieved to find that he didn't go commando.

I woke up one night smelling smoke and rushed out into the lobby to find Butta and two other men sitting around a table playing poker and smoking Cuban cigars.

"I'm sorry, there's no smoking at Seaview."

"No wonder we couldn't find any ashtrays," he said with a laugh, tapping ash into a coffee mug he had pulled off the sideboard. "Want me to deal you in?"

I pulled my robe a little tighter. "No, thank you. I'm going to ask you to finish your game and call it a night."

The three of them groaned.

"Man, I'm on a hot streak," said Butta, patting a pile of dollars on the table in front of him.

One of the other men scooped his stack of bills into his pocket. "Maybe it's a good thing we quit now while I've still got some cash left." He stood up to leave. "Sorry to disturb you, ma'am." He stuck his cigar in his teeth and nodded at the other man. "Come on, Charlie, let's let this lady get back to sleep. G'night, Butta. Good game."

Butta looked up from shuffling the cards. "Good night, Charlie, Gabe, good game. Thanks for the money." He laughed.

I folded my arms across my chest. "Put out your cigar, please, and go to your room."

He stubbed out the stogie in the coffee mug. "What are you, my mother?" He put the pack of cards in his shirt pocket and the cigar in his mouth. "I'm going. Oh, and we're outta beer." He waved his hand at the beer bottles on the table. "I was sure you wouldn't mind."

Instead of going up to his room, he sauntered across the lobby and followed his friends out the door.

For the life of me, I couldn't imagine where he was going. It was after two o'clock. Johnno's was closed at one o'clock, as were the rest of the bars along Road Bay. I followed him to close and lock the door behind him. I hoped he had his keys because I didn't relish being awakened by him pounding on the door when he came back.

He must have had his key because there he was at the breakfast table the next morning. He wasn't alone. There was a young Anguillan girl seated at the table with him. They each had a mug of coffee. Butta looked a little worse for wear, and the girl was staring at the mug in her hand.

"I should go," she said.

He put a hand on her wrist to keep her in place. "Go after breakfast. Breakfast is good here."

It was a good thing that I glanced into the lobby before making the breakfast tray. I hurried out to lay a placemat and silverware in front of her, then went back into the kitchen to make four plates of egg bake and ham slices. Carrying the tray into the lobby and setting a plate in front of each of them, I said, "There's bread and jam on the sideboard if anyone would like toast."

Butta stood up. "I'll make you some toast. You want jam on it?"

"No, thank you." She kept her eyes on her plate.

I was having a second cup of coffee when Geneva arrived for the day. She said good morning and put her purse on the shelf in the back room. She came back into the kitchen, tying on an apron. "I will just get the breakfast dishes started."

"Would you like some eggs or ham?"

"No, ma'am, Mrs. Rose, I had breakfast at home."

I kept one ear cocked to hear when the guests left the lobby so I could go out and collect the soiled plates. Geneva was faster.

Suddenly, a raised voice came from the lobby. It was Geneva. "Emerald, what you doing with the likes of this man? Don't you got no respect for yourself than to go off with a strange man?"

I heard a chair scrape on the wooden floor. "Now, just

a minute. Uh, Emerald and I aren't strangers. We met at the jump-up on Sunday and we're in love," Butta said.

"In love? In love! You met four days ago and suddenly you say you are in love?" Geneva's voice was high and loud. "Emerald, you tell me the truth. You love this... this man?"

I heard a low mumble.

"You want to go to the States, and you think that cozying up to this man will get you there? Is that what this is about?" Geneva laughed. "He is never going to take you home with him. He only likes you for a good time when he's on holiday. Ask him. Ask him if he is ready to take you home to meet his mama."

I couldn't help myself. I walked to the doorway into the lobby to watch the drama unfold.

Emerald looked up at Butta, tears in her eyes. "Will you take me home with you?"

Butta stood looking down at her, his hands hanging at his sides. "I, uh, I don't think I can. See, I got a girl at home that thinks we're going to get married. This was supposed to be my bachelor party trip, but my friends couldn't make it, so I came alone. I've spent the week partying and when I go home, the wedding is in two weeks." He ran a hand down his face. "I'm sorry, Emerald, that I gave you the impression that we were something more than a fling."

Emerald's face crumpled, and she folded in on herself. She started crying in earnest, tears dripping down her cheeks. "Oh, what am I going to do now? Who will be my baby's daddy?"

Butta backed up so fast he knocked his chair over. "Baby? Oh no, not me, I am not anybody's baby daddy."

"What are you saying, Emerald?" Geneva reached a hand to the younger woman's shoulder. "Are you having a baby?"

"I'm outta here." Butta looked at me. "I'm leaving just as soon as I can get packed."

"There are no refunds," I told him.

"I don't care. I'm going home. All I wanted was a little

fun." He turned and sprinted up the stairs and I heard the key scrape the door as he tried to get it into the lock with hands that shook.

Geneva pulled a chair over and sat down, her arm around Emerald's shoulders, while the younger woman silently cried. I gathered up the dirty breakfast things, loaded the tray, and carried it all into the kitchen.

True to his word, Butta was packed and back at the registration desk to check out within thirty minutes, his duffel bag at his feet.

"I'm sorry you're leaving early. Do you have a flight arranged? I could check online."

He shook his head. "No thanks, I'm taking the ferry to St. Martin. Then I'll go to the airport and find a flight home. I'll just wait until someone has room for me on a plane."

I charged his credit card for the week and handed him a printout.

"I'm sorry I made such a mess. I've gotta get out of here before Emerald's dad comes looking for me with a shotgun." He glanced over at the table where Emerald had been. "All I wanted was one last fling before I got married. All I wanted was a week in the Caribbean with sand and sun and good times. Evidently that was too much to ask." While he spoke, he folded up the printout, tucked it into his duffel bag, and pulled his rental car keys out of his pocket. "Well, I'm off. Thanks for everything, Rose. I hope I wasn't too much of a pain." He surprised me by leaning across the registration desk and kissing my cheek.

I put my hand up to my face. "Goodbye, Douglas. I hope you find a flight."

He turned at the front door. "It's Butta remember, I'm smooth." He winked at me and disappeared.

"Yeah, too smooth for your own good," I said to the empty room.

That left me with two guests for the last couple of days of the week. I could tell that the women were happy that Butta was gone. No more beer belches at breakfast and no more loud music after the bars closed. "He was a nice enough guy," said one of them. "But he was kind of a caveman."

As I bussed the tables, I mused on the future Mrs. Butta. I wondered what kind of woman she was. With husbands like that around, I was glad to be unmarried. Except Iggy would never be like that.

Geneva and I made short work of cleaning Butta's room so that it was ready for the following week's guests. The next week I had two scuba diving couples and their teenage daughters coming. That meant all the rooms would be full. I wasn't sure how that would work out because I didn't have any place for the divers to hang their gear to dry. Maybe they would arrange with Thomas to leave their gear hanging in his storage area in between dives.

On Saturday morning, the guests checked out and Geneva and I got busy cleaning and doing laundry. This week there were only two rooms to clean and reset because Butta left two days early. That moved things along nicely and gave us a breather before the new guests arrived in the late afternoon.

When I did my shopping for the next week's breakfasts, Mrs. Richards in Vista Market was suddenly a little nicer to me. Had she heard that I had sent Iggy packing, so Mrs. Whiting was crowing about having him back at her side? I had taken a dozen muffins up to the Market like Elizabeth suggested, and Mrs. Richards seemed to thaw a little. Maybe if I kept her supplied with muffins, she would go back to smiling when I came in. Maybe we would even go back to being on a first-name basis.

CHAPTER 29

The Larsons and the Petersons came in together, all six of them burdened with heavy bags. "We can't wait to get underwater," said Gene Larson as he signed his family in. "As soon as we're checked in, I'm heading next door to get us signed up for tomorrow's boat dives."

I nodded. "I'll make sure that breakfast is served early enough so that you don't have to rush to get to the boat."

"That'll be great."

They carried their bags upstairs, bumping the treads with every step. I cringed, thinking of the hours spent sanding those treads so that they were perfectly smooth. Ah well, it was a hotel, not a house. I had to expect that things would get abused.

The parents had ocean-view rooms, and the daughters had garden-view rooms. There was a lot of back and forth as they unpacked and loaded their dive bags. Then Gene and Steve Peterson went to Tamarind Dive Shop next door to get them all signed up to dive. When they came back, Steve poked his head into the kitchen and said, "The guy at the dive shop wanted to know if you're going to be diving with us. You're welcome to come along."

"Thanks. I'll come diving at least one day. Did you ask if you could hang your equipment in his storage locker? I don't have any place where you can hang wet gear."

"Yeah, we figured you wouldn't want all of our stuff dripping in the bathrooms, so we asked. Thomas said we could leave it there, that they lock up all the gear at night. It'll be safe."

"Good. I'd hate for it to be hanging on the back porch where any passing person can see it and get ideas."

I handed each man cheese and fruit plates for their families and offered wine, which was declined.

Angela Larson poked her head into the kitchen. "Where did you two get to? We're starving and want to go find food." Gene held out the nibble plates that I'd just handed him. "Oh, good. Thanks, Rose, that will tide us over until we can figure out a restaurant to go to." She took the plates and turned to carry them upstairs.

The Larsons and the Petersons were happily in and out of Seaview, going diving in the morning and sightseeing in the afternoon.

Dru stopped over for a visit on Sunday after church. We sat down in the kitchen with glasses of iced tea and talked. She thanked me for hiring her son to fill in the hole left by the mango tree.

"Jed is a good boy and works very hard to get his business started," she said.

"He did a good job for me. He even threw down some grass seed so that I don't have a dirt hole where the beach dogs can dig."

She turned her glass in its ring of condensation on the kitchen island. "I am sorry that Calvin is bothering you. He has never been this bad before. He hardly comes home anymore, and when he does, he berates me for not being more like you. I tried to convince him to leave you alone, and he hit me." She started to cry.

"Oh, Dru, I'm so sorry he hit you." I laid my hand over hers on the kitchen island. "I've done nothing to encourage him; I seem to be his latest obsession. Iggy says that he's always chased other women. That can't have been an easy life for you."

"For the longest time I didn't know what he was doing, but then my cousin called me and told me that Calvin was at some woman's house in the afternoon when he said he was working. I confronted him, and he admitted it. He told me I wasn't enough woman for him, so he had to look elsewhere." She choked out the last sentence and sobbed into a tissue she pulled from her purse.

Just then the guests returned from their morning dives. Sonya and Angela came into the kitchen with their families' wet bathing suits and towels. "Can we hang these on your clotheslines?"

"Of course, go right ahead."

Dru tucked her tissue into her purse and stood. "I will go home. I just thought I would stop to apologize for Calvin's behavior and tell you I do not believe a word of what Mrs. Whiting and her cronies are spreading around."

"Thanks, I really appreciate that. Let's meet for lunch one day soon." I reached out to give her a hug.

She leaned into me. "I would like that."

I sent all my guests down to Johnno's for the Sunday night jump-up.

Almost as soon as my guests left for the party, there was a knock on the front door, and Edward was there. "I know you don' want to dance, Mrs. Rose, but you have to come. It no good for you to sit here feeling bad. You shouldn't have chased Ignatius away, but since you did, he not at the jump-up so you can come."

"I don't feel like dancing, Edward. I'm just not in the mood."

Edward reached for my hand and swung me into his arms, and danced me around the lobby. "The music and the people will make you happy, you'll see. Come with me, please."

I didn't want to have everyone stare at me. "No, I don't want everyone talking about me and looking at me. I'm not the evil woman that Mrs. Whiting paints me to be, and I don't want to see her words in people's eyes."

"No one really believes that you are evil. They are just a little curious about how you really are and what you mean to do in Anguilla. Come to the party and show them you will not be chased away by one mean woman."

"Oh, all right. Give me a few minutes to change and freshen up."

Edward waited for me. He held on to my arm as we walked down the beach as if he was afraid that I'd turn and bolt for home.

The first person I saw when I stepped onto the floor of the beach bar was Iggy dancing with Mrs. Whiting. I turned to leave. Edward tightened his hold on me.

"It will be just fine." He escorted me over to our usual table against the wall and sent Silas to get me a rum punch. "Stay for one dance and one drink." He leaned over and looked me in the eye. "You can't hide from your friends alla the time."

I didn't want to hide from everybody, just Iggy. I watched as he and Mrs. Whiting circled the floor in the crush of dancers. Iggy looked as miserable as I felt. Mrs. Whiting looked triumphant. It seemed like Iggy's feet were sticking to the floor. He was hardly moving, and she was steering him around in a circle. I took a sip of my drink.

Edward took my hand and pulled me to my feet as the band started the next song. "Come on, Mrs. Rose, let's dance."

I tried to pull my hand away. "I don't want to dance, Edward. I want to go home."

"Just one dance," he said as he spun us toward the crowd.

I kept my feet still and then realized I looked just as unhappy as Iggy did. I thought that standing in the middle of all the dancing people made me more of a spectacle than blending in with the crowd of dancers.

I gave in. "All right, just one dance." Once I was in the middle of the crowded dance floor with Edward and couldn't see Iggy all the time, my mood lightened a bit. I might have even smiled. When the song ended, we went back to the table where Silas was unloading a tray of food.

"You have to stay and eat," Silas said, "Dad always makes too much."

I wished I were sitting in a chair with my back to the room so that I couldn't see Iggy and Mrs. Whiting sitting at a table across the way. She kept smiling at him and then in my direction as if she was showing me he was with her now. I took a few conch fritters, some plantain chips, and chicken fingers that I nibbled at. The band was taking a break, and the Larson and Peterson daughters came over to the table laughing. "Mrs. Rose, thank you for telling us about this party. We're having a blast."

"I'm glad you're enjoying it. I'll send some of these guys over to dance with you if that's okay. They're my friends; they helped fix up Seaview, and they're excellent dancers."

The girls looked at each other and said, "Great."

Just then the band came back from their break, started the next song, and Luke and Melvin got up and asked the girls to dance. Suddenly the dance floor was jammed, and Silas asked me to dance.

"No, thanks, Silas. Tonight, I'd rather watch. I'm not staying too much longer, anyway. I'm just not in the mood for a party."

He leaned over to speak in my ear. "It is no good you sitting here watching them and feeling bad. Uncle Iggy does not look any happier than you do. Come on, Mrs. Rose, just one more dance."

"Oh, I guess so." I put down my drink and took his hand. He did a good job keeping us far away from where Iggy and Mrs. Whiting were dancing.

When the song ended, I finished my drink, said good night to my friends, and left. On the way out, I passed my guests.

"Are you leaving so soon?" Angela said.

"I've got to get up early to make breakfast," I said with a laugh. "You stay and have fun."

It was a short walk down the beach to Seaview. I didn't hear Calvin behind me until he grabbed my arm and spun me around.

"Leaving the party so soon? I hear you sent Ignatius packing. Now there's room in your life for me." Calvin leaned toward me, flabby lips puckered, pulling me to him.

"Oh no, there isn't." I balled up my fist and let him have it right in the nose.

He staggered back, his hand up, trying to staunch the blood pouring out. "Why, you little..." He reached out his bloody hand toward me. I tried to duck away, but his reach was longer than I thought, and he grabbed me.

"Help!" I cried.

Calvin pulled me tight to his chest and growled, "Hold still or I will hurt you."

I struggled in his grasp, my flailing hands splashing his blood all over us. In the dark, I saw his face looming over me as he leaned in to kiss me. I turned my face away so that he couldn't reach my lips and yelled again. "Somebody help me."

He strengthened his grip, and I felt his chest heaving as we struggled. "Hold still," he said through gritted teeth, his powerful hands gripping my upper arms.

That's as far as he got. We stood in front of the police station, and Officer Matthew came running out as soon as he heard what was happening. He pulled Calvin away from me.

"Mr. Brooks, you are under arrest for assault and for violating the restraining order that Mrs. Lambert swore out. Come with me, sir, you'll be spending the night in the cell." He had Calvin's arm twisted behind him and was propelling him over the sand and into the station. "Good night, Mrs. Rose. I will take care of this."

"Thank you," I said, stunned at what had just happened.

I stumbled the few remaining steps to Seaview, climbed up to the doors, and let myself in. I had blood on my arms and my clothing. One of my favorite shirts, too. I hurried into my bathroom and got busy trying to get the blood out. I used a bar of old-fashioned laundry soap and cold water to scrub the bloodstains. They eventually came out. Then I got into the shower and scrubbed myself. I could still feel the strength of

Calvin's grip as he pulled me to him. I'd have bruises on my arms in the morning. My hands were shaking so hard I could barely dry myself off, but I managed, got into clean night clothes, and went to bed.

I thought how safe I felt in Iggy's arms and how miserable he had looked on the dance floor. Part of me wanted to call Iggy back just to wipe the smug smile from Mrs. Whiting's face. I decided I was a better person than that. That thought brought tears to my eyes. If I'd been a better person, I wouldn't have chased Iggy away the way I had. I would have listened to what he said instead of getting all up in arms because he wanted more of my attention.

It was a long time before I fell asleep.

CHAPTER 30

I got the coffee made and started cracking eggs for scrambled eggs. In the pantry I found a can of processed meat that I could slice and fry to serve alongside, since there had been no bacon or sausage in the stores that week. The guests were moving around upstairs, so I set out placemats, napkins, and silverware and put a loaf of coconut bread by the toaster along with an assortment of tropical fruit jams.

Sonya Peterson was the first one down. She poured herself a mug of coffee and came into the kitchen for a splash of milk.

"There's a pitcher of milk by the sweeteners," I said as I whipped the eggs to a froth and poured them into the hot frying pan.

"Oh, sorry, I missed it. Are you making scrambled eggs?"

"Yes, I hope you all like them."

"Steve will be pleased. Any form of eggs is his favorite breakfast food. Is there anything I can do to help?"

I thought about it. "Actually, yes. You can take those bowls of fruit out and put one at each place while I keep the eggs moving. Thanks."

She loaded the tray with the six bowls of fruit, carried it into the lobby, and returned with the empty tray. "Is that canned pork?" She was pointing at the plate of fried slices I took out of the oven.

"The Dutch version, yes, it is. I hope that's okay. It's all there was at the market this week." I was serving the eggs onto six plates and putting a couple of slices of meat alongside.

"I've never had it before," Sonya said. "I'm sure the girls

haven't either. What does it taste like?"

"Kind of hammy, kind of porky, a little spicy. I like it. I hope you do too."

By then the other guests were downstairs pouring coffee and talking about where they might go on their dives that morning.

Sonya heard the chat and said, "You should come along diving today. Our daughter Lizzie is sitting this one out, so we're a buddy short. Come on, Rose, come diving with us."

Geneva came in the door and slipped into the back room to put her purse away and tie on an apron.

"Let me see if Geneva will mind. Here, let's get these plates served so everything is still warm and I'll talk to her." I carried the full tray into the lobby and set out the plates.

Gene Larson was already making toast. "I've got toast for anyone who wants it," he said, handing toasted and buttered bread to his daughter. "No jam for you. Who else wants toast?"

I left the two families to their breakfast and went back into the kitchen where Geneva had already started washing the dishes. "Would you mind if I went diving this morning?"

"No, ma'am, Mrs. Rose, you go on ahead and enjoy the day. I can clean the bathrooms and get the towels washed by myself."

"Thanks."

I hurried into my apartment to put on a swimsuit and make sure that I had all of my dive gear in my bag.

Silas came in the back door as I walked into the kitchen carrying my gear bag. He walked over and dropped a kiss on Geneva's cheek. "Good morning," he said, laying a soft hand on her shoulder, then he turned to me. "Going diving?" His eyes dropped to the fingerprint bruises that had bloomed on my arms overnight. "Are you all right, Mrs. Rose? I heard that Calvin Brooks lay in wait for you last night."

"Yes, I'm all right. Thanks for asking." I hoisted my bag onto my shoulder. "Geneva said she doesn't mind, so I'm taking the morning off to go diving."

"Do you have any little jobs that need doing?" he said.

Geneva spoke up. "Yes, there are a few. Mrs. Rose, you need to get going so you do not miss the boat."

"I'm going."

Silas walked out with me and snagged his toolbox from the back of his truck. "Geneva will put me to work, I guess."

"There's always something that needs doing around Seaview. She knows what to tell you. I'll be back around lunchtime." I waved, hoisted my gear bag on my shoulder, and went next door to Tamarind.

I put my gear on the bow of the boat and waded around to the boarding ladder.

Sonya Peterson saw me and said, "That looks much easier than trying to haul myself up onto the bow. I'm right behind you."

After making sure that there were tanks and weights on board for me, I got my BCD vest and regulator set up on a tank.

Angela Larson sat down next to me. "I guess we're buddies today. Gene and Nan are buddying up, so Mom's the odd woman out."

We spent a few minutes discussing the way we liked to dive and learning each other's favorite hand signals so we could communicate underwater. Happily, both of us liked to swim slowly and look in, around, and under things.

While we were getting acquainted, Thomas pushed the boat away from the beach and climbed aboard. Freddie steered us out toward the deepest dive site around Anguilla. Thomas gave the briefing. "Author's Deep is where a tongue of deep water creeps into the Caribbean just north of Anguilla. It's calm today, and that's why we're headed there. Make sure that you wear your wetsuit because the water's a little colder. That upwelling of cooler, nutrient-rich water is responsible for the healthy life in the area. Max depth is one hundred ten feet, so monitor your bottom time and your air consumption. There's a pinnacle at eighty-five feet that's wrapped in plate corals and there are black coral bushes around too. No touching." He waggled a finger at us. We all chuckled.

"Yes, sir!" Gene Larson saluted.

After a longer than usual ride, the boat slowed, and Freddie hooked the mooring buoy and secured the boat to it. There was a flurry of activity as all six of us got suited up and ready to dive. Angela and I met up at the mooring buoy and decided to descend along the mooring line until we hit the bottom and then evaluate the current to choose a direction to swim in. Steve and Sonya headed straight for the deep pinnacle, and Gene and Nan followed them down. We swam along, feeling the cooler water wash over us. I was glad that I had a full-length wetsuit. There was no danger of getting overheated on this dive.

Angela and I got to the pinnacle and swam around it, seeing Spotted Moray Eels in nooks near the bottom and all kinds of shrimp living in niches in the coral. After about forty minutes, I checked my air and was down near one thousand psi. I signaled it was time to ascend. We swam up toward the mooring and were engulfed by a school of Yellow-tail Snappers. The fish parted to let us pass through. It was a fun feeling to be part of the school for a minute. We paused at fifteen feet to make a safety stop and were soon joined by the rest of the divers.

I was first up the boarding ladder, took my fins from Freddie who had stopped giving me dirty looks, and made my way to my spot along the side of the boat. I slid the butt of my tank into the rack behind my seat and slipped out of my BCD. By then, Angela was coming across the boat with a big smile on her face.

"That was a terrific dive. Did you see that Green Moray Eel? It had to be as big around as my thigh."

I nodded. "It was a big one, all right."

One by one, the rest of the party climbed onto the boat.

Gene talked about the size of the lobsters that they saw in the sand at the base of the pinnacle. "Too bad we couldn't take them. They'd have made a great supper."

Thomas said, "Good thing you didn't. We don't have a permit to catch lobsters. We'd have all been in trouble."

"I'll talk to one of the fishermen who lives in Sandy Ground," I said to Gene. "He usually has lobsters. You can grill them on the patio."

"That'd be great."

"Oh, yum," Nan said.

Freddie unhooked the boat from the mooring and steered us back toward home, the wind generated by the movement drying our hair into spikes. We stopped off Sandy Island for a second, shallower dive on a reef. There were a lot more fish to see on the reef. We even caught sight of a shark cruising by out where the water got deeper.

I rinsed my gear and repacked my dive bag to hang my equipment on the back porch. "Thanks for inviting me to come along on your dives," I said. "It was great."

My guests were rinsing their gear and getting it hung in the storage locker. "We enjoyed having you come along," said Sonya. "Maybe we can do it again before we go home."

"I'd like that. I'll talk to Billy the fisherman and see if he won't drop off some lobsters for you."

"Excellent," said Gene. "Let us know how much they cost."

"I'll do that." I shouldered my wet bag and headed back to Seaview.

Geneva was taking a load of towels out of the dryer when I got back from diving. "Did you have a good dive?"

"I did. How's the laundry coming? Do you need help?"

"This is the end of the laundry. I will fold it and get it put away. Silas is fixing the lock on the white and green bathroom."

I hung my dripping scuba gear on the pegs on the back porch. "Good. That one is the only one that sticks. Maybe taking it apart will help. I know that spraying it with lubricant didn't do any good. Did he get all the burned-out light bulbs replaced?"

She nodded. "He did, and he said that we need to fill up the shelf. He used almost all the bulbs you had there."

I made a mental note to add light bulbs to my shopping list the next time I went to Sint Maarten to the big home store. It made sense that all the bulbs would burn out at the same time since they all got installed at the same time, but it was still frustrating.

"Hey, beautiful, I got the doorknob fixed so it doesn't stick anymore." Silas came out onto the back porch with a big smile on his face. "Any more jobs that need doing?" He stopped behind Geneva and wrapped his arms around her waist. "More jobs means more kisses." He nuzzled her neck. "I enjoy doing jobs when Mrs. Rose is gone."

Geneva elbowed him away. "Mrs. Rose is back, fool. Maybe she has more jobs for you. I don't." She picked up the basket of clean and folded towels and turned to carry them back into Seaview. He reached to take the basket from her, but she held it away. "Your hands are dirty. Keep them away from the clean laundry."

Silas pulled his hands away. "I washed my hands when I finished with the lock, but I will let you carry the clean laundry." He turned to me. "Do you have any other jobs that need doing, Mrs. Rose?"

"No, thank you, Silas. The burned-out lightbulbs and the sticking bathroom doorknob were it." I couldn't help thinking that if Iggy were still around, I wouldn't have had to enlist Silas' help; Iggy would have taken care of those things as they happened. Maybe I should call Iggy and apologize for flying off the handle. I missed him. Had I been taking advantage of Iggy? Anyone could do those jobs. Was I counting on him, using him, taking advantage of him, the way I wondered if he just wanted me for sex?

My guests came in from the dive shop and I heard them looking for Lizzie. Soon, Sonya Peterson came to the kitchen doorway. "Did Lizzie tell you where she was going?"

Geneva looked at me and then at Sonya. "She was in her

room when I put in fresh towels. She said hello; I said hello back. That is all."

"She isn't in her room and didn't leave a note. What was she doing when you went in?"

Geneva shrugged. "Looking at her phone like all the youngsters do these days."

"Maybe she's taking a walk along the beach," I said. "Did she tell Nan what she was planning to do while you were diving?"

"No, Lizzie wouldn't confide in Nan. She thinks Nan is a goody-two-shoes, that she'd rat her out. I told her to stay around the hotel. Ooh, that kid, I'll murder her if she's gone off without leaving a note."

I looked at Sonya. "Are any of her things missing? Did she maybe take a daypack out to Sandy Island for the morning?"

Sonya shook her head. "No, that's what we were planning to do this afternoon. She knew that. We'll have to split up and see if we can't find her. Where would she have gone?" Sonya turned to go back into the lobby. I heard her say, "She didn't tell Geneva where she was going."

Leaving Nan behind at Seaview in case Lizzie came back when everyone was out, the two couples set off up the beach. There were a lot of beach bars and a couple of snack shacks where a teenager could meet up with locals and lose track of time. I watched them talk to everyone on the beach and go into every business along the way. Sonya's body language showed that she was close to panicking over Lizzie's disappearance. I thought about where else she might have gone. Seeing a trio of young men hanging around the end of the town pier gave me an idea. Calling out to Geneva that I was going to walk down to the little neighborhood of houses at the north end of the village, I set out. Old Reynaldo's house was the first one I passed. He was sitting on his porch smoking and waved at me. I waved back and called out, asking if he'd seen an American girl. He nodded and waved toward the salt pond. I cut between a couple of houses, petting dogs, shooing chickens out of my way, and climbed the dike that surrounded the salt pond. At the far end of the pond there was a lean-to made of driftwood and palm fronds. There was a group of kids sitting in and around the shack, and in the middle was Lizzie. I started toward them and could smell the weed. Oh, man, if it had only been tobacco, that wouldn't be too bad. One of them caught sight of my approach and there was a flurry of movement, stubbing out the joints and hiding the evidence.

I called out as I got closer. "Lizzie, your parents are worried. You need to come back to the hotel."

"What if I don't want to go back?" She had her arm draped around one of the young men.

I folded my arms across my chest. "Then I'll tell them where I found you and what you were doing."

"You wouldn't."

"In a heartbeat. Now come on. Let's go."

I turned to make my way back along the dike and heard her say, "I gotta go."

I walked slowly enough that she caught up to me.

"How'd you know where to find me?"

"I didn't, but I figured a girl would seek kids her age and I know there's a big group of teens that hangs out down at this end of the village, so I tried here first. I sent your parents and the Larsons up the beach toward Blue Harbour Resort. You have time to shower off the stench and change your clothes before they come back."

We walked along for a few paces.

"Why are you helping me?"

"I like your parents and don't think they deserve to have their vacation ruined by an ungrateful daughter. You straighten up, go diving every day, and hang with your family, and I won't tell them I found you smoking weed with a bunch of young people old enough to know better. How'd you meet them, anyway?"

She shrugged. "They were at the jump-up and Marco

asked me to dance. He invited me outside for a little smoke. I said I couldn't get away that night, that I'd blow off diving today and meet him. It was easy. I'm not an all-gung-ho diver girl like Nan, so it didn't surprise them when I bailed today. I said I got my period. Mom bought it."

I looked at her, all goth-ed out in black jeans, a black tank, and hair dyed black, and smiled. "Your mom gave you the day off. She didn't believe you got your period. Mothers know when their daughters' cycles are."

"You think?"

"Yeah. I always knew when my daughter's cycle was just like she knew when mine was. When women live together, their cycles tend to coincide." We reached the back of Seaview. "Go up and shower and change but be quiet; they left Nan here in case you came back."

She fixed me with a squint. "Nan won't rat me out. She's got her own secrets." And she slipped through the screen door, took off her sandals, and headed upstairs.

Sonya and Steve were both pale and scared looking when I caught up to them just past the pier.

"I found her," I said. "She's back at the hotel."

"Oh, thank God."

"Where was she?"

"She met some kids from the jump-up and was visiting in the neighborhood at the other end of the village. She's fine. She said she was going to take a shower."

The Petersons hugged, and Gene Larson clapped Steve on the back. Angela looked suspicious but said nothing. It was a much happier group that got back to Seaview. Sonya went right upstairs to make sure that their daughter was really back and safe. Steve and Gene got out an Anguilla dive guide to talk about where they hoped to dive the next day. Angela pulled me aside.

"What was Lizzie doing with those kids?"

"Nothing much."

"Something illegal, I'm sure. That girl attracts trouble

like bees to honey. She's already been kicked out of school twice for smoking. I'll bet she was smoking. Come on, Rose, you can tell me."

I shook my head. "If you'll excuse me, I have some work to do in the kitchen." And I left the lobby.

The rest of the week was quiet and uneventful.

On Saturday the Larsons and the Petersons packed up and left, saying that they'd had a wonderful vacation. Even Lizzie hugged me goodbye and whispered her thanks for not telling on her.

CHAPTER 31

Saturday was its usual hectic round of cleaning and laundry. The only difference was I had only one guest arriving that day, and it was a single man. Having only one guest did little for my bottom line. I cheered myself up by looking at the reservations and deposits for the next few months.

Peter Norton arrived on the afternoon ferry from St. Martin, picked up his rental car at the ferry terminal, and arrived at Seaview around cocktail time. I was standing behind the registration desk when he came in, rolling his suitcase behind him.

"Welcome to Seaview," I said.

"We'll see about that." His abrupt and rude reply took me by surprise.

"Is there a problem?"

"Not yet, but it's early days."

He handed over his driver's license and credit card so I could get him checked in.

"I hope you enjoy your stay with us." I offered him a cheese and fruit plate and a split of wine. He refused.

"I'm allergic to cheese and I don't drink wine."

I could feel my smile slip. "Do you have any other food sensitivities I should know about?"

"Dairy. I'm allergic to all dairy products so no milk, butter, cream, or cheese."

My mind reeled. No dairy? Most of my breakfast recipes had a dairy product in them. Take muffins, for instance, they have butter and milk in them. No muffins for Peter Norton. Egg bake has milk and cheese in it. Maybe I could find some almond milk at the market and just leave out the cheese. That meant until I got to the market on Monday, it'd be scrambled eggs, breakfast meat, and toast for breakfast. It was a good thing that there had been bacon in the meat case when I shopped last, so I laid in a good supply. "Thank you for telling me. I'll be careful when I make breakfast."

"See that you are." Norton picked up the handle of his suitcase. "Which one is my room?"

I had put him in the yellow room. I grabbed that key fob and escorted him upstairs. Sunlight was streaming in the windows when I opened the door for him, and he stepped back.

"Awfully bright in there. Don't you have shades?"

"I'm sorry, I don't have shades. You can close the curtains for privacy. Most guests like the light and the view."

"I am not most guests. I suppose it will be all right." He pushed past me into the room, rolling his suitcase over my foot.

"Ouch."

"You should have gotten out of the way. That will be all."

I laid the keys on the bedside table. "The key with the blue cap is for the front door, which I keep locked. The plain key is your room key. Be sure to take towels when you use the bathroom as there are none in there. Enjoy your stay." I backed out and pulled the door shut.

I walked downstairs, wondering how the next week would go. Peter Norton wasn't like my usual happy guest. He seemed like he was going to be a challenge, and there wasn't another guest to dilute his effect. What would Iggy think of him? Would he be worried that I was alone in Seaview with a man like Peter Norton? And what was happening with Iggy and Mrs. Whiting? Would she grind down his resistance and finally get her way?

Peter Norton was sitting in the lobby reading a newspaper when I went in the next morning to make coffee. "I'm an early riser," he said. "I expect coffee to be ready at six."

I bit my tongue to keep from retorting, "Then make it yourself." "All right, I'll get the pot ready to go before I go to bed, and you can turn it on when you get down here. I hope that's okay."

"I suppose it will have to be." He rattled the newspaper at me. "This issue of the New York Times is from yesterday. Where can I get today's copy?"

In Anguilla? Where did he think he was? "I'm not sure. I'll call around to see where you might find a daily paper. Maybe one of the larger resorts gets the Times delivered." By then I had the coffee made and got the toaster out of the sideboard. "I'll go make scrambled eggs and bacon. Can I bring out some bread and jam for you to make toast?"

He frowned at me over his paper. "I have to make my own toast? Why don't you make it?"

"If I make it and carry it out here, it'll be cold. I'll be happy to make toast for you if you don't mind that it's cold."

"You make it."

How would an entire week with this man play out? I knew for a fact that I wouldn't be worrying about him like I had my previous guests. It was hard to warm up to such a demanding guest.

I unplugged the toaster and carried it into the kitchen. I scrambled a couple eggs in a small bowl and put a few slices of bacon in the skillet. Once they were crispy, I slid them onto a plate and into the oven to stay warm while I cooked the eggs. I toasted two slices of coconut bread that I also kept warm in the oven. Figuring Mr. Norton had said nothing about fruit allergies, I made a small bowl of berries, mango, and pineapple to go with his eggs. Once everything was ready, I loaded a tray and carried it out into the lobby.

"Here you go, breakfast is served." I slid the placemat, napkin, and silverware over to where he was seated and put the plate of eggs, bacon, and toast on the mat. "Be careful, the plate is hot."

He looked around the edge of his newspaper. "What's

this? I didn't order this."

I took a deep breath. "Mr. Norton, this is a bed-and-breakfast hotel. There is no menu to order from. I make breakfast, and you eat it. Today and tomorrow there will be scrambled eggs, bacon, and toast, with a bowl of fruit on the side if you'd like. I hope to find almond milk at the market tomorrow so I can make an egg casserole for Tuesday. Wednesday, I plan to serve Rudolf's Banana Bread if there is margarine to be found. Thursday we're back to eggs any way you like them. I usually make muffins, but my muffin recipe calls for butter and milk. If I can find almond milk and margarine at the market, I may try to make muffins. Don't count on it. Supplies on the island are limited." I stopped talking and waited for an explosion.

"Oh. Well, in that case, what kind of jam is there for my toast?" He folded the newspaper and laid it across the table from him.

I reached for the jars on the sideboard. "We have passion fruit and guava jams."

"Thank you. That will be all." He waved me away like some servant.

I walked back into the kitchen and couldn't decide whether to laugh or cry. Obviously, Peter Norton was used to a completely different level of accommodation. I wondered what had brought him to Seaview. If he treated me like a servant, how would he treat Geneva? I wouldn't stand for him abusing her, verbally or physically.

Whatever had convinced him to come to Anguilla and stay at Seaview, it was my job to see that he had a pleasant stay. I picked up the phone and started calling resorts to see if anyone got the New York Times delivered daily and if I could send him over to get a copy. Or more likely go get one for him myself.

I kept an ear out to hear when Peter Norton was done with his breakfast and went out to gather up the dishes and unplug the coffee pot. "How was everything?"

He was engrossed in his newspaper and just grunted.

I had the tray loaded and was nearly out of the lobby when he said. "What's for lunch?"

That stopped me in my tracks. I fought to keep my voice level. "I'm sorry. This is a bed-and-breakfast. I don't serve lunch or dinner. You'll have to find those meals on your own. Many of my guests purchase lunch food that they keep in my refrigerator and then go out for dinner. You're welcome to do that."

"How will I know where to go?"

I wondered when his manservant had fled. "Just a minute." I carried the tray into the kitchen and set it on the kitchen island, then went back into the lobby. From a pigeonhole behind the registration desk, I pulled out an Anguilla tourist guide that I carried over to where Peter Norton was sitting. "Here. This is the latest tourist guidebook. It has listings for lots of restaurants and snack shacks all over the island. This is the hotel copy, but you're welcome to use it to get started. There are also listings of historical sites and other attractions that might interest you."

He put down his newspaper and picked up the book. "It isn't very thick."

"Well, Anguilla is a small island."

He flipped through the pages. "Where can I get one of these?"

"I saw a stack of them at Vista Market up on top of the hill last week. They're closed today, but I'll pick one up for you tomorrow, or you could stop for one yourself. Either way works for me." I watched him run his finger down the listing of restaurants.

"Are any of these close by Seaview?"

"All the ones listed in Sandy Ground or Road Bay are in this neighborhood. You can walk to them. The rest you have to drive to."

He nodded his head and pulled a small notepad and pen out of his shirt pocket. He started writing names and phone numbers. "I guess I'll start with the closest ones and work my way out."

"Good plan." I left him exploring the little guidebook and went back into the kitchen to wash the dishes, then I remembered something. I went back to the doorway. "I forgot to tell you, there's a jump-up tonight at Johnno's Beach Bar, almost next door. My guests have enjoyed going to the party and meeting some locals." Some more than others, I thought.

I had to explain what a jump-up was, how everyone was welcome, how he could find a corner and observe, but usually everyone ended up dancing.

The next time I glanced into the lobby, Peter Norton had gotten the map out of his car and was marking places on it using the guidebook as reference.

Once again Edward came to Seaview's front door asking me to come to the jump-up. "Come dance with me." He slid his feet across the floor and swayed to music only he could hear.

Rather than argue with him, I gave in. "Okay, give me a minute to change my shirt."

Peter Norton came down the stairs as I got back to the lobby from my apartment. "Oh, Mrs. Lambert, I will see you at the party. I am interested in local customs. I am something of an amateur anthropologist, you know."

I wondered what happened to the grump of the morning. "No, I didn't know that." I introduced Peter Norton to Edward and the three of us walked down the beach to Johnno's. I looked carefully around to see if Iggy and Mrs. Whiting were there, but didn't see them.

Edward grasped my arm. "He not here. You don' have to worry about seeing Iggy tonight. He at church."

"Okay. What's going on at church?"

"Some choir thing that Mrs. Whiting is part of. She won' let him miss that."

Silas, Luke, and Melvin were all at the table holding chairs for us. Peter Norton followed Edward and me across the room and stood looking lost when I was greeted by my friends. I introduced them, and Silas pulled out a chair for Peter Norton.

"Sit here by me, Peter. You will have a good view of the dancing."

I asked Peter Norton what he'd like to drink.

"I might as well try the local drink while I'm here."

I went to the bar to get two rum punches.

Edward claimed my hand for the first dance. We whirled around the floor amid the crowd. I barely had time for a sip of my drink before Melvin asked me to dance with him. Then it was Luke and finally Silas that I danced with.

I plopped down, sweaty, and out of breath, into the chair next to Peter Norton. "How are you liking the jump-up?"

"The mixing of social strata and races and ages intrigues me. How do they manage it?"

I laughed. "There's no managing it; it just happens. People dance and mix organically. I think it's the music and the location—and the rum doesn't hurt."

He looked at the tall glass sitting, half empty, in front of him. "There's rum in this?"

"Yes, that's why they call it a rum punch."

"I thought it was just fruit juice. I see so many young people drinking them. They can't all be drinking rum."

I sipped the last of my watered-down drink. "The children aren't but the drinking age on Anguilla is eighteen years old so the rest of them probably are. Eighteen-year-olds look very young to me these days. Would you like another?" I made to get up to go to the bar.

"I suppose it's my turn to buy." He picked up our glasses and made his way around and through the dancers.

I saw Johnno glance over at me and knew that he'd make my drink light. To be honest, he could leave out the rum altogether and I wouldn't mind. I'd be just as happy with all fruit and soda and no booze.

When Peter Norton came back with our drinks, the band

was just starting to play a ballad. He put down the drinks and stood looking down at me. "Would you like to dance?"

This Peter Norton was far and away from the grump who had checked in yesterday and had crabbed about coffee not being ready at six and being asked to make his own toast. I wondered what made him change.

"Sure, I'd like to dance."

Peter Norton held me away from him in a classic dance pose and stepped off in the box step like we were in a ballroom. He led me around the floor, gracefully avoiding the other dancers, most of whom were swaying in place or shuffling their feet in a small circle. When the song ended, he kept my hand in his and escorted me back to the table. "Thank you for the lovely dance. It's time for me to turn in." And he walked away through the crowd, leaving a fresh drink sitting on the table.

I watched him go and shook my head. Peter Norton was surely a contradiction. I stayed for a few more dances with the guys, enjoyed eating some conch fritters, chicken fingers, and plantain chips, finished my second drink, and left before the band quit for the night.

Walking down the beach, I kept listening for footsteps and looking over my shoulder, thinking of Calvin sneaking up on me the week before, but no one came. Instead, Iggy was sitting on Seaview's front steps when I walked up. My heart started fluttering and my breath got tight. "What are you doing here?"

He kept his eyes on his clasped hands. "I have something to tell you. I did not want you to hear from someone else."

My heart sank. "What's that? Are you marrying Mrs. Whiting?"

"No, not that." He gave a dry chuckle which quickly turned sober. "Um, I have to tell you I heard from Dru just now. Calvin is dead."

My knees buckled, and Iggy reached out and steered me to sit down on the step beside him. "What happened?"

"Jed went over to the shop to borrow some tools this evening and found him. He had been dead for a while. Dru said it looked like a heart attack."

That explained why I hadn't seen his truck parked up the road the last few days. Relief washed over me. No longer would I have to worry about Calvin following me around in his green truck or trying to sneak into Seaview. I could leave the doors unlocked during the day for the convenience of my guests and not worry about coming back from errands to find him hiding somewhere inside. "I'm sorry you lost your friend."

"He was not my friend anymore, not since he started stalking you." Iggy laid a soft hand on my back. "Rose, I want to come back. I will move in if you want me to. I will sell my house and live here with you. I miss you. I love you. Please."

I turned to look at his pleading face in the light from the porch. "You don't have to sell your house. It was selfish of me to demand that you either live with me or leave. I was rigid with fear that Calvin would invade Seaview and do more damage, damage that I couldn't afford to fix." I leaned over and rested my head on his shoulder, amazed at how well we fit together. "I've missed you. Can we go back to the way we were before? You can stay with me sometimes when you want to, but still keep your house and your independence. I've been trying to get up the courage to call you and apologize."

Iggy put his arm around me and snuggled me to his side. "I have been waiting to hear from you."

"What about Mrs. Whiting?"

"Mrs. Whiting is a nice enough woman, but she is no Rose Lambert."

I wondered how Iggy could ignore the weeks of slander I'd endured at Mrs. Whiting's instigation. I was glad to have him back but wondered if Mrs. Whiting's campaign against me would be even stronger.

"What did Dru say when she called?"

"She said that when Jed found him, he had been dead for several days. He had pictures of you plastered all over his little sleeping alcove in his shop." His arms tightened around me. "You were right. Calvin would never leave you alone."

I refrained from saying I told you so.

We sat for a long time just enjoying being with each other again, then we went inside. Together.

The reunion with Iggy was passionate and sweet. We lit the small lamp and enjoyed slowly undressing each other in the dim light. Iggy's hands roamed over my shoulders, down my arms, to my breasts, raising goosebumps as he went. I shivered.

"Are you cold?"

I shook my head no. "I'm glad to feel your hands on me again."

My hands weren't still. They caressed Iggy's chest and slid down his back to his firm backside. When we could no longer endure the waiting, we slid between the sheets and joined our bodies in passion. Twice more during the night we awoke to pleasure each other.

The sun was barely up when there was a persistent rapping at my door. "Mrs. Lambert, Mrs. Lambert..." It was Peter Norton.

"What?" I said. "Is there something wrong?"

There was a pause, then he said. "There is no coffee made, and it's after six o'clock."

I groaned. I had forgotten to get the coffeemaker ready to be turned on the night before. "I'm sorry, I'll be right out." Iggy groaned into his pillow.

"See that you are. I've already gotten the paper, and I'd like coffee to go with it."

I scrambled out of bed, scooped up the clothes that I had on the night before, and put them on. I hurried out into the lobby and got the coffeemaker filled with water and grounds and turned on to brew.

Peter Norton was sitting at one of the tables with his nose buried in his copy of the New York Times.

"Give me a few minutes and I'll make breakfast," I said.

He grunted.

I slipped back into my apartment to find Iggy curled up with my pillow. "I have to get dressed and make breakfast. Sorry, I can't come back to bed. Peter Norton is an early riser and rather demanding."

"I like the way your pillow smells," he said, inhaling deeply. "I like the way you smell better."

I stretched out on top of the covers and slid between my pillow and his arms. "I like the way you smell, too, especially when we're making love."

His grip tightened and I could feel his response. "We could have a quick…"

"No, we can't, sorry. I need to brush my teeth, get dressed in clean clothes, and get into the kitchen. Can I have a rain check for later?"

He groaned and slowly relaxed his grip. "I suppose I can be patient."

I got clean clothes out of the dresser and went into the bathroom to wash up. It only took a few minutes, and I was in the kitchen frying bacon and scrambling eggs for three. Iggy wasn't too long behind me and went into the lobby for a mug of coffee.

"Who are you?" I could hear Peter Norton close his newspaper and I heard the clink of a china mug as Iggy took one from the shelf.

"I am Ignatius Solomon, Mrs. Lambert's paramour. Welcome to Anguilla."

"Weren't you sitting on the steps last night when I came home from the party?"

"I was. I was waiting to see Rose and give her some news. I hope you enjoyed the jump-up."

"I did. It was a very interesting anthropological study of third-world life." Peter Norton expounded on the mating rituals and habits of what he called "lesser peoples."

I was horrified hearing such blatant prejudice and waited for Iggy to explode. Anguilla wasn't a third-world county, and the natives of the island weren't "lesser people." If anything, the tourists were the lesser people because they left their morals and their etiquette at home. Iggy held his tongue, said through gritted teeth he was glad Mr. Norton had a good time, and came back into the kitchen.

"Oh my god, that had to be the worst thing I've heard in a long time. I'm sorry he said those things to you."

"It's all right. Many people judge others by the color of their skin; very few of them are so blatant about it."

I looked down at the skillet of scrambled eggs on the stove in front of me. "Makes me want to put something nasty in his eggs." I looked at Iggy and smiled. "But I won't. Paramour, huh? I like it, even if neither of us is married."

Iggy put down his mug and looked across the kitchen island to where I stood at the stove stirring the eggs. "We could be. Married, I mean. To each other."

My heart beat faster. "Uh, hold that thought." I fixed a plate of eggs, bacon, and toast for Peter Norton, then carried it out into the lobby to serve to my guest. I hurried back into the kitchen.

I turned off the burner and slid the frying pan to a cool spot. "What do you mean, we could be married?"

He fiddled with the handle of his mug. "We could get married, you and me. We're both single and we love each other. I thought maybe we could, you know, get married." He looked at me with pleading eyes. "Help me out here. It has been a long time since I proposed, but I think this is the way it is supposed to be." He got up and came to stand in front of me. "I do not have a ring to give you or a date in mind. It just came to me when I was watching you cook, and I thought I wanted to watch you cook breakfast every morning." He put his arms around me. "What do you say, Rose?"

"I don't need a ring." I put my arms around his neck and pulled his lips down to mine in a kiss. "I say yes, let's get married."

The eggs and toast were cold by the time we got around

to eating them.

CHAPTER 32

The week passed in a haze of the afterglow of Iggy's proposal. I never thought that I'd want to get married again after Jim died, but when Iggy asked me, it seemed like the most natural thing in the world to say yes.

Peter Norton continued to be an enigma. One day he would be cheerful and friendly, and the next he'd be grumpy and complaining. When I went into his room every other day to change his towels it looked like no one was staying there. His suitcase stood in the corner, the bed was always smooth and wrinkle-free, and the towels were folded just the way I folded them when I hung them. The only thing that changed was the growing stack of New York Times newspapers I went to get from Blue Harbour Resort for him every morning. I was very glad that the nearest resort had an extra paper I could buy for my guest. I didn't think that sending him on a wild goose chase across the island for a paper would make his mood any better.

I couldn't help but notice Peter Norton's comments about local people and how they were nearly "like the people at home." I don't know how Iggy kept his temper when Peter Norton went on and on about the artifacts in the local historical society museum, how they showed remarkable intelligence for "ignorant natives."

On Thursday, a middle-aged man came into Seaview's lobby as I was clearing the breakfast dishes. Peter Norton had just left, climbing the stairs to his room with his newspaper under his arm. The stranger came over to me, holding out his hand. "I'm Detective Mick Jacobs, NYPD."

I shook his hand. "Rose Lambert. How can I help you?"

He reached into his shirt pocket and pulled out a photo. "Have you seen this man?"

I took the proffered picture and looked at it. "I'm sorry, it's my policy not to say who is or isn't staying here." I tried to hand it back, but he shoved my hand toward me. "Have you spoken with the local police?" I said. "I could call them. There's a station just up the road."

He flipped out his badge. "I liaised with the locals. They sent me to your place. Just tell me if he's here now. I've been chasing him for months and I know he's staying here."

I put the photograph down on a table and picked up the tray with the dirty dishes and turned to go into the kitchen. "If you know he's here, what do you need me for? What's he done?"

"He's a con man. He cozies up to little old ladies and cons them out of their savings, jewelry, and anything else he can get. I need you to confirm my suspicions. Now, Mrs. Lambert, is Elias here or not?"

I set the tray down on the kitchen island and turned to face the police detective. "Peter Norton. He's registered as Peter Norton. He said he had retired from the corporate world."

"Is he here?"

I nodded. "He just went up to his room."

"Show me."

I sighed, went behind the check-in counter for a key, and led the way upstairs. At the door of the yellow guest room, I stopped.

Jacobs knocked on the door. "Open up, Elias, we have to talk." Silence. He knocked again. "Come on, open up. I know you're in there." He gestured to me to unlock the door, then he shoved me aside, pulled a pistol out of a holster on his belt, and shouldered the door open.

The room was empty. One window was open, the screen removed, and the curtains billowing in the ocean breeze. The room smelled of the sea and expensive cologne.

Jacobs stuck his head out of the window. "Dammit. He must have heard my voice and climbed out." We heard tires on gravel. "And there he goes." The police detective pushed past me and raced down the stairs. "I'll be back."

Thinking that I should call the local police, I noticed that Peter Norton's suitcase was still standing in the corner. I left it alone, closed the door, and relocked it. I went back into the kitchen to wash the dishes but found Geneva had beaten me to it. It was weird but kind of cool to have a New York City police detective chasing one of my guests, like on TV. But how would it affect my reputation if word got out? Just what I needed: more gossip.

"I just had a New York City policeman here asking for Peter Norton." I picked up the photograph that lay on the kitchen island and showed it to her.

"Really? What has he done?"

"According to the officer, Peter Norton cons old ladies out of their money and then vanishes. And his name is Elias." A thought occurred to me. "Either I'm not old enough or he figured that I'm not rich enough because he didn't try to cozy up to me."

Detective Jacobs came back in a couple of hours. "I lost him. How can he hide on such a small island?" He shook his head. "Did he leave anything behind?"

"His suitcase is still in his room."

"I'll take it." He handed me a search warrant. "Maybe there's something in there that will help me find him."

By then Officer Matthew had come down from the local police station and said that his commander had vetted Detective Jacobs. He said that I should cooperate with anything the detective asked. So I led the NYPD cop back up to the room that Peter Norton had stayed in and let him take the suitcase after signing a receipt for it. The detective searched the room first, peered into all the drawers, flipped through the stack of newspapers, and ran a hand between the mattress and box springs, but found nothing.

I half-expected Peter Norton to show up later that day looking to pick up his belongings, but I never heard from him again. It disgusted me to learn that the credit card he used to pay for his room was stolen, so I never got paid for his stay. I was happy to see the back of Mr. Peter Norton and took extra care in cleaning the yellow guest room to remove any trace or taint of such a prejudiced and criminal man.

I wasn't sure how I could turn my experience with Elias, alias Peter Norton, into a way to ensure that none of my future guests were fugitives from the law, but I would be more careful checking that credit cards weren't stolen.

The four guests who arrived on Saturday afternoon were in great vacation moods. It was a pair of friends and two single women who all got on famously. They swam and snorkeled, walked on the beach, and explored the island by car. Breakfast was a lively meal where they shared their adventures around Anguilla and traded restaurant recommendations.

That week was also Calvin's funeral. Since I liked Dru and Jed so much, I went to the service with Iggy. I was surprised at the number of women who came up to me privately to say that they were glad he was dead, that he had made their lives hell with his unwanted advances. All I could do was hug them and agree. Dru didn't cry.

I kept trying to talk to Mrs. Richards at Vista Market about the rumors that Mrs. Whiting spread about me, but the market was never empty when I was there although the muffins that I took to her went a long way toward thawing her attitude toward me. I didn't want to have someone overhear me plead my case. Since Iggy had come back to me, Mrs. Whiting redoubled her efforts in that area. Iggy started his own campaign telling everyone that we were back together and that the things Mrs. Whiting was saying were lies. I heard from Rebecca O'Neill that Mrs. Whiting was spreading increasingly wild tales of my hold over Iggy and that many people had stopped believing her.

My daughter Marie called to say that she was planning to come down in a few weeks' time to see Hernando Gomez, the Customs agent, and ask if there would be room for her at Seaview. She hadn't called in a while and was glad to catch up. I checked the reservations and was happy to tell her that there would indeed be a room for her. I cautioned her that the room wouldn't be free, that I'd charge her the same discounted rate that I'd charged Will and Elizabeth. There really wasn't room to expand my living quarters to have a place for family when they visited. I thought about putting a daybed in my sitting room, but hadn't gotten around to it.

"I thought you did that because they showed up unannounced."

"No, I can't afford to feed and house you for nothing. I have to charge something if only to offset the room tax."

She sighed. "Okay, I guess."

Next, I had to decide if I was going to tell Marie that Iggy had proposed. I didn't want to do it over the phone, and I wasn't sure that I wanted to tell my children at all. Iggy and I hadn't decided when we wanted to tie the knot. We had joked about doing it at a Johnno's jump-up, and the idea was growing on me. I wasn't sure what the Anguillan wedding traditions were, but since I wasn't a churchgoer, I wasn't thinking of a church wedding. Maybe Iggy would want that. I thought that a marriage by a justice of the peace in the middle of a party would be just fine. We had a lot to talk about.

CHAPTER 33

Iggy and I were enjoying the next Sunday's jump-up at Johnno's. I enjoyed sitting at the big round table with Edward, Silas, Luke, and Melvin, drinking rum punch and having bar snacks for supper. It made me happy to be back there with Iggy. I had missed him so much. I had just finished dancing with Edward when a hand touched my shoulder. A proper British voice accompanied it.

"May I have this dance?"

I turned around to find a gray-haired man smiling at me. "You may," I said and turned away from Edward. "I'm Rose Lambert. I own Seaview, the bed-and-breakfast almost next door. We haven't met."

The man smiled at me. "I'm George Clemment. My wife, Susan, and I are staying at Blue Harbour Resort at the other end of the beach." The steel drums started playing. "Let's dance."

George led me around the sandy dance floor with confidence. This British man could really dance. He wasn't as energetic as Edward, and I found it easy to follow his lead. After the song ended, George led me over to meet his wife, who had been dancing with Silas. She was tall and thin with graying blond hair that framed her flushed face. "Susan, my dear, meet Rose. She owns the bed-and-breakfast that you were admiring on our walk down the beach the other day."

Susan thrust out a hand. "It's good to meet you. I watched that building decay over the last few years. I was happy that someone was saving it from falling down."

I laughed. "I fell in love with Seaview forty years ago when my late husband and I came to dive in Anguilla. I'm glad I'm not the only one who saw the potential."

Iggy came up behind me, bringing my drink from the table. "Here, Rose, I thought you might need something to drink."

"Thanks." I introduced Iggy to George and Susan, and we stood talking while the band took a break.

"How are you liking your stay in Sandy Ground?" Iggy said.

"Oh, we love it here," George said. "I especially like diving on all the shipwrecks."

My smile widened. "Are you divers?"

"I am; Susan is not. Do you dive, Rose?"

"I do, and I'm always looking for a dive buddy. Maybe we can dive together while you're here."

George looked at Susan, who nodded. "Well, I'm signed up for tomorrow's two-tank morning dive. Do you think you could make it? I'd love to have a dive buddy I could trust."

"How do you know you can trust me, George? We just met."

George shrugged. "I'm tired of being buddied up with young men who swim too fast and go off chasing turtles and barracuda all the time. I suspect you swim slowly and enjoy the scenery."

"You're right, I do." I felt Iggy touch my waist and squeeze his approval. "I'd love to be your dive buddy tomorrow, George. I'll get the guests fed and meet you at Tamarind just before nine o'clock."

A big smile wreathed George's face. "That's great. I'll see you tomorrow."

The band started playing, and Iggy and I leaned on the bar to order fresh drinks. Johnno was careful to put a paper umbrella in my drink so that I knew there was half of the rum as in a regular one.

"You made a new friend."

"I guess so. I wonder what led him to ask me to dance. We'd never met before."

Iggy leaned down to my ear. "Maybe he liked the way you

shake your booty."

"I don't shake my booty when I dance, do I?"

"Oh, you do, but in a very restrained way. Yes, you do."

The next song was a slow one, so we moved onto the dance floor and swayed to the music. When the song ended, we moved back toward the table with the rest of our crew.

Iggy set down his drink. "I think I'll go ask Susan to dance since George danced with you."

"Good idea," I said as Luke claimed my hand for the next dance.

At around ten-thirty, I told Iggy that I was tired and ready to head home. We said our goodbyes, waved to my guests who looked like they would never tire of the party, and stepped out onto the sand.

George and Susan walked out behind us.

"I'm so glad that you're leaving," Susan said. "We were getting tired but didn't want to be the first to go."

"Glad we could help. See you in the morning, George."

We turned toward Seaview and walked slowly home under the waning moon.

I got the guests breakfasted the next morning and as soon as Geneva started washing the dishes, I checked my scuba gear to make sure I wasn't forgetting anything, put on my swimsuit with a sun shirt, and hurried over to Tamarind. There was a crowd of people boarding the boat.

George was loitering in the shop and gave a sigh of relief when I arrived. "I was afraid that you wouldn't be able to get away."

I poked my head into the equipment locker to get some weights and grinned at him. "I'm not about to miss a chance to go diving. I hurried through breakfast and got the cleanup organized, and here I am." Turning to Lomira, I asked her to charge me for a two-tank dive on the "locals" plan, then followed George out to the boat. I slung my gear bag up on the boat and then waded around to the stern to climb the boarding ladder that Freddie lowered for me.

When I appeared next to him, George said, "Where did you go? One minute you were beside me and the next you'd disappeared?"

"I didn't disappear, but I have a hard time boosting myself up on the bow of the boat, so I wade around and use the boarding ladder. I get wet but don't mind." We were assembling our gear on the tanks behind our seats to prepare for the first dive. "Where are we going? Did anyone say?"

George shook his head. "I guess we'll find out in the pre-dive briefing."

By then all the divers were on board, most of them fussing with their gear, getting it set for the first dive and tucking their gear bags under their seats. Freddie started the motor and Thomas pushed the boat away from the beach.

Once the boat was moving, Dougie called for everyone's attention. "Today we'll be diving on the MV Commerce. She was a 145-foot cargo ship that was wrecked by Hurricane Klaus in 1984. Her bow is intact and lies on a coral slope beginning at 45 feet. The stern is also in one piece and lies down the slope at 80 feet. In between the deck is collapsed and littered with old cars, machine parts, and a broken crane." He described the rich sea life that had colonized the wreck and cautioned everyone to "keep your hands off the big lobsters that lurk under the side of the ship. It isn't lobster season." Everyone sighed, and I knew everyone would be down at the bottom trying to catch sight of the big crustaceans.

I leaned over to George. "I've been tempted to nab one of those beauties but don't want to risk the steep fine that goes with getting caught."

Once Dougie had finished the briefing, George and I planned our dive. We would follow the group down to the propeller and then slowly work our way up the wreck until we emerged onto the reef at the bow. It was a relief to dive with a conscientious partner rather than have to buddy up with a group or trail the divers to make sure no one swam off. Dougie came over to ask if we wanted to follow the group or dive on our own.

George and I glanced at each other, looked back at Dougie, and said together, "On our own."

Dougie nodded, "I thought you might," and he went off to snag the mooring buoy at the dive site. Our dive worked out exactly as we had planned it.

We saw big lobsters waving their antennae at us as we swam from the stern toward the bow, but we just waved back and swam on by.

The second tank dive was at Sandy Deep on the east side of Sandy Island, the little, one palm tree island you could see from Seaview. On the reef there was an explosion of colorful fish and critters, sponges, and forests of sea fans. Every time I dived Sandy Deep, I wished I had a camera. I used to have one; it flooded on a dive, was ruined, and I never replaced it.

When we climbed the boarding ladder after the second dive, George said, "I hope that you'll consent to dive with me again. It was a relief not to have to chase down my buddy as he swam off into the abyss."

I sat down and nestled the tank butt into the rack, then slid my arms out of the BCD. "I'd love to. How long are you and Susan going to be on the island?"

George peeled off the top of his wetsuit and used a chamois towel to dry his face and chest. "Maybe forever. We've been looking for a place to buy. Winters are getting too cold for us in England and we're thinking of moving here."

I felt the smile stretch my lips. "Oh, that would be great. I'd love to have a dive buddy on the island instead of having to rely on a diver guest or go alone." I invited George to stop at Seaview and have some lunch with me. "Call Susan and ask her to walk down to meet us if she hasn't eaten yet."

"I'll call her when we hit the beach. Don't want to risk getting my phone wet."

He looked around at the other divers, some of whom had their phones out and were taking pictures, taking selfies, or poking at the screen sending texts.

Once the boat slid onto the sand, he pulled out his phone and called Susan. "All set," he said, slipping the phone back into his dry bag. "She will walk down to Seaview and meet us there."

"Great."

We waited while the rest of the divers jumped off the bow of the boat and retrieved their gear bags before rinsing and hanging their gear on the rack next to the shop.

"If we take our time, we should be back at Seaview just about the time Susan arrives."

George looked at me. "What's for lunch?"

"I made another batch of gazpacho yesterday, and we can make either pimento cheese sandwiches or grilled cheese to go with them. How does that sound?"

"Sounds good."

Susan was just walking up to the front of Seaview when George and I came from the other direction carrying our wet dive gear.

"Let's go around to the back where we can hang this stuff and let it drip on the back porch. I had Silas mount some pegs for drying equipment. There should be enough room for all of our gear." Once we had the dive equipment hung up, I showed George my bathroom where he could wash the saltwater off before lunch. Susan and I pulled out the big bowl of cold tomato soup.

"Would you rather have pimento cheese or grilled cheese sandwiches with the soup?"

"I'm not familiar with pimento cheese. Is that an island thing?"

"No, it's a southern Indiana thing. It's a cold shredded cheese and mayo sandwich on white bread. My grandma made them when I was a kid and I've been addicted to them ever since."

She grinned. "Let's have those then. Maybe I'll become addicted too."

"What are you going to become addicted to?" George came into the kitchen and pulled Susan to him for a kiss.

"Rose's grandma's sandwiches. Oh, stop, you're wet." They laughed.

Susan said, "What can I do to help?"

I directed her to where the soup bowls were while I pulled out the jar of pimento cheese spread. I sliced Italian bread, the only white bread I'll eat, for the sandwiches.

"George, pull out some placemats from the center drawer in the kitchen island. Napkins are in the right-hand drawer, and silverware is in the left-hand drawer."

I made three generous sandwiches, cut them in half, and piled the halves on a plate. Susan ladled gazpacho into three bowls, and George set places for us at the kitchen island.

"What would everyone like to drink? I have water and sun tea."

"What's sun tea?" Susan said.

"It's just iced tea brewed by leaving the jar in the sun. You don't boil the water; you just let the sunshine do the work."

"Is there sugar in it?" I shook my head no. "Then we'll both have that."

I dealt out small bread and butter plates for the sandwiches, and lunch was ready. "I'm starved. Let's eat."

The three of us sat around the kitchen island, slurping the chilled soup and munching on cheese sandwiches.

"I see how you could get addicted to these," Susan said, brandishing hers at me.

I nodded. "They're good, aren't they?"

Dimitri, one of my guests, walked into the kitchen from the lobby. "Sorry to disturb you, Mrs. Rose, I would like some tea."

"No problem, Dimitri, help yourself."

As he walked to the refrigerator, George stopped eating, his spoon stopping midway between his bowl and his mouth. "Dimitri?"

Dimitri straightened up, holding his water bottle in one

hand and the tea pitcher in the other. He turned slowly to face us. "George?"

Susan inhaled her spoonful of soup and coughed. George was distracted and turned to pat her on the back. "Are you all right?"

"I'm fine," she croaked. "I'm fine. Is that who I think it is?"

George nodded.

I looked from one man to the other. They were both unmoving, their gazes locked. "You know each other?"

"In a manner of speaking. What are you doing in Anguilla, Dimitri?"

"Vacationing. The same as you."

"We're looking for a home here. Is Irina with you?"

"Da. Where else would she be? Do you vacation without your wife now that you are retired? You are retired, aren't you?"

George stared straight into Dimitri's eyes. "You know I'm retired the same way I know that you're retired. Are you staying here at Seaview?"

"Yes, we are staying here. We like it here. I am going snorkeling, and Irina is walking on the beach and writing."

Susan snorted.

"Are you sure you're okay, dear?" George turned to look at her.

"I'm fine."

George stood. "I think we need to have a chat, don't you, Dimitri?"

The Russian put the tea pitcher back into the fridge. "No, I do not think that we have anything to talk about, George. I will go now." He turned and walked out of the kitchen, carrying his empty water bottle.

"Well, I'll be damned." George sat back down on his stool.

Susan put her hand on his arm. "One of your old competitors from work?"

"Um-hm. Someone from way back. The last person I ever

263

expected to see in Anguilla."

I saw the way Susan and George looked at each other and knew that they were saying a lot more with their eyes than their mouths. "Anyone need more gazpacho?" They both started as if I had shouted.

"No, we're fine. It's time we got moving and let you get on with your day." George finished the last of his pimento cheese sandwich, stood, and carried his plate, bowl, and glass to the sink. "Would you like me to rinse my dishes? Susan has me trained."

I laughed. "No, thanks. I'll take care of the dishes. You two run along." I went around the end of the kitchen island and stuck out my hand. "It was great diving with you this morning. I hope we can do it again."

"Oh, I'll definitely be calling you to schedule another dive. You're a good buddy. I haven't enjoyed a dive so much in a very long time."

Susan carried her dishes to the sink, too. "Thank you for the lovely lunch, Rose. I enjoyed every bite. Will you share your recipe for pimento cheese? I think I'm becoming addicted to it too."

"Sure, it's simple to make. The hardest part is grating the cheese, but that isn't really hard, just tedious since it's so much cheese."

"Maybe I can make half a recipe. That way I won't be tempted to eat it three times a day."

"Good luck. I usually only make it when I know I'm going to have company so that I'm safe from too much temptation."

We went out onto the back porch. George packed his partially dried dive gear, and Susan and I talked about children and hobbies. I discovered she was a knitter.

"Oh, do you have knitting with you? Come back this evening," I said. "I'm having a group of locals over for a knitting circle and I advertised it in the island newspaper, *The Anguillian*. I'm hoping for a good turnout. There'll be little pimento cheese sandwiches. Other kinds of sandwiches too."

Susan laughed. "Yes, I have knitting with me. I never travel without it. Tell me what time, and I'll be here. You had me at knitting and sealed it with those sandwiches."

"Great. I'll see you around eight o'clock then."

"I might be a little later; we have dinner at seven."

"That's fine, just come when you can. I'm sure we'll still be knitting, chatting, and eating."

Dimitri appeared at the back door. "I think a chat is in order after all."

George put down the dive bag that he had slung over his shoulder. "All right. Let's take a stroll."

As the men crossed the backyard and stepped around the bougainvillea hedge, I turned to Susan. "What's going on?"

"I don't know. I think they're marking territory."

I was confused. "I don't understand. If they worked together years ago, why would they need to do that?"

Susan looked at me. "Well, uh, they worked for competitors."

"Yes, you said that."

"And the competitors still don't get along very well, so their relationship is rather fraught."

"What kind of work did they do?"

"Government work." Susan's answer was short and said in a tone that ended my questions.

We went back into the kitchen to wait for the men to return. I ran hot water into the sink and started washing the dishes. Susan insisted on helping, so I gave her a dishtowel and let her dry. We talked about what she liked to knit (sweaters) and what I liked to knit (socks) and passed the time, neither of us able to keep from watching the door to see if George and Dimitri were coming back.

The dishes were washed, dried, and put away, and I had time to find a card and write out the pimento cheese recipe for Susan before we heard them talking in low voices as they crossed the backyard, both of them looking serious.

"Are you ready?" George said, shouldering his gear bag

again.

Susan tucked the recipe card in her shorts pocket and said, "I'll be back this evening after supper with my knitting in hand, Rose. See you soon, and thanks for the lovely lunch."

George leaned in through the doorway to say that he had enjoyed the dive and would get in touch to go again later in the week. And they were gone.

Dimitri had walked across the kitchen, through the lobby, and mounted the stairs to his room without saying a word.

I was itching with curiosity to know what these two such opposite men had done for their respective governments that made them so wary around each other.

After supper with Iggy, I wiped off the tables and chairs in the lobby and set about making a big platter of little sandwiches for what I hoped would be a good turnout of knitters and crocheters. I had said in my ad in *The Anguillian* that all crafts were welcome.

Eight o'clock came, and no one arrived. I had pitchers of sun tea and lemonade on the sideboard beside the platter of sandwiches. I heard voices and went to the lobby doors. There was a group of about five local women standing on the sand talking about who was going to be first to mount the steps and come in.

"Come in," I said, "please. All of you are welcome."

They stood aside and let Lomira, my friend who worked at Tamarind Dive Shop, come in first. I got everyone settled with a beverage and a plate before making the little welcome speech I had been planning in my head all week.

Just as I spoke, three women, obviously tourists, poked their heads through the door.

"Is this the knitting group?"

I nodded and welcomed them in. It didn't surprise me when the three tourists sat together across from the local women. I figured it would take a few minutes for people to warm up. Maybe I could help with that. I started introductions.

"Hi everyone, and welcome. I'm Rose, the owner of Seaview. I'm a pretty experienced knitter and missed my knitting group at home when I moved down here so I decided to see if I couldn't start one up." I held up my project. "Tonight, I'm working on a Gramma's Favorite dishcloth because I realized I use the ones I have for cleaning and doing dishes all the time and I need more." I turned to Lomira, sitting next to me. "Lomira?"

She introduced herself and then held up the lace table mat that she was crocheting. Introductions moved around the room until everyone had spoken. Seeing what everyone was working on broke the ice. In just a few words and a few minutes, we went from strangers to a band of fiber friends.

Susan arrived and fitted into the laughing, talking circle of women with the sweater she was knitting for her granddaughter.

Susan sat down next to Lomira and leaned over to admire her crocheted lace table mat. "That's so beautiful," she said.

Lomira fingered the lilac wool that Susan was knitting her sweater with. "I have never worked with wool. It is too hot here for wool, but that is beautiful and so soft."

One of the tourist women was knitting a sock, and the islanders were transfixed at the architecture of it. "How do you make the stitches curve to fit the heel?" an islander asked. That turned into an impromptu lesson where the knitter explained the short-row technique that lets the stitches make that ninety-degree angle.

Iggy stayed out of the way in the kitchen, tinkering with the balky bathroom door lock that kept sticking. He laid a piece of cardboard on the surface so that he could keep the parts together and in order, and not get any grease or oil on the stainless-steel island top.

CHAPTER 34

Marie arrived in Sint Maarten and Hernando Gomez met her at the airport. I said I would be happy to pick her up, but she said, "'Nando insists on picking me up. He said he'd bring me right to Seaview."

It was good to have Marie with me. I saw little of her for the first few days of her visit. 'Nando wanted to take her around and introduce her to all his friends and relatives. That made me a little nervous because he was conservative and religious, and Marie was not. I was afraid that they would endure some pushback, and it turned out I was right. I came back from running errands one afternoon in the middle of the week to find Marie crying in the kitchen.

"Where have you been?"

I lifted the shopping bags I was carrying. "Grocery shopping and picking up a few things. What's the matter?"

She sniffled into the tissue she held. "Oh, 'Nando says that I can't wear shorts anymore."

"What? Why not?" I looked down at my shorts-clad legs. "Everyone here wears shorts."

"Not everyone. Not 'Nando's mother, grandmother, and aunts. They wear dresses. He wants me to wear dresses too, and not skimpy, sleeveless sundresses. He wants me to wear frumpy old lady dresses with sleeves and a high neck and skirt down to my knees."

I hefted the bags onto the kitchen island and started putting the food away. "That's ridiculous. He liked you well enough when you were in shorts and little dresses when you were here before. What changed?"

"He says that we have a reputation to uphold. That we represent the Anguillan government, and I have to be... what's the word he used... proper."

"Baloney. When he's at work in his uniform, he represents the government, but when he's off, he's just a guy. You don't represent the government; you're an American woman here on holiday."

She dabbed at her still-streaming eyes. "I told him that, but he's adamant." She put her head down on her arms on the island and sobbed. "This was a big mistake, Mom. I should have never come back down here."

I folded the bags, put them in the basket that I used for produce from the market, and set it all by the back door. I'd put it back into the car later. "Don't be silly. It's a good thing that you found this out early before you have a lot of time and emotion invested in the relationship. You've had a nice flirtation long-distance and now you've learned that it's not working out in person. Dry your eyes. We can salvage your visit. Let's plan a dive trip for tomorrow, just you and me. Did you bring your mask, snorkel, and fins?"

She sniffled, hiccuped, and nodded yes.

"Good. I'll call Tamarind and get us signed up on the morning boat. Geneva won't mind if I go off diving with you. I'll let her know right now." I hurried off to find my right-hand woman.

We had a nice dive, two nice dives, and were on the catamaran coming back into Sandy Ground when I blurted it out. "Iggy asked me to marry him, and I said yes."

"What?" Marie turned to look at me, eyes wide and mouth hanging open.

"You heard me. Iggy and I are going to be married."

"When?"

I shrugged. "We haven't set a date. We're taking things slow."

"Oh my god, Mom, have you told Will?"

"No, I didn't want to tell him over the phone, and I'm afraid that he'll take it badly. You know how he gets when things change."

"Tell him. This is not a secret I'm going to be able to keep. You know how I am. I can't keep a secret."

The boat slowed and slid onto the sandy beach in front of the dive shop. We packed up our dive gear and followed the other divers to the bow and then off onto the sand. We stopped talking while we rinsed our gear, returned Marie's rental gear, and I left mine there to drip. "I'll pick it up in an hour or so," I told Thomas.

He nodded and then leaned over to whisper, "Congratulations. I like Iggy. I think you'll be good for each other."

My hand flew to my mouth. "Oh, I didn't think you could hear me. Please don't say anything to anyone. We haven't made an announcement. We want to do that together when we're ready."

"You can count on me, but talk to Freddy before you leave. I'm sure he heard you too."

I was reluctant to talk to Freddy because he'd been giving me dirty looks for weeks. But I hurried back to the boat to talk to him. He said that his mother had told him about Mrs. Whiting's lies and promised not to tell anyone, not even his mother, so my news stayed secret a little while longer.

Iggy brought over lobsters to grill for supper. He brought enough for Marie and 'Nando too. 'Nando never showed. "I think he and Marie are quits," I said. "He wanted her to be something she isn't, so they broke up."

Iggy laid the lobsters on the grill. "That is too bad. 'Nando is a nice boy, but I do not think he was the right one for your Marie."

I was glad he said it because that's what I was thinking about the relationship all along.

Marie came out of the kitchen door with an armload of

fabric. "I thought we could eat out here on the patio," she said. "I have a tablecloth and napkins. Is that okay?"

"That's fine. I enjoy dining *alfresco*." I turned on the string of lights over the patio. "I'll get the plates and silverware. Marie, you bring the salad and melted butter, and we'll be ready."

It was a fine meal, even if the sight of that last, unclaimed lobster made Marie tear up.

I made lobster scrambled eggs with homemade Hollandaise sauce for breakfast the next day. I used the sauce recipe I got from my knitting friend, Carol. It was very popular with my guests.

Marie kept after me for the rest of her visit. "You have to call Will, Mom. Tell him you're getting married. Oh, he's going to flip when he hears that."

"Don't you think he likes Iggy?"

She was folding her clothes out of the laundry basket and putting them into her suitcase. "I think he likes Iggy just fine as your boyfriend. I can't imagine what he'll say when he finds out Iggy's going to be his stepfather."

I reached in for one final tee shirt to fold. "Iggy's not going to be his stepfather, he's going to be my husband."

Marie looked at me, threw back her head, and laughed. "Oh Mom, you're kidding, right? When you get married, Will and I will have a stepfather. There's no getting around that fact."

Iggy and his first wife had no children, but he was close to his nieces and nephews, of which there were many. I knew Silas wouldn't mind us getting married, but I wondered what the rest of them would think. I had met a lot of his family members at jump-ups, where they were very friendly. Would that change when we announced our engagement?

The thought had never occurred to me. Now that the kids were adults, I guess I had imagined some sort of space between them and me. I tried my best to stay out of their lives, but especially in Will's case, he couldn't stay out of mine. Will had a lot to say about me buying Seaview and renovating it, and I was certain that he'd have plenty to say about me getting married. I guess I had to call him. I checked the time and picked up my phone.

"Hey, Mom! How're things? What's up?"

I held the phone a little tighter. "Things are fine, Will. Marie has been here for the week. She's packing for home now. What are you doing?"

"Right now? I'm driving home from work. Why?"

"Can you find a place to pull over? Maybe into a parking lot?"

"Okay. You're scaring me. What's going on?"

I heard the sound of his tires change as he turned off the highway.

"All right, I'm parked. What?"

"I told Marie in person, but I have to tell you over the phone because I don't want to keep it a secret." I took a deep breath. "Iggy proposed, and I said yes. We're going to be married."

"Yeah, okay. When?"

I let my breath out and waited for him to really hear me. "Did you hear what I said? Iggy and I are going to get married."

"Well, it's been nearly five years since Dad died and you've been dating Iggy for at least a year so, okay, you're getting married. When?"

"I don't know when. We haven't gotten that far. We're not in a hurry."

"That's good. You don't want to rush into things. Take your time and make sure it's what you want. Tell Iggy congratulations from me. I've got to get moving. Elizabeth will think something's happened to me. Bye, Mom. Tell Marie I said hey." And he hung up.

I looked at the phone in my hand and wondered who I'd been talking to. That didn't sound like my ultra-cautious, change-averse son at all.

"What'd he say?" Marie folded the last of her clothes into the suitcase.

"He said to tell Iggy congratulations and to let him know when."

"Is that all?"

"No, he said to tell you hey."

We looked at each other, both of us at a loss for words.

Finally, Marie spoke. "Do you think he has a fever or is maybe on drugs? That totally didn't sound like my brother."

I was staring at my phone. "I don't know."

CHAPTER 35

It took us a while, but Iggy and I finally decided on a wedding date in early June, which meant we'd be engaged for just enough time to get the wedding organized. The weather was near perfect in June and there was little danger of a hurricane crashing the ceremony. We decided to invite Pastor Davis from the local Anglican church to come to Johnno's one Sunday evening and marry us on the beach at the party. At first Iggy wanted a proper church wedding. We talked to Pastor Davis, and she assured him that Johnno's Beach Bar was just as good a wedding venue as her church.

"God will oversee the rite no matter where you have it, Ignatius," she told him, laying a comforting hand on his forearm.

As the news of our engagement spread over the island, we received congratulations and disdain in about equal measure.

Dru Brooks was one of the first Anguillans to extend her congratulations. "I knew that you and Iggy were made for each other that first night we met. And now that Calvin is out of the way, you can relax."

It surprised me that she mentioned her late husband and acknowledged the tension he'd brought me. I will admit that I was relieved that Calvin was dead and no longer stalking my every move. I could leave the doors of Seaview unlocked during the day for the convenience of my guests and not have to worry that I'd find him lurking somewhere ready to pounce on me or damage the plumbing.

Mrs. Whiting and her coterie of single, divorced, and

widowed ladies who had been chasing Iggy since his first wife passed had a lot to say about our wedding plans, none of it positive. We had a few chilly encounters when we met in the grocery, but I rose above most of the remarks.

Marie went on about having a stepfather in her weekly phone calls, and Will counseled me about keeping our financials separate. I reassured them both that Iggy and I were making a prenuptial agreement to protect each other's estates. Although Iggy had no children from his first marriage, he had nieces and nephews he wanted to provide for. Iggy's family couldn't have been more welcoming. Over the weeks since I'd told Marie and Will and Elizabeth about our engagement, they'd gotten used to the fact that their mother was getting remarried, and they planned to come down for the wedding. I blocked off the two garden view rooms for that week and promised that I'd only charge them the room tax. That made Will happy. Elizabeth offered to make food for the party, and I gladly accepted even though it disappointed me she hadn't been able to figure out the secret ingredient of Johnno's conch fritter sauce.

I needed a dress. I went over to St. Martin to look through the shops and ended up in downtown Phillipsburg on the Dutch side of the island where I found the perfect dress. It was a tropical print of red hibiscus on a white background with a fitted bodice, wide straps over the shoulders, and a full-ish skirt. Now I just needed a pair of red sandals to go with it. Red, not white, never white.

Life at Seaview went along fairly smoothly in the months before the wedding. Guests came and went, leaving a blur of laughter and sandy floors in their wake. I decided not to have guests the week of the wedding so that I didn't have to wake up and feed strangers on the morning of the ceremony. That made Will happy because they could have an ocean view room for their stay. Iggy would go back to his house for the night before the wedding.

Iggy and I had a few meetings with an attorney to get the prenuptial agreement settled and signed. For the immediate future, Iggy decided to hold on to his house in West End Village. He was considering offering it as a long-term vacation rental. He moved some of his things to Seaview and remodeled the back room so that there was room for his tools and electrician's supplies. Having less room for linens and kitchen items somehow made the storage more efficient. Geneva worked with Iggy on it. I credit her organizational skills for the improvement.

Marie called in May saying that she wanted to bring a guest to the wedding. Would that be all right?

"Sure, what's her name?"

There was a brief pause, and then she said, "Justin."

"Oh. Will Justin need a room, or will he be staying with you?" I prayed I had kept any judgement out of my voice when I asked the question.

"That's up to you, Mom. Justin's willing to pay the room tax if you'd prefer that we had separate rooms."

Huh. That left me with a quandary. Justin wasn't family, so I felt like he should pay something more than the tax for his own room, but he would be Marie's guest. "We're all adults," I said, "He can stay with you if you're comfortable with that."

"Good, because we're kind of living together."

"Oh. When were you planning to tell me?"

Her voice tightened. "I'm telling you now. It hasn't been that long since he moved in. You don't have to get snippy."

I took a deep breath. "I'm sorry. I feel a little snippy. The first time I hear the guy's name is when I hear that you're living together. Catch me up."

She said that Justin worked for the cable company and had come to her place on a service call about six months ago. They had clicked, and he'd asked her out for coffee. He was a diver too, so they'd gone on a few dives in a group last fall and gotten along even better underwater. A few coffee dates had led to dinner dates, and about a month ago he had moved in.

"It's too bad that Iggy doesn't dive, Mom, all six of us could go diving when we're down there."

"I'm trying to convince him to take a Discover Scuba class, so keep your fingers crossed."

I did a little mental math and realized that she had been dating Justin at the same time she was involved with Hernando Gomez. Maybe breaking up with 'Nando hadn't been the heartbreak I'd imagined it was. I resolved to let Marie make her own way in the relationship world and just be a sympathetic ear if she needed one.

CHAPTER 36

Will and Elizabeth, Marie and Justin all flew in the day before the wedding, and we had a nice family supper around the kitchen island. This was Justin's first time in the Caribbean, and he was excited to have the chance to dive in "water you can really see through."

Elizabeth had been emailing Johnno, and they'd worked out a menu that combined his usual bar snacks and a few special items for the wedding party. Marie and Elizabeth teased Iggy that he had to go back to his house for the night or he'd jinx the marriage.

"I was planning to go home for the night. I know how you are not supposed to see each other before the ceremony. It is bad luck." He kissed me on the cheek, and I walked him to his truck.

I put my arms around his neck and hugged him close. "Next time I see you will be on the beach in front of Johnno's and Pastor Davis will be there to make it official."

He slid his arms around me. "Nervous?"

"A little. You?"

"I am not nervous at all. I have wanted to marry you almost from the moment we met. It has taken longer than I hoped, but we are getting there now. No, I am not nervous." He leaned down and kissed me, then pushed me away. "I had better be moving along, or I will forget about the bad luck and stay here tonight." He got into his truck, started it, and pulled away, waving out the driver's side window.

I watched his taillights fade into the distance until I couldn't see them anymore. "I love you, Iggy," I said to his diminishing lights. I thought about the night before my marriage to Jim, how I'd been so confident in my deep love for him and realized that my love for Iggy was just as deep but in a more mature way. I would always miss Jim, but now I had Iggy to spend the rest of my life with. I shed a few tears, wiped them away, and turned to go inside.

When I got back into Seaview, the kids had put all the food away and washed and dried the dishes. Elizabeth and Marie had their heads together over a sheaf of papers.

"What's that?" I asked.

"Never you mind," Elizabeth said. "These are the plans for the food, and I need to go down to Johnno's. We have some last-minute planning to do." She gathered up the papers and left by the back door.

Will got up from his stool. "Wait up. I'll come along."

"Mom, do you mind if Justin and I go for a walk down the beach? We'll probably stop at Johnno's for a drink too. Do you want to come along?" Marie stood in the doorway to the lobby.

"No, I'm not in the mood for Johnno's tonight. You kids go on."

"You won't mind being alone?"

I shook my head. I spent a few minutes getting all the clean dishes put away and wiping the island to make sure I wouldn't have any overnight visiting pests. There were no guests this week, so I had Seaview all to myself for once. I poured a glass of wine and took it out onto the front porch to sit in a rocker and watch the sunset. Tomorrow at sunset I'd be pledging my vows to Iggy. I thought about all I'd gain, a steadfast partner to lean on and support when he needed me. I'd be marrying someone my children accepted as part of their family, and I'd get to be a part of Iggy's large extended family.

The wedding day dawned a little cloudy, and there was a brief rain shower but soon the clouds moved off and the sun dried up the rain. Marie and Justin were up and out on the dive boat. There was no reason for them to hang around with me.

The wedding wasn't until six-forty-five in the evening so that we'd be married during the sunset. I wanted our vows to be bathed in pink and gold light.

Elizabeth was in the kitchen making wonderful smells and not letting me help. She had shanghaied Will as her sous chef, so he was chopping and measuring, and washing dishes at her command. Maybe having no guests this week was a bad idea. I was bored with nothing to do. I spent part of the morning cleaning the bathrooms, but that was all I had to do all day.

Marie and Justin came back from their dives, and Justin raved about the wrecks and the water clarity. I could tell that he was going to be in the water as much as possible during his week on the island. That was fine with me. I hadn't been able to convince Iggy to take a Discover Scuba course, but he insisted I go diving with my children while they were there. I didn't argue. We weren't planning a honeymoon trip. I couldn't afford not to have paying guests two weeks in a row.

Elizabeth sent Will out into the lobby with sandwiches and a pitcher of iced tea for our lunch. No one was allowed in the kitchen. "I don't want to spoil the surprise."

I didn't want to tell her I could smell my favorite buttermilk brownies baking and figured that she was making them instead of a cake.

After lunch I lay down to take a nap, but I was too nervous and excited to sleep. I watched the ceiling fan slowly spin while I tried to remember the vows and listened to Elizabeth bossing the other three around in the kitchen.

It was finally time to get ready. I took a nice shower, not a speed shower like I usually did and spread on a layer of sunscreen and moisturizer. Marie knocked at my door.

"Mom, do you need help with anything?"

"Yes, can you come in and clasp my necklace for me, please?"

She fixed my necklace and then looked at me in the mirror. "You look lovely, Mom."

Her voice cracked as she said it, and I turned to hug her. "Don't cry, sweetheart, your mascara will run."

"Oh, I'm not wearing any. I planned knowing I'd cry sometime today." She held my upper arms and looked me in the eye. "You can still change your mind if you want to."

I lifted my hands and clasped her arms. "I'm sure that I want to marry Iggy. I've got a minor case of the jitters, but only because I want everything to be perfect. I'll be fine."

"Okay. Just so you know, I'm ready to drive the getaway car if you want to flee."

I had to laugh. "This is such a small island; where would I go?"

She shrugged. "I don't know, Sint Maarten?"

"Yeah, the next island. Are you planning to hijack the ferry?"

"I will if I have to."

I pulled her into a hug. "Come here." We stood together for a minute, not saying anything. "You know that I'd give the world if your dad were here with me, but he's not and there's nothing I can do about it. Iggy is a good man and I love him. We'll have a nice life together."

"Yes, you will. I know that you'll be happy and safe with Iggy. Especially now that the crazy plumber isn't around."

I groaned. "Don't remind me. Calvin was certainly a lost soul. I'm happy he's at peace."

Will knocked on the door frame and poked his head into the room. "It's time to go, Mom. Time to get hitched."

"Elizabeth got all the food organized?"

"Organized and delivered to Johnno's. Everything is set except we need a bride and groom." He held his elbow out to me. "May I escort you?"

I let out a breath, slipped my feet into my flat red sandals, and linked my arm with Will's. "Let's go."

The sun was slightly above the horizon as we walked down the beach toward Johnno's. So much sand got between my feet and shoes that I made Will stop so I could take them off and continue on barefoot. I could see Pastor Davis standing next to my groom. Iggy wore a long-sleeved white shirt, a tie, and dark slacks. He was barefoot, too. Soft steel drum music wafted out of Johnno's with an undercurrent of voices. Word had gone out that we were getting married at the jump-up tonight, so the crowd was even bigger than usual.

Will walked me up to Pastor Davis, turned me to face Iggy, and slipped his arm out of mine. He leaned over and kissed my cheek. "I love you, Mom."

I reached up and touched his cheek. "I love you too, Will." Then I turned to face Iggy.

He smiled at me and said, "Do not look so nervous. I will not bite."

The sun was just about to set, and the world was bathed in golden-pink light. Pastor Davis cleared her throat and said, "Let us begin."

The ceremony was short and traditional, read from the Book of Common Prayer. We repeated our vows, leaving out the obey part because neither one of us was particularly obedient. We exchanged rings, simple ones that we got from a jeweler in Phillipsburg, Sint Maarten.

"I now pronounce you husband and wife. You may kiss your bride."

Iggy softly put his hands on my shoulders and pulled me toward him. He leaned down and touched his lips to mine. A cheer rose from the assembled partygoers, and the steel drum band played a flourish. Marie gave me back my sandals, and we walked over the sand and into the beach bar where we were surrounded by friends and strangers wishing us well. My construction crew had

given up their table so that my family could all sit together.

Edward took my hand and whirled me onto the dance floor. "I want to be the first to dance with the bride."

I looked over my shoulder at Iggy, who smiled and nodded. "I will get us something to drink." So, I had my first dance as Mrs. Ignatius Solomon with another man.

I was glad that my sandals were comfortable because I don't think that I sat out any songs all night long. I saved the slow songs for Iggy, of course, but I think every man in the place wanted a dance with the bride. By the time the band finished playing for the night, I was exhausted and starving. Marie and Elizabeth had saved me a plate of goodies that I gobbled down even though it was nearly midnight. I had been right; nestled on the side of the plate was a buttermilk brownie. My favorite.

I felt hands on my shoulders and Iggy leaned down to my ear. "Are you ready to go home, Mrs. Solomon?"

I reached up and covered his hands with mine. "I'm ready, Mr. Solomon."

THE END

If you enjoyed Open For Business, please consider going on Amazon or Goodreads and leaving a review. They tell me what and how you liked the story and they help others decide to read the book. Thanks.

Seaview Muffins

2 cups all purpose flour
1/2 cup granulated sugar
2 teaspoons baking powder
1/2 teaspoon salt
3/4 cup milk (can substitute buttermilk, sour cream, or plain yogurt)
1/2 cup flavorless oil (vegetable, canola, coconut, safflower)
2 large eggs
Coarse sugar, for sprinkling

1. Preheat oven to 350 degrees. Line muffin pan with paper liners or grease well, set aside.
2. In a small bowl, whisk together the dry ingredients.
3. In a medium bowl, whisk the milk, oil, and eggs together until well combined.
4. Add the flour mixture and stir until just combined.
5. Divide the batter into the muffin cups evenly (I use an ice cream scoop) and sprinkle the tops with sugar, if desired.
6. Bake for 20 to 25 minutes or until a toothpick inserted in the center comes out almost clean.
7. Cool muffins on a wire rack. Muffins are best the day they're made but can be stored for later consumption.

Note: You can use half butter and half oil if all oil makes them too soft for your taste. Melt 1/4 cup butter and let it cool before adding to 1/4 cup oil.

Mango Lime Muffins: add 1 teaspoon vanilla extract to the wet ingredients and add 1 tablespoon fresh lime zest to the dry ingredients. Once wet and dry ingredients are just combined, gently stir in 1 cup diced fresh mango. Continue with steps 5-7 above. Mango muffins may take longer to bake. Be sure they're done by inserting a toothpick in the center which comes out clean. Cool on a wire rack. Make a little lime glaze with a few tablespoons of powdered sugar and enough fresh lime juice to make it slightly runny. Drizzle over cooled muffins.

Banana Walnut Muffins: replace granulated sugar with brown sugar, add 1/4 teaspoon nutmeg to dry ingredients, and add 1 mashed ripe banana and 1 teaspoon vanilla extract to the wet ingredients. Once wet and dry ingredients are combined, gently fold in 1/3 cup walnut pieces, if using.

Continue with steps 5-7 above. Banana muffins may take longer to bake. Be sure they're done by using the toothpick test.

Seaview Egg Casserole

4 cups cubed crusty bread
8 slices bacon, cooked and crumbled (or 1 cup cubed ham or 1 lb. breakfast sausage cooked and broken into bite-size pieces)
1/2 of a large onion, chopped
1 garlic clove, minced (optional)
1 bell pepper (any color), chopped
8 large eggs
1 1/2 cups milk (can use 1 cup sour cream or plain yogurt with 1/2 cup milk)
1/2 teaspoon salt
1/4 teaspoon black pepper, or to taste
1/4 teaspoon dried mustard (optional)
1 1/2 - 2 cups shredded cheese (can be cheddar or any combination you have on hand)

1. Dry bread cubes overnight or in the oven a 300 degrees for 10 minutes.
2. Saute the onion, bell pepper, and optional garlic in the same skillet you used to fry the bacon or sausage.
3. In a large bowl, mix together eggs, milk, salt, black pepper, and optional mustard powder.
4. Grease a 9x13" pan, arrange bread cubes in an even layer on the bottom.
5. Spread bacon, ham, or sausage evenly over bread cubes. Spoon sauteed onion and bell pepper evenly over meat.
6. Carefully pour the egg mixture over the meat and vegetable mixture, making sure that the bread cubes are evenly moistened. Sprinkle with shredded cheese.
7. Cover with plastic wrap or foil and refrigerate for at least 1 hour and preferably overnight. When ready to bake, remove covering and let sit at room temperature while the oven heats.
8. Preheat oven to 350 degrees. Bake the casserole, uncovered, until the top is golden, the edges are crisp, and a toothpick inserted in the center comes out clean, about 40-50 minutes.
9. Cool for 10 minutes, then slice and serve.

Serves 8.

Note: recipe can be halved and baked in a 9x9 baking dish to serve 4.

Rosanna's Pimento Cheese

Mix together:

4 cups shredded sharp cheddar cheese or 1 large bag of preshredded cheddar cheese
1 small jar of pimentos (undrained)
3 cloves of garlic, pressed
1/2 teaspoon celery seed to start, add more if desired
Enough mayonaise (not Miracle Whip) to make it gloopy and spreadable. Start with 3 heaping tablespoons and go from there.

Refrigerate overnight to allow flavors to meld. Serve on white bread.

Rudolf's Banana Bread

1 cup butter, softened
1 cup granulated sugar
1 cup brown sugar
4 cups all-purpose flour
3 medium ripe bananas, mashed
1 teaspoon vanilla
1 teaspoon nutmeg
2 teaspoons baking soda
3 eggs

1. Preheat oven to 350 degrees. Grease two medium loaf pans.
2. Cream butter and sugars; beat in eggs until well blended; mix in mashed banana; add vanilla.
3. Fold in flour, baking soda, and nutmeg.
4. Pour into greased pans.
5. Bake 1 - 1 1/4 hours or until tester comes out clean.

Mother Malcolm's Never-Fail Coffee Cake

4 cups all-purpose flour
1/2 lb. butter or margarine
Cut butter into flour as for pie crust.
Mix in 1 package dry yeast, 1 teaspoon salt, 1/4 cup sugar.

Separate yolks and whites of 3 eggs. Set whites aside, keep at room temperature. (Yes, overnight.)

Beat the yolks, add 1 cup milk and mix into dry ingredients. Cover with plate or cloth and refrigerate overnight.

When ready to bake:
FILLING: whip egg whites and gradually add 1/2 cup sugar, beat until stiff. Set aside.

Soften 1 stick of butter.

Preheat oven to 350 degrees. Divide dough into as many as four parts. Roll each part, one at a time, fairly thin. Butter dough lightly to 1" from all edges. Divide filling into the same number of parts as dough. Spread filling over dough, then sprinkle with brown sugar and shake cinnamon over the whole mess. Roll up, jelly roll style, seal edges with water and pinch. Place on baking sheet. Let rise awhile (about an hour). Bake for 25 minutes at 350 degrees--watch it--take out when light brown. Frost if desired.

Summertime Gazpacho

I like to shop the Farmer's Market for fresh from the garden ingredients and make a batch of this refreshing soup for those summer days when it's too hot to cook.

2 cups chopped tomatoes
1 sweet onion, chopped
1 bell pepper, chopped
1 cucumber chopped
2 green onions, chopped
2 fresh lemons, squeezed (at least 3 Tablespoons)
2 Tablespoons red wine vinegar (apple cider vinegar works in a pinch)
1 clove garlic, minced
1 teaspoon dried tarragon
3 teaspoons fresh chopped basil or 1 teaspoon dried basil
1 teaspoon white sugar
4 cups tomato juice
Salt and pepper to taste
Pinch of dried red pepper flakes (optional)

Combine all ingredients in a large bowl. Use a stick blender or blend in a food processor or blender in batches until well combined but slightly chunky.

Pour into a serving bowl and cover. Place in the refrigerator and chill at least 2 hours to let the flavors blend before serving. Recipe can be halved.

Serves 10

ACKNOWLEDGEMENT

I want to gratefully thank the women in the Women's Writing retreat at The Clearing Folk School led by Sharon Nesbit-Davis for their invaluable help and encouragement as this manuscript was in progress.

Thanks to my aunt, Barbara Rehder, for her advice on how hurricanes act, how to ride them out, and when to flee. (We are ignoring Hurricane Ian.)

The members of WWA Novel Critique groups deserve thanks for their insightful comments and especially Lisa Lickel for her continued encouragement and greatly appreciated critiques as this manuscript grew to completion.

Thank you all. I couldn't have done it without each and every one of you.

ABOUT THE AUTHOR

Barbara Angermeier Malcolm

Barbara Angermeier Malcolm, a Green Bay native, is an avid traveler and former retail SCUBA sales professional.

She has journeyed to countless islands with her family on diving vacations, collecting inspiration and stories along the way. A passionate storyteller, Barbara has been crafting tales for years.

When she's not writing, you'll find her sketching, painting with watercolors, knitting, cooking, or doting on her grandchildren. She is an active member of the Green Bay writing community and a proud member of the Green Bay Area Writers Guild and Wisconsin Writers Association.

THE SEAVIEW SERIES

Follow along as Rose Lambert navigates rebuilding and opening her four-room bed-and-breakfast, Seaview, on a Caribbean beach. She convinces her son that she can manage on her own, rebuffs the persistent attentions of the plumber, and sparks a romance with the electrician. Meet her changing cast of guests, a throng of islanders, and interesting expats in The Seaview Series novels.

The Seaview

She knew it would be hard work, but what she didn't plan on was the electrically charged subcontractor and the way he made her feel.

Despite her son's vehement objections, Rose buys the ramshackle Caribbean beachfront bed and breakfast. She's confident that she can oversee the work in time for the start of tourist season. That is until the Health Inspector locks them out of the building.

Desperate to get the crew back to work she pleads with the plumber to get the key and finish at least one bathroom. The plumber has his own agenda. Rose's confidence is nearly destroyed by this major setback.

Can Rose and her crew finish the job before the first guest arrives?

The Seaview is the first book of The Seaview Series. If you

like engaging islanders, breathtaking scenery above and below water, and a little romance this book is for you.

Open For Business

It's opening day, and Rose eagerly awaits her first guest. Juggling excitement and nerves, she's determined to keep her new bed & breakfast afloat despite bad weather and a lecherous plumber.

Now that Seaview is refurbished and reopened Rose's dream seems to be coming true, but the arrival of Hurricane Alphonso might end her dream before it can really begin. Her first guests are in residence and one of them acts like the hurricane with its wind, rain, and power outages is a personal affront.
Her attempts to fit into the island community are thwarted by nasty rumors spread by a local woman who resents Rose's romance with Ignatius "Iggy" Solomon. And a lecherous plumber just won't take "No!" for an answer.

In Open For Business, the second book of The Seaview Series escape to the Caribbean island of Anguilla. Enjoy Seaview with its changing cast of guests and the ever-faithful Iggy for delectable homemade breakfasts, beachside dancing, and rum punch as you dive into a tropical women's fiction story. Grab your copy today! BONUS: includes Rose's most popular recipes!

Spies Don't Retire

Some secrets refuse to stay buried... even in paradise.

Rose is settling into being a newlywed and hosting guests at Seaview Bed & Breakfast on the Caribbean island of Anguilla. Whispers of spies on the island begin to circulate. Someone threatens to unmask them. Rose's peaceful retreat risks becoming a battleground.

At a lavish party, the hostess introduces a British couple to a Russian one, and the tension seethes. Recognition. Sizzling hostility. Delicious gossip makes the grapevine hum. Were the men spies on opposite sides? Or do the wives share a more dangerous past?

As rumors fly, Rose finds herself caught between keeping Seaview's reputation intact and navigating the conflict between feuding friends. In the meantime, she's fighting to clear her name from the lingering lies of her nemesis.
Can Rose mend fences with the local women who distrust her? Will the two warring couples declare a truce—or set the island ablaze with old rivalries?

Spies Don't Retire, the third book in The Seaview Series, takes you back to the tropical shores of Anguilla where intrigue, scandal, and delectable island fare await. Escape to paradise.

Christmas At Seaview

Her daughter wants to get married. At Seaview. In four days.

Rose is excited about Christmas. Her children and their partners arrive on Christmas Eve at Rose's bed-and-breakfast on the island of Anguilla in the Caribbean. Two bombshell announcements on Christmas Day make her ecstatic. But her happiness turns into panic when her daughter makes a decision that turns the week upside down. Can Rose plan a wedding and take care of her paying guests during the most stressful week of the year?

The days tick away, and Rose is powerless to slow things down. Friday is coming fast. Will her guests feel ignored in all the wedding prep hubbub? Food, flowers, officiant. How will she get everything arranged before it's time to say, "I do?"

Pick up your copy of Christmas at Seaview, a novella that takes you along on Rose's wild ride through the week she never expected. Escape to the Caribbean this Christmas for a heartwarming story filled with joy, chaos, and family cheer.

BOOKS BY THIS AUTHOR

Horizon

Gail Logan, a widow in her mid-fifties, has lived her life by what other people think. That has to change.

Signing up for a watercolor class and thrifting a new wardrobe with a young classmate makes a good start. Replanting her regimented flower garden is another idea, but at the garden center, Abel Baker dismisses her plan and tells her what to buy. Gail doesn't appreciate his interference.

Widower Abel turns up in Gail's path again and again, but she buried one bossy man, and she's not interested in another. Should she give Abel a chance?

Her sons and her best friend feel threatened by all of Gail's changes. Should she go back to her dull existence or keep moving forward?

Better Than Mom's

Better Than Mom's is a neighborhood diner in a small city in Wisconsin where good food and interesting people come together.

Meet Brady, the warm-hearted owner who takes pride in making homemade food for his customers, Fay, the sassy morning waitress who cares for people more than she lets on,

Naomi, the welfare mom who cooks like an angel and needs a job, Steve, who sits in the back booth and won't let anyone see what he's writing, and Officer Bates, who comes to investigate a crime but ends up sweeping Fay off her feet.

Stop in at Better Than Mom's for a bowl of homemade soup, a lighter-than-air biscuit, and a visit with people who could be your neighbors.

Island Dreams

He found his dream job. She's reduced to cleaning vacation rental homes.

Ella Thomas and Dan Martinson are excited to leave their families and friends behind in Green Bay and move to the island of Bonaire in the Caribbean to pursue their dream of owning a dive shop.

Dan finds a job as a diving instructor immediately, but Ella can't get a work permit. The excitement and beauty of the coral reefs fill Dan's days. Ella's stuck cleaning up other people's messes for cash under the table.

They're dedicated to saving as much as they can so that when a dive shop becomes available, they can act fast. An unexpected opportunity threatens to drive a wedge between them.

A frustrated Ella comes up with a plan to maximize their savings by chasing that once-in-a-lifetime opportunity. Will Dan go along or stubbornly insist that they stick to their original plan?

Follow the ups and downs of life with Ella and Dan as they chase their Island Dreams.

Anneke's Legacy

Lucia answers the buzzing phone on her desk, and her life changes forever

Tasked with settling her great-aunt's estate on the arid Caribbean island of Bonaire, cynical editor Lucia Vandersteeg clashes with Burke, a rugged fisherman living on the property. As she uncovers her family's past and confronts a dangerous treasure-hunting scam that puts her in peril, Lucia must decide whether to trust the man who infuriates her most, or return to her lonely life in the city, leaving behind a chance at unexpected love.

While navigating the island's slow pace and the complexities of the estate, Lucia develops a simmering attraction to the fisherman, all while being pursued by the more suitable attorney.

Can the tangled lives of the people on this small island be sorted out before someone gets hurt? Will Lucia and Burke acknowledge their attraction before it's too late?